the guy in the middle

AN UNDERDOG LOVE STORY

KATE STEWART

1st Line Editor: Donna Cooksley Sanderson
2nd Line Editor: Grey Ditto
Cover by Amy Queau of Qdesign
Formatting by Champagne Book Design

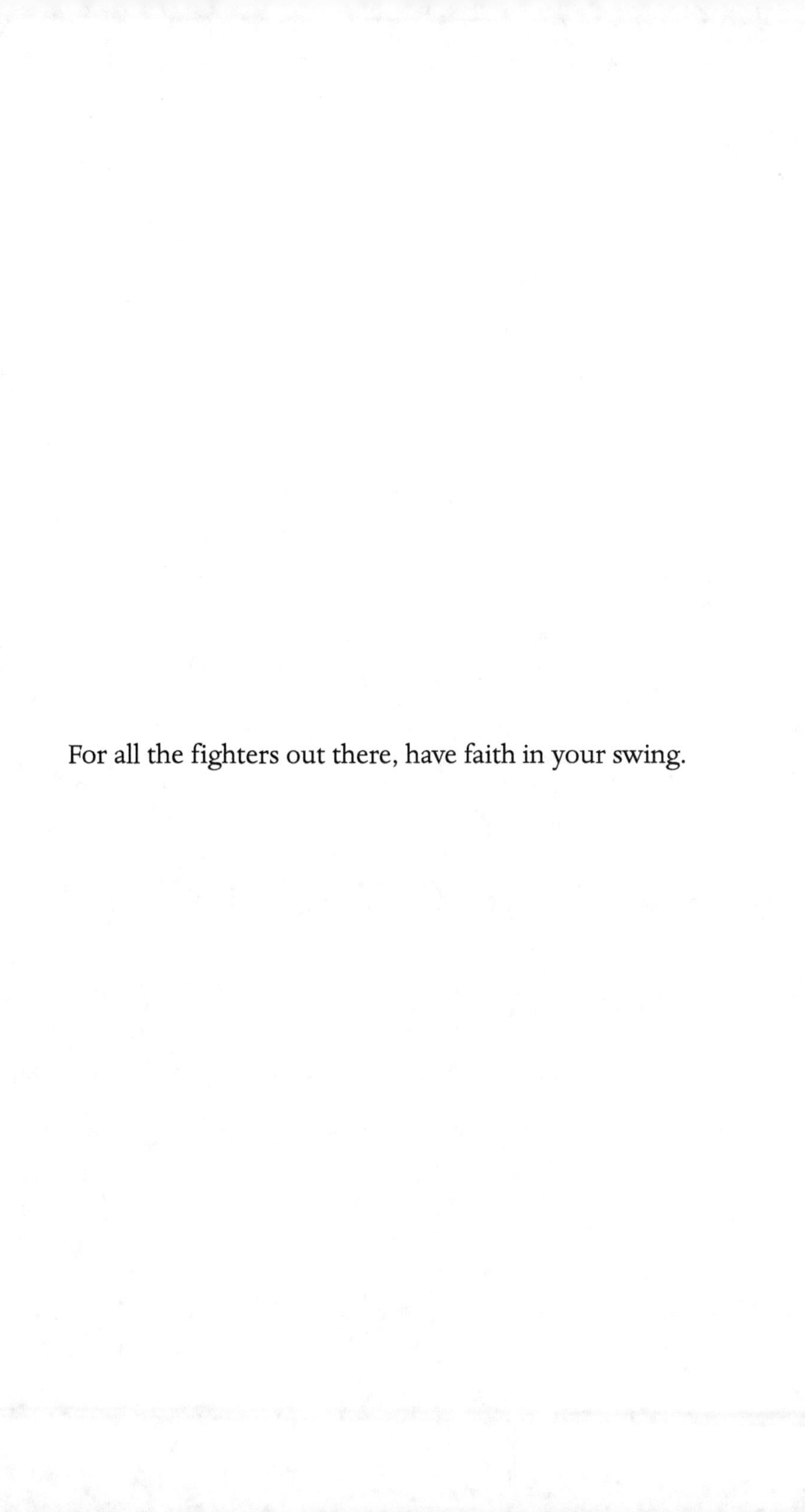

For all the fighters out there, have faith in your swing.

ROUND
1

one

HARPER

Sweat skates down every muscle, every crevice, every solid indentation on the wall of his massive chest.

Blink.

Blink.

Blink.

His deep voice rumbles from above me and I look up, and up, until my eyes land on the face of dark, raw masculinity. "Did you hear a word I just said?"

No. I didn't. I'm still gawking, mystified, while doing everything in my power to keep my mouth closed.

I've been privy to a lot of eye candy in my twenty years, but none had the jarring impact of the man standing in front of me. My first eyeful of him gives way to an electric shock. He'd been hitting the bag on the other side of the gym when I came in a few minutes ago, and I'd immersed myself in my dancing until he charged over and rudely shut off my speaker. Shaking my head, I peer into light grey eyes set under thick, dark, slashed brows and find myself caught in the tumultuous weather there. He snaps his fingers in front of my face. He's pissed and I have no idea why. The man's demeanor screams, "don't fuck with me, this dog will bite." Despite the dangerous air about him and his reputation, I'm not afraid of him. I'm more amped with him in my space than anything.

"You can't run your drills or whatever you're doing in here. I own this gym from six to nine on Wednesdays and Fridays."

"Pleasure to meet you too. My name is Harper, it's called dancing, and I was told—"

"Wrong," he crosses bulging forearms along his expansive chest, "you were told wrong."

"You don't own this place," I snap. "I have just as much of a right to be here as you."

He doesn't roll his eyes; he just looks up at the ceiling and leaves them fixed there as if trying to subdue his temper. As if I'm not intelligent enough to read the situation.

"You're a jerk." It sounds a little like a question coming out of my mouth, but I continue. "There's a polite way of telling someone they've made a mistake."

"Then whatever way that is, let's pretend that's how I said it. The gym is mine tonight."

"There's plenty of room, and it's huge," I point out. "There's enough space for the two of us."

"I'm not listening to that shit you call music," he nods towards my Bluetooth speaker, "while I'm trying to concentrate."

"Now my music is shit? You're just dick out and ready for the pissing contest today, aren't you, buddy? It's a good thing you've got your looks and are decent with a ball or you wouldn't get anywhere in life with that attitude."

His lips tip up briefly, then the smile's gone.

"Don't flatter yourself," I huff at the amusement still gleaming in his eyes. "I have no room in my life for another asshole."

"Don't flatter *yourself*. You're not my type."

"I'm sure I'm not. Anyone with an IQ to rival that inflated ego of yours would be too much hassle."

"You don't know a damn thing about me."

"Lance Prescott, aka 'The Blanket.' Cornerback for Texas

Grand, number twenty-two. TGU should have been your last pick, but I'm guessing you settled because campaigning yourself to a worthier school, with your temperament, would have blown your chances all to hell. I assume you took the easy route, figuring you'd defend your way onto a winning team."

His brows lift higher with my every word. "Am I supposed to be impressed that you follow football?"

"I follow *Grand* ball. It's in my blood."

"Is there a point to this rant?"

"It'll be a miracle if you get drafted."

Too far, Harper!

But I don't stop because today's been a shit sandwich and he's just served me a cup of fresh piss to wash it down with. My best friend, René, just got an audition to dance in an off-Broadway show. And while I'm truly happy for him—to work off the sting of jealousy—I came to this rinky-dink gym, only to be greeted by an entitled asshole.

Accusing eyes blaze a trail down my form. It's always the legs they check out first. I was blessed with a decent set of legs, an ass, killer metabolism, and good hair. That's where the blessings end from my perspective. We're all our own worst critics, but I have no grandiose illusions about my appearance. My nose—gifted from my mother—is too sharp in contrast with my father's chin. I have dull brown eyes and lips on the thin side. It's not low self-esteem talking; it's acceptance. I work with what I've got, and as far as I'm concerned, it's enough. I wasn't born perfect, very few are, with the exception of the man in front of me.

Lance Prescott is a triple threat; face, body, and infuriating confidence. Three attributes every athlete needs to feel superior. It's a formula that's had panties dropping since the days of yore. I'm not into guys who hide behind any of it.

"Rumor had it last year that New England had their eye

on you, but you have to stop letting your frustration best you if you're hoping for any more draft talk."

"Who in the hell are you to pass out advice?"

"Someone who knows enough about ball to see when a player is pissing away his shot. And it's for this very reason, right here. But don't worry, knowing the NFL and their dangerously low standards, you might just slither in." I cock my hip and face him head-on, well, as much as I can with our difference in height.

"Are you done?"

"Not quite. You're good, Lance, *really* good. Undoubtedly one of the best in the conference, but you need a new personality. Especially if this is the way you introduce yourself to a stranger."

He opens his mouth in rebuttal, but I lift my hand to cut him off.

"Spare yourself the breath you'd waste trying to convince me you aren't anything more than the conclusions I've drawn within a minute of meeting you."

"Sweetheart, I couldn't give two shits about your opinion of me. But I do find it a bit ironic you know so much about me and are conveniently *here* at the exact time that I use *this* gym."

He thinks I'm one of *those—a helmet hoochie.* The type of girl who sees a ballplayer as a ticket to a swanky life, a future paycheck. I'll let him assume away because it will send the right signal, not that guys like Lance give me a second look. And I don't miss his assessment of me. He dwarfs me by height and weight. I'm in the skimpiest shorts I own—which fit more like underwear—along with my sports bra and see-through tank.

"Do you really believe that I schemed my way into using this gym, in hopes of gunning for *you?* Please, believe me, if I was desperate enough to use those bullshit antics to get a ballplayer, yours isn't the number I'd go to any lengths for."

"Whatever," he lifts his chin to cue my send-off, "you can go."

"Actually, I think I'll stay until I talk to someone of authority. I'm not bothering you. It's the opposite."

"Look," he reasons as I shift my weight from one foot to the other, "it's only three hours. You can come back another day."

"So could you," I challenge.

"My friend's dad owns this gym."

"Congratulations, Jake's my friend too. He also gave me permission, hence the key."

"Fuck it," he sighs, stuffing in his earbuds. "Just turn that shit down, all right?"

"Whatever," I huff as he walks off. I can see his reflection more clearly in the mirror when I try to resume my practice. I've never been self-conscious about my dancing before, but after watching his retreat, I notice that the bag is facing me. Now that I have the asshole's attention, any misstep on my part gives me the potential to embarrass myself. There's a newly renovated multi-million-dollar gym he's privileged to abuse, so why isn't he lifting on campus with his friends, pounding beers or looking for fresh flowers to pollinate?

Dismissing my wandering thoughts, I turn my music back on and take my position as the sound of glove to bag resumes. It takes only a few minutes, but I find bliss when I finally lose myself.

two

LANCE

WHAT THE FUCK?

Who in the hell does this chick think she is?

I just had my nuts snipped off and handed to me in a matter of seconds *and* by none other than a ball busting little witch with a superiority complex.

And she had the nerve to call me entitled?

I can't see this girl being a friend of Jake's in any scenario. And I'll make it my mission to get rid of her.

Feeling the singe of her words, I smash the bag to release the pressure, baffled by how a complete stranger managed to press so many of my buttons in a matter of minutes.

There's nothing I hate more than someone who assumes they know me because of ball.

I don't want to be one thing. I want to be many things. And the split-second assessment she just made of me is enough to drive home my point. I'm not just a ballplayer, or a student, or a rancher's son. Those are the things that matter most to me, but they aren't all that I am. I don't want to look back—like so many other ballplayers do—and think this was the best it's ever going to get for me, my high point or peak because it feels like anything but. I've seen what that can do to a man, namely my father. I grew up listening to his "glory days" stories. At first, it was fascinating, and now it's just sad.

Dad and I don't agree on much these days, except when it comes to the ranch. Our love for that land a common bond, our need to preserve the legacy and protect my mother and brother the same. The ranch might be my future, but first I have to save it, and that's where the strain in our relationship lies.

Dad's been writing checks that my ass may not be able to cash for the last eighteen months; his faith in me unwavering, the pressure a constant. That's why I find solace alone, unleashing my frustrations on my own body, strengthening the tool needed to eradicate the look of terror I constantly see on my mother's face.

I don't have to play poster boy to play ball. I'm not going to campaign myself because I'm not a man who minces words. I don't tap dance for attention I don't want. I don't need to be anyone's favorite anything; I just need to play ball, keep my head down, and get through this season.

That means working longer and harder than I ever have in my ball career. It all comes down to this year. It means a strict schedule, a whole lot of self-deprivation where the extra-curricular is concerned and cutting all distractions. I'm so damn close. With my stats what they are and the promise of a decent upcoming season, I may just pull it off. I've already put in my mandatory field time to enter the draft but didn't pursue it last year because of my obligations at the ranch. That hesitation may have cost me, especially with the way the season ended. Now it might be too late. Only a small percentage of college players are picked to join the league. Regardless of what Miss Priss decided about me, I refuse to let arrogance guide my quest or my temper destroy my chances. This year, no mistakes. I'm a changed man and my ability to withstand that character breakdown without blowing a fuse proved as much.

When they aren't hosting geriatric jazzercise in the dank gym, this is my place to unwind. It's the only time I get to nail the bag, to let my anger rule so I can exorcise it to the point it's beneath me, not a weakness I can't manage. The rest of the week I'm stuck in practice, lifting or training to milk out the rest of the summer before school and regular-season starts.

Every single day I remind myself why I'm here, and it's to save that ranch. To save my parents the embarrassment of losing everything and to protect three generations of blood, sweat, and tears. It's all up to me.

Twinkle toes had been on the receiving end of my latest blow, which was the shit news that my father had gotten a fair price for my Silverado. A truck I don't have a replacement for. I'm now a man without a horse, but it bought the one thing my family seems to have very little of lately, time. Not only that, it will cover the room I've rented for my last two semesters. As far as getting around, I'm on my own, but my family has what they need, so it's worth the sacrifice. Selfishly, I'm still pissed at the fact that I just lost the truck I'd worked five summers for. All that effort gone in a blink. So yeah, I'm pissed, constantly stressed, and always frustrated. The future swings over my head like a bladed pendulum.

As many truths as she nailed, I could fill a book with the shit she doesn't know.

Movement draws me from my thoughts as I glance over at the tiny girl and watch her choreographed steps.

The way she moves shows she's comfortable in her own skin and the way she told me to fuck off says she's got a backbone; but when I'd approached, her shaky demeanor alluded that she may be on the inexperienced side.

Jake told me the room was mine. If he thought this chick would be a welcome surprise, he's wrong. I do my best thinking isolated, and this girl is buzzing in circles around me. I can't adjust the bag to get a different view, and even if I did, I can see her in my peripheral, in the reflection of the long-ass eyesore mirror that takes up one wall of the gym.

This is jacked.

I pound away, doing my best to ignore her…until she catches fire. She's dancing like a pro, her body made for movement.

It's fascinating…and distracting.

Heavy bass no longer thrums out of her impressive little speaker, but you wouldn't know it with the way she's stepping into every beat while manipulating her form in ways that have me dizzy.

Motherfucker!

I thrash at the bag, my nerves fraying as she slides, glides, sashays, and then cuts the song off abruptly. It's on the edge of my lips to protest with "why did you stop?" before she restarts the music.

Irritated, I watch.

I can't help myself.

I watch.

three

LANCE

I TAKE ADVANTAGE OF MY POSITION BOTH ON AND OFF THE FIELD, which at times makes me a hypocrite, falling into the one and done stereotype. Callie slides on her panties and eyes me over her shoulder, a bright smile on her face. I grin back at her.

"Well, someone had some issues he needed to work out tonight."

Feeling the pull of sleep, I punch my pillow and position it behind me.

"You can stay."

Callie's eyes run appreciatively down my chest. "Sweet, but no. I don't want to meet your new roommates after that show we just put on, and you're out of toilet paper."

"Sorry," I offer, unsure if said offer was obligatory or self-ish. If she stays and I get a second wind, it's convenient. I'm not much for conversation, sharing my bed is about as intimate as I get, and Callie understands that about me. It's an unspoken agreement between us.

I've been seeing Callie for a few months. She's nice and we get along well enough. That's really all I need. She graduated last spring and decided to stay home for the summer before joining the workforce. She comes with perks, meaning she'll be gone soon, so no commitment pressure, with the added bonus of no baggage—win/win. I've been down the monogamy road in high school, and it was nice—while it lasted—but a relationship hasn't been a priority with the amount of shit I have going on. The minute I stepped on Texas Grand University campus, I decided women had to take a back seat. I had enough expectations to deal with. I've kept that promise to myself for three years. With my focus solely on ball and saving the ranch, I refuse to jerk any woman around.

"Night," she leans over, her hair tickling my face as she takes my lips in a parting kiss. "Damn," she whispers with a grin, shaking her head when she pulls away. "It's a good thing I know better about you."

"Yeah, what's that?" I can't help the edge to my voice. I've dealt with enough judgment for one day.

"I just know if I catch feelings, I'll be messing up."

"So, don't."

"Obviously, it's never happened to you," she sighs while sliding on her flip flops. She really is a beautiful girl. If I was in a better position to date, she'd be the type to consider long term.

"Not really."

She laughs. "Oh, you'll know."

I sit up. "Have I treated you badly? Disrespected you? If so, I apologize. I'm shit at this, Callie. I told you from the get-go."

She seems to read the sincerity in my eyes. "No. I'm sorry. I didn't mean to imply anything."

"Then don't imply anything."

"And don't show me you're different. You know, maybe it helps me to think of you this way. Have you thought of that?"

She grimaces. If she thinks she's said too much, she has.

I grip her hand while she stares down at me with murky eyes. "Look, I'm just staying in my lane because we're both about to make an exit," I say simply. "There's no point."

"Right."

"Callie," I softly scold, knowing we're done. She reads my posture, the tone of my voice.

"Shit," she says. "Okay, let's do this now."

I nod, eyeing her. "If that's what you want."

She leans in and I kiss her, holding back. At the door, she glances back at me over her shoulder, a sad smile tilting her lips.

"Did you just manipulate me into breaking up with you?" She shakes her head and snorts. "Unbelievable," her laughter tinged with incredulity. "You son of a bitch, you totally did. Lord help the woman you fall for."

When she shuts the door, sleep comes easy and I know I'm a bastard for it.

four

HARPER

He's everywhere. In my new gym, my favorite coffee shop, and last week I spotted him leaving Jake's apartment, no doubt in an attempt to get my gym privileges revoked. He failed.

Take *that,* asshole.

Jake and I went to high school together, but he was in the dorms with Lance freshman year. Jake said he's rough around the edges, misunderstood due to his hermit ways, but deep down a good guy.

Jake's advice? Stay out of his way.

I'm taking it.

I've dodged him twice to keep him from seeing me. He's always alone when I spot him, which is odd because typically the giants rule together.

Athletes have always been a part of my life. I'd grown used to being around them from an early age. I was never wary of them until my body started reacting to the testosterone. But after years of watching athletes, I assume I was bound to develop a little hero worship. Not to mention these men are in the prime of their lives, it's hard to ignore how in tune they are with their bodies—and how in tune mine has become with theirs. I'm a fan of the art of the human body and the beauty of movement; whether for sport or dance, anyone who can manipulate their physique in such a way has both my attention and admiration.

And Lance Prescott, even when throwing simple punches at a gym bag, is mesmerizing.

I wasn't lying to Lance when I told him football is ingrained in me. My father and I have a mutual love for the game, he takes his far more seriously and with good reason. His legendary status at the school and the break in tuition is what keeps me here. The deal is simple, four years for a degree, and then I can actively pursue my dancing dream. I'm starting this year a sophomore, year two of a four-year sentence. But four years in a dancer's life is an eternity. The next three years I've decided to look upon a bit like Olympic training. If I fail, at least I'll have tried and have my accounting degree to fall back on.

There's just one issue, I don't want to be in a classroom when I could be dancing. At all. Every day is agony and the more that come to pass, the more I feel I'm missing out. It's all about location when it comes to excelling in a career in dance, and College Station, Texas, is not prime real estate. Until graduation, I'm stuck here. I'll bide my time, do my homework, hone my skills, ace the dance program, and avoid the jocks that seem to take up all the space in the street. Affirmation made with my daily pep talk, I turn the corner of the gym bathroom and run into a wall.

"Oof," I tumble backwards before strong hands reach out to steady me.

"You okay?"

I feel like I just got run over by a truck, but I nod.

"Fine," I reply, jerking out of his grasp before I adjust my clothes. I have on a ripped tank, and I don't miss his eyes on the extra flash of skin.

He lingers and I patiently wait, staring at his Nikes. "Talked to Jake."

"And?"

"Said you went to high school together. Anyway, the gym is booked up for the rest of the summer, so we'll have to share it."

I lift a shoulder. "I'm not the one who has a problem with it."

"What do you say to an hour and a half each?" As he starts negotiations, I shake my head.

"I need more time."

"I'm trying here," he blows out a frustrated breath. His hands taped at his sides, his fingers tense as if he's ready to spring and attack. It's the only thing I notice as I keep my eyes down to avoid ogling him.

"It would probably help the conversation if you looked at me." I hear the hint of a smile in his voice and snap my gaze to his. "Better."

"I need more time." There, simple. I don't take note of the way his shorts hang from his hips at his narrow waist. Or the way his T-shirt clings to his biceps screaming, 'look!' Or the way his thick, dark-brown hair curves naturally away from his face. No, not at all. Satisfied with my attention, he smirks down at me. "Look, we'll just get used to it, all right? I need all the time I can get."

"Why?" he asks, "you have something coming up?"

No. "Yes."

"Well, I do too. I want to be able to hit the bag as much as possible."

"You're going to box?"

"No. It's a pastime."

"Pity."

"Why?" He crowds me and I swallow while the scent of him invades my nose. Clean, masculine, tempting.

"Because someone needs to knock the shit out of you."

"Wow," he chuckles, "you really don't like me."

"You made a bad first impression. Now, I'm indifferent. And you don't really care if I like you."

"I owe you an apology," he takes a step forward. He loves his effect on me, it shows in the twinkle in his eye. Typical. "I just got…well, it was a bad day, so I apologize for the way I acted."

"Accepted. But we don't have to be best friends to share this space. So, let's just divide the sandbox and go our separate ways."

"What do you have coming up?"

"None of your business."

He ignores my snark. "Is it like an audition?"

I wish. "Why?"

"Maybe I'm curious."

"I'm not a pastime, so go find another to entertain yourself with." I push past him and hear his gravelly chuckle behind me before he speaks up.

"You really should do something about that."

I glance back at him.

"About what?"

"About that thorough fucking you need."

My lips part as he stalks towards me before standing uncomfortably close. He bends down until we're eye level with each other. "You get to assume shit about me, well allow me to join the party because clearly, you don't accept my apology. That chip on your shoulder isn't sexy, *at all*. There's a tiny division of men who will jump through hoops to try and get past it, but they aren't going to entertain *your* attitude long. Loosen up, Priss, or you're going to find yourself with your own shitty reputation."

"Says pot to the kettle. Stay out of my way, Prescott."

"No problem, sweetheart."

"Don't bother with the pleasantries now, you basically just called me an uptight bitch."

"If the Nike fits." Like an idiot, I glance down at my solid hot-pink Nikes before I catch his smirk.

And with that, he makes his way towards his bag.

five

LANCE

T THE ATM, I ENTER MY CODE FOR CASH ONLY TO GET rejected a second time. Slapping the side of the machine in aggravation, I lower my head and let out a slow breath, knowing the culprit.

"Hey, man, you done?" I glare at the asshole behind me, who clearly decides not to give me the moment I so obviously need.

"Fuck off," I grumble, punching in the numbers again, deciding to check my balance. Nineteen dollars minus the three fucking dollars it cost me to check my balance. I have sixteen dollars to my name. Gaping at the total, I dial my dad as I walk away from the machine with my cell to my ear.

"Hey, son, I was just talking to Pete about you."

"Dad, where's the money?"

"Yeah. About that, son, meant to call you. Pete gave me a good deal on a few heifers and I needed to borrow a little."

"A little? You wiped me out!"

"I'm sorry, son. I couldn't pass it up. I'll put it back by the end of the week."

"You can't just *take it*, Dad, it's my money."

There's a hesitation. I know I've embarrassed him, something I never want to do to the man who's given me everything. "It's a loan, son. Temporary. I swear, I'll replace it. Just give me a few days to move things around."

I pace the parking lot. "Fine. But a heads-up would have been nice."

"It's just temporary."

"Yeah."

"Let me just tell you about what I'm working with," there's an uncomfortable edge to his voice, one I'm all too familiar with. It's the same tone I've dealt with for the majority of my life when he wheels and deals, doing his best to make ends meet. He got us through those times and he'll get us through this, I just have to be patient. But it doesn't change the fact that my stomach is growling, and I have no solution.

"I gotta go, Dad. I'll call you back."

"All right, son. Don't worry. Leave that on me."

"Sure. Bye."

"I love you—"

Guilt shadows the anger knowing I've hurt him by cutting him off. I order an Uber, knowing the commute home is going to wipe me out. In the back of a white Taurus, the driver, Dave, makes polite conversation with me as I fume in the back seat. Though the ride is costing me, I need the bag right now a lot more than I need a meal. I need the release. Thanking Dave, I shut the door and approach the gym, knowing I just have to hang on a few more seconds. Opening the door, the smell of the sweat-infused pleather equipment brings me comfort the way it always has since day one.

"Mr. Prescott, we're waiting," Mrs. Sheffler prompts me expec-tantly as all eyes in the classroom dart my way. It's the last thing I want.

"Lance, get up, man, it's your turn," Chad mutters under his breath as I stare down at the gaping hole on top of my shoe, his new Nikes gleaming in my periphery. I shake my head, keeping it lowered.

"Freak," I hear uttered behind me.

"*Lance, I'm going to need you to come up and do your presentation.*"

I kick at the poster board leaning against the front of my desk. I'd worked on it for three days, but it's the hole in my threadbare shoes keeping me in my seat. This morning I'd tried to cover it with black electrical tape, but it only made it look worse. So I shaded my shoes with a permanent marker to try and match the tape, but I'd jacked them up even more, and they're my only pair. If I stand up in the front of the room, everyone will see what I'm attempting to hide.

"I'm going to have to pass, Mrs. Sheffler." That comment earns me a few laughs and I sink in my seat, knowing this isn't going to end well.

"This isn't optional," Mrs. Sheffler says, her fingernails tap, tap, tapping against the notebook she's holding.

Tap. Tap. Tap.

Tap. Tap. Tap.

Knee bouncing, I reach for any excuse I can come up with to keep from standing in front of the room to be scrutinized. I can feel Channah's stare on me. Last night she'd helped me finish my board and as a reward, I'd kissed the life out of her. I should never have brought the board to class. It only makes my lie more damning.

"I didn't finish mine."

Mrs. Sheffler isn't buying it. I wouldn't either. "Lance—"

"Chickenshit," I hear from the same voice behind me. Mark, it's always Mark. I've already kicked his ass twice this year. Doesn't change the fact he doesn't have holes in his sneakers. He doesn't have to worry about thirty sets of eyes judging his clothes.

"Who said that?" Mrs. Sheffler barks, just as I snap and snatch up my poster board.

RIIIIIIIIPPPPPP

I toss the pieces on the floor and grin up at her. "Like I said, I don't have it."

Her tone turns to ice. "Lance, you need to go to the principal's office."

Picking up my pencil, I study it as if it's more of a fascinating artifact than a writing tool, wishing I could use the end of it to erase the last few minutes. Dad warned me if he or Mom gets called into Principal Hatter's office again, he'll have my ass. I'm not sure which music is worse to face at this point, but the decision has been made for me.

"Mr. Prescott, did you hear me?"

"Rarely ever do," I mutter as laughter erupts around me.

I'm not moving; I don't want anyone staring at me. Knee bouncing uncontrollably, I shake my head as my palms begin to sweat. "I'm pretty comfortable here. Have you tried this seat? You really should sometime."

"Mr. Prescott. Right now."

I ignore her, keeping my head down, clamping up tight in the hope she'll give me a pass, just this once and deal with me later—no such luck.

"Lance, get your bag and go. Now."

Eyes lowered, so I don't have to see their judgment, I collect my backpack and leave the classroom making the trip to the principal's office.

An hour later, in the bucket chair that's been a second home since school started, I lean in, straining to hear the conversation with my parents, the principal and the school counselor.

"We can't have this type of insubordination. He's already been in two fights this year," Principal Hatter says. My dad comes quickly to my defense.

"It's normal for kids his age to get into a brawl or two. Testosterone is kicking in. He's just blowing off steam."

"Mr. Prescott," Mrs. Eve, the school counselor chimes in. "There's a big difference between 'boys will be boys' and this incessant, blatant display of disregard for authority. There may be more going on inside

Lance than growing pains. Are there any issues going on at home we should know about?"

The sound of metal scrapes against the floor as my dad erupts. "Don't you dare, lady! In my house, it's family first. We're getting along just fine at home."

"Have you even asked him?" My mother interjects, "I know there's a reason. Lance is a good boy. He never exhibits this type of behavior at home."

Principal Hatter speaks up. "We feel, at this point, he should be evaluated, and you should consider counseling. Despite his punishments, he's only gotten more aggressive."

My dad is still standing; I can hear it in the way his voice is pitched. Temper flaring, I sense the accusation in his own voice. "He didn't want to read a presentation out loud, and you call that aggressive?"

"Mr. Prescott, no need to get upset."

"You're right, just like there's no need to go pointing fingers about bad parenting. We're raising a man. He's not some punk kid with an attitude problem. He has a lot of responsibilities at home, aside from his schoolwork. Maybe it's catching up with him."

I close my eyes, feeling the guilt of letting them both down. My shit just put them in the position to defend themselves as parents, and honestly, I couldn't think of two better heroes.

My mother speaks up with evident heartbreak in her voice. "Maybe we've been working him too hard."

"Don't go there, Jeannie," Dad erupts as my knee kicks up. "He needs a punching bag and a good talking-to, not a fucking shrink. And you can forget about meds. I'm not poisoning him."

"Mr. Prescott, we don't use that kind of language in these meetings. Is that understood?"

"Lady, I'm not your student, and my boy may have a little bit of an attitude problem, a temper, but it's ours to manage. We're his parents.

Get on with his punishment. He'll serve his time, both here at school and at home, I assure you. He's not a threat to anyone."

"Lance, please stop kicking your chair," Mrs. Estrada, the school receptionist says, peering over at me while pulling me out of the conversation. I hadn't realized I was doing it. I look down to see my hands balled into fists and stop the swing of my heel against the metal bar of the chair. "Sorry."

Pulling on my gloves, I can still feel the shame from that day. It was undoubtedly one of the worst. The day I vowed not to let anyone get too close, the same day my girlfriend, Channah, decided to kiss Mark instead of me. But it was also the day my dad changed my life by gifting me my first set of gloves and an outlet. My bouncing knee slowed a bit, my palms got less sweaty, my confidence spiked, and my life changed. I had a place to escape. In the ring, against the bag, I had freedom, a way to even the score with my faceless opponents—embarrassment, shame, anger, frustration.

The day I discovered boxing was the day I embraced a side of me I knew no one else would truly understand. The hardest part to swallow was how much I liked it when I let it take hold. Maybe I am a bit of a freak, but I choose to embrace it.

The day I turned eighteen, I got the barbed wire tattoos symbolizing my fight to keep my inner beast on a leash. And in the ring is where I learned to get along with it, where I let it reign.

Cranking up the music, I tap my gloves together and open the floodgates.

Six

HARPER

SEVENDUST'S "BLACK" BLARES THROUGHOUT THE GYM AS I unlock the door and make my way towards my half of the sandbox. When I turn the corner my breath is stolen by the sight of Lance ripping into the bag. Powerful arms deliver precise and devastating blows making the bag jump on the chain. Covered in a heavy sheen of sweat, his face drips with exertion, his focus undeterred by my presence. He's not dressed in his usual attire. Tonight, he's jean-clad in an old faded grey TGU T-shirt and sneakers. It seems as if he couldn't be bothered to change into his clothes in haste to get to the bag.

Something's…off.

It's clear he came to vent, and I can *feel* the anger and frustration emanating from him, even from my side of the room. It does something to me that I'm not prepared for. At a machine-gun pace, he lands one solid blow after another, the music fuel. Anyone on the receiving end of those punches wouldn't be standing at this point, I'm sure of it.

I stand back, stunned, listening to the words of the song as understanding washes over me. He's not some jaded, entitled jock. In this moment, *he* seems to be the only person he's waging war on. If the lyrics are any indication of his situation, he's in a place of complete and utter turmoil in his own skin. I've heard the saying 'battling demons' a thousand times or more in my life, but I've never seen such a physical example. The heavy guitar rift rattles the walls, the floors, *me,* as I watch him exhaust himself, never giving up the fight, but owning that he could never win it.

Guilt for some of my agitated word vomit upon meeting him comes to the surface as I watch his struggle between vulnerability and anger. It's so blatantly obvious there's a lot more going on with Lance Prescott than he lets on. A fierce and unexpected need to protect him washes over me as I round the room when the song begins to fade. He leans in hugging the bag, his breaths coming out ragged, his eyes closed as if he's just come down from an uncontrollable high.

I grab a water bottle from my bag and approach him with it out in offering. "Are you okay?"

When he opens his eyes, I'm startled by what I see—a mix of hurt and defeat.

"Not a good time, Priss." His voice is chalky, his gaze sliding to the floor between us as if he's ashamed of himself in this state.

"I know. That's why I'm asking. Drink this."

He nods and then starts to work his gloves off, ripping at the Velcro with his teeth. I still his efforts and take one of them in my grasp, unlatching the wrist strap and free one hand.

He remains silent, just watching me, and the hairs on the back of my neck rise.

"So metal, huh?" I say with a small smile, braving a glance at him as I work to get his other glove off. "That's your bag?"

"Old Metal and Rock. I grew up on it."

Gloves off, I hand him the plastic bottle and he thanks me before draining it.

"Do you want to talk about it?"

"No."

"Look, if you need—"

"This is why I like to work out *alone.* No offense, but this is my time to do my thing. All right?" Biting my lips, I nod and take a step back. He didn't say it in a way that offends me, but I feel the sting of rejection anyway.

It's then I fully understand why he doesn't want me in the gym with him. "I-I can come back."

"No, you're good. I'm done. Just going to rope for a while."

"Okay."

I turn to make my way towards my corner and glance back. "For what it's worth, I'm sorry for the shitty things I said."

"Yeah, same." He gives me a nod before making his way to his locker room. As I start my own music, I can't help but glance over at him when he emerges a few minutes later in his usual attire. He begins with his jump rope, clearing it easily at an exhausting pace. It's as if he's tapped into some sort of reserve and is hell-bent on fatiguing himself. Curiosity piqued, I spend a few minutes stretching, just watching as he wears himself out.

What are you hiding, Lance Prescott?

As if he hears my question, his gaze meets mine briefly before he packs his duffle and leaves me staring in the direction he left.

seven

HARPER

BEING OVERLOOKED ISN'T A BAD THING, ESPECIALLY IF YOU PLAN on being a back-up dancer. The only thing I want people to recognize when they see me is how in sync I am while dancing. I don't want the spotlight, that's not my goal. Winding my hair into a bun, I check my reflection. I'm wearing my favorite black shorts and cut to midriff T-shirt. Clothes only get in the way of watching my form as I execute. Though my outfit borders indecent, I didn't see Lance anywhere when I arrived at the gym. Just as well. I want to try something new, and it would be hard to get the kinks out with him around.

I've noticed his pattern in the last few weeks and been quick to avoid it. He's at the coffee shop I frequent in the mornings, either on his laptop or reading. We've kept mostly to ourselves since the night I saw a few of his true colors, a polite nod here and there with little to no conversation.

Cardi B's "I Like It" fills the gym as I dig into the routine I memorized on YouTube. Jerking my head, I follow it with the smooth transition of my torso sliding left and right within the same second before I whip back into starting position. Gyrating my hips, I use my arms to emphasize every step before gliding along the floor in seamless and purposeful movement. It's a level 'insane' routine, but it's near the difficulty I'm looking to conquer. Before I know it, I'm lost. Whipping my body, dominating my steps, twisting my frame. I bounce on my heels and push-off, jerking, sliding, breaking my body down twice the tempo of the beat.

Satisfied once the song ends, I jump back when I see Lance in the mirror casually leaning against the wall with his arms crossed. He's in his typical attire of mesh shorts and a form-fitting white tee, his eyes intent on me as I audibly swallow.

"That was pretty…fucking amazing."

eight

LANCE

She's…pointy. She reminds me of a little bird, in a way. But when the girl starts to move, she takes flight. I was honest when I told her she's not my type. She's not, but I can't stop watching. The minute she starts to move, I'm fixated. It's witchcraft what she does on those killer legs. She's perfectly toned, and I can't deny the jolt to my cock when she works herself like a contortionist. Today the music doesn't suck, and neither does her routine. If I'm honest, I've been impressed with her talent from the get-go.

Whatever she's auditioning for, I have zero doubt she'll make the cut.

She's that good.

I watch as she bounces and transitions like she's floating on air, liquid, fluid but never mechanical, every move purposeful, calculated and perfectly executed. When the music stops, my mouth moves before I have a chance to think it through.

"That was pretty…fucking amazing."

I take satisfaction in the surprise on her face when I pay her the compliment.

"Take that compliment," I push off the wall, "it was genuine."

"Even if I don't care for the supplier?" She grins, and I grin back.

"Suit yourself," I walk past her and drop my duffle before pulling off my shirt. I catch her checking me out in the mirror, and my smile widens.

"What made you come to this school? It's hardly the place to hone your skills. Wouldn't you be better off at a dance academy or something?"

She tilts her head, surprised at my line of questioning. "In-state tuition."

I nod. "I get it. If I didn't have a full ride, I wouldn't be in college at all. But, with the way you dance, you couldn't get a scholarship?"

She blows out a breath.

"Humor me, Priss."

Her nose scrunches in distaste for her pet name. "My dad is on faculty here. And no, the dance program at Grand wasn't my first choice, but it's decent. It just made more financial sense to do it here." She shrugs. "I'm not going to let it stop me."

"No doubt you won't."

"I can't tell if you're sincere or if it's this chip I'm carrying keeping me all icy and suspicious." Another grin, but I can tell my digs grated on her the way hers did me.

"Sorry about that. But you can be a little frigid, especially when someone is trying to apologize."

"You're right. I'm just as guilty. The day we met was a shit-show for me as well, so I'm sorry for what I said."

"We're cool. And you really are good. I mean that."

"Thanks," she says, a slight heat creeping up her face. "So are you, at ball, I mean. But you're still in need of a personality makeover."

"Whatever," I shiver in exaggeration. "Is it cold in here?"

"Shut up," she says, cocking a hip, making her legs look even better.

We eyeball each other as I unzip my bag and pull out my gloves. She takes a step towards me and turns the tables.

"So, what's your story?"

"We sharing now?"

She shrugs. "Why not?"

"Don't really have one. Grew up on a ranch a hundred miles from here."

"Wow, that's cool, didn't picture you as a cowboy."

"You still shouldn't."

"I don't know. Kinda seems like it'd be a good look on you."

"Oh yeah?" I grin. "Am I headlining your fantasies tonight in a Stetson and nothing else?"

She rolls her eyes. "So, have you always boxed?"

"I've been doing both for a while. If I had my way and I could afford it, I'd be training in both. Ball is more accessible."

She walks over to where I stand. "So, don't let it stop you. Are you good?"

"Money doesn't grow on trees, Priss. College is expensive enough. I boxed a lot when I was younger, amateur stuff. I was pretty good. I've kept up with the conditioning, but I put the gloves down when ball started sabotaging all my time." It's not the complete truth, but it's close.

Twisting my torso in a stretch, I crack my neck and catch her checking me out. She's...cute in an odd way: gorgeous halo blonde hair, deep brown eyes, and nose with character. Her lips are on the thin side but shimmer under a layer of something glossy. Her body and attitude are a lethal combination. I like the sassy personality that collides with the sweetness in her voice. She catches my raking gaze and shies away from my appraisal, crossing her arms.

"Whatcha thinking about over there, Priss?"

"Nothing, enjoy your…whatever."

I lift my fingers as if I'm tipping a hat and give her a slow, suggestive wink.

Red-faced, she heads to her side of the box.

nine

LANCE

"LANCE," THE BARISTA BELLOWS OUT AS SHE SITS MY COFFEE at the end of the counter.

I pick it up and take a sip. "Thank you, Laney."

"Put an extra shot in for you today."

"Appreciate it."

"Anytime," she drawls out, "you're one of the few I like around here cause you always leave a tip." She lifts an expectant brow and gestures towards the half-empty jar sitting on the counter. I chuckle, emptying my pockets before stuffing a few dollars into it. She's a cute, petite, doe-eyed brunette, with an adorable accent and feisty attitude, but I refuse to shit where I've eaten seven mornings a week for the last year. And she's got one hell of a 'don't eff with me' vibe going on.

The coffee shop is close to campus, and lately, I've had to bide my time here after practice until gym time in an attempt to save what little Uber money I have. I didn't plan to sell my truck when I rented a room fifteen minutes from campus. The decision so far has been a hard pill to swallow. Between the safety of the coffee shop and snagging rides where I can, I may make it to the end of the season without landing myself into more debt. Another reason I don't mind frequenting the shop is the girl sitting on the torn-up pleather couch flipping through her tablet while pretending to ignore my presence. In all honesty, it's the insanely toned, mile-long legs that draw me in as I make my way towards her.

"Morning, Priss."

"Jolly Green Giant," she says without glancing up.

I'm chuckling as I take my favorite seat opposite her. "What are you reading?"

"I'm not, I'm watching a video," she says, turning the screen my way so I can get a look. "Couldn't get into a book so I'm studying a new routine."

Stretching out on the overused chair, I sip my coffee. "Not listening to the music?"

"This thing is so ancient the sound goes in and out."

"Sucks."

"Uh hmmm…staring is rude."

"I'm having a hard time believing you're shy."

She shrugs. "I'm not shy."

"You hardly ever look at me when you speak to me."

She rolls her eyes before lifting them to meet mine.

"Better."

"Careful, that coffee may stunt the growth of your ego."

"I can't help you're good for it. Though I'm taking it, you're not a morning person?"

"Negative."

"Shame," I stretch my legs out on the ottoman in front of me. "I'm a wake up with the birds, hit the gym, sunny side up type of guy."

"Opposite. I'm a wake up, throw my alarm clock, curse the breath of life, and stomp around with my eyes closed until I hit water type of gal." She smirks down at her tablet, and I chuckle.

"So, what are you doing here?" I look around the mostly empty shop. "School hasn't started yet, why are you hanging out so close to campus already?"

"Creature of habit. This is where I get my cram sessions in. And I still live at home, so this place is my getaway."

"I've never seen you here before."

Her eyes dull. "You've never noticed me here before."

"Don't take offense, Priss. I keep mostly to myself."

"Oh, I'm not offended, but it seems I'm not lucky enough to go unnoticed today."

That has me grinning like an idiot. "Admit it, you like me. And last night you bit your lip more than once thinking about me in the *nude* wearing only a hat."

"Puh-lease, unless your name is Shawn Mendes, you are not in my fantasies."

"What's a guy got to do to get in your fantasies?"

She tips her coffee, her eyes alight with surprise.

"Cat got your tongue?"

"You're more like a hairball, Prescott."

"Ouch."

"Yo, Lance," Patrick calls my name as he enters the coffee shop. He barely glances at Harper and kicks the bottom of my chair. "What are you doing?"

"Drinking coffee and talking to Harper," I grit out in annoyance. He barely spares her a glance.

"Harper, this is—"

"Number thirty-four, Patrick Wallace aka 'Loose Ends.'"

This piques his interest. "You the dancer girl?"

"Yep," Harper says, popping the 'p' without looking up from her tablet. "That's me. So," she says, scrolling, "how much shit has he talked about me?"

"Little bit," Pat replies with a smile. He's a tank, twice my size and one of the best linebackers in the state. He looks like a hulked-up version of Opie—*Sons of Anarchy*, not *Andy Griffith*—as he glances between us trying to figure out what I'm up to. I'm unsure myself.

He lightly kicks the side of my chair again. "So, we going, or what?"

Sipping the last of my coffee, I stand. "Later, Priss."

"Mr. Grinch," she gives me a curt nod in dismissal, and I bark out a laugh before leaning down to whisper in her ear. She smells like vanilla and coffee.

"What color hat was I wearing?"

Her reply is instant. "Black."

"I knew it."

She scowls as I back away with a satisfied smile. "Busted."

She shakes her head, heat evident on her cheeks as I join Pat at the door.

He glances back at her, confused, and grills me the minute we step outside. "You into *her?*"

"I told you, we work out together at Jake's dad's gym," I glance back before the door closes, catching her eyes on me before she flicks them back to her tablet. Grinning, I turn back to Pat. "And I don't dislike her. Why?"

"Well, that's surprising considering a few weeks ago you did nothing but bitch to Jake about her… She's not your type, is she?"

I'm already offended. "What do you know about my type?"

"I know enough to know she's not it. She's plain and not exactly…hot, dude."

"What the fuck? What does it matter to you?"

"It doesn't. You barely socialize at all, let alone sit and chat with a girl who's clearly not your type." He glances back, "decent set of legs, but yeah, that face ruins her for me."

"Good thing she doesn't give a damn about you or what you think. Don't be such a dick. There's nothing *plain* about that girl, I assure you." I shrug. "I was having coffee, so was she."

"Huh."

I climb inside the cab, slamming the door behind me. Pat joins me, staring a hole into the side of my head. I take three seconds to cool my shit before I turn to him on a growl. "What?"

"You like her."

"A lot more than you right now. Drive the truck. Coach will have our asses if we're late."

ten

HARPER

TWERKING. HE CAUGHT ME TWERKING. I ADMIT I GOT A LITTLE carried away once I saw what it was doing to him. Some days my ass has a mind of its own and today, it got lost in the music, and in *him*. I blame Lizzo and her bad bitch self. The minute the music started; my ass took the cue. I must admit I broke it down and got a little nasty. Even when I caught sight of him standing at his bag—I didn't tone it down, no I turned it up…octane. And damn if he didn't deserve a little payback with the way he struts around the gym, just as close to indecent as me. Fine, he's got shorts on, but it's not enough to cover his raw sex appeal. The man is tall, dark, trim, tanned, muscular perfection and the barbed wire tats around his arms deserve the attention they've gotten. The Gods slapped that man with sexy, and his skin drank it in. I worked myself stupid, basking in the attention of his smoldering gaze. And the payback was worth it.

He got hard. I know he did because I watched him adjust his junk…twice. Stamina is something that comes naturally to me after years of dance, so the show lasted far longer than intended, and not once did his gaze waver. He enjoyed every second. For fifteen solid minutes, his gloves didn't touch the bag, arms at his sides, he'd watched me, and I danced for him.

And it was the most erotic fifteen minutes of my life.

When I finish the last of a five-song set, I begin packing my bag, thankful when I see my sister's name flash on my phone and I shoulder my duffle before answering. I spare a glance back at Lance to see he's still speechless and not doing a damn thing to hide his arousal. My heart skips several beats as our eyes connect.

"Sis, you there? You answered the phone. Harper? What in the hell are you doing?"

Eyes locked, my throat goes dry. I see the intent in his eyes, the hesitation in his posture. Was that an invitation I just gave him? And why? It's not like he deserves one. But that was clear flirtation on my part. Maybe he's just as confused at the signal as I am.

"HARPER! I'm about to hang up."

"H-hey."

"Are you okay?"

Am I?

I can't see shit past the look in his eyes. I burn that look to memory because I know later, I'm going to use it.

I raise my hand to Lance in goodbye, and he barely lifts his glove before I walk out the door.

eleven

LANCE

"Wake up, Prescott!"

I move to position and curse my lack of concentration.

She's fucking killing me. That body, Jesus, that body is perfect. The more I watch her, the more I want to play with it, play with her.

I've been in a daze since she danced for me. And there's no mistaking it was all for me. What in the hell was that show all about? I got so hard the other night I thought I was going to load my shorts and that was just from watching her. The way she moves is addicting. An hour into practice and I'm still cloudy just thinking of how she made that ass jiggle. Jesus Christ, I've never been so hard. I had to snap two off that night. In her wake at the gym, I had my gloves off and my cock in hand before she could lock the door. I was jerking my shit like a sick fucking lunatic. It was only after I came long and hard that I realized there might be cameras. I had to call Jake to verify there wasn't video evidence of me losing my shit over this girl and stuttered out an excuse as to why I needed to know. In my prayers that night, I thanked God his dad was too cheap to spend the money on security.

Harper is torturing me at this point, and I have no idea why, but I'm letting her. For the last few weeks, she's been taking up my thoughts and every bit of my sexual imagination. I don't know what's happening, but there's static in every corner of that gym and it's not just on my side. I'm so tempted to cut the bullshit and just ask her what her game is, but I'm not sure she knows. She's a good girl, that much I'm sure of. Though she's quiet, there's an inkling of something in her eyes, her stare, that I'm all too familiar with.

There's a lion inside that little lamb, and if that was an invitation—I'm all too ready to unleash her.

I'm not in the mood to box tonight, but I showed up. I'm here. Hoping…for what? Honestly, it's enough just to watch her dance. It's quickly becoming a new favorite pastime. Watching her brings me a sort of peace. It lets me know I'm not the only one out here working on my hustle alone. She's like me in a way, at least I think she is. Every time I see her, she's alone, and I think she prefers it. She doesn't seem uncomfortable without the company of others.

"Hey," she greets me, walking out of the locker room.

"'Sup?" I say, throwing a punch.

"You not in the mood tonight?" She asks, reading me all too easily. I speed up my throws, and she rolls her eyes. "It's cool, Prescott, no need to showboat, you must be exhausted since you had two practices today."

"How do you know?"

"I told you, I'm a fan."

This has my attention. "You watched practice today?"

"For about fifteen minutes. My sister was at the school, bringing my dad lunch. I met her there."

"Huh."

"You're looking good out there."

"Thanks."

"I just ordered a pizza. You want some?"

"What kind?"

"Does it matter? This is your third workout today and you're barely standing."

"Good point." I work my gloves off just as a sharp knock sounds on the tin door of the gym. Harper disappears briefly before hauling a huge box back in along with a plastic bag.

"You ordered that not knowing if I'd want any?"

I approach her and take the box, setting it down on a stack of mats.

She shrugs. "Leftovers. Someone at home will eat this if you don't."

She unveils some plates and napkins from the bag and passes them between us. I take the seat opposite her on the mat. Lifting the lid, I see it's plain cheese, New York style.

"Shit, you did good. This is my favorite."

"Mine too. This is the only place that makes it right. Like authentic New York."

"You ever been there?"

"Oh yeah, it's my second home. I'm a half Jewish New Yorker, Mom's side. Double major; dance and accounting. I work some summers for my nana at her accounting firm in New York City. Nana knows her numbers and thanks to her, I've been invested since I was young. She's a wizard. After I hang up my dance shoes, I plan to run my own firm and later, live off dividends. If you need help getting your investment portfolio started, I'm your girl."

"I'll keep that in mind." I chuckle dryly at the irony I don't have much in my account due to the fact my dad swiped it to pay for a couple of Red Angus.

"We're supposed to see a Broadway show this Christmas. I can't wait."

I question her while devouring the perfect bit of gooey bread and cheese. "Is that your goal? Broadway?"

"Any dance troupe. I'd love to dance backup in a tour. What about you? Ever been to New York?"

"Nah, we didn't travel much when I was young. We had too much work to do at the ranch."

"I'll bet it must have been awesome growing up there."

"It was. Lots of vitamin D but a shitload of hard work."

"Yeah. I can imagine."

She lifts the pizza to her mouth and takes a huge bite.

"How in the hell did you get all that in your mouth?"

She wrinkles her nose and pulls the pizza away, a string of cheese floating in the air behind it. "Talent," she says around a bite.

"Impressive." I finish a slice in record time and am grateful. "This is good. Thank you."

"Welcome."

Grabbing a second piece, I look up to see she's watching me. "You look…less stressed."

I want to tell her I've been beating off more regularly thanks to her weekly shows, but I don't think that will go over well. "I've been sleeping a lot better lately."

She quirks a blonde brow. "Any particular reason?"

"Excessive workouts."

Her eyes dart down at her empty plate. "Do you have a girlfriend?"

"If you want to ask me a question, Priss, you need to look at me."

She doesn't hesitate, though I know it costs her a little pride. But if I'm honest, I'm tiring of the cat and mouse routine. My interest is past piqued. Our eyes connect, and I feel…something shift. It's a connection, along with the low-lying pulse that's been strengthening since the minute we met in this gym.

Her eyes dart to my lips as I lick them clean. "Harper, you had a question?"

"Just asked if you had a girlfriend."

"I've been avoiding it most of my time here because I'm not sure where I'll end up. I'm concentrating on the game. Wouldn't be fair."

She nods. "Makes sense."

"What about you?"

"I was seeing this one guy for all of ten minutes a couple of months ago, but I swear he was only into me when I danced."

I choke on some cheese and clear my throat with my chuckle.

Her eyes snap up. "What?"

"Nothing."

"Tell me," she prompts.

"Harper, you know damn well you get dirty as fuck at times when you dance."

A guilty grin covers her lips before she gives me a full smile that kicks my pulse up. "I do know that, but if my ass is all he's drawn to, we don't have much to go on."

Remorse blankets me because, in a way, I'm guilty of the same. But it's not just the way she moves; it's the way she looks at me, it's her backbone, the way she smiles. The way she lights up when she sees me. The way I feel lit when I look at her.

"True."

"So, yeah, single. I'm too into my goals to take anyone se-riously." She sips her soda.

Silence lingers, and I'm comfortable in it until she speaks up.

"Don't feel obligated to hang out. It was pizza."

"What?" Confused, I stare at her.

"It's Friday night, Lance. Don't feel like you need to make conversation…or hang because I bought pizza. You got quiet."

"I'm in a carb coma," I say, laying back on the mat. "I'm not going anywhere."

More silence. I open my eyes and find hers trained on the exposed skin at my stomach.

"Busted. You know you check me out almost as much as I stare at your ass."

"More ass talk," she rolls her eyes.

"It is one *amazing* ass you have. And those legs."

Red creeps up her cheeks as her chewing slows, and she swallows loudly.

"Are you innocent, Harper?"

Shit, Lance, subtle much?

I can sense her deer in headlights vibe. "Don't answer that. I had no right to ask."

"I'm not. Not exactly. I fooled around when I was way too young." She slides closer to me, and I tuck my hand behind my head and peer up at her. "I, uh, made a big mistake in judgment and let's just say, I compensated with my virginity. My parents found out. It was a bad time. So innocent, no, far from it. But I haven't…uh, done much since."

"Much?"

She frowns. "Why are you so interested?"

"Because I am."

"That's too vague. If you want to pry, you're going to have to give me a better reason than that."

"Because I think about you. A lot lately."

She pauses her drink halfway to her mouth and stares down at me before recovering.

"I'm thinking it's not about my sharp wit or pizza ordering capabilities."

"It's not like you've given me much of a chance to get to know you, Priss."

"Well, it's not like you're the most receptive man in the world with your mastery of resting bastard face."

We both laugh until I lift her hand and put it on my chest.

"I'm serious, Harper. I think about you. I wonder what it would be like if we just cut the bullshit."

"You want more of a chance to know me?"

"Yeah, maybe."

"That clears things up," she spouts sarcastically, tossing her half-eaten slice down and pulling her hand from my grip to clear her fingers of the crumbs.

"Look, I'm not much into tap dancing around subjects."

"That's obvious."

"I'm just saying let's not waste time denying there's something going on here."

I reach out and run a finger down her cheek, and she freezes. Our eyes lock and my cock stirs. "I know you feel that."

"I do," she says, a little breathless. I grip the back of her neck from where I lay and pull her towards me, my thumb sliding along her throat. "Closer, Harper, I want to run something by you."

She leans in, her breath catching with each stroke of my thumb.

"W-w-what?"

"What if I told you I wanted to pull you to me right now and murder those lips of yours?"

"I would say that," she swallows, her chest rising and falling, "sounds painful and like a bad idea."

I loosen my grip. "Message recei—"

"But," she sputters nervously, "you should totally do it."

In a flash, she dumps her plate on the mat and straddles me. I'm already in motion, rising up and thrusting my fingers in her hair right before our mouths crash together. It's more than a kiss; it's recognition of the fuse we lit the second we met and the fire we've spread up until this point of explosion. Her kiss as eager as mine, I go deep, sweeping my tongue into her tiny mouth, the sweet taste of soda fresh on her tongue as she grinds on my lap. It's instant, our rhythm, like we've been practicing for months for the big show. I devour her, cradling her head, my hands in a place where I know she feels safe. It's incredible kissing her, being this close, after wanting her for what seems like an eternity but has only been a matter of weeks. When we pull away catching our breath, we share a smile before she speaks.

"So, this is an ass thing?"

"I told you, it was your legs first."

twelve

HARPER

LANCE GRINS AT ME FROM WHERE HE SITS BENEATH ME, HIS hands still tangling in my hair. I'm drunk on his kiss, the situation surreal. It's his words that slap me back into reality. *"It was your legs first."*

I hide the piece of me hurt by his comment and my offense. He doesn't know or understand why this would irk me. He doesn't see me the way I view myself. Just once I wish my body wasn't the physical attribute that draws a man in, especially this man.

"You've got to admit," he says hoarsely. "I'm not the only one guilty of that."

"No, you're not." It's the truth. I've been just as attracted from afar as he has. It sure as hell wasn't his personality that drew me to him initially.

He'll be the perfect man to experiment with. And maybe that's what he should be for me, an experiment with my newly revived sexuality. Because since he stepped into the gym with me, the part of me I've kept dormant has sprung back to life. Watching him this summer, I've worked up quite a thirst, and suddenly he's quenching it. His eyes never straying from mine, I can feel him hard beneath me, feel the heat emanating from his skin, from his bold touch. Most girls would have a condom strapped on him by now, and a part of me wants to be that girl, but the other knows this experiment could go horribly wrong, not just for me but for us both.

He presses his forehead to mine, the bulge beneath me impossible to ignore. "Harper," he huffs before leaning in to bite my neck. I grind on his dick fully aware I'm stoking the fire and hear the breath leave him. "We both know you're not about to get naked, be kind."

"Sorry, can't help it."

"Neither can I."

"I like that I have this effect on you."

He pulls back, his eyes seeking my permission as his hands gently explore. He trails them down my sides before he grips my ass in his palms, and I swear I hear him whimper before his lips again crush mine. Then we're kissing again and it feels like flying. I know this high—it's dangerous. This high is a liar that tells you that nothing is more important than chasing for more, but the importance lies in *who* is behind the kiss. I'm kissing Lance Prescott, one of Grand's most eligible bachelors. His palms glide up my waist, his thumbs sliding along the underside of my breasts while I moan into his mouth. I'm in nothing but cotton sports shorts, my clit rubbing along the hard ridge in his thin mesh shorts. It's the perfect friction. Gasping into his mouth, I pull away electrified and he studies me. I swivel my hips, spurring him on and his eyes flare.

"Jesus," he groans thrusting up to meet my movement, and with that, my thighs begin to shake.

"Look at you…" I don't have a second to react to his compliment before I'm on my back, his hands pinning me, grinding into me. "Can I make you come?"

Gazing up, I can't believe what I'm seeing. Lance is hovering over me looking at me like I'm the eighth wonder of the world. To him, this may be nothing unusual, to me, it's everything.

It's like I'm being seen for the first time, center stage. It feels so spectacularly real.

"Are you…being honest?"

He draws his brows, his breaths more like grunts.

"What?"

"Look, I know, I mean I can *tell* you're being careful, and you don't want to hurt me…"

"Are we having *that* talk already? I want to Make. You. Come. Not start a conversation."

"Right, sorry. Yes."

"Yes, what?" He taunts in a slow grind. I'm soaked. With no shame, I meet his thrusts until he backs away, taunting me. "Yes, what? Harper?"

"Yes. Make me come."

He leans down and takes my lips while slowly grinding into me. With another leisurely stroke and thorough kiss, he pulls away, his hips still in motion, and I feel every inch of his dick sliding along my center.

"Fuck, this feels so good," he breathes. "It does, Harper, you," he shakes his head. "God, the ways I want you."

"I'm right here."

"You're not ready for what I want to do to you."

"Make me ready."

"Damn, woman."

Grind. Thrust.

Grind.

Thrust.

My needy clit pulses with each slow stroke as he does it again and again. It's agonizing for both of us, a lot of tease without re-ward but the view of him hovering above is more than enough. He's looking right at me, deep cloudy eyes filled with heat, long dark lashes flitting over his cheekbones as he gives in to the pull, closing his eyes, biting his lips while he works me.

"I'm going to lose my shit," he rasps out. He drives then, his hips hitting me perfectly. And that's when I feel it, the edge of an orgasm. It's small, subtle at first but it creeps up in a tiny wave climbing until it unfurls through my whole body. I go over, pulsating everywhere, my body catching fire as Lance thrusts again spurring it on, milking it, while gripping my jaw to watch it happen. No man has ever watched me come, and I'm fascinated by his response to me. Somehow it means something, and I don't think either of us isn't aware of it. I could be romanticizing. And maybe I am, but I have a beautiful man between my legs, and that *is* something. I appreciate it for what it is. Lance buries his head in my neck, his cock rock hard on my thigh.

And then I go limp, my pulse still humming, my body covered in a thin veil of sweat.

"That was…"

"So good." His voice is all I hear before he claims my mouth in a hungry kiss. When he pulls away, I look up at him with a new perspective. I want to hand him an award of some sort, but I grant him my awkward reaction instead.

"You are *really* good at that."

"What do you think about doing this again?"

I grin up at him. "Not much in it for you."

"Let's rectify that." He lifts one side of his mouth and takes my hand in his. Together we palm his cock. He groans into my mouth taking it with a possessive kiss as I take over, dipping into his shorts and pumping his length with my hand.

"That's it, this will be quick," he rasps out seconds before he pulses in my hand. He lets out an exaggerated breath, his face straining, his mouth slightly parted before he stares down at me with wonder. After, we lay spent on the mat for minutes in silence, our bodies tangled.

Once rested, he pulls me up to sit with him.

"I had fun tonight, just…hanging out. Fooling around. I don't see the harm, if you don't."

"I don't fool around, Lance." I lift from the mat, realizing where we are and how far we've come from casually sharing pizza and conversation in mere minutes.

What in the hell?

I just let a guy dry hump me on a gym mat. I look over to see Lance isn't at all weirded out by this. To me, it might as well have been voyeurism.

"Oh my God, what if there are cameras?"

"There aren't. I asked Jake the other…"

I narrow my eyes.

He winces, "when I got my key?"

It's obviously a lie, but I let him have it. All that matters is that we weren't on camera. It's my worst fear and for good reason. What in the hell was I thinking? I pull myself together while Lance reads my change in demeanor.

"What's wrong?"

"Just something…nothing. Paranoia."

"I can prove there are no cameras."

"What?" I ask, still dazed. I've never done anything like this. Not even close. I feel free and terrified at the same time.

"I believe you," I say, mind reeling.

"I'm not sure you do, come on," he stands and grabs my hand. I take it as he escorts me to the office. It's pretty basic, nothing to see.

"If there were cameras, there would be a monitoring system in here. Text Jake, he'll tell you."

"Okay." I breathe a little easier.

"Did we go too fast?" He's on edge, and I put him there.

"No. Not too fast. I just had a moment. I'm good."

Slightly at ease, he pulls me to him and lifts my chin with his palm. "So, what do you think? I mean about doing this again? Food, conversation, fooling around?"

"Are you asking me out?"

"I'm asking for more of what we did here. No pressure."

"I don't know about *here*."

"I still want to watch you dance."

That comment lights me up from inside. "I can dance anywhere."

"For me?"

"Maybe. I need to go."

He draws his brows. "Okay."

"I'll see you Wednesday."

It's clear he's not happy about my quick retreat, but I need council. Like now. With my sister or René. Either will do for the moment. I'm in unchartered territory. I need to pull up my big girl panties, but right now, they're soaked, courtesy of Lance Prescott. Gathering my things, I leave him standing in the middle of the gym.

thirteen

HARPER

SAFELY INSIDE MY TOYOTA. I SHOOT OFF A TEXT TO MY BEST FRIEND René.

SOS. Call me now.

My phone rings and I answer, starting my RAV4 and putting my phone in the cradle when the Bluetooth connects.

"Mami. What is it? I have three minutes until my Uber gets here.

"I just got dry humped by a hot-ass ballplayer."

"Tell me everything. Is this the guy from the gym?"

"YES!" I press my forehead to the wheel. "God, René, it was like my whole body lit on fire."

"So hot. Did you finish?"

"Finish?"

"Get off?"

"Off. Yes. What do I do?"

"Send him a thank you card."

"Really?"

"Hell no. Oh God, you're a hopeless and dopey romantic, and you chose a jock to fool around with? Not smart, Mami."

"I know. Trust me, but he's so damned sexy."

"They always are. Until they steal your favorite shirt and go have sex with another man while wearing it!"

"I don't think I'm in that same danger."

"Lucky you."

"You know whenever you say that it sounds like you're calling me a lucky Jew."

"Aren't you?"

I grin. "Tonight I am."

"Look, have fun. Don't over think things. This is probably a fling."

A knock at the window has me jumping out of my skin. I look over to see Lance holding the pizza box. Mortified, I roll down my window and narrow my eyes.

"How long have you been standing there?"

"Pretty much your entire conversation." Lance chuckles. "You forgot this, and my ride is here." He points to a white Taurus. "I couldn't hold out any longer."

"Who is that? Mami?" I turn the volume way down; my eyes bugging out of my head. All the blood rushes to my face as I snatch the box out of his hands.

Lance leans down, his presence stealing my breath. "So, no thank you card?"

"It's rude to eavesdrop."

"Just wanted to make sure you didn't fake that orgasm."

"You know damn well I—"

He snatches my face into his hands and plants a long hard kiss on my lips. When he pulls away, his eyes are shining with amusement. "Goodnight, *Mami*."

fourteen

HARPER

L ANCE'S TONGUE SWIRLS AROUND MY CENTER IN A TEASE before he begins to lap me up while I rip at his thick hair. Since we've started to get intimate, the minute we enter the gym, we enter a different world.

Tonight, the second I locked the door he crossed the gym to meet me, and we collided. There wasn't an ounce of hesitation on either of our parts. The trust he's been earning evident now as he keeps me pinned, his hands around my wrists, his mouth devouring me.

For the last two weeks, we've been taking it as far as we can go without actually 'doing' the deed. Some nights we study. Others he works himself stupid on the bag until he collapses, mostly silent due to his frustrations. It's getting easier to gauge his moods. And it's also getting easier for me to see the weight on his herculean shoulders. Today he's been more talkative than usual. Taking a break from his workout to watch me dance. Sometimes he sits atop the mats and just watches, quick to compliment, always ready to give soundless approval with the look on his face alone. He's replaced every single man in my fantasies, and tonight, after touching and tasting me the way he has, I doubt he'll be excluded in any of them in the future.

"Yes, right THERE!"

His gravelly chuckle sounds throughout the room as I sink further into the mat, my legs over his shoulders, thighs spread wide as he goes as deep as his tongue will allow. Shaking uncontrollably, I come on his tongue, and he laps me up, a master at his craft. He's gone down on me twice and never asked me to return the favor. I plan on reciprocating soon but have been gun shy due to lack of experience. The more he touches me, looks at me, the bolder I become. Content with a sigh, I lay back as he moves up my body and takes my mouth in a kiss, my flavor on his tongue. Deep groans erupt from his throat, his stone erection pressed against me until he pulls away, frustrated. "Harper, I want you alone," he rasps out. "I need to get you alone."

"We are alone," I answer between kisses, goosebumps covering my flesh. I feel safe with him. The way he touches me, covers me, it's all I think about lately. That and his infectious laugh, the way he strokes my skin, his tender words surprising in contrast to his rough exterior. I'm enamored, and honestly proud to have the attention of a man of this caliber. For other women, I'm sure a football star is all they see, but I see the accompanying stars that make up his constellation. Football is such a small part of who he is. Between our talks about ambition, love of family, and all they entail, I know the matter, the makeup of this man and trust it to be the truth. I feel it with his every word, his every action. It's then I make the decision.

I separate us so I can look up at him, tracing the barbed wire tattoo around his arm with my fingers.

"I want you in my bed." He carefully weighs my reaction. "Tomorrow night. Unless you think—"

"Now."

"Now?"

"Right now."

"Lance, I want, I want…"

He exhales, warm breath hitting my center, my back bowing from his mattress. We've been at it for what seems like hours, unable to go more than a few seconds without attacking the other.

"Now, I want you now, all of you."

He rises to hover above me and shakes his head. "Harper, I don't know if this is a good idea."

"What? Why?"

"I'm not going to be the one to take it."

"I'm not a virgin. I mean, technically, I'm not. I told you that."

"My intentions aren't pure for the moment. I can't think past fucking you. And you deserve better."

"And?" I wrap my legs tightly around him. "You had every intention of following through when you brought me here. Don't bullshit me, Lance."

"It's just that I like you," he murmurs against my mouth. "And I don't know what happens after."

"Sure, you do," I say softly. "We both do." I lean in and suck his lip. He groans as he thrusts into me fully clothed, making me gasp out his name. "I want this."

"Harper, if we take this further, we take it further in and out of this room. I can't guarantee I'm the best guy for you."

"I know you are. I don't need your assurances."

"It should be with someone who can promise you a future."

"Lance," I pull back to make sure he hears me. "Please don't be offended. But I'm not asking you for your future. I don't need you to promise me forever or even tomorrow. When I think of *my* future, it has little to nothing to do with a man. I'm not planning my life around a man, now or *ever*. I'm a dancer, that's what I want to be."

His eyes do nothing to shield his surprise. "*Wow.*"

"Yeah, so don't worry, I don't need you to put a ring on it, I need you to put a condom on it. As long as we're being honest," I slide my shorts down along with my panties and wrap my legs around him. "I want this, right now, with *you.*"

"Harper," he groans, dropping his head in my neck.

I boldly reach between us and untuck his cock from his shorts, running my thumb over the silkiness of the head.

"It's so soft."

He growls, ripping himself from my neck. "That's not *soft.*"

"No," I giggle, stroking him lightly. "The skin is so soft. So silky," I rasp out.

"Great, you talk dirty too. Perfect," he groans.

"So hard. I want to taste this," I play with the moisture at the tip.

"Fuuuuuck, I may die."

"Lance, look at me." He brings grey eyes to mine. "I want this inside of me, *now.*"

"Harper, I don't want to hurt you."

He reaches between us; stretching me, rubbing me, beckoning, playing me perfectly.

"Would you rather it be someone else?"

His whole body tenses, as my heart thunders. And that's when I lose my breath. His fingers stop, his breath stutters before he brings answering eyes to mine. In them, I see jealousy, possession, and I take those seconds to enjoy them. His hungry mouth descends as we lose the rest of our clothing. Once bare, he sinks between my legs, his eyes roaming appreciatively down my body before he plants his forearms next to me and we lock gazes.

"Sure?"

I nod again, and he reaches for a condom in his bedside table.

Once fitted, he slowly presses in, stealing my breath. Hands on his chest, I stare up at him breathing through the discomfort and nod my head. He presses in again, and white-hot pain sears through me as I arch off the bed into his chest. He holds me there, to him, his breaths ragged at my ear, I feel torn, I feel breakable, I feel precious to him. It burns, and I do my best to control my whimper.

"I'm not really getting the fuss," I joke stupidly before silvery eyes meet mine. And then he kisses me, so deeply that the burn fades briefly, the thrust of his tongue is hypnotizing. It's everything, *everything*. I know I feel for him, it was inevitable, but the feeling that it's fleeting has me hanging onto every second. I bat that thought away and let him kiss me, let him shower me with the affection I've been starving for.

Because underneath him I feel perfect, not just adequate or passable.

I *feel* precious.

I *feel* beautiful.

He gently presses me back into the pillow with his kiss, his hands pushing away my hair.

"Tell me if it's too much."

He gently rears back, and then it's burning again. I don't make a sound, I just stare up at him with parted lips, trying to soak in everything, the curve of his biceps, the strain in his chest, the longing in his eyes, his fast breaths, the way the sheet drapes over the curve of his ass.

"Harper," he whispers, gliding in and out easily now. The pain still lingers, but it's the pulse at his neck I'm studying, the weight of him on top of me, I'm memorizing. Girls like me don't often get to keep guys like Lance.

I want to make that a lie. I want to believe we're different. I want to believe that he's capable of committing to me, of looking at me the same way for a thousand days to come, and a thousand days after. But I meant what I said. I won't ever put my dreams on hold for any man, no matter how magnificent said man is.

So, this is what obsession feels like.

I'm smitten. Totally rapt, and I allow myself to warp and be shaped by it. It's incredible and consuming. It's everything I thought it would be.

"Better?" He prompts, his thrusts picking up.

"No, how are you doing?"

His grin is misplaced in the moment due to my uncontrollable mouth, but beautiful, and I love the sight of it.

"Fucking perfect."

"Should I be doing something here?"

"Not this time," he whispers through a pleasure-filled grunt.

"I'll improvise," I wrap my legs around his back and squeeze his hips with my thighs.

"Jesus, Harper," he moans.

"Ah, like that? You're so simple, Prescott."

A chuckle escapes him as he speeds up. And then I feel it, something close to pleasure and a moan escapes me.

"That's it, baby," he urges, his mouth hanging as he brands his touch to memory and burns his name across my heart. That term strikes me deep, and then I'm in a haze, drunk on his rhythm, soaking up the feel of his eyes hot on me.

I'd be his personal whore to keep this feeling. No wonder women make this a bad habit. I can see the appeal.

Moaning again, I thrust up to meet him and regret it because of the resulting pain, when he curses, drunk on pleasure.

My moans spur him on as I tighten myself, wrapping around him and he loses control.

He burns through me, knocking us both into orbit an inch past blissful oblivion, his eyes opening as if in shock as he convulses and pants out his orgasm. And then he's kissing me, so long and so hard that I fight for breath. His lips cover every inch of my face, my neck, trailing down and laving one nipple then the other before he collapses in a heap on my stomach.

A smile graces my lips as I stare at the blades of the fan on his ceiling.

It was pleasure and pain, worship and consummation.

In head and heart, it was my first time, and it was perfect.

Lance, now a pile of hair and muscle on my chest breathes out his contentment as I run my fingers through his hair.

"Well, that's one way to lose your virginity."

His body bounces slightly against mine.

He rests his chin on my stomach, peering up at me while he massages my sides. "You okay?"

"Stop asking me that, this has been done before."

"Just don't want you hurting."

"Well, I didn't realize your dick was *that* big."

A loud laugh erupts from him, and he pulls away to gaze down at me, his lips smiling, his eyes filled with a mix of scold and concern. "Stop making jokes."

"I don't know what else to do."

"How about telling me if you're hurting."

"Hell, yes, I'm hurting."

He winces. "I'm sorry."

"I'm not," I say softly.

He holds himself above me his face glistening with the aftermath—a drop of sweat sliding down his temple. "Harper, that was a gift you gave me."

"Was it? It seemed kind of awkward."

His laugh rumbles through his words. "Stop making jokes."

"Stop giving me material."

"You can play off of anything." His gaze rakes over me. "This is where you're supposed to let the hormones kick in and get emotional."

"Sorry to disappoint."

His grin widens as he presses a gentle kiss to my lips and moves to exit the bed. "I'm going to get us some food and water."

"I'll straighten up your room. You're quite the slob." It's just the opposite. There's not a single thing out of place. His books piled neatly on top of a cheap IKEA desk, while all his clothes hang in a small closet. On top of his dresser sits his watch and a bottle of cologne. Even his pocket change is stacked neatly. He's a neat freak, and I love it. It's definitely the room of a bachelor, but not wholly devoid of life. There's a picture of his family on the nightstand. Covering myself with the sheet, I study the image and what must be the eighteen-year-old version of Lance on his graduation day, his smile sincere, carefree, a different version of Lance than the one I met. The man sliding on his sneakers is a far cry from the boy in the picture. When I get a glimpse of that boy here and there, I hang onto it. It's the side I love the most. A side I'm sure only a few see. I'm one of the lucky ones. He's let me in, and it both elates and terrifies me.

Lying in his bed naked in more ways than one, the reality

of his words set in. My emotions are getting the best of me. I've let myself be vulnerable with him, something I don't take lightly. Something I wasn't sure I'd ever be capable of again. But because he is who he is, because of his understanding, it feels like I'm with another version of myself. We are alike in a lot of ways; ambitious, hard-working, goal-oriented, family-oriented, and loners who don't easily trust. And I want so badly to trust the version I know; the version whose touch makes me feel beautiful and breakable, fragile and worthy.

I share a reassuring grin with him as he leaves the room, burying my fears beneath that smile. It's only when I hear his footfalls on the stairs that I let the tears slip. But they aren't tears of regret or pain. They're tears that let me know I made the right decision by choosing Lance Prescott, no matter where that decision leads us.

fifteen

LANCE

"OH NO. OH, MY GOD!" HER SHRIEK IS LOW, BUT IT wakes me from a dead sleep. Raising my head from my pillow, I squint in the dark to see Harper shuffling around the room dressing frantically.

"What's wrong?" I click on my bedside lamp, and she freezes, one leg in her shorts. Closing her eyes, she hangs her head.

"There's something I need to tell you."

I grip her hand and pull her to sit on the edge of the bed, distracted by how her hair cascades down her back. I'm so tempted to pull her back to bed, but the look on her face has me on edge.

"Tell me."

"It's bad. Brace yourself."

"Tell me."

"I didn't mean to. Swear to God."

"To what?" I glance around the room and then back to her. "What could you have done in this room in the last few hours?"

"I'm so sorry."

"Out with it," I growl impatiently and she jumps. "Sorry. But the suspense is killing me."

"I may have just Snapchatted a picture of your ass and the top of your jersey to my sister. Well," she says a blush creeping up her neck, "it was meant for my sister."

"What?" I chuckle. "Why?"

"It's not funny," she says gravely.

"It's kind of funny."

"Lance, I Snapchatted your ass to my father!"

I freeze.

"I sent it to my whole family. I meant to just get the top of the jersey without the number, I was cropping it that way and didn't see your ass in plain view behind it."

"Did you add a caption?"

"Yes."

I can't help my laugh.

"Lance, it's not funny!"

"Okay," I say, unable to hide my smile. "Sorry," I do my best to keep a straight face. "What did it say?"

"I've taken a lover. Grand man, indeed."

"Oh, shit," I lay back as laughter rips out from me.

"It's not funny!" She whisper-yells before her face falls.

"Why would you do that?"

"You wouldn't understand. It's a sister thing. She's been trying to get me to take the leap for a hot minute."

"I'd say you did a pretty good job." I rub her silky hair between my fingers, itching for another go with her.

"Lance," she shakes her head, her eyes filling with tears. "I really screwed up."

"Okay," I sit up doing my best to get my shit together as I try to pull her to me. She shakes her head and pushes at my chest.

"Hey, it's going to be embarrassing, but it will pass."

"Dad is fiercely protective of me because of what I told you."

"I get it, but you're twenty."

"Doesn't matter. It was a really serious deal."

"Okay, so you don't tell him who I am."

"That was always the plan. I never thought I'd have to explain this and I-I didn't tell you, didn't think it was important. I didn't know what was going to happen here." She gestures between us.

"Out with it, woman."

She hangs her head.

"My last name is Elliot."

That wipes the smile off my face.

"Elliot?"

"Yes."

"As in Coach Ryan Elliot's daughter?"

Her eyes fill with fresh tears, and she nods.

I spring out of bed and glare down at her. "Your dad is my fucking coach!?"

She nods, her eyes tracking my movement as I slip on mesh shorts. "Let me get this straight. You woke up in the middle of the night and took a shot of my jersey and ass and sent them straight to my fucking coach!?"

"That's, uh, that sounds creepy."

"Yeah, well, sorry, maybe I don't understand. I've never slept with a woman and Snapchatted her ass to my brother. What were you thinking?"

"I was thinking I was happy for five seconds and wanted to share it with my sister." She pulls the hem of her shirt down. "I have to go."

"Did you get my number in the picture?"

"No, I told you I made sure I got just the top of the front of it and snapped your ass on accident."

"Dammnit, Harper." I palm my face and shake my head. "Why didn't you tell me before?"

"You know this was a spontaneous hookup."

"The first time. The second time. Not today."

"You're right. I'm sorry. I'm so sorry. I'll go home and face the music. It's not like he can see the pic again. He can't study it and try and figure out who you are."

"Thank Christ." Anger boils beneath the surface, and I try to remain calm. "When you say protective—"

"He's unreasonable. What happened years ago broke his heart. It was humiliating for the whole family."

"Can't you delete it?"

She swallows. "No, you can only delete text, not pictures."

"It's dark in here, maybe he won't be able to make out much."

"Except I took the picture with flash. I'm so sorry." She gathers her bag from the floor. "I screwed up. I'll own it. I'll make it so you're nowhere near this."

I bite the inside of my cheek so hard my eyes water.

"Lance, I'm sorry."

"Just go, Harper."

"Please don't hate me."

"I don't, but you need to go. This could ruin my whole season and all of my plans."

"I meant to tell you…"

"But you fucking didn't," I seethe and see the hurt in her eyes. I'm seconds from an explosion and don't trust myself.

"No," she wipes a tear off her cheek and sniffles. "I didn't. I wanted to keep you to myself a little longer."

"Didn't keep you from bragging about it, huh? I know it wasn't your intention to broadcast, but it doesn't make you much better than the others."

Her eyes flare. "Don't you dare."

"You need to go before I say something else I know I'll regret."

She shakes her head, her eyes refilling. "I'm sorry, Lance."

"Just go."

"Don't do anything, okay? I'm going to go feel them out, maybe I can get to their phones before they view it and then it will be like nothing ever happened."

"Except I just deflowered my coach's daughter."

Tears stream down her cheeks. "You want to erase that too?"

"Harper, you purposefully deceived me. What do you want me to say?"

"I want you not to have meant that. But you did. Don't worry," her voice cracks along with my chest at the devastation on her face, but I'm too angry to stop her from leaving. "I'll make it disappear on my side. I'm sorry," she whispers one last time before closing the door.

sixteen

HARPER

CREEPING DOWN THE STAIRS OF THE HOUSE LANCE RENTS WITH two other guys, I'm safely at the front door and nearly sigh in relief.

"Hey."

Jumping back, I turn towards the source and see Troy fucking Jenner, the wide receiver for TGU sitting at the kitchen table. He's kicked back in his seat, playing with a beer cap, a bottle in one hand, his eyes on the deck just outside the door. The moon lights up his face clearly, though I know I'm safely shrouded in the dark. Troy is devastatingly handsome and for some reason I know if he were to look my way, he would see right through me. He's lost in his own head. I don't bother replying, but haul ass out of there. Once safely on the other side of the door, I sprint to my car parked on the other side of the street, praying I don't hit any other landmines. In the driver's seat, I start up my Toyota and glance up at Lance's window. He's standing there, watching me. He'd thrown me out, not with malicious intent. I know I deserved it. I'd kept my identity from him in a way. I wonder if he would have entertained me at all if he had known. Then again, with how pissed he is, I guess I got my answer.

When it comes to women and ball, the alphabet wins. The B always comes first. And for once, I let myself get lost in the moment, and this game already cost us both. He disappears from the window as I drive away.

seventeen

HARPER

"TWENTY YEARS OLD, AND YOU'RE HIDING IN YOUR ROOM because you had sex," I mutter around my toothbrush. I've been waiting my parents out. My parents—who are early risers. I haven't slept a wink and I got home too late to sneak into their room without being caught. Knowing them, there's a good chance they won't even open it today. They're not exactly social media experts and only downloaded the app so my sister, Kandace, could snap them pics of my nephew. I send my twentieth text to Kandace praying she calls me back. Briefly, I consider running through the house, jumping in my SUV and hauling ass to Houston where she lives and is capable of having sex without announcing it to the whole damned family. Just as I curse her for not coming to my rescue, my phone lights up, and I see her name.

"Kan—"

"Oh, my God, you idiot. You just killed our father!"

"Shut up! Shut up! What do I do?"

"Get a fucking crash cart," she yelps over the phone before she bursts into laughter. "Has he seen it?"

"No. Not yet."

"You've got to get that phone. Steal it. Smash it. *Both* of their phones."

"I will. Just…how?"

"I'll tell you, but can we talk about that ass for four seconds. Jesus. Way to go big or go home."

Panic courses through me. "Did you notice the jersey?"

"Yeah, seriously, what were you thinking?"

"I just wanted…" I don't know how to answer that. We're close, she knows why. She's just as nervous as I am.

"I get it. I do. But Harper…"

"I was giddy. And I couldn't sleep."

"How do you feel?"

"Mortified. That's a good description."

"Well, just tell Dad you meant to send it to me."

"Because that will go over well," I scoff. "This is serious. You think he'll kick him off the team?"

"You know he can't. Don't be dramatic. Who is it?"

"Not telling. Ever. So don't ask." I vow to myself then and there no matter what I face with my dad I won't ever crack.

"Was it awesome?"

"It was until I told him who I was."

"Oh, shit. You didn't tell him?"

"No. The whole first month we met we were kind of at odds, and then it just, you know, happened…God." I bury my head in my hands. "How am I going to explain this to Dad?"

"Tell him you wanted to brag to your sister that you bagged a hottie."

"Hey!"

"It's the truth, and I tell you all the time you're pretty and you don't believe me."

"Because I'm not. Not for a guy like that."

"He disagrees."

"Right." I cringe at the idea I may never feel what I felt beneath him last night in his bedroom again. Worshipped is a good description. Fresh anger surfaces when I think of how he threw me out of his room.

"He threw me out of his room. He took my virginity and threw me out of his room."

"You are kind of in the wrong, sis, seeing as how you Snapchatted his ass to his coach."

"He could have brainstormed with me, or at least walked me to the door."

"Self-preservation is evil. When that kicks in, all bedside manners have a tendency to go out the window. You're so green."

"Meaning?"

"Meaning, you have a lot to learn about men. The good part about them screwing up is that they have to grovel to get back in your good graces. Stand your ground early."

"Will do."

"Okay, so here's the plan. Until you hear Mom's voice morph, you're safe."

"I know, when she goes nuts her New York accent kicks in, and she sounds like that prude mom on South Park. What, what, what!?"

Kandace giggles. "That's dead-on, but Harper, focus. I'm going to call Mom on the house phone and gauge her mood. I'll fake an emergency and create a distraction."

"Uh-huh," I'm eager for the help.

"While I've got them all riled up, you—"

"Harper!" My mother screams from the kitchen.

"Oh shit," Kandace's voice deflates. "Maybe you forgot the trash…"

"Oh my God! Harper Jean!"

"What in the hell?" My dad's voice booms from the same room.

"Well there goes that theory. Babe, you're twenty. Stand firm. He knew you wouldn't be innocent forever."

"Harper! Get in here, right now!"

"I took a lover," she giggles. "You idiot."

"Thanks," I reply dryly as footsteps approach my door and my mother shrieks behind him.

"Ryan, Ryan, don't go in there, don't you dare, let me talk to her. Ryan, stop right now! You need to calm down."

"I should thank you," Kandace chirps. "I'll be the good daughter for at least six months."

"He's coming," I tell Kandace as my heart beats in my throat. "Bye, love you."

"Love you," she sighs. "Call me after."

"K."

Just as I hang up, my door bursts open, and I meet the livid eyes of my father.

eighteen

LANCE

IT'S BEEN NEARLY A WEEK SINCE I'VE SEEN HER. SHE'S NOT answering my texts and hasn't been to the gym since that day. School started a few days ago and I've been frantically searching campus between classes for any sign of her.

Through texts, I've apologized for the way I reacted, though I know for a fact, coach did not miss that message. He's been a prick since the summer program started, but now he's being unreasonable, riding us harder than he ever has, looking at each of us with clear accusation. Harper wasn't exaggerating. We got a thirty-minute lecture on respect just yesterday, most of which, coach growled out. The team was understandably confused as to why we were being lectured for half of practice, rather than on the field. It took everything I had to meet coach's eyes yesterday and not flinch. Most of the last few practices I wanted to speak up and name myself the culprit so I alone can deal with the backlash, other days I want to call him out for being such a dick. If I thought for one second this would blow over, I was dead wrong. Coming up empty on my search for her, I ignore the gnaw in my chest and shoot off a text.

Lance: Talk to me, Harper. Right now. At least tell me if you're okay.

Bubbles pop up and disappear the way they have for the last few days. She wants to talk, but she's afraid of the asshole that kicked her out of his room. I get it. But the situation was shit, and I was not at all prepared for the bomb she dropped. I see both sides of this, and I can't understand why she can't or refuses to see mine. I've told her enough for her to know how important this season is to me.

She's stubborn as hell. And most days it's an attribute I like about her, but for the last week, it's pissed me right the hell off. Staring at my phone, I will her to text back until it lights up with an incoming call.

"Hey, Momma."

"Hey, you. How are you?"

"Good, sore from practice yesterday and walking to class."

"They're working you hard, huh?"

"Every day."

"Well, I raised a warrior. You'll make it."

"How are you? How's Dad?"

"Good. Good. Dad's good, but your brother is a nightmare. I knew I should have stopped at one child. The little shit took off with the tractor last week to impress some girl. He actually drove it down the highway and picked her up. Stole my picnic basket with the good china and everything."

I can't help my grin. For years, Trevor thought his name was 'little shit.'

"He's in the dog house. Your father nearly skinned him."

"He's just blowing off steam, Mom."

"Is that what you call it? You weren't much more intelligent sneaking over to Becky Ballenger's house when you were only fifteen. Or was it Becky Rendon? I could never keep up. I was certain I was going to be a grandmother before you graduated."

"Mom, can we change the subject?"

"Fine. But you know I'm right. You gettin' around okay?"

"So far yeah, the room I rented is a little far from campus, so it's a bit of a pain in the ass, but it's cheap rent, so it's working out."

"Do you need money?"

"No, Mom, I'm okay."

"You don't know how sorry I am that you had to sell your truck. I promise you once we get the herd to auction and—"

"Stop beating yourself up. I swear, I'm good."

"Okay. Be there to pick you up this Friday? Dad could use your help with a few things. And I'll get your laundry."

"I can do my own laundry, Mom. There's a machine at my new place."

"I like doing it."

"Liar. I'll text you the new address."

With the season about to start, my trips home will be fewer and fewer, I'm going to have to work sunup to sundown while I'm there. Sighing heavily, I rub my forehead and clear all selfish thoughts until familiar, fair white-blonde hair distracts me from my pity party and conversation. My body jolts in awareness when I see my inkling was right and Harper comes into full view walking across campus alone, towards the parking lot.

"Momma," I start at a dead run, "I gotta go."

"K, son, see you Friday. Love you."

"Love you too." I stop a few feet away from where she walks and adjust my backpack so I can shoot off a text.

Lance: You can't avoid me forever.

Harper stops walking when her phone buzzes in her hand. Reads the text, bites her lip, before raising her phone to respond. I study her profile as she types out another reply, she has no intention of sending. She looks beautiful in a fitted sundress, her curves hugged by the thin material. Her halo hair in a braid along her crown while the rest of it flows down her shoulders. My dick recognizes the need for her as I wet my lips, tempted to sweep her up in my arms and carry her away. I can't decide if I want to kiss the life out of her or punish-fuck her into oblivion. Either way, it's time to face the music.

"You ever going to send off that text?"

She hangs her head, letting out a breath of defeat without looking my way.

"Go away. We can't be seen together."

"No one is around," I confirm, scanning our part of campus. "It's just you and your *lover*." I chuckle, but it dies in my throat with her reaction.

"Yeah, well, I don't want *him* around either," she retorts dryly.

I close the space between us, determined to front her out. "Look, avoiding me isn't cool. You're the one who screwed up." I raise my hand as she opens her mouth to object. "But not telling me how it went down at home or letting me know if you're okay isn't either. I must've texted you a hundred times."

She narrows her eyes. "*After* you threw me out of your room."

I nod. "I was upset. I had a right to be."

"You don't get to treat me like that no matter what I do wrong. You hear me?"

"I apologized. If you were good at accepting them, maybe we could have resolved this by now."

"I'm new to this, and you know that!" She looks so innocent glaring at me with a mixture of hurt and determination. "I will not be treated that way!"

"I heard you the first time. And here's a tip. You have to communicate with the person you're arguing with or else it isn't an argument."

"Don't you patronize me, *Shrek!*"

Loud laughter bursts from me, and she harrumphs.

"Oh, come on," I call to her back, "that was a dig at me and it was funny!"

More aggravation takes hold the further away she gets, and the boom of my voice at her back stops her in her tracks. "Harper, stop!"

She turns to me with her arms crossed.

"Okay, you've got me, I'm through the first hoop. You win, I'll juggle, I'll do whatever you want, just stop fucking walking away and talk to me."

She stares at me, her mouth opening and then closing.

"Talk to me," I urge more gently.

"Look, this week was hell on earth, and I know you've got enough going on. It's just…I felt like we were getting close and you just shut me out like that. So easily, *too* easily. You shut down on me. I know it's my mess, but it made me feel like shit." She tilts her head, her eyes raking over me. "If I'm so easily disposable, I don't think I should *play around* with you anymore."

"If that's what you want, it's probably best." It's my line. I'm sure I've said it half a dozen times, and I've never hated myself fully for it until now. I don't say it because I don't care, I say it because I genuinely have never wanted to commit to any woman, *until now.*

"Well, it's *not* what I want, if you want honesty from me. Damn you," her eyes rake me, and I see her face fall, "now I have to start over."

"What?" I cover the distance between us, studying the gloss on her lips. I've missed her. The increase in ache lets me know as much. Being this close to her and being unable to touch her hurts a lot worse than the separation. But she's forbidden, the key to my demise. She could be the one person to ruin every best-laid plan for me. Why can't I shake what I feel for her and chalk it up to curiosity? Why am I standing so close to the fire doused in kerosene?

Because I like her, and I like spending time with her. Because I see a lot of myself in her. Because I feel the need to protect her. Because I love being inside of her just from the taste I've acquired so far. I love kissing her, touching her, hearing her moan my name. I'm enamored by her. There's not one thing about her that grates on me, not even when I'm pissed at her. Nothing about this girl rubs me wrong. It's just the opposite.

"God, could you not stand there looking at me like that!" She shakes her head. "I made it nearly a week," she mutters. "I was giving you an out. So just take it. Go away. And if you see me in the future, turn the other way. This can't happen, right? So, let's cut the head off the monster before it gets us both."

She resumes her walk towards the parking lot. I fight every inclination to follow, though everything in me is screaming to go after her. Having her the way I had did shit to stifle my want. My appetite has only grown. She's under my skin, filling my veins, changing my makeup. She wants this, us, to be a thing. How can this be a thing? The coach's daughter? It's career suicide, and I don't even have a career yet. But it's the throbbing in my chest that wins as my legs pump to catch up with her.

"Harper," I grab for her hand.

"Go, Lance. I mean it. You need to go. You wanted to erase the other night, right? It's erased."

Her words sting so much, my throat clogs. In a barbaric act of stupidity, I throw her over my shoulder and carry her towards her Toyota. This move officially makes me the dumbest fucking man in the history of ever.

"Put me down, you ass!"

"We were in the middle of a conversation, a *lover's quarrel,* if you will. If you want to lecture me about manners, it might be good to gain some yourself."

"We were done."

"Unlock your truck."

"What?"

"The keys are in your hand, Harper, unlock it."

"Why?"

I slap her ass and duck behind an Escalade to avoid a few students.

She yelps at the contact, and I hear the distinct beep and head in the direction of the noise.

"You want this to be real?" I ask hoarsely, my mind racing as I haul her through the parking lot.

"It's already real. A little *too* real, if you ask me. And this is not a conversation I want to have when my ass is in the air."

"If we do this thing, heads up, your ass will be in the air *often*."

I open her driver's door and sit her behind the wheel. She keeps her eyes down. "I'm trying here, Prescott. I'm trying really hard to do what you need me to do."

"And what do you think that is?"

"Disappear, not exist in your world. I know this world you're in, maybe better than you because you can't see outside of it. And you can't see anything outside of it for months at a time. I get it. That's how I feel about dance. And I'm a fan of yours, Lance, not because of whatever this is, but because you have real talent. I've watched you grow. I don't want to get in the way of your goals. Honestly, I wouldn't let you get in the way of mine. And we both know you're going to get drafted."

"We don't know."

"You have a good chance, depending on how the season

goes. Walk away from me, this, now, and you'll have an even better chance."

I groan in frustration because I know she's right, but I don't move, not an inch.

"What do you want to happen?"

She pushes out a long breath and shrugs. "The impossible. I want it to be *easy* like it was, but it's not now. I thought we were connecting. I liked being with you."

"Me too," I say softly. "I've missed you, Harper."

She nods. "Me too."

Silence passes as we both try and find a way around the shitstorm we've created. But she's so close I can taste her; a new addiction, the needle within reach. With her, I can exhale. With her, there's no pretense. She knows exactly who I am and what I'm about. I let her in, and I did it willingly, no resistance. There's a reason. I'm into her too much to walk away.

"Maybe our season was summer, you know? And now it's almost over."

I lift her hand and she fits her fingers between mine.

"I just don't want to cost you something I can't replace, Lance."

"What if it's you?"

Her lips part and I know that I mean it. Fuck, I'm falling for this girl.

"We do this and we're going to have to hide it until the season is over. This is more than just about ball. This is a lot more."

She draws her brows. "What do you mean?"

"I mean if this was just about *me*, it would be one thing. I'd face coach, I'd try to make it right between us now, but it's not just about me. It's about a lot more, and I can't take a chance on it knowing the outcome might not go in our favor. This season is a life changer for me. I *need* to get drafted."

She rolls her eyes. "Every player does."

"No," I shake my head and catch her gaze, "this is serious."

She swallows. "I would never do anything to jeopardize ball for you."

"I need your word that you won't tell anyone."

"I wouldn't, but, my sister already knows. And my best friend. He lives in New York and doesn't give a shit about football."

"Damn it, Harper."

"You want me to trust you? Well, you're going to have to trust me. These are my people. They would never hurt me or anyone I care about."

"Fine. That's it."

"Swear."

"No Snapchatting my dick."

She rolls her eyes. "It was your ass and—"

I grip her chin and crush her mouth with mine. I kiss her as deep as I can before pulling away.

"That's the first and last kiss I can give you in public until December. You okay with that?"

"So, what does this mean?" She's glowing, and it does something indescribable to me.

"I'm yours for the season, whatever that means."

"No other girls?"

"Are you serious? I can barely handle you."

She grins. "Tell me why the draft is so important."

I lean in and press a kiss to her temple. "One day I'll explain, but for now you're going to have to trust me and believe that this secrecy isn't about me."

"I trust you." She hesitates, and it puts me on edge.

"What?" I ask, pushing her hair behind her shoulder.

"This isn't an ass thing, is it?" I see her pride overtake her features. This girl is a force.

"No, it's not an ass thing."

"You have feelings for me?"

"You're asking for a lot of confessions in one day."

"I expect a lot. I want respect, manners, and an occasional dinner."

"It'll have to be breakfast in bed."

"Good breakfast?"

"Can we negotiate later? I'm late for class." I lean in and force her eyes to mine. "Don't disappear on me again. If we're having a fight, I need the opportunity to defend myself."

"Okay."

"Promise me."

"I promise."

"Come to my place at eleven tonight. Text me when you pull up, and I'll sneak you in. There are always ballplayers over when my roommate is home, so we'll have to be careful."

"K."

I shut her door, and we share a smile through the window before I turn and make my way towards campus, reeling with how easily I just gave in to what I wanted. It's the first selfish thing I've done since I started TGU. Harper will be for *me*. She's the one thing I want out of the rest of my time here, even if it's running out. But deep down I know there's more truth. I couldn't deny this girl anything.

I'm definitely falling for her.

nineteen

HARPER

ELATED ON THE DRIVE HOME, I DIAL RENÉ'S NUMBER. I MET him at dance camp in sixth grade, and we've been inseparable since. He's the true best friend in the way time and space don't matter. Even without speaking for weeks or months, we remain thick as thieves.

"What's up, Mami? They have three openings left in the show. Come to New York, now, I know you'll get one of them.

"He wants to be exclusive."

My phone beeps and I see it's René requesting FaceTime.

I answer and mount my cell on the dash.

"This is not an announcement for a phone call!"

"I'm driving," I giggle, giddy as hell. I call this feeling 'The Lance Effect.'

"All the stress this week for nothing. Do you have a picture?"

"Don't go there right now."

"Too soon?"

"Way too soon."

"Oh, Mami, you are glowing. I'm so happy for you. So, he likes to play with balls too?"

"Cute."

"Be careful with this one. If he's too pretty, he probably got a mean streak."

"He can be bitchy but not with me. He's patient with me. And I think you would love him."

"I can't wait to meet him. Bring him at Christmas."

"I'm going to try."

"You know I miss you so much. Is so cold here already. Did I tell you, I'm with Ricky now?" René's conversations are always a mile a minute and probably a result of a case of undiagnosed ADHD, but I'm always able to keep up.

"Yeah. He's the hot one?"

"No, he's the ugly one. I love him, I think."

"You think?"

"I don't know. I'm feeling a little needy lately. When can you come to New York?"

"I told you before Christmas."

"I mean to *live,* Mami."

"Two and a half years?" It seems like a lifetime.

"Do your parents know what they are doing to you?"

"They just want me with a diploma before I hand myself over to dance."

"You are the best dancer I know. This is a waste of your youth. School can wait. You know Ricky got an audition to do a tour? He won't tell me who with because he thinks I show up."

"You will."

"Does no one trust me?"

"I don't. But I love you."

"Do me a favor, Mami, send me a picture of him shirtless, so if Ricky pisses me off, I can make him jealous."

"Absolutely not."

"It was worth a shot."

"I have to go, Mami, I have chicken in the oven. Love you."

"Rainbows."

"Rainbows."

twenty

LANCE

COACH SLAMS HIS DOOR, AND WE ALL FEEL THE VIBRATION, our heads collectively turning towards the hallway.

Texas in August is hell on earth. Two of the guys threw up today and that ended one of the most hellacious practices I've ever had as a ballplayer.

"Hope that ass was worth it, fucker!" Yates tosses his helmet across the locker room as everyone groans in agreement.

"What the hell is he going on about?" Orlando questions to my right, and I shrug as if clueless while dread cloaks me. Orlando taunts Yates on the other side of the room where we all are stripping off our newly ruined knee pads.

"What the hell you going on about, man? You need a tampon?"

"Fuck you. Secret's out, asshole!" Yates snaps, his accusing eyes landing on a few of us individually before he rips his jersey over his head. Fear courses through me and I know what's coming.

"What the hell is your problem, Yates?"

"My problem? It's *our* problem. Some stupid asshole dicked the coach's daughter, and we're all paying for it."

Stunned reactions circle through the room.

"How do you know?"

"I overheard it," Yates rants as inside I fight the urge to silence him *permanently.*

"You've got to be shitting me, man. *This* is why he's riding us so hard?"

Yates rolls his eyes. "Ya think?"

Voices sound out throughout the room.

"Who the hell would be dumb enough to do that?"

"What's her name, Parker?"

"Harper," one of them corrects, "she's a sophomore."

"The ugly one?"

That remark has me tensing so tight when Orlando looks over at me, it's all I can do to mask my fury. Keeping my head down, my hands busy, I take deep breaths to calm myself. There are two ways this can go, and one is off the table. It means outing us both.

"She's got a decent body," another voice spouts while I grip the back of my neck and close my eyes.

What in the hell have we started, Harper?

They're baiting me. And by committing to Harper, I've voluntarily thrown myself into the biggest test of wills.

I can't be a part of this conversation, or I'll hulk out. Or maybe this situation is just what I need to prove to myself that I've changed. That my temperament is different. I can do this. I just have to master control. For her, for me, for my family. Nothing else matters. Even though I'm a part of the team, by deciding on Harper, I've alienated myself further. No one can know. I won't trust a soul with the secret, and that's to protect us both. And then there's her side of things. Jersey chasers can be nasty, and if they're half as cruel as these judgmental assholes I'm playing with, things can get a whole hell of a lot worse. I fight the urge to text her, to warn her.

"I think she's cute," a voice sounds from somewhere in the

crowded space. Maybe they're going after her to spite me. That fear has me reeling. Part of me wants to backpedal from the decision we made earlier today. To protect her.

What the hell was I thinking? Surely none of these bastards would dare touch her, hurt her? No way would they be balls enough. If so, Coach's wrath would only intensify.

"Maybe when you're done with her, I can get a taste." Snickers pass through the room as I unlace my cleats.

This is where I make my decision. Not back in that parking lot with Harper, but here in the locker room, where our situation is the biggest threat. By doing what I promised her, promised myself, I'll keep everyone I care about out of harm's way. Mind set, I shut my locker and head towards the showers. I know my temperament, and this too shall pass. This will all pass.

"No fun if your friends don't get none," someone spouts as a few guys snicker around me. "Come on, be a *team player*."

Fists clenching, I reach for my earbuds. Another minute of this and all my good intentions will go straight to shit.

"Didn't coach just lecture us about respect?" Troy snarls from a few lockers down. "How about you take that advice to heart and shut the fuck up." He doesn't look my way. He can't know. And between these walls, he's considered a god, and by his record, the only other draft competition in the locker room. And when God speaks, these disciples listen.

I need an ally, but we're on opposite sides. Though he's my roommate and on my team, we don't talk much or run in the same circles. His circle is far larger. While he's considered 'the man' on campus, I do my best not to be seen on anything other than the field. It's not his house I'm renting, and I owe him nothing. But in this moment, I'm thankful for his gospel and will never be able to show it.

twenty-one

HARPER

I SHOOT OFF A TEXT TO LANCE AND WAIT. THE HOUSE IS EERILY quiet—it's not late enough for anyone to be asleep. With a Honda sitting in the driveway I assume someone is home, or there would be no need for the Bonnie and Clyde routine.

Harper: I'm here.

Lance: I see you. I'm coming for you.

Harper: That's kind of scary.

Lance: I'm coming to get you.

Harper: Worse.

Lance: Damn it, woman. I'll be there in a minute.

Harper: Better. But I can still feel the aggression in your text. We need to work on you.

Lance: Did I say I missed you? I must have hit my head.

Harper: Zero points for today. You're scoring nothing.

Lance: I have a very persuasive tongue.

Harper: Is this a bad idea?

Lance: Yes, but we should totally do it anyway.

I grin at his use of my own words against me before turning off my engine and rolling down my window. I sit in wait for mere seconds when I hear a voice sound off just as a little boy bursts through the door onto the neighboring porch.

"Mommy! I can't be on the porch at night!"

"You will stand out there, young man, until you can talk to

me with respect," her reply sounds out as the little boy crosses his arms and glares inside.

"This house is a prison!"

"You need some new material," she calls back.

"No, I need a *new* mommy who will let me do my work in *peace*."

"Boy, watch yourself. I'll extend your time. Five minutes. Think about the things you say before you spray them."

"That's not funny. You rhyming like that."

"Well, *I* think it is."

"Who cares what you think! *I* don't."

"Adding three minutes. You just hurt my feelings."

"I can't hear you from the porch. You need to come closer."

"Sorry, I'm making your crappy mac and cheese."

"I didn't say it was crappy."

"Yes, you did."

"I said I was tired of having it!"

"It was implied."

The little boy throws his hands up. "I didn't say anything about flies!"

Laughing, I jerk in my car seat when Lance appears out of nowhere and takes the passenger seat next to me.

"What are you doing? I thought I was coming inside?"

"Trust me, you don't want that kid to be the one to spot us," Lance says, slinking down in the seat.

"I really don't think this little SUV is equipped to conceal a gladiator. And that kid is hilarious."

Lance glances at the little boy a smirk upturning his lips. "His name is Dante, and he reminds me of my little brother Trevor."

Dante speaks up from the porch.

"Fine. I'm sorry, Mommy. For what I said. Can I come back in?"

Her voice rings out clearly. "What did you say?"

"I don't know!"

"Five minutes left."

"Fine. Whatever. Hand me my pillow. I'll sleep out here."

Seconds later, a pillow flies through the open door.

"I *will* sleep out here!" He threatens before looking around, the fear in his eyes, proving his threat empty. "I will."

"Well, there's your pillow, 'man of the house.'"

"You are supposed to be *nice* to me. I'm your son!"

"Works both ways, kid. You have an attitude problem."

Lance and I chuckle before he speaks up. "It's eleven. He's usually in bed by now. He's up way later than normal."

I lift a brow. "You know the bedtime routine next door?"

"I'm home a lot."

"Why?"

"Because…" he frowns. "Long story."

"I have time."

He turns to me, his hair damp. I can smell his body wash. He's got on a T-shirt and black mesh shorts. My mouth waters at the thought of curling up next to him, inhaling that scent.

"I lost my truck not too long ago."

"Lost it?"

"Sold it."

"Why?"

"Had to."

"Elaborate."

"Naw. Not tonight. Not something I want to think about right now, okay? Just forget I brought it up." He *does* want to talk about it. It's eating him up inside, I can tell, but I nod.

"You can come in," the woman calls out before Dante disappears inside.

"She puts her kid on the porch often, huh?"

Lance grins. "Clarissa is her name. And yeah, they fight like an old married couple. To be honest, he reminds me a little bit of me too, when I was his age. It's entertaining. Come on," he takes my hand before I can prod him further, "I think we're good."

"So, who's home?" I ask as we approach the porch to the older two-story house.

"Just Theo."

It's then I hear the sound of a guitar coming from the basement.

"Wow, he's really good."

"Yeah and he'll be at it most of the night."

"Hmm. And Troy?"

"He's gone most nights. I think he works graveyard." He turns to me. "Wait, how did you know Troy lived here?"

"He saw me the other night when you kicked me out," I say with an edge to my voice.

"And you're just *now* telling me? Did you miss the point of our argument?" His voice carries a much more dangerous edge.

"He was three sheets to the wind or lost in thought or something. He didn't even look my way. He just said, "Hey," like he was on autopilot. He was at the kitchen table, staring out the window. I didn't answer him. He was on another planet."

Lance seems satisfied as he walks me up the stairs, the sound of guitar filtering throughout the house. "Wow, he's incredible. You said his name is Theo?"

"Yeah, he plays in the Grand Band."

"What does he play?"

"I don't know, we don't talk much." Lance leads me up the stairs before closing the door to his bedroom and caging me behind it. "I didn't kick you out," he says, his masculine scent filling my nose.

"Threw me on my ass," I clasp my hands behind my back. "Tossed me like garbage." Lance bends, so we're eye level.

"You really aren't going to let this go, are you?"

"I do believe you mentioned something about your tongue and an apology."

His eyes pool dark. "I didn't mention an apology."

He leans in, slightly lifting the hem of my T-shirt with his finger and lazily running it along my abdomen.

"You should apologize."

"I did."

"You should do it again."

His deep chuckle sends goosebumps over my flesh as his finger runs up between my breasts before tracing the underside of my bra. "A little bit demanding tonight, aren't we, *Mami?*"

"Maybe."

"Well, let's hear them."

"Hear what?"

"Your other demands."

"I don't know yet. I'm new to this."

"I'm sure they'll come to you."

Breathless, I lean into his touch and am rewarded when he takes it a step further, his erection pressing into me. "We should ease you into this."

Something about being with this man makes me bolder. It's been that way since the day we met.

"Then I'll have your tongue first."

twenty-two

LANCE

I STROKE THE SKIN OF HER HIP, MY ARMS WRAPPED AROUND HER AS we listen to Theo's latest concert. It's been an hour-long mix of Santana and Jimi Hendrix. "He should join a band or something."

"I told you, he's in the marching band."

"You know what I mean." She looks up at me, her eyes filled with curiosity as her cheeks heat. "You, uh, did something different this time."

"I have a lot of different things I'd like to do to you."

She turns her tight little body to lay on her stomach, all her goods hidden aside from the spectacular view of her ass which I unveil by moving the sheet. I love our late-night chats. I've been sneaking her into my room every night this week. Though stuck in the small space, we've managed to keep ourselves entertained. Sometimes we study until passed hungry looks get the best of us. Other nights we order food in, sharing Chinese takeout across a stack of pillows. It's an escape for both of us, to say the least. In this room, we're free to just…be.

"Are you ever going to tell me what happened with your dad?"

She winces. "Is he still going hardcore on you all?"

"Every damn practice. It's like he's been waiting for the chance to make us pay. It's hell on earth."

"I'm so sorry."

I chuck her chin. "Tell me."

"He yelled, a lot. More than he ever has. It was pretty scary. And then he apologized for it, which only showed me how hurt he was. I told him it wasn't meant for him to see, but it didn't matter. Mom hasn't made it any easier on me. They both went silent for a few days after the initial blowup, which was the worst. Mom is coming around a little day by day but Dad, well he's submersed himself into the season. I've spent the last few days trying to talk to him, assure him it's not a thing which is like shooting my own foot off. I hate lying to him."

"Harper, I can't—"

"I know," she says softly. "I-just, if he ever finds out he may never trust me again. We're close. I've always been honest with him. It's my guilt. I'll deal with it. He's just, really protective of me because of what happened."

"Tell me what happened."

"With that guy?"

I nod.

She swallows, her eyes cast down. "I was fourteen. He told me he really liked me and talked me into sneaking over to see him. He'd been my crush since third grade. I wanted so badly to believe him. Being with him was… he made me feel…high. You know what I mean?"

"Yeah. I do."

"He pressured me, sweet-talked me into it, but he didn't *make* me. It wasn't like that. I was willing, but I still knew it wasn't right. I knew I wasn't ready. Anyway," she looks down, picking at non-existing lint off the sheet, "it lasted only seconds, but it was painful and horrible. But that wasn't the worst part. He recorded it to show his friends."

"Jesus, Harper."

"Yeah, well, he's the one who should have been embarrassed, he's the minute man."

"Don't joke."

She runs her fingers over my chest lost in that time. "Trust me, it will never be funny."

"It's no wonder why coach is ready to kill us. If that happened to my kid, I'd flip shit."

"It circulated through the school. My sister didn't speak to me for months. After that, my whole life imploded. I was totally out of control and I couldn't stop crying. My parents pulled their hair out. I had to go to therapy. Bad, bad time."

"Yeah, but you're speaking so casually about this."

She frowns. "I know, it's just…I think when you've been through possibly the worst thing that will ever happen to you, it changes you a little. I feel for other people, like *really* feel for them, I can empathize, but that incident kind of made me, I don't know, tougher…harder to hurt? Less quick to bruise."

I lift her to lay on my chest and thread my fingers through her hair.

"I'm sorry that happened to you," I whisper to her temple.

"It was just a mistake, you know? Something that I could've lived with and learned from, but Dad said modern technology made it impossible. At least that's his take. And that's why doing what I did to you makes me a frigging idiot."

"That's different, you didn't mean to take a picture of my ass."

"Different, but I'm still guilty."

"Let it go," I nudge her with my chin, "I have."

"Promise?"

"Swear."

"Thank you."

She lifts my hand and measures ours in size against my palm, and I lace our fingers. "Since then, Dad's kind of watched me like a hawk in that respect. He just doesn't want to see me hurt like that, ever again."

"Understandable."

She smiles up at me. "And since then, I've been afraid to pull the trigger with guys. Until you. That's why I was hesitant to walk away from this but knew I had to. That *we* both needed to."

"This is a mutual decision."

"I know. And you should know you're the first guy I've ever really trusted. And I know," she says softly resting her chin on my chest. "I just know you won't hurt me. Not like that."

"I won't."

She smiles. "I said I *know*."

"How?"

She shrugs. "With you, things are just different. I'm not afraid of you, even though you're a mammoth meathead with a nasty temper."

"Nice."

twenty-three

LANCE

I HATE SURPRISES. THEY GIVE ME ANXIETY. BEING PUT ON THE SPOT is a fear of mine. I always end up freezing, making a fool of myself or lashing out. So, when my girlfriend asked if she could plan my birthday, I was hesitant, but gave her permission. I glance over at her as she drives, my knee bouncing. For the last month and a half, it's been smooth sailing. With the season underway, it's been a tough gain for every win. Coach hasn't let up much at all, and we've all been paying for my secret relationship. My resentment for him is growing, but I leave Harper out of it.

Our days at the gym have been cut down to one, and we utilize that day, and every other I'm not out of town for a game. I'm always eager to watch her dance while we're at our gym and she's always at my feet while I'm boxing, quick to point out whatever YouTube advice she's learned on the sport the night before. I humor her, though it's not much help. We've hit a groove. Our bond only growing as we spend endless hours learning each other, and not just physically. The more we stay together, the more I'm convinced we made the right decision. Even with all the time we've spent exploring the other, she's not wearing on me a bit, my need for her only grows.

"At least give me a hint."

Harper exits onto the interstate and shakes her head. "Is it, or is it not, your birthday?"

"Yes."

"And did you, or did you not, agree to let me plan something tonight?"

"I did."

"There's your answer."

"Damn, you're stubborn." I draw her hand from where it rests on the gear shift and kiss the back of it. "I don't need anything but you. *Naked.*"

"Charming, but you're still not getting a hint."

Expecting a long drive, I kick back in my seat, body aching after a week of hellacious practice. I feel good though, loose, though coach is still working us harder than he ever has, I feel more in tune with myself, with my capabilities.

"He'll ease up."

"I'm good. I was just thinking of how good I feel."

"Yeah?"

"Yeah." I kiss the back of her hand again. "Are you…"

"Am I what?"

"Are you okay with our arrangement?"

She glances over at me from the wheel. "Fine, why?"

"I just hope you know things would be different if we weren't in this situation."

"I do. And look at you, being all considerate."

"I'm trying."

A mile of comfortable silence passes and when she speaks up, I know exactly what's coming.

"Lance?"

"Yeah?"

"Can I ask you a question?" She spares another glance my way.

I nod. I've seen the question in her eyes more than once.

"Tell me what happens when you put your gloves on."

Sighing, I close my eyes. I've never told anyone about it. Not even my mother and she's the closest thing I've ever had to a best friend.

"I become my truest self." It's the truth, but I can see that's not the explanation she was looking for, so I do my best to explain.

"When you dance…whether you know it or not, you're the most honest version of yourself."

She remains silent but nods.

"Your dancing is beautiful because you're not trying to hide anything, you unveil everything. Your sexuality, your thirst, your motivation, your hunger. It's what attracted me most to you. I prefer that type of honesty over inch-thick makeup and a push-up bra any day. That's how I feel when I'm boxing."

"I get it, I really do. But if that's your truest self, are you really that…angry?"

"No. That's me letting it all out. Kind of exorcising my urges. I have a side of me that's prone to erupt. I've always been a bit of a shit. It started when I was young but got worse when I was around twelve. My dad bought me a bag and taught me how to channel it. I fell in love right away."

"Why did you stop?"

This is where it gets tricky. My honesty may scare her away.

"In high school, I snapped and put a kid in the hospital. It was the same prick who'd been messing with me since middle school. I heard he'd fucked with my little brother, and I just lost it, went too far and made him pay for everything along the way. It's the one thing in my life I'm most ashamed of. That fight got me benched the last six games of my JV season. I decided ball was a safer outlet and put the gloves down until this summer."

"Was the guy okay?"

"Broke his nose and a rib, but yeah, he recovered fine."

"Jesus, Lance."

Closing my eyes, I let out a breath. "That's the last time I did anything like that. And it's why I stay mostly to myself."

"You're afraid you'll hurt someone?"

"Not so much anymore. At this point it's nervous energy that triggers me more than anything. And it's due to the pressure I'm under. God, I can't believe I'm telling you this."

"I'm glad you are." Her silky voice is comforting, and she takes our clasped hands and kisses the back of mine the same way I did hers. "I want to know you. More than anything. Okay? Don't be ashamed to tell me something like that, especially the truth. Deal?"

I nod.

"So, how does your love compare in ball to boxing?"

"I love ball. I love thieving it just as a wide receiver opens up, it's a natural high. I love the speed, the energy, the hustle, getting lost in the chaos. Boxing…it's just me. And I like that part of it. And the minute I glove up, it's like…permission. I missed it a lot. That's what got me back in the gym."

She nods in perfect understanding. "I get it."

"I think you're the only woman I've ever met that might. I see how you let go, Harper, and it's beautiful. *You're* beautiful."

She pulls into a gravel parking lot in front of what looks like a warehouse and parks her Toyota. I glance around confused, and she turns to me with watery eyes.

"Was it too much? Did I freak you out?"

"God, what you told me? No. *Hell*, no. Without trying to sound condescending, I'm proud of you." She unbuckles her seat belt, and before I can open my door, she climbs to my side straddling me before kissing the hell out of me. When she pulls away, her eyes are still shimmering.

"Thank you."

"For what?"

"Saying," kiss, "what you mean," kiss, kiss, kiss, "and meaning what you say."

"O-*kay*," I chuckle as she showers me with affection.

"I'm serious."

"Want to tell me which part made you so grateful?" I grin. "Happy to repeat it."

"Nope. Can't be repeated."

"Shame."

She kisses me again and then nods toward the building. "Come on. Let's go in."

"I have a better idea. I'm wiped. How about we go home instead of doing whatever you have planned, so I can put *into* you what's left of my energy."

She frowns and then moans when I bend and kiss the delicate flesh of her neck. "Why did I have to meet you this year? Why not last year? School's going to be over—"

I silence her with a kiss. When I pull back, she's smiling. "I promise you're going to love this."

"You going to tell me what *this* is?" I look for signs or a marquee and come up empty.

Her face lights up. She's never looked more beautiful. "It's a weigh-in. You're already registered with USA Boxing. You're here to meet your trainer."

I shake my head, anger simmering from embarrassment. "I can't afford a trainer. I told you that." I nudge her to move her from my lap. "Let's go."

"Not so fast. He's paid up until the end of spring semester. Just two three-hour sessions a week."

"What the hell, Harper?" Exiting the car, I take her with me and let her down on her feet. I give myself a few seconds to chill and form the right words. Scanning her delicate face and hurt expression, I'm pissed at myself for ruining her gift. "It's a nice thought, generous, really, but I can't accept it. Too much."

"It's not, I assure you. I'm good with money, remember? I'm a wealthy woman already because of my penny-pinching Nana. And besides, if you're so adamant about it, you can pay me back when you win your first big fight. Until then, you accept this as a birthday present."

"I'm sorry, but I can't."

Palming my jaw, she pulls my face towards her. "Lance, listen, you just sweetened this surprise for me by telling me how you feel about boxing. You *want* this, a lot more than you think you do. It's so easy to see. You need this. You *deserve* this. You owe it to yourself and your talent."

"All you've seen me do is hit a bag."

"I just have a gut feeling, and it's a good gut. I know you will excel at this."

"Harper, I can't juggle ball, school, and boxing. Again, I appreciate it, but it's too much."

"No, it's not." Cold wind gusts through the parking lot, and Harper shivers, her eyes darting between mine.

"I don't want to add any more pressure to your plate, but what if…"

She trails off as I free a piece of hair from her lip gloss, my eyes intent on hers. "What if what?"

"What if *football* is your pastime?"

"You think the season's going that bad, huh?" I joke, but she's serious. More serious than I've ever seen her.

"I'm not wrong. You are good at this. You'll be an exceptional boxer with the right trainer. And this guy, Tony, could be the right one. I've talked it over with him and he's willing to work around your ball schedule. I'll be with you the whole time. I'll take you to and from, and we'll do this thing, *together*."

"You'll get bored."

"I won't. I'll love it. Every minute of it, because you'll shine in that ring. I'll know inside you're excited, even with your resting bastard face, like I know you are now."

I shake my head staring at the building behind her, adrenaline already pumping. She's right. I want this.

"Lance, look at me."

I do. I stare down at her as she gazes up at me, and the wind shifts, lifting blonde strands from her shoulders.

"Who cares how you got the opportunity if you've worked for it. Pride aside, just freaking take it. Please, *take* it."

I cover my mouth with my hand and run it down my jaw, and she pulls it away, commanding my eyes.

"What if this moment, *right here*, is the moment that changes your life?"

I feel those words down to my core, penetrating further inside than any woman has ever gotten. It's then I know I'm in deep with her. The way she looks at me, it's trust, it's belief, and if I'm honest, it's more expectation. But I want it, and I want it from her.

Eyes dancing, she knows she's gotten to me and that I'm on the edge of yes. "Damn it, woman, you're so…"

"I'm so what?" She asks, a smile lighting up her face.

"Incredible," I whisper, pulling her to me, before gently taking her lips. "Infuriating," I murmur as she grips my shirt in her hands while I inhale her neck, "and I can't wait to hear you calling my name tonight. All. Fucking. Night. Long."

"Well, I have a cake for you, but that sounds a lot better, for *me*."

"We'll get to that cake." I wink. "We'll work it in."

"Freak."

"Right back at you." I can't help myself. I kiss her again and again until we're both floating a foot off the ground, eager, needy. When I pull away, her eyes remain closed for a few seconds, and it's all the affirmation I need. She's worth the risk.

I cup her face. "Thank you, Priss. This is the nicest thing anyone has done for me in a very long time."

She smiles up at me. "Are you ready, Champ?"

"Hell yeah. Let's do this."

Hours later a half-eaten cake lays on my nightstand as we separate, panting together in a sweaty heap. There's so much noise downstairs that tonight it was a free for all. We lay on our sides, facing each other as I run my palm down her arm.

"Happy Birthday."

"Best birthday I've had in forever, thank you." I kiss her temple.

"So, you were quiet on the way home. What did you think?"

"I was still a little shocked about what you did."

"You're just a physical away from getting started. He said you'd be eligible for heavyweight and you can bulk up after the season."

"I haven't fought since I was eighteen."

"So, you're rusty. You'll get back into it. Tony said you'd be sparring in a month," she adds as if I wasn't there soaking up the surreal situation. "Do you like him?"

"A lot more than my other coach at the moment."

She frowns. "I know."

"He's a former heavyweight. He's got connections. This could be a real thing."

"I think you stunned him with what you know."

I grimace. "He said he's going to have to correct a lot of bad habits I've formed training alone."

"You've so got this." We're whispering now and the more we talk, the closer we're being drawn to the other. It's as if we physically can't be separated. My head's a fucking mess full of her. I'm having a hard time keeping my distance, and I've just had her. I can't get close enough.

"You really believe I can do this, don't you?"

"Without a doubt. You're the best investment I've ever made."

"Then I'll do the work. I'll prove you right."

"I know."

I sink further into the bed pulling her to me. "What do you want?"

"I told you, I want to dance. It's all I've wanted since I was a little girl watching videos over and over in my parents' basement. It's all I want now."

"And after?"

"Nothing past that goal. Nothing. I'm good just getting to that point. Making it happen."

"I get it. Getting drafted is all I've concentrated on for years."

"Are you ever going to tell me why it's so important? You said it was more than just playing in the NFL."

"It is."

"Tell me."

I exhale a stressed breath. "Our ranch is in trouble. In the last auction we got bottom dollar for our cattle because Dad was desperate enough to take it and the vultures were circling. The drought took out a few head we couldn't afford over the summer, and our overhead at this point is eating us alive. With the way things are, we've got a year at most, and that's generous."

"I'm so sorry."

"There's a lot more going on, but that's the gist of it. A signing bonus could save our necks and keep us flush in cash for a while."

"Is that why you had to sell your truck?"

"It was either that or quit school. My parents can't afford the housing, and I can't take a job because I have to spend every spare minute back at the ranch when I'm not playing."

"Is there a way to cut costs? You know I'm really good at this kind of thing. Maybe I can come with you to the ranch sometime and try and help out."

I glance down at her. "You would do that?"

"I don't know that I'd be much help." She shrugs as if she hasn't just offered to save our hides. "But yeah, of course, for you, I would."

"I'll think about it and talk it over with Dad, thanks."

"Anytime."

She moves to get up, and I voice my protest. "Stay."

"I can't."

After gathering her clothes, she fastens her bra and looks down at me as if leaving is the last things she wants to do. "My dad is already suspicious with my sudden late-night study sessions, and all the time I've been spending away from home. And I've been coming in later and later lately. It's a good thing we are actually getting some studying done in here, and my grades reflect that, or else I'd be a lot more on his radar." I groan when she tugs a dress over her hips.

"But it's my birthday."

"You going to play that card, huh?" She glances at the football-shaped clock on my nightstand. "I'll give you ten more minutes. What's your pleasure?"

I curl a finger at her, and she walks over feigning irritation. I start to tug her dress up.

"Lance, I just got dressed."

"Fine, I'll take your panties."

"And you say *I'm* insatiable." At the edge of the bed, she slides down her panties and straddles me where I wait, already standing at attention.

"Just a little ride," I grunt as her bare pussy, slick and ready slides along my dick.

"Mmmm," she moans, already wet from our last go. I reach over to grab a condom and realize the box is empty. "Shit, change of plans." I move to lift her to my face, and she stops me.

"Wait," she says, biting her lip, lost in an idea. "We know I'm clean. And I know you're safe. We haven't once had sex without a condom. What if we…I'm on birth control," she murmurs, gauging my reaction. "How about I ride you…" her brows shoot up, "birthday bare."

I'm already nodding. "Fuck, yes, please."

"It's just us, right? No one else."

I run my thumb along her bottom lip. "I don't want anyone else, Harper. No one. You have to believe that by now."

"Yessss." She rotates her hips, already lost in the sensation before she kisses me. I cup her head, kissing her back to reiterate my point while licking the taste of cake off her tongue. Somewhere in the midst of this kiss, she lines our bodies up before slowly lowering onto my rock-hard dick. The stretch, the heat, the slickness of her middle sending my desire into overdrive. I pull away groaning and lock eyes with her. It's then I want to tell her, this isn't an ass or leg thing, or even a physical thing at all. My attraction to her stems from all sides, especially the inside. But it's her hunger I feed at that moment, the fire and heat radiating from her skin, the lust drunk look in her eyes.

"Dance for me," I order, thrusting up so she's fully seated.

The second she moves I go blind with pleasure.

"Fuck, again, Harper, that feels so, *FUCK*," I practically shout as she expertly swivels her hips, my cock swelling unbearably hard inside her, the friction too much. "Just like that, damn, damn," my words spur her on, the tips of her angelic hair hitting the top of my thighs. The way she fits me, perfection. I can't think past the glow of her skin, the sensation of her tight pussy surrounding me.

"Lance, I feel...I think I can—" her own gasp cuts her off and she leans forward rubbing herself along the edge of my cock, in a steady rhythm. Licking my thumb, I take over and press it to her clit as she picks up her pace. She pulses around me, in tune with her body as surprised eyes fly to mine. She's in the middle of discovery, and I'm too wrapped up in the feel of her to do more than stare at her, open-mouthed and overwhelmed. Grappling, I finally take control and thrust into her movement, our breaths mingling as she hovers above.

"You fit *me*, this pussy, fits *me, only me*." Possession, borderline obsession, it's all I can do in this moment to keep from completely claiming her. I buck underneath her, and we both call out to the other. Her lust-filled eyes glaze over just as her orgasm hits mere seconds before I fill her up.

I'm able to sneak her out easily due to the collective commotion in the living room. The irony is that half of that room is filled with teammates. I'm halfway back up the steps when I hear Troy call my name.

"Yo, Lance."

"'Sup?" My whole body is thrumming at the possibility he just saw her leave, but the air about him is relaxed. "We're watching the game. Want to come down and hang? I've got a beer with your name on it."

"I'm good. Got shit to do."

He gauges me as if he's trying to figure me out and I simply stare back.

"All right, man, suit yourself, but consider it an open invitation."

"Will do."

Troy takes the stairs up two at a time until we're eye level.

"Something else?" I ask, my guard up.

"Yeah." He looks back at the front door and then to me. "Is she worth it?"

Shit. I hang my head. We've been too careless, and a part of me just wants the secret out. I want to be in the open with my girl. I'm not much into PDA, but I have a feeling with Harper I won't give a damn. Problem is, at this rate I'll never know.

"Troy, I can't—" I scrub my jaw, "this isn't just about me."

"Hand to God, man, your secret is safe."

"If you say a word, it will end me."

"Trust me, I've done my fair share of locking it down when it comes to important shit. But do us *both* a solid. Give me a text or heads-up next time she comes, so I can make sure the coast is clear. Neither of us needs the drama."

"Will do."

He makes his way down, and I call after him. "Troy?"

He turns around and grins up at me. "Swear to God, it's safe with me. You're just gonna have to trust me on this."

"Thanks, man."

"Sure." He taps the edge of the staircase before disappearing back into the living room.

twenty-four

HARPER

Harper: Good luck today. You've got this.
Lance: Thanks, Priss. Are you coming?

My chest zings at his term of endearment. What was initially an insult is a namesake I now hold dear. The first two games were a solid victory for the Rangers. Lance's interception and thirty-yard gain at the last game has been the talk all week long in the halls and in classrooms on campus. Though he's pretty incognito, I know he's being watched, not just by the school but by those who matter to his end game. And for the first time in my life, I have a boyfriend. We've been seeing each other a little over two months. When we aren't together, I keep a sane schedule to keep suspicion low for my parents. My dad is slowly coming around. We've resumed our game day breakfast. He stares at me now across the table at The Pancake House.

Harper: Wouldn't miss it.

"Who is that?"

"René. He was telling me to quit school and join him in New York."

Dad's shoulders tense, and he pauses the work of prepping his pancakes. "And you told him?"

"Two more years, Dad. We made a deal. I'm not planning on backing out of it." I take a large bite of the fluffy cakes. "So, what's your feeling on tonight?"

"Not sure. The defense has stepped up big time. Prescott is a beast. We're going to use him a little on special teams. Got a couple on offense stepping their game up."

"Prescott is good," I nod without looking up. "You think he'll get called up?"

"It's not looking good for him, no," he says easily. "I think his hesitation to enter last year may have cost him. But if he keeps it up and gets an invite to camp this year, he might have a shot."

Dread fills me. I know how much he needs this, but I can't linger on him.

"What about Troy Jenner?"

"Hard to tell. He's gotten some interest. They're talking about him. I think he's a shoo-in and will get an invite to camp. But he seems a bit distracted this year. He's going to have to get it together if he really wants it. We need this season."

"I know, Daddy."

I thank God I haven't raised suspicions with my questions, but Dad is too focused on tonight's game at the moment. The Rangers barely snagged a bowl game last year, and in the last five years, the team has declined in the rankings.

We spend the next thirty minutes mulling over the team and the possible outcome of the season, his strategy, along with his other favorite subject, my mother and sister. He's a family man through and through. Most coaches wouldn't wake up at five a.m. to have game-day breakfast and indulge their daughter in ball talk, but most coaches aren't Ryan Elliot. Though his concern for my personal life is now mostly misplaced, I understand his protection of me. And that fierce protection in my eyes equates to nothing but love. My dad's demeanor might be hard to penetrate, his moods sometimes impossible to navigate safely around, but his priorities never change, his family, his team, all of it comes down to his love and his respect.

But as we leave the diner and I kiss my father's cheek, I can't help but think back on the beginning of our conversation.

If Lance doesn't get drafted, what will he do? How will he survive? How will his family fare if they lose the ranch? Clearing my head, I focus on faith; the faith I have in Lance, in what he's done on the field so far this season, faith in his capabilities. It's then I get an idea of just how much pressure he's under and vow then and there to do anything in my power to help him.

He's become far more than my experiment. For the first time in my life, my father isn't the only man who's taken up residence in my heart. Driving away from the restaurant, it sinks in, I'm falling.

twenty-five

LANCE

"EVERYONE, THIS IS HARPER," I GRIP HER HAND IN MINE and squeeze. I can feel the slight tremor in her stance. She's nervous. And I have to admit, I am a little too. I used fall break as a chance to bring her home for two reasons, one to possibly help us with the books, and two to introduce her to my family. The shitty part is I only have her for one night and have to get her back to her family for Thanksgiving tomorrow. I caught my dad's gaze when we walked in, and it was one that told me, 'we needed to talk.' Ignoring it, I made quick introductions. "This is my Mom, Jeannie, my Dad, Jack, my Aunt Dotty, and Uncle Pete, and this little shit here is my little brother, Trevor."

"Nice to meet you all," she says cordially. "You have a beautiful home."

This earns points all around, and I'm quick with my weaponry when my dad scrutinizes her further. "She's all about ball talk, Dad, so I hope you've got more beer than usual."

"Fan?"

"You have no idea," I spout proudly, wrapping protective arms around her briefly before letting go. I don't miss the shock in Mom's voice when she speaks.

"Just about time to eat," she says, clearing the emotion from her throat.

"Can I help with anything?" Harper offers.

"No, hon, all set. Everyone grab a seat at the table."

Harper sits to the left of me as everyone joins hands. After short grace, the ball busting begins, and Harper is quick with every quip, even joining in on the cracks on me. She fits in, just like I thought she would, but I can clearly see the change in her expression when she watches my dad's hand tremor while he attempts to get a bite on with his fork. He's concentrating on his task, too fucking stubborn to ask for help and I can't say I blame him. Harper's eyes begin to shimmer before meeting mine, and I see the instant realization sets in.

"You know for all the driving we did, I forgot to wash up. Would you all," she drops her eyes just as Dad drops a heaping glob of mashed potatoes in his lap, "excuse me."

Trevor, Dad, Uncle Pete, and I stand, and she holds up a hand. "No need to get up. So sorry. I'll be right back." She calmly makes her way from the table.

"You know, I didn't wash up, either. I'll be right back." I toss my napkin down and stand before I make headway down the hall and catch Harper just before she shuts the door. I lock us both in the bathroom, my hands behind me on the knob.

She stands in the middle of the small room, her back to me. "I have to go."

"What?"

"To the restroom." Her voice is filled to the brim with emotion, "give me some privacy."

"You're lying."

She turns on me, her eyes filled with tears. "How does it feel?"

"It was an omission."

"It's lying! You didn't tell me he was sick!"

"The tremor's gotten worse since I saw him a few weeks ago."

"So what? You didn't think I'd notice? Doesn't change the fact that you didn't tell me!"

"The last thing that man wants is your pity. Trust me."

"You should have told me." She's on the verge of bursting and I can feel the crack inside her. "Harper, I don't understand. Are you angry I didn't tell you or that you have to look at him?"

"Are you kidding me right now?" She practically shouts, but I don't flinch. We're too far from the table for anyone to hear.

"I'm dying inside just watching him." Tears fill her eyes and quickly soak her face. "That poor man." She points past my shoulder. "Is it early-onset Parkinson's?"

I nod. "Yes."

"And this is why the ranch is in trouble?"

"Yes. I mean we've always been hand to mouth but, yeah, it's gotten dire since his symptoms have worsened. We can't afford help or the medical bills. It takes him three times as long to do the work now. Trevor helps, but he's only fourteen, and well, he's Trevor."

"Jesus," she sniffs. "You could have told me, prepared me."

"I didn't realize you would care so much."

"Care? I'm in love with them already from what you've told me and now being here," she says, her face falling so far I feel it in my bones. I move to gather her to me, but she shakes her head. "Don't, I've already ruined my makeup, if you touch me, I'll lose it." Her eyes burn with more tears. "I'm sorry. I've embarrassed myself. They probably know something's wrong by now. You should have told me. I don't want your dad to know I'm upset." She furiously wipes away her tears as I stand there feeling like the shit I am. I should've told her. There's no excuse.

"I'll be right back."

"What? No!"

"Trust me."

Her glossy eyes find mine. "Do I have a choice?"

"No." I make my way back to the table. Mom is fully aware when our eyes meet, but the rest of the family is clueless. "She's, uh, got an upset stomach, so let's give her a minute."

"Got some Pepto in the cabinet, son," my mother says, passing me a message, sympathy pooling in her expression.

"On it."

I make my way back to Harper and see her eyes water over again. "I told them you had a stomach ache."

"Great, now everyone thinks I have the shits."

I burst out laughing, and she slaps my chest. "God, you are in so much trouble." She pulls me to her and cries in my neck. "I hate you so much right now."

"Harper, I'm getting whiplash."

She sniffs, bringing her face to mine, her cheeks splotched. "I'm sorry. I know this isn't happening to me. It's you. Your dad, your family, I just…"

"Well, you're a drama queen."

She musters a smile. "Exactly." Her face falls, and I chuckle when she starts blubbering again.

"Jeez, am I glad I invited you. Life of the party right here, folks."

"I hate you."

"No, you don't."

"I want to."

"You can't. You've got the best heart of anyone I've ever met," I say, pulling her to me despite her protest. She gives way in my arms and rests her head on my chest.

"I'm so sorry, Lance. I'm so sorry. This has got to be so hard on your family."

"We're making it through. It's going to be okay. You told me, I'll be drafted, right?"

"Right."

"And if I don't, I'll be a rich as fuck boxer."

"Exactly."

"That means better medical care and fixing this place up. Hiring help. Letting Trevor be a kid. Getting Mom a nurse to help her out when it gets hard. And a motorcycle for me."

"Gotta be something in it for you, huh?" She sniffs.

"Well, I am the one who's gonna have to ice my knees for the next ten to fifteen years."

"You say *I* have a good heart. Look what you're doing. What you've been taking on. It's like I read the story in seconds without being told." She sniffs again, and I tip her chin up so I can see her eyes.

"Tenderhearted thing, aren't you?"

She blows out a stuttered breath. "Any ailment, any illness like that, when I see it in person, I just lose it. And the fact that it's you, your dad. God, I just can't imagine. My whole life is about movement, Lance. I can't imagine not being able to dance, to move when I will myself to. It's my worst fear."

"I get it. I think it's mine too. The more I see him, the more I realize how lucky I am."

"I'm sorry," she crumbles again.

I hold her tightly to me. "It's okay, baby, it's going to be okay."

"I know, I mean it's horrible, but that's not why I can't stop crying."

"Then, why are you crying?"

"Because I fell in love with you, Lance Prescott, and I'm not quite sure it was the best move to make on my part."

That statement zings through my chest, lighting me up in a way I've never imagined possible, and I do the only thing that comes naturally. I laugh. I throw my head back, and I laugh hard until small fists pummel me.

"You. Total. Asshole."

"I'm sorry," I chuckle. "God, I'm sorry. It's not that I think it's funny."

"Don't look so pleased, you smug bastard. I'm terrified."

"Me too."

"So not what you're supposed to say," she tries to mask her own smile.

"No, I mean, I feel for you too."

"Oh, well, good. I'm glad you can pick off a ball because you're shit at sentiment, Shakespeare." We both crack up as she looks on at me, her eyes softening. "Hook, line, and sinker. I'm officially a sucker for your ridiculous and inadequate charms."

"I'll get better at the Shakespeare, I promise."

"Coach's daughter falls for a football player. Like how cliché can it get?"

I lift my palms. "We can wear matching Christmas sweaters, adopt a dog, and take 'almost a family' photos."

"Sounds good to me. Can we give the dog a ridiculous name?"

"Sure." I wipe the tears from her eyes

She nods. "Just give me a minute to glue myself back together."

"You've got two."

I open the door as she primps in the mirror, wiping the black beneath her eyes. "It's so obvious what just happened. I'm mortified."

I kiss her cheek. "Hurry up before I change my mind and keep you locked in here."

"Lance?"

"Yeah?"

"You're okay, I guess."

We share a smile, and I wink before I close the door. After dinner, beers with dad, and two rounds of pie, I whisk my girlfriend away from the chaos and make love to her all night in my childhood room. Skin to skin, we wordlessly bind ourselves, nose to nose, chest to chest. The next morning after breakfast Harper locks herself in Dad's office for a few hours with the books before she calls my parents and me in.

"I've found you five grand, I think."

My father looks skeptical but walks over to where she stands.

"This is owed, right? You have this crossed-out, but I've checked, and double-checked the numbers, and this makes sense, here." She leans in analyzing my dad's chicken scratch. My father pulls out his phone and steps outside.

"Whitty, you didn't pay me for those heifers I sold you. Nope. Looking at the books right here. All right, see you after a while." My dad walks in and nods. "Thank you. So much, really." He's too proud to show much more than that, but I know he means it.

"Jeannie," Harper summons from dad's desk and my mother walks over to stand behind where she sits. "I've put a few suggestions here and here," she says. "They may work for next month."

"Thank you," my mother says, staring down at her with adoration before looking up to wink at me. I wink back.

"We need to get on the road," I remind Harper, who looks up at me and nods. And I feel it, without her saying it. I feel it to my bones. She loves me.

We hold hands the entirety of the ride home. I drive her RAV4 as she sings Christmas carols while I try to find the right words to tell her what a difference she's made in my life in the months

I've known her. Rehearsing and re-rehearsing in my head how to put into words the way she makes me feel. Words that stem from any emotion have always been my weakness. But for her, I want to try. I want to tell her so much. How much she's surprised me. How I never thought I could feel as much for any woman the way I feel about her. That I love her too, though I'm positive she knows.

Our smiles are never far from our lips as she rattles off future plans for Christmas. Our plans. And I don't object once, because it's a given for me as well. The transition from friend to confidant, to much more has been so effortless on both our parts, I wouldn't object to any decision she made regarding us at this point.

Put simply, Harper makes me happy.

Turning into my neighborhood, I glance her way as she sings, committing the moment to memory while dreading her imminent departure to spend the rest of the holiday with her family. Her smile disappears and shock covers her features when I pull into the driveway. Following her line of sight, I hit the brakes a little too hard when I see her father, my coach, standing in front of his pickup, his arms crossed and hellfire in his eyes. Dread tightens my chest and defeat creeps up as I throw her SUV in park and put on my game face. Though the only thought racing through my mind at that point is *game over*.

twenty-six

HARPER

I'M THE FIRST TO JUMP OUT OF THE TOYOTA, BUT LANCE ISN'T FAR behind.

"Daddy, please don't go off without hearing us out."

"Go home, Harper." He's not even looking at me, his blazing blue eyes on the man standing behind me.

"Coach—"

"Don't. Out here I'm not your coach, I'm this girl's father."

Lance doesn't miss a beat. "Woman. She's very much a woman and you raised her well, Mr. Elliot. So well, in fact, that my family and I are smitten with her."

"Go home, Harper. Your mother and sister are waiting."

"Daddy, he's right. I'm no longer your little girl. I have a right to see whomever I choose, and Lance is a good man. He's a great man and you would—"

"You lied to me. You told me this was a one-time thing. You lied to everyone!"

"I was trying to avoid this! It's *ridiculous*. It's like you expected me to stay innocent forever!"

"I didn't raise you to sneak around like this, whoring yourself out to one of my ballers!"

"Sir," Lance barks, the level of threat in his voice terrifying. "Uncalled for."

"Don't you dare lecture me, Prescott. Who in the hell do

you think you are? This is blatant disrespect. For me, and for your team."

"I thought we were leaving ball out of it?"

Lance means nothing by it, but my dad takes an aggressive step forward on the verge of explosion. "I should fucking end you."

I'm speechless as I watch their exchange.

"You very well could, sir."

"Why bother with the formalities now? You took and soiled what was precious to me and behind my back, like a fucking thief."

"Jesus, Dad, this is ridiculous. I'm twenty years old. I'm no saint."

My father's eyes find mine and what I see in them levels me. "You humiliated me."

"You did that to yourself," Lance snaps from behind me. "You couldn't keep it under wraps. Maybe if you hadn't worked the team to the fucking bone and pitted us against each other, we wouldn't be a pack of wild dogs at the moment ready to rip one another's throats out. You want a reason? There's the reason."

"Couldn't be a man and own up to it?"

I come to Lance's defense. "He's plenty man, but his entire future—life is riding on this season, Dad!"

"Harper," Lance's volume rises in warning. "Not your story to tell."

"He needs to know!" I glance back at Lance and see the shake of his head, but I'm too overcome with the need to protect him.

My dad looks between us. "Nothing is going to help his case."

"His father is about to lose everything he's worked for!"

"Harper!" Lance barks.

"No, no, his dad is sick, and his whole family depends on their ranch to survive. They are about to lose everything! And if you found out what would you have done? Benched him? Ruined his season?"

Lance explodes next to me. "Damn it, Harper!"

Dad takes a menacing step towards Lance. "Don't you dare go near her."

He turns to me. "You still live under my roof, and you have the audacity to lie to me, about one of my players? He's a coward. Ask his team."

"You need too much control, Daddy. I don't know what's gotten into you, but you have no right to act this way. I love this man. I will see him whenever I choose."

"You finally get some attention, and you're going to call it love?"

Tears burst out of me and I sob into my hands.

"You fucking asshole," Lance lashes out, his voice venom as he sweeps me into his hold, but I push away and stand in front of him, separating them both before I face my dad head-on.

"I know you're hurt. And I know this space I put between us wasn't fair, but this has gone too far already. He's your kind of man, if you would just get to know him."

"I know plenty about *him*. I know he's got an explosive temper that put a kid in the hospital." Lance glances down at the driveway. "You think your good boy here didn't fuck half a sorority house last year? Think *again*."

"Don't, please don't. Anything he's done doesn't matter."

"Go home, Harper."

"Go," Lance whispers at my back. "Just go. He's not going to listen to you. You're talking to a wall."

I turn back to Lance to see his jaw set, and there is nothing but regret in his eyes.

My whole demeanor drops. "Please don't believe him. You are not those mistakes."

"I know, baby, go."

"She's not your goddamned baby!"

Lance closes his eyes, dropping his head.

"Dad, please, just be reasonable," I plead before I turn to Lance.

"It's okay," he assures me, standing his ground. "He's right. We should have come clean months ago."

"Lance—"

"I'll call you later."

I nod, fear-filled tears sliding down my cheeks that he pushes away with his fingers. "This isn't your fault, Harper."

"As much as it is yours," I sniff. "Promise you'll call?"

"Swear."

I look back at my father who looks like he's just getting his second wind.

"Please, Dad—"

"Just go home, Harper."

twenty-seven

LANCE

I'VE DEALT WITH MY FAIR SHARE OF LIVID COACHES IN MY LIFE, BUT none of their wrath has come close to that of Ryan Elliot. If looks could kill, I'd have been a dead man the minute his eyes connected with mine when Harper drove away. His voice equally as damning. "You let them suffer."

"You made them suffer, and for what? I've *never* mistreated her. I've never done anything but care for her."

"She's not like other girls. She won't recover if you rip her heart out. She's been through a lot, and you're subjecting her to a lot more."

"I'm aware."

"You have no fucking clue! Why her? You know she doesn't fit your mold."

"What mold would that be? Surely you can't think so damned little of her that my interest or affection surprises you?"

"Be honest with yourself, you preyed on an innocent girl who's starved for attention."

"You underestimate her. I wonder if you know her at all. Look, this is just as much of a surprise to me as it is you, but not for the reasons you think. In fact, you need to understand right now, I'm not going anywhere. I'm in it for the long haul with her."

"I don't want you on my team, in my life, or with my

daughter and not because of what you've done in the past but because of the way you snuck around behind my back and had my daughter do the same."

"You're partly to blame for that, and that's just tough shit, *Coach*. And before you object that this isn't the field, you might want to remember that you're the one who brought the personal shit into the locker room, not me."

"So easy for you to say. You're a punk-ass kid without a family."

"That's where you're wrong. I have a family, and it might not be identical to yours, but they depend on me just as much."

"She might have fallen for the sick dad routine—"

"Wow, you've really gone off the fucking deep end, haven't you? You think I need to make up stories about a sick daddy to get a girl into my bed?"

Murderous eyes meet mine, but my anger boils over.

"With you for a father, no wonder she's starving for affection."

"You're done, Prescott!"

"I was done the minute I pulled up."

"Fuck you, punk." He walks towards his truck as I counter.

"With all due respect, sir, fuck *you!*"

He turns back to glare at me.

"Don't bother showing up to the game on Friday."

"Wouldn't miss it for the world. You'll have to toss me out in front of everyone."

"Don't think I won't."

"Then I guess I'll see you there."

LANCE

TROY TOSSES HIS HELMET IN MY DIRECTION, HIS ANGER EVIDENT. Tonight, we fucked up, majorly. Both offense and defense. The team is completely at odds, everyone to blame. The whole game was a shitshow, and it had little to do with skill and everything to do with miscommunication. We're on a losing streak. I shake my head in apology towards Troy, who has just as much riding on being drafted as I do, and tonight, I was benched for half of the game. Technically, I could go over his head if I wasn't getting fair play and coach knows it, so he's playing me the minimum which is costing us games. I'll never understand how he could throw a season out of spite, but I do understand his love for Harper. Because it's all I know anymore. We're all circling the drain with morale alone, and that has the team screaming for answers. The village is demanding someone to crucify, and everyone's house is being searched. Accusations are flying, but it's the one flying to my right that grabs my attention.

"You," someone says, and all of our heads snap up. "It's you, isn't it, Jenner? Can't keep your fucking dick out of *anyone.*"

Troy shakes his head and slams his locker. "Fuck yourself, Altman, it's not my fault you threw the game away." This is something I've never seen, the quarterback and the wide receiver at each other's throats. It's gone too far.

"Chill out, man, don't point fingers," someone calls out. "We're a team; therefore, we *all* fucked her."

"Yeah, well I didn't cum," someone spits to my left as my pulse kicks up.

"Everybody knows Troy's the yes man," Altman mutters with disgust. "He'll fuck *anything*."

"Back off, man," Troy grits out. "I'm with someone."

News to me. From what I've seen he's not been bringing anything in off the street for a hot minute. His room's been a no-fly zone.

"Yeah? Who?"

"None of your fucking business," Troy growls.

"You need to back the hell off, Altman," I grunt. It's one look. One look from Wallace when I know I've just implicated myself. Pat eyes me for a long moment before dropping his head. I'm sunk. And I don't even care at this point because I can't handle another comment about Harper. But to my complete surprise, he doesn't say a single word. Instead, he waits for me in his truck in the parking lot sitting mute with his eyes straight ahead, the heat blowing at us from the vent. After a long, uncomfortable silence he finally speaks up.

"It's her, isn't it? The dancer from the coffee shop."

"Yeah."

"What the hell, Lance? We've been boys since freshman year."

"My silence was for her just as much as it was me."

"Jesus, I would understand if she was good-looking but—"

"Don't you fucking dare," I hiss in his direction.

"All this shit, *all* of this because of you and her."

"It didn't start like this. I didn't even know she was coach's daughter until after, even then I wouldn't fucking stop so if you're going to tell them, go ahead and tell them."

"She's a six at most, why are you wasting time with a six?"

"Add five to that."

"What?"

"She's my eleven."

With a loud sigh, he puts his truck into gear and turns to me. "Hope it's worth it."

"You know it's Coach Elliot that's throwing the season, *not* me."

"We all see it. And I'm not going to say shit, but this better be the girl you marry. You owe us all that much. She better be worth it."

"She is."

twenty-nine

HARPER

Harper: Hey you.
Lance: Hey baby. You here?
Harper: Just pulled up.

Tears streak my cheeks as I try my best to hold in my sobs. Lance appears in a long-sleeve T-shirt and beanie, his eyes lighting up when they find mine. He frowns when he sees me standing by my car and nods towards his front door.

"Come inside." He blows in his hands. "It's cold."

I shake my head. "I can't."

He looks past me at my loaded SUV. "What the hell? He kicked you out?"

I swallow. "No."

He closes the distance between us and sees what I'm trying hard to hide.

"I'm leaving. I'm taking my shot, Lance. Things at home, well, they aren't good, and there's a casting call for something off-Broadway. René is going to let me stay with him."

I can physically feel the crack in my chest when his features twist. "Priss, don't."

"I can make up school later. I can't get a dancing year back, *ever*. It's for the best. Our relationship is wreaking havoc on your life, your team, the season, my relationship with my father. His career. There's more than just you and me to worry about. I really," I sniff. "I really care about you and your family, but I've been selfish. We've both been selfish. Other people are paying for this."

"They'll get over it." His eyes search mine, and I shake my head, losing my battle as more warm tears fall.

"You know you gave me…," I breathe through the pain, "you gave me a love story, a *real* love story, even if it doesn't have the ending I was hoping for."

"It doesn't have to end."

"It does," I reason with a shaky voice. "It does, Lance. And it's okay. I'm okay. We're both going to be okay. I'll still feel the same way about you, even years from now. I know it. I know myself. I probably won't ever stop loving you. And who knows," I say as his eyes glaze over, "maybe one day the timing will be right, and my father won't hate us both, and we can try again."

"Harper, listen to me. The secret is out. It's not going back in."

"My dad can't even look at me right now. I can't stay there, not now."

"Then stay with me. He'll get over it. You can't be a daddy's girl forever."

"But I wanted to," I admit as I push away more tears. "And I want to be your girl too. But it's not going to work out that way. At least not right now."

"You are *my* girl."

"In every way. *Always*. You have my heart. Please don't make this any harder on me. I have to go."

"Bullshit. This will all blow over, you'll see. This isn't for the best; this is you running away."

"No, this is me using this shitshow as an excuse to go after what I want and to grant you the freedom to do the same. I'm standing in the way of things for you right now, and I'm not going to stay here and watch you throw it all away for me."

"That's dramatic."

"No, it's the truth. You're so close, Lance. We betrayed him for months and rubbed his nose in it. He's not going to give you the game time you deserve if we continue to parade around like what we did didn't hurt him. He's good at holding a grudge, even against his own daughter. He may come around with me, but there's no time for you."

"Fuck this, I'll go talk to him. I'll apologize."

"It won't work, and you know it." I palm his chest. "You take the field. I'm going to go take the stage." I push up on my toes, and he pulls me to him, holding me tightly. I feel every word he's not saying in his reluctance to let go. "Harper, please, fuck, don't do this."

"I deserve my shot too. Now is just as good of a time as any." I feel his nod in my neck. "But I do love you," I whisper before I press my lips to his jaw. "The crazy big kind." It's agony already, the separation I feel when he finally releases me. "Don't be too much of a stranger, okay?"

He opens his mouth, and I hold up my hand.

"Lance, stop," I demand, the last of my strength leaving me. "Don't use this as a convenient time to return sentiment or you'll ruin it for me."

Thumbing away my tears, he bends capturing my mouth, kissing me, his tongue diving deep, his body radiating the pain that I feel, his mammoth embrace just enough comfort to keep me standing when he pulls away.

"I'm not sorry," he says hoarsely, his eyes shimmering with unshed tears, "fuck them all. I would do it again in a heartbeat."

I muster up a smile and step away. "Me too."

"Text me when you make it there, okay?"

With that, I get into my car, adjust my mirror, back away, and cry past two state lines.

thirty

LANCE

Three weeks later

SITTING ON MY BED, I OPEN THE BOX TO REVEAL A NEW PAIR OF high tops in my size, a black silk boxing robe embroidered with Lance "The Blanket" Prescott and matching trunks. She had to have spent a fortune on it. Chest aching, I shoot off a text.

Lance: It's perfect, thank you. I fucking love it.
Harper: Yay, you got it. So happy you love it.

I love you. I want to reply, but I type out something else entirely.

Lance: Did you get my gift?
Harper: Not yet.
Lance: Should be there tomorrow. Merry Christmas.
Harper: Merry Christmas. You know you didn't have to. I can't wait to see you in that robe.
Lance: I miss you.
Harper: I miss you too.
Lance: Come back to me.
Harper: It wasn't you that I left. It's opportunity that I'm chasing. Please understand.

Lance: I do. I'm trying to. It just sucks. It's a cruel world without you in it.
Harper: I love you. Always. Make me proud, Lance. Keep fighting.
Lance: Give me a reason to.

I swallow, knowing I won't be able to move on unless I ask.

Lance: Are you happy?
Harper: Not completely, no.
Lance: It's me you're missing.
Harper: Every single day.
Lance: Wait for me.
Harper: Neither of us can make those promises.
Lance: I can.
Harper: Please don't.

Hurt flares up when I think of how easily she left me standing there with my chest slashed. Even if there were tears, I'll never understand how she could just drive away. We meant more than that. At least to me.

Lance: I guess you've already chosen.
Harper: I love you.
Lance: Maybe I don't believe you.
Harper: You don't mean that.
Harper: Lance?
Harper: Lance, please talk to me.
Lance: Take care, Harper.

The next day I spend twenty minutes coming up with an apology only to send it and have it bounce back. She blocked me. Not out of spite, but to give us a clean break. She's unwilling to commit to me, and I can't have it any other way. I'll go crazy seeking it from her, and she knows it. She knows this is the only way. She always told me her dreams would come before any man, I should have believed her. I just never thought she'd discard me for them so easily.

Anger like I've never known boils through my veins. Another raw deal. Another punch life has decided to throw to break me down.

Regret eats me alive as I think of all I should've said, could've given her.

I could have loved her so much better, given her so much more if she'd given me a chance.

She's already blocking me out of her life. It's only been weeks, and I'm already a part of her past. I know she thinks this is the best decision for both of us, for *now*. But the tie she's so boldly cut already feels like a molecular change in my makeup. It's a change I don't want, can't stand to deal with. I feel like I've been ripped in half by loyalty and ambition.

Loyalty won on my part, and our mutual ambition just severed us. But the decision was made for me and for that I can't forgive her.

But she would never let me choose. She would never make me.

I should be grateful. Instead, I'm pissed.

Sentence passed. I'm serving day one. My conviction in knowing I never truly got to fight.

My bedroom is now a tomb.

I have no way to go after her, not the means or the way. There are no magic words to change her mind. All I have left is this vessel I dwell in to turn things around, to change my fate, to save myself.

The problem is that it feels like she took the biggest part of it. I no longer feel the beat in my chest, the strength in my veins, nor the will to fight.

This test she left me, I fear I won't pass. But I've got to believe her.

I've got to make our sacrifice worthy of the cost.

But first I have to inhale, exhale, remember my own dream and I have no idea what it is at this point.

I lace my sneakers and stalk out into the wind scattered rain, and I run. I run five miles until I feel the blood pounding at my temple, another five miles until my inhales are painful, and the breaths scrape my insides in search for the beat. I run another five until I convince myself I'm still breathing, that pound in my chest is a heartbeat, that I can still bleed. And so, I run. I run until I bleed out.

thirty-one

LANCE

6 months later...

"H EY, MAN." I APPROACH MY ROOMMATE, WHO SITS deflated on a barstool. "What are you doing here?"

Theo looks like hell, his eyes moving over me in assessment before he scours the outdated shit shack I've been frequenting since Harper left and the season ended. The hole in the wall reminds me of a bar back home where I sip much-needed whiskey after backbreaking days.

"What are *you* doing here, this isn't your scene, is it?" He's just as surprised to see me.

"Not my scene, no," I say, sipping my beer. I glance around the musty bar. Skeletons of longhorns hang sporadically around the place while stapled signed dollar bills pose as wallpaper. "This is where you come to hide, and it's cheap."

"Yeah."

"You look bummed."

He shrugs. "Girl shit."

"Something to do with that beauty you used to bring home all the time?" I know her name because she's my favorite barista, but I don't want to let on that I do. He's protective of her and has a bit of a complex. I was in my bedroom the night he had a blowout with Troy when Theo thought Troy had been pining for her. It couldn't be further from the truth. I know firsthand just how off base Theo was with his accusations. Troy needed a distraction from the ache of missing the person he truly wanted. Don't we all?

With Harper gone, I spent more time in my room observing life around me after exhausting myself at the gym. Six months without a word. Six months of pounding out my frustrations. Despite my best efforts, I was on a losing team. And this year I lost in more ways than one, I lost everything.

"You saw her?"

"Heard her mostly. She cracked me up."

Theo frowns, his eyes roving over me with suspicion I expected. For a little guy, he's oddly intimidating. He's got an air about him I respect. And an immense talent that few have. He'll go far. I've been so wrapped in my training, I've barely spoken to either of my roommates in the last few months, though Troy and I have become tight. But it's been hard to put words to anything, especially after the way the season ended. Troy's been distracted, but he's been there, as silent support, when I needed him most. Daily, he's still struggling, fighting for the future he wants, and the outcome he's aiming for still seems possible, where mine is totally up in the air. Though wrapped in my own headspace, it was hard to ignore Theo and Laney and what they had brewing when they thought I wasn't around.

"Thin walls," I offer in the way of an apology. "Couldn't be helped."

"Sorry," Theo mutters.

"Don't be. Seems like you had a good year." I grin and sip my beer.

"Well, my good year is ending on a shitty note. Garçon!" Theo calls to the bartender, who gives him a tattooed bird before pouring more shots.

"So, what's your story?" He asks. "Seriously. I've never seen a jock be such a recluse."

"I'm a creature of my routine." It's the truth. The other half of it is a bitterness that has been eating me alive. "I break out once in a while. But I stick to my circle, and it's small." After alienating myself from the team and losing Harper, it's never been truer.

"I get it. Mine is dwindling."

"Yeah, be careful with that." Lifting our freshly poured shots, I clink my glass to his. "To the graduating class of 2019."

We toss them back, and I welcome the burn as it slides down my throat.

"So, are your parents coming to your graduation?"

Dad's deteriorating rapidly in his mindset without the right meds and most likely won't be able to make the trip. Mom is feeling more helpless by the second bearing witness to it. The situation is as fucked as it is impossible. "Nah."

"Really, why?"

Tony nods toward me, cue stick in hand. "I'm up," I say, avoiding more small talk that'll lead to reminders about my failures, about a future I'm not ready to face. "See you, man."

"See you."

"Jesus Christ, man, if I hear that song one more time, I'm going to fucking lose it. Do you hear me?" Tony mutters in his thick New York accent. "Seriously, this kid is your roommate? Make it stop. They're about to turn on him." A group of bikers taking up residence at one of the long tables glances over to where Theo sits next to the jukebox listening to the same song on repeat, his fingers in the air as if he's playing piano along with the melody. He's got it bad, and I feel for him.

"Motherfucker," the bartender spouts over the music. "I told that idiot to slow it down."

Theo looks seconds away from passing out. The minute the song dies, I hear a collective sigh of relief throughout the bar. But when the opening notes to "Everywhere" by Tim McGraw sound again, I feel the tension in the air rise.

"Fuck this," I hear muttered nearby as two of the bikers stand, and I hold up a hand to stop them. "I've got this."

By the time I reach Theo, he's sliding to the floor. I scoop him up and get a number of odd looks before nodding over to Tony. "Can I use your truck to get him home?"

Tony pulls out his keys. "He pukes, you buy the fucking thing."

"Got it."

"See you back in an hour?"

"Yeah," I catch the keys and make my way out of the bar with Theo hanging limply over my shoulder. The second I get him in the passenger side, he looks up to me, broken in every way a woman can break a man.

"I fucking lost her because I'm too afraid to lose her. Ironic, isn't it?" His head bobbles on his neck, his voice cracking as I shut the door and round the truck before hopping in. He's still talking as I turn the engine. "What kind of idiot does that? Me."

It's emotional vomit, and I feel every word of it to my core. But Laney isn't halfway across the country. I'm jealous of his advantage. Harper is where she wants to be, where she chose to be, over us. I can't demand or stand in the way of her path, the way she can't do the same to me. She knows I understand it, even if I don't want to. I'm at a loss, I'm angry with her, not for leaving me, but for the way she cut us in half, tore us clean apart without anything, not an inch of flesh, bone or vein to cling to. I stay somewhere in a mix between anger and resentment at this point because I'm helpless to the situation. This man is mere miles away from his solution.

"It'll work out if you want it to."

"You say that, but women are a little more complicated than drive-thrus."

This pisses me off. "Newsflash, band boy, I'm capable of carrying a ball, intelligent dialect, and a mature relationship."

"Sorry, shit," he slumps in his seat. "I didn't mean anything by it. No offense."

"Offense taken. Don't be so quick to judge. It's rough all over when it comes to *girl shit*. Believe that."

"I'm sorry. It's just, it's got to be easier for guys like you."

"Believe what you want. I'm telling you different."

There's no point in talking to whiskey, it does nothing but lie to you. It tells you you're stronger than you are, more re-silient than you are, and that your dick will work when you've drunk too much of it. All lies. But the numb it sometimes pro-vides makes it necessary.

Theo's out cold by the time I get him back to the house. Collecting him from the truck, I hoist him up the porch steps and into the house and kitchen before nabbing one of my fro-zen Gatorades out of the freezer.

Bloodshot eyes open briefly when I set him on his mattress. "Shampoo."

"What's that?"

"Shampoo," he repeats as if it will give me more clarity.

Chuckling, I head to his bathroom in search, and grab a bot-tle of what I assume is her shampoo and hand it to him where he's sprawled on the bed. He doesn't bother opening his eyes but pops the cap and inhales. "Thanks, man."

"Just don't drink it. And anytime. Thanks for the room."

"Lance?" He calls weakly from the bed as I get to the door.

"Yeah?" I look back to see he's out.

But I know his question and scribble both my reply and my regret on a Post-it I find on his desk, before leaving it in a place he can't miss it.

> *Do yourself a favor and don't make the same mistake I made. Tell her.*
>
> *Lance*

Problem is, I was never good at coming up with the words to tell Harper how I truly felt. Maybe if I had, she wouldn't have cut me out of her life so fucking easily. And even if I managed to find them, I'd never get a chance to tell her because she took the ability away from me.

thirty-two

Sixty-three fights later…

THE SHOUTS COMING FROM ALL SIDES OF THE RING DULL INTO a collective thrum. I'm dancing on air, light as a feather, my arms the only thing weighed down by exertion. Six rounds, and he's fazed. I crack my neck, arms loose at my sides just as the bell rings, and the dance begins.

He's dizzy, weakening by the second. It's only a matter of time.

I come at him with my winning combination, and he swerves, knowing my tactics. This I was prepared for, so I change the sequence.

Body, body, body, uppercut.

I'm still fighting.

I've been as low as a man can get in the last two years.

No girl.

No draft.

And the bank is about to foreclose on the ranch.

Draft day came and went, and I retired my number.

Football is over.

Harper and I are long over.

But this, here, this is my future.

Not every dream is realized. That's the hard truth, and the lesson I've come away with and survived.

Not all hard work pays off. Not every guy gets the girl. And sometimes, even the most carefully laid plans get changed, interrupted or abandoned because life has other ideas.

I've been on my knees more times than I can count at this point. From the ashes of the past twenty-four months, I know who I am, it's become abundantly clear.

I'm a born fighter.

No matter the outcome, I've always got fight left in me, no matter how many hits I take. And I took them, eager for more, covered in those ashes, hungry and thirsty, and it all led up to tonight—my last amateur fight.

Pivoting forward, I end his misery and deliver one last blow, letting gravity take care of the rest. He collapses at my feet, and I take a step back, satisfied as my arm gets lifted while the ringside roars.

Though I know her distance, it doesn't change the fact that I search the crowd for her face after every fight in the hope she'll be there, a pride-filled smile on her face, an 'I told you so,' ready on her tongue. But she's not. I'm her past, a moment in time, a memory. Her college boyfriend. A blip. And I have yet to fully believe that for myself.

Every fight I come up empty, but it doesn't change my routine. I'm always going to look for her because even though she asked me not to, inside, I've been waiting.

Because of tonight's win, the ranch is safe, at least for another few months. My family is safe.

Harper is thriving. I've been keeping up with her progress on social media. She's joined a dance troupe that travels, working various shows all over Europe, exploring places we only dreamed of together in the double-sized bed we tangled to fit in.

The smiles in her pictures seem genuine. She's with people who care about her, believe in her. She's living her dream.

And my dreams have changed.

With the NFL unattainable, boxing saved me. She was right. Football was a pastime, and boxing has become my obsession.

And so I fight, for myself, for my family, and for her, in hope she looks for me in the crowd at the foot of her stage. Where I want to be, instead of sitting on a bench while Tony cleans my eye.

"You did good, kid. Two months and we're in Vegas. You earned this. But we've got a few things to work on."

Tony's been with me since Harper introduced us, conditioning me for the heavyweight circuit. He believes in me so much, he trains me at the ranch. I've become his pet project. My family has taken him in as one of their own. He's as obsessed as I am. We're so close we can both taste it. Aside from Harper and my family, Tony is the only other person in my life who believes in more for me.

Harper.

Closing my eyes, I let the lingering loss of her eat me from the inside as he cuts the tape from my hands. Some days it seems like a lifetime ago we were in that gym, other nights, like tonight, I feel her with me.

"Kid, I figured you for a better mood since you just dominated that fight. Not a bad payday either. I told you those amateur rounds would pay off."

I lay back and stare at the gaping hole in the tile on the ceiling as Tony inspects the damage to my ribs.

I'm a world away from his conversation, struck with how much truth has been revealed to me tonight in the last few hours.

Why the hell am I waiting?

Springing up from the table, I start to pace the locker room.

"What the hell, man?"

"I'm good. Ribs are sore, but I'm good."

"You need to let me make that decision. Get back here."

"I'm good." I pace the room, thoughts racing, my pulse picking up as something inside me tells me now's the time. The *only* time.

"I don't like that look," Tony says, crossing his arms from where he stands at the table.

"I need a few days."

He shakes his head. "We don't have time to miss a few days. We've got that charity match in a week, and we need every minute together before Vegas."

"We've got months. I'll make it."

"We need every spare minute we can get."

"I won't miss a day. I'll keep up with it on my own."

He sighs, pulling up his phone. "Where?"

"New York."

Tony's head jerks up. "Now, you're doing this *now*?"

I nod.

"Why now?"

"Because I want to see if I'm right."

He sighs. "I'll book us on the next flight out."

I answer with the shake of my own head. "I need to do this alone."

"No time for that. I'm coming."

"This is personal, and you know it. I'll need some space."

"I'll make it work." He sighs and taps furiously on his phone. "Did you sign?"

"I haven't looked at the contract."

"Jesus, kid, he's one of the best agents in boxing, and he's not going to wait forever. Don't piss this away. I can't get started on negotiations for Vegas without him—"

"Book it," I snap, gathering my bag, "I'll sign it on the plane."

"Hey, man, before you laser my damn head off with that look, I like Harper. I'm not saying she's not worth the effort, but the timing is shit. And you're about two years too late. We don't have time for you to play Romeo. You know we've got a limited window."

"I'm not going to blow it."

"What if she's moved on?"

I pull a T-shirt over my head, batting away the ache. "She hasn't."

"How do you know?"

Because I have to believe she hasn't dismissed us as easily as she's made it seem with her silence. I have to believe that every day she battles the same urge I do. To come back, to get us back—there—to that place where nothing can touch us. Where we aligned our separate planets and revolved around each other, protected each other, shielded one another, and grew together in our own universe—one we created to simply exist. With her, I felt safe, accepted, more like myself. I grew into a better version of me with her. Without her, I'm a lonely planet.

I've spent enough time denying myself.

It's time to fight for what I want.

"You going to throw this all away if it doesn't work out the way you hope?"

Shoving my gear in my bag, I rest in how right it feels to go after her, that this could be our chance. I never should have let her end it. I was never okay with her goodbye or a single minute after it.

"I wouldn't, and she wouldn't let me." I grin down at my discarded gloves that lay on the bench. "I'm her greatest investment." I've got another swing left, another round inside of me. Her words strike like lightning as I pack my shit.

"What if this moment, right here, is the moment that changes your life?"

When I met Harper, she was a fair catch. At any point in

time, I could have tapped out, signaled the flag, and claimed her despite the onslaught of hurdles we were up against, the opposition running toward us full force. Against those odds, we cracked and were forced off the field.

This is a whole different playing field, with a completely different set of rules. And this round, winner takes all.

Ding, Ding.

ROUND
2

thirty-three

HARPER

ONE BREATH, ONE STEP.

"Harper, watch your frame."

It was just a dream.

"Harper!" I'm tanking. I've never backed down from a challenge in the entirety of my dancing career, but I can't seem to mold myself to fit this woman's demands. She's freaking Cruella de Vil, plain and simple. I'm sure the rug in her 2nd Avenue penthouse is what's made of the puppy fur because she's sporting nothing now but an outdated nude leotard and raging camel toe. Camel toe everyone sees, but no one *ever* discusses. In this company and most circles, she's considered the Madam of Dance, and because I've just landed the first solo of my career in her new show, *Retro*, I'm glutton for this punishment until the final curtain drops.

In the last couple of years, I've traveled the world, having been fortunate enough to dance in numerous shows with the troupe. It's been the best two years of my career, a living dream, aside from the regret that gnaws at me most nights I lay in bed. The last few days he's been on my mind because of a different dream, one that felt so real, I woke up crying. He was inches away, but I couldn't touch him. I kept calling his name, begging for him to see me, but he couldn't hear me. It was one of those agonizing dreams that seemed to last forever. Even though my heart has never forgiven me, my head sometimes decides to join in the war while I sleep.

Since that morning, I've been battling myself just to reach out, but the coward in me always wins. It's been too long to strike up a casual conversation, to check in, in a friendly way. At the time, leaving Grand was undoubtedly, the best decision for me, maybe for us both, so why can't I live with it?

I guess I never thought moving on would be so debilitating.

Although moving is all I seem to do, the ache of missing him still lingers. It's days like today when I'm failing that I wonder just how far I'll go. Or how far I would already be with the man who made me feel everything with a single look.

So movement it is, until I can escape any lingering doubt that I'm where I should be.

"Again." The dreaded word has my body aching. My toes are bleeding, I can feel the wetness between the tape.

One breath, one step at a time.

I've been dancing since I was two. Ballet, tap, jazz, modern dance, sway, I've even signed up for a summer of ballroom. I can still remember the exact movements to the 'hop, shuffle-foot, step' routine I memorized for my very first recital. My first memory is dancing in that lineup of snot-faced babies wearing a pound of tulle.

Dancing never made me cry, *then.*

This is what it takes, Harper. This is what it takes.

And I'll take it, to keep the dream alive. Dancing is in my blood, my bones, it should never stop being fun. Especially not because of Camel Toe Cruella.

"Jesus, Harper, I picked you, I chose you, this better be your only *off* day, and it better be due to that period bloat."

Face reddening, I throw myself into the routine and manage to get out of rehearsal intact.

"Jesus, she's gunning for you. You must have stared at the camel toe too long." Grinning, I turn to see Casey catching up with me as I exit the building and welcome the cold slap of New York winter on my face.

"I can take it."

He regrips the duffle on his shoulder. "Yeah, well, she's miserable, and the only reason she's got any say is because she owns the center and is on the board of directors. Her time is almost up, and she knows it. You were fine."

"Fine?"

He smirks, giving me a side-eye. "You want a compliment?"

At twenty-eight, Casey is one of the youngest and best choreographers in the business. I've worked with him on other shows, and he's been helping me with my number for *Retro*. My pointe is rusty, and he's been conditioning me. Although my confidence could use a lift, I don't want false compliments. It does nothing to help me. "Fine will do. I know I was off today."

"Not by much, and shit happens. She's drilling hard. You still have plenty of time."

"Thank God we're on break for a few days."

"I'm surprised she's letting us have it. And I'd be even more so if that bitch knows a thing about Jesus."

I throw my head back and laugh. "You make a fortune off her, don't you?"

"Doesn't mean I have to like her." He smiles down at me. "You going home for Christmas?"

"To Texas?" Inwardly, I cringe at the thought. That place is now a ghost town of my former life. "No. My nana lives here, so I'll be celebrating Hanukkah with her. How about you? Do your parents live here?"

He shrugs. "They both passed. My sister lives in Ohio and

has a thousand kids, so I'm passing on that this year. So it's just me and my dog Romeo."

My cheeks heat. "That's right, you told me that, didn't you?"

"Once or twice."

I've made out with Casey a couple of times at various parties the past few months, sending him mixed signals. On Halloween, we spent the better part of an hour doing some heavy petting in one of the guest bathrooms of a director's house. As soon as he produced a condom, I tapped out. He asked me out as I adjusted my flapper dress in an attempt to reel it in, and I'd turned him down with some bullshit excuse brought to me by Grey Goose. Since then, we've been friendly, and he hasn't pushed.

He lifts my duffle off my shoulder, adding it to his.

"Come on, I'll buy you a piece of lettuce to help you get rid of that period bloat."

"Har, har."

"Coffee?" Casey isn't what I'd call ruggedly handsome. With dark brown hair and deep-set brown eyes, he's got a boyish charm to him that's alluring, along with an incredible build.

"Sure. I have time for coffee."

He pauses on the sidewalk and turns to me as a cab horn sounds next to us, and the wind kicks up. I can feel Christmas in the air due to the amped chaos and those bustling around us. Very little compares to a New York City Christmas.

"Just so you're aware, this is a date."

"What?" I gape at him, surprised at his changing demeanor. "I agreed to coffee, not a date."

"It's a date," he says adamantly. "I've been patient. Whoever you've been waiting for isn't coming."

The words strike deep, and I feel slapped.

"Pardon? Who says I'm waiting for someone?"

"I do. This is the third show we've done together, and I get this vibe, this not available vibe, but I keep waiting for this guy to pop up and he never attends shows or meets you after rehearsal. So, the way I see it is that you're waiting for someone. Or maybe you were, *or*," he gives me a hopeful grin, "he's been waiting for you for three *long* shows."

"You know I like you, Casey, but—"

"Shit, kiss of fucking death." He gives me a sheepish grin. "Too bold. I came on a little strong in the end, didn't I?"

I can't help my smile. "Little bit."

"Sorry."

I sigh, hating that I'm making this so awkward. "You know what's crazy? I've never been on a *real* date."

"What?" He frowns.

"It's true."

"Well then, what's the holdup?"

The holdup is a six-foot-plus ballplayer turned boxer than I haven't been able to get over since I left him standing in his driveway. 'I belong to dance' has been my motto most of my life. I kept it true by pursuing my dream and letting Lance go so he could pursue his own. But it's been *years*, not days, not months. It isn't healthy. I never thought the ache would last this long. I knew I would regret it, that I would never stop loving him, but I never expected to mourn our relationship this much after so much time had passed.

Lance still dominates my heart. As for sex, I made the mistake once of giving my body away for the sake of attention. I have no intention of repeating that mistake ever again. With the handful of flirtations I've had the past few years, I've never once broken that promise to myself. It's never felt right. I've never wanted to hand myself over as freely as I did with Lance. With him, sex was love, and I don't know the difference between the two. And I just know, I'm not the girl that wants to separate them.

Looking at Casey now, I wish I was.

And he's right, I've been waiting, and for what? *I broke us, and I did it intentionally.* I gave Lance no reason to come for me. I gave him no reason at all. I denied commitment and shattered us both. But the bond we made; I can't seem to escape from. Every single step I've taken since, I've made with him in mind. I can still feel him as a presence in my life, and no matter how far I travel, I carry him with me. His smile, his blunt charms, his love. The look in his eyes. I'll never get over Lance Prescott, that's what time and distance have told me.

Or am I just not trying hard enough?

Am I trying at all? It's been two years, and I'm mourning my first love like a widow. At some point, dance won't fill every space in my life. Casey's handsome, educated, funny, and one hell of a dancer. I'm attracted to him and way past the rebound point. If I was looking for a prospect, I have one hell of a con-tender right in front of me.

Contender.

It was just a dream, Harper.

I blow out a frustrated breath and level with Casey.

"You're right. And it's been this way for far too long. I can't make any promises. That said, do you still want to date me?"

"I already knew that, so yeah." He pushes the hair away from my face. "So, what do you say? We start slow. Coffee first, and then we can work our way up to dinner."

I pull on my beanie and nod. "Okay."

thirty-four

LANCE

I CAN'T FEEL MY BALLS. I'VE NEVER IN MY LIFE BEEN THIS DAMN COLD. I was nowhere near prepared for a New York winter when I got on the plane. All of my rounds in the amateur league consisted mostly of bouts in the Southeast. This cold is far more bitter. Mouth closed tight, I tread the sidewalk with my hands stuffed in my jeans eyeing each apartment building. Most days, I could give zero shits about posting my status, but tonight I thank God for social media. While waiting to board, I'd searched for Harper. I knew she no longer lived in the same place that she moved to when she took off to the city. She told me then that they were looking for something bigger. This led to stalking those closest to her to search for any clue of Harper's address. I'd started with her sister, Kandace, who'd visited a little over a year ago. She'd posted a picture of the place John Lennon lived and died, so I know Harper lives on this street because the caption said, "my sister lives on the street John Lennon lived and died." Morbid, but factual, and the reason I'm on 72nd Street.

It's not like I could call and ask her dear old dad. The last time I saw him, he was in the headlines, and it had little to do with coaching ball. There was far more going on with Ryan Elliot that year than we all thought. It hadn't been so much me dating his daughter that had caused a rift in the team, though I know it had everything to do with his hatred for me. It appeared

Coach Elliot was hiding a few secrets himself, and that scandal had rocked its way into national news. It was all I could do to keep from reaching out to Harper.

But I didn't.

Another regret.

Coach might have been the wedge to come between us back then, but he was no one to regard or respect now.

Fuck him.

But that was then and there. This place may be the perfect backdrop for a fresh start for us, at least for the time being. Though this city is anything but welcoming. Stepping over the lines on the sidewalk, I try to picture it through Harper's eyes. So far, New York City is a whole lot of sensory overload—brightly lit marquees, metal and glass skyscrapers with residential huts in between corner stores and eateries. Horns are a constant background noise, in addition to the piss-poor hospitality, and mind-numbing cold. For Harper, it's home, for me, it's a different universe. One I'd gladly enter just to get a glimpse of her in it.

Searching for any sign of the lit front door, I begin to question my tactic. This half-assed plan is straight from a lunatic's imagination. René had been the key to getting me this far. After seeing Kandace's post, I searched for René and found he recently posted a selfie in front of his building, where I know they still live together. Behind him in the shot were twin lit candy canes on the front door of the lobby, the numbers blurred by the vanity filter magnifying his face.

I have a street and a clue as to which building, and if I was taking stalking 101, I'd ace that shit. I'm not sure what that makes me, but I'm assuming somewhere between desperate and creeper.

Desperate seems the right word for the moment.

I can't shake her. No matter how much time has passed.

With every step I take, I curse the fact that at any point, I could have made this same trip two years sooner and maybe salvaged our relationship.

It's been two years.

Two years.

Do I even know her anymore? Have I changed?

Am I chasing what was and what no longer exists?

"Fuck it." Pushing those thoughts away, I cross the street and resume my search. I'm determined to see this through, to either fuel or snuff out any lingering hopes.

I'm a few blocks down when I see the lights on the door. Speeding up, I'm there in seconds and through the doors looking at *her* mailbox.

Medrano / Elliot 21B

Surely it can't be this simple?

Entering the elevator, palms sweaty, I keep my eyes trained on the threadbare maroon carpet.

"I'll still feel the same way about you, even years from now. I know it. I know myself. I probably won't ever stop loving you."

Harper is the only woman I've ever let get close enough to truly know me, but I can't help the doubts creeping in. Then again, I've been living those words on my own side of things since she left my driveway.

And it's time to find out if they have proved true for her as well.

Sharply, I knock twice on the door and shove my hands in my jeans. The slight swelling in my eyes has my vision blurry. The fatigue I feel after going six rounds before the trip here vanishes when the door opens. René stands in front of me in a black tank and blue jeans. He's shorter than me, attractive and built. If I hadn't seen his Instagram and known who he was, I would have been on edge with him answering the door, especially with his scrutinizing brown eyes and the way they're taking me in. Nothing about this man's appearance seems anything but hetero. That is until he opens his mouth and calls behind him.

"Oh, dear Christ. Mami! Santa came early, and my delivery finally showed up!"

I can't help my grin when he turns back to me.

"I dreamed you. Thank you, Jesus." He does the sign of the cross and blows a kiss to the heavens before lifting his hand on the frame and leaning in. "So, what should we do first? A picnic sounds so *romantic*."

"It's December."

"Never underestimate the power of body heat."

"Do you greet all strangers at your door like this?"

"If they look like you, yes." He deadpans.

I shake my head with a grin. "Is Harper here?"

"And all my hopes, splat like shits." I throw my head back and laugh. This guy is something else. He calls back over his shoulder again. "Harper, GQ just showed up, and he is hetero!" He turns back to me. "What's your name?"

"Lance."

He opens his mouth and freezes, his expression turning grim.

"Lance?"

"Yes."

He lifts a brow as I lift my chin, ready for the inevitable.

"Huh, I thought you look familiar. Cowboy Lance."

I cup the back of my neck. "Not exactly."

He steps out into the hall, crowding me before yelling back into the apartment. "Never mind, Mami, it's for *me*."

"What the hell, man?" I say, backing up so he can close the door.

He crosses his arms, unfazed. "Aren't you about, oh, *two years* too late?"

"She's here, right?"

"Oh, tough guy, she here, but you are not welcome."

"And why is that?"

"Because she smiles now, without being told to, that's why."

It's like a knife to my chest, but at the same time, it angers me. Why didn't she reach out? I'm the one she left. If she had regrets, she should have voiced them to me.

"I just want a word."

"No."

"Jesus, man, it's been a long flight, a hell of a long night, and I need to talk to her."

"Fine, first a test."

"You're serious?"

"Are you Lance?"

"Yes."

"Then yes, a test."

"Come on with it, man."

"How did you find her?"

"The internet. I follow you, and her sister," I shrug, "easy to piece together."

"So you stalked?"

"I guess so, yeah. I mean, I've kept up with her because I care about her."

"But, you were not invited."

"No. We've established that."

"So, hot man, what makes you think she wants you to come now after all this time?"

"Dude, I know you're her best friend, and you're trying to protect her, but I've never hurt her."

"Why you wait so long?"

"She left me."

"No, she didn't."

"Yes, she did." I say mocking his accent.

"It's not nice to make fun of my accent."

"I apologize, but you're pissing me off."

"I am a US citizen."

"I'm happy for you. We're in the same club."

"Are you always this grumpy? You know it's Christmas time, right?"

"Are you fucking serious?"

"About Christmas, yes." He shakes his head. "Yeah, no, with this…" he thrusts his hands my way, "disposition, this is not good. You come back when you have a better attitude."

The door opens behind him, and for the first time in two years, I get a look at her. My heart slams into my chest when her mouth parts. Seconds of silence stretch as we take the other in.

"Hey, Priss." Despite my irritation and the obstacle between us, I can't help my smile. René's gaze ping-pongs between us before resting on Harper, who is still gaping at me, a mist in her eyes.

"Lance…W-what are you doing here?"

"Just thought I'd fly to New York to stand on your doorstep and get my nuts snipped by your roommate."

"René," Harper scolds, gripping him by the arm and pulling him inside. "Come in, come in," she says, ushering me in behind him.

"Mami, you know this man—"

She gives him a stern eye that cuts him off mid-sentence.

René crosses his arms. "Don't you look at me like this. You came to New York with plastic bags and a broken heart."

Harper's expression hardens as her ears redden. "Enough,

or I'm calling Ricky and telling him you hated his Christmas present."

"You wouldn't *dare!*"

"I would so."

"That's just wrong," he snaps. "He got me a fiber optic angel. Who wouldn't hate it?"

Harper raises a brow, and he sighs. "Fine, do you, Mami."

Winning the debate, she wastes no time grabbing me by the hand and leading me through her living room, past a sad excuse for a kitchen before yanking me into her bedroom. When the door closes, she throws herself in my arms, and I catch her without hesitation. Holding her tightly to me, I get a whiff of the vanilla in her hair, and I'm back, there, in Texas, in the place of *then* while gripping tightly the reason why I'm here, the *now*.

We hold each other for several beats, neither of us speaking before she gazes up at me with a watery smile. "You know, I always knew deep down I would see you again. Someday, somewhere, I just wasn't sure when." It's when she pulls away, I finally get a good look at her. Her gorgeous hair is a little longer, she's filled out, some in her curves, some in her face. Eager brown eyes scour me, drinking me in just as greedy.

"How, God…" she lets out a nervous laugh. "How have you been?"

"Good, busy. I fight full-time now."

"Yeah, I know, I've been following your progress. Lance, I'm so proud of you." She removes a few sweaters off a vanity chair. "Sit down."

I take the seat as she sits on the edge of her mattress across from me. Glancing around, I see she doesn't even have a closet. Just a tall dresser and a rack of clothes sitting next to it. It's the smallest bedroom I've ever been in. Much like the city, chaos seems to be the recurring theme in her corner of the apartment.

"I've been wanting to message you for a while now, to tell you how proud I am. Going pro, huh?"

"Yeah. Got my first fight in Vegas in a few months. It's not Caesars Palace or anything but—"

"You'll get there. Your record is forty-seven and—"

"Forty-eight, I fought tonight. KO."

"Oh my God," she exclaims with pride-filled eyes. "Look at you," she moves in and gently turns my head. "Barely a scratch. I've seen you throw. I watched a few videos. Lance, the things they're saying about you—"

"Shhh," I wink, "let's not jinx it."

"K," she says easily, "but I am proud of you."

"Yeah, what about you, hot shit? You've danced your way across Europe."

"Yeah." She bites her lip. "That was something else. The budget was shit, so we stayed in some pretty sketchy places. But yeah, it's been incredible."

"I don't know who's taking those pictures and videos of you while you dance, but wow."

"Yeah?" She asks, seeming surprised that I've kept up. "Thanks."

We share a silence that lasts long enough for us to smile and again drink in the other.

"So are you—"

"What are you—"

We're still smiling, and I point to her. "You first."

"How is your family? Jeannie, Trevor? Your dad?"

"All good. Dad's shake has gotten a whole lot worse…but you know what? Let's skip that part of the conversation for now."

She gives me a slow nod. "How long are you staying in New York?"

"A few days, I have a fight in a week."

"So, you fought here, tonight? In the city?"

"Yeah." I'm flat out lying. Would it be so hard to believe that I came here for her? This is fucking embarrassing. Am I alone in this? Is she feeling what I am? I can't tell. I'll just focus on the fact she's happy to see me. It's enough.

She lifts a piece of golden hair away from her neck, and my fingers itch to slide through it. "You look good, beautiful."

"Yeah? Thanks. You, well…" her eyes roam over me appreciatively. "You're a monster. You wasted no time bulking up," she gives me a wink.

"Fighter training is a lot different from ball."

She bites her lip briefly before she speaks. "I'm so sorry about the draft."

"Don't be. I'm better off."

"Really?"

"Fuck yes, I-I," I shake my head and dart my eyes to her scratched up hardwood floor, "I have you to thank for that."

"That was all you, Lance."

I give her a pointed look. "I think you know better."

"Hush," she says. "So, tell me. What's it like?"

"Boxing?"

She grabs a pillow from her bed and hugs it to her body, obstructing my view before resting her chin on it. "Yeah."

"It's exhilarating. The best kind of high."

"They say you could be the next Sugar Ray."

"I'd rather be Marciano."

"Going for undefeated, huh?"

"We'll see."

She scrutinizes me. "You seem…happy."

For the moment I am, so I let her believe it. "You do too." I stand because I'm fucking nervous and take the only space the room will allow to study the canvas printed photos that line her walls. Several of them highlight her talent in colorful costume. I get fixed on one where she's mid-leap, the perfect picture of a prima ballerina.

"These are epic."

"Yeah? Amazing what cell phones are capable of these days. René snapped that. It was cheap to print too."

I glance at her over my shoulder. "Still can't take a compliment from me, huh, Priss?"

She darts her eyes to the floor, her chin quivering.

"Hey, hey," I say, reaching her in one step. "What did I say?"

She shakes her head, the smile she's wearing a farce, her eyes glossy. "I just…it's good to see you."

"You too."

I clear my throat. "Can I ask you an intrusive question?"

"Of course."

"Are you seeing anyone?"

"Sort of…" she says distractedly as if she's in another place before bringing her eyes back to me. "To be honest, I went on a coffee date today, but it's nothing serious. It's new."

Heart thundering, I clear my throat for the second time. "So, if I'm not stepping on any toes, what do you say we spend Christmas together?"

It's then, while in wait for her answer that I see the invisible tie to her appear wrapped around my enslaved heart. The idea she might pass, along with her confession of something *new* has my stomach rolling.

"You want to spend Christmas with me?"

"Why not? I'm here. You're here. It'll be fun. I've never been to the city. You can show me around."

"I have a break until the day after, so yeah," she nods and nods, her expression dazed before her eyes lift, "I'd love to spend Christmas with you."

"All right then, it's settled." I glance at her bedside clock. "It's late. I should go, let you get some sleep."

"I'll plan it all out. What time do you get up?"

"Early crow, around four-thirty."

"Lance," she looks at the clock. "That's like four hours from now."

"I'll sleep in then and be up at six." I give her a wink. "Just, uh, text me when you wake up." I pass her my phone, and she takes it, her eyes darting down when our fingers touch. It's then I see it, guilt. Guilt I would've loved to have seen two years ago for the way she banished me. I bat that away, my anger with her low-lying. Where it will remain. I'm not about to screw this up by punishing her. I can't bring myself to do it yet, but oh, how I want to. What I want more is to punish her shimmering lips, rip off her sweater and leggings and fuck the hell out of her until she's whimpering out regrets and apologies. Instead, I pocket my phone once she's programmed her number in and head for the door.

"I'm gonna head out."

"See you tomorrow?" She pipes up behind me when I open it.

"Yeah."

"I'll walk you out, so my little bodyguard doesn't attack."

"I can handle him."

"He was tired. Just wait until he's had some coffee tomorrow."

I chuckle as she walks me to her door. The apartment quiet, my steps heavy on the hardwood. The last thing I want to do is leave, but I'm still fighting the gnawing resentment, and I need to get a handle on it before I keep more conversation with her. How she can be so completely foreign and familiar at the same time is screwing with me.

Once on the other side of her door, I linger, as does she.

We stare silently, time and past between us before she speaks up. "I can't believe you're here."

"Yeah," I say softly, before leaning in to kiss her cheek. When I pull away, I do it just a hair from her lips. "It's good to see you, Priss."

She licks her lips, and her eyes slowly lift to mine. "You too."

"Night."

thirty-five

HARPER

WATCHING FROM MY BEDROOM WINDOW, I WAIT UNTIL Lance disappears out of sight before I turn towards my bedroom door. "You can come in. I know you were listening."

The door bursts open, and René stands with his nightly smashed avocado face mask on in a white robe he stole from a posh hotel that Ricky took him to on an anniversary.

"What are you doing?"

"I'm sitting on my bed. What are you doing?"

"You're going to take him on a tour of New York?"

"That's the plan." I can't hide my elation, and I don't want to.

"Mami, you let him go for a reason."

"Yeah, the timing was off."

"And you don't think it's off now? Your career is thriving. You just landed your first solo."

"So?"

"So, what you going to do? You going to go to Texas and have his massive babies and throw it all to shit?"

"No, I'm not. Stop spitting hatorade. He's in town, and he wants to catch up."

"In town for Christmas? You don't find that odd that he here without no family?"

"I don't know. I'm not going to waste time that I could spend with him worrying about it."

"Fine, he your first love, I get it. But you made a conscious decision to end it with him. You both have different lives. You told me so over and over."

"It's a tour of New York, not marriage."

"He wants you back. Mark my words."

"That's hard to do."

"Shut up," he snaps, sauntering in my room and sifting through products that he will eventually steal off my dresser. He flips a cap off my body spray. "Mmmm."

"Don't you dare. I just bought that."

"A little spray."

"It's a bit flowery."

"I like flowery. My parents named me René, a girl's name," he sighs, "what did they expect me to do with that?"

"Your name doesn't make you gay," I say, taking the bottle from him and capping it, "your attraction to men does."

"Exactly, it's a sickness though, these men, they break your heart." He gives me a side-eye I'm sure he considers subtle and is anything but. The man is shit at keeping secrets, and that's why I'm careful with my deepest around him, but he's all heart. And I love him like no other.

"I'm okay. And I'm going to be okay, no matter what happens the next few days."

"He wants you back," he singsongs, giving me a pointed look while swiping some of my new balm across his lips.

"It's been two years," I shrug. "Maybe he's curious."

"Curious if you still look the same *naked*."

"And would that be so bad?"

"He broke your heart, broke your family up, and it made you miserable."

"My father broke my heart. I left Lance so that we no longer had to suffer for it. He did nothing wrong. I've explained this. You want a villain where one doesn't exist."

"I just don't want to see you in that much pain ever again."

"Goes with the territory," I say, knowing Lance leaving me in mere days will probably feel like a wrecking ball to the chest. "I chose dance, I chose his well-being. I chose my own well-being. I ended it."

"Okay, Mami. You're all grown up now, I guess."

"*Yes*, I am."

He rolls his eyes. "Just be careful. What about this guy who took you to coffee?"

Casey doesn't hold a candle to Lance. The flickers I felt today during coffee don't have shit on the flame that ignited in my chest the second I saw Lance at my door.

I shake my head, and René sighs.

"Okay, just know I'll be here."

"You better be here, always."

"I just said I will. Now, I make another mask, and pick some clothes so you can be ready for tomorrow."

"No, thank you, I just want to sleep."

"Oh no, we doing this."

The decision is final. For the next hour, I'll be buffed and polished.

These are the perks of having a best friend with a self-care addiction and great fashion sense. And when I say best, he's the best I've ever had. He leaves the room to go hammer and nail out my makeover while I stare at the vacant chair Lance just left.

I've been watching his progress closely since clips of fights started on social media. Seeing a highlight reel was just posted to his page, I watch as he knocks his contender to the ground with little effort. Two years ago, he was the most alluring man

I'd ever seen. Even with evidence of a broken nose, the man is now God-like and more attractive than ever. He's bulked up so much, I barely recognize his width, but those grey eyes and thick lashes and smooth full lips I would know anywhere. Not to mention the way they make me feel. The way I feel with him in the same space, period, is enough. Flipping through his feed, I see the location of his fight, the fight he said took place in New York. I scroll up and see the time stamp. Seven hours ago, Lubbock, Texas. Clearly, he's not the one running his own social media page.

And he lied. But why?

thirty-six

LANCE

Brisk air slaps me in the face as I get acquainted with Manhattan. Twice I've dodged a cab, my focus on the view. It only took me a mile to realize how brave Harper is, how brave anyone is to try and conquer a city such as this. As for my own opinion, so far, it's the same—chaos. A clusterfuck of skyscrapers, streets filled with loud traffic, and people scattering in all directions on life's everyday missions. It's everything and nothing like the movies. A bit less glamorous, but I'm going to let my time with Harper here sway my final decision. I'm three miles in when I take a detour to Ground Zero. Even though I was six when it happened, I'll never forget the panic on my parents' faces as they watched those buildings go down. It was the first time I've ever felt real fear. I stand in place, staring at the memorial in awe of what those people have endured and decide it's a plus for the city. New York is an overpopulated army of survivors who stood their ground and reclaimed their city as not one of fear, but as a place of resilience. It's heroic just to live here. New York is full of fighters, so maybe there's a place for me here too.

But how can I fit in her life here?

Is this a fool's errand?

My life is at the ranch, and when it's not, it's on the road. I dedicated myself to the purpose years ago. But if my inkling is right, maybe it doesn't have to be complicated. Going heavyweight means I can split my time between fights. I'll get much better pay, more leisure time to prepare between bouts. I'll hire help at the ranch. I'll do whatever it takes if we manage in a few days to reclaim what we lost.

Dreams change, they evolve, because of the people in your life.

Mine are evidence of just how drastically it can happen. But any new dream I've conjured up has always involved Harper, dead center. I can't imagine her out of any scenario that won't complete me. And I can't will myself to forget her. I don't want to. My motivation for being here is selfish. She may be able to live without me, but I'm convinced her asking the same of me is too much to ask of my heart, which has been slowly suffocating without her. I don't love her any less than I did two years ago, that was clear to me the minute I saw her on the other side of that door. If she's changed, maybe I can change to suit her. I have to believe that life is a series of truths and that some are absolute while others get too muddled amongst youth, aspiration, and ambition.

Harper is a truth for me. What I feel for her is the truest of truths.

It's love, the kind that changes people, pure and simple, because she changed me by just believing me, in me, to the point she possessed a part of me. Maybe I can't move on because I'm not supposed to. Or maybe I'm too late. Either way, I have to know.

There's been plenty of available women down the line, but I've rarely indulged and after, fucking hated myself for it. At one point, I damn near self-sabotaged and then blamed Harper for the guilt, for discarding me like I was disposable which made me a hypocrite. I used those women for solace, to try to ease the ache. Another old habit reemerged, and right now, I'm fighting against them all.

This is either a sick fascination with the past, or I'm finally running in the right direction. Time will tell. In the next few days, I'll know.

If given the chance, I'll love her better than I did, wholly and unconditionally, the way she loved me. I thought I had loved her right, but I must have missed something because she didn't hesitate long enough, and she didn't walk, she ran away.

I never wanted to be one thing, anyway. I don't want to be a fast definition.

Ballplayer, rancher, fighter...I can switch hats to whatever she needs because I want her back in my life.

With every light tap of my sneaker to concrete, I try to convince myself this isn't a manic attempt to escape my reality back home.

I need this.

I need this.

My phone rattles in my hoodie as I stop a few feet from my hotel. I assume it's Tony wanting to get some training time in. He's already managed to arrange a few hours at a gym later tonight.

Harper: Just woke up. Ready to see the city?

Lance: I've already run the whole thing, but I'm happy to browse more.

Harper: Show off.

Lance: Early bird gets the worm.

Harper: I couldn't give a shit. The worm is all yours.

Lance: I see we're still a pleasant morning person.

**Harper: I just punched René in the throat for using the rest of my peppermint creamer. You might want to give me an hour and another cup. Don't take any chances, save yourself the sore throat.

Lance: An hour. Got it.

Harper: Did you see the statue?

Lance: You mean that small ass action figure off the harbor? Seriously, a lot smaller than they make it out to be.

Harper: That's what she said.

Lance: Aww, look, sweetheart, you made a joke even in your wretched state. I'm guessing you're happy someone is in town.

Harper: Yeah, I heard Lucas Walker is staying at the Four Seasons for his press junket.

Lance: You're an asshole.

Harper: Happy face and hands emoji

Lance: Eye roll emoji. See you in an hour.

thirty-seven

HARPER

I'M NERVOUS IN A STAGE FRIGHT WAY. LESS THAN TWENTY-FOUR hours in and I've already lied to Lance. I threw up in the shower due to nerves. I'm not in a bad mood, I'm terrified. What if René's right? What if he's here because he wants me back, or worse, what if he doesn't?

I've barely slept. I can't stop thinking about how amazing it felt to be on the receiving end of his attention, in his arms. I haven't forgotten how thoroughly I got wrapped up in him when we were together, of how certain I was, of how much I trusted him, in us. And now? Now I'm a girl whose once sure steps are unsteady.

"Chill out," I scold myself, brushing my teeth for the fifth time in an hour. I can't sit still. I can't stop fidgeting. Why is he in New York?

"Mami, door."

"I'm coming." I gloss my lips and do a final once-over in the mirror. Hair down, beanie, sweater, jeans, and short boots. It's my go-to girls' night outfit, and René approved. When I get to the living room, René is in a silent stare-off with Lance, who's politely making small talk.

"…you ever lost?"

"Oh, yeah, plenty when I first started. But none in the last six months."

"How many fights is that?"

Lance grins. "A lot." He catches sight of me. "Hey, Priss. You look beautiful." I avoid direct eye contact as more nausea threatens.

Woman the hell up, Harper.

My stomach rolls and I smile so wide, René gives me an odd look. In an attempt to tone it down, I busy my hands wrapping my scarf around my neck before gathering my bag from the hall tree. "Thank you. Good Morning."

"It's noon," Lance says, trailing after me to the door.

"Like I said, Good Morning."

"Don't dancers have to get up early?" He chuckles behind me.

"Life's a bitch to me that way."

"Should I wait up for you?" René calls from behind us.

"You shouldn't," I say, blowing a kiss toward his questioning eyes before closing the door. "Sorry about that. He's a bit of a menace in the man department."

I make a beeline for the elevator, my nerves still getting the best of me as Lance speaks up behind me. "It's fine. I like that he's protective of you."

"Do you?"

"Yep. But his instincts need work. I'm harmless."

"Says you," I hit the button for the lobby and turn to face him, and that's when I'm struck stupid by the sight that greets me.

"So," he asks as the elevator door closes, "what's first?"

"It's," I fight the urge to gape at him, "...a surprise."

"Yeah?" He looks over to me with his silvery gaze and amused smirk. It's clear that last night I was drenched in too much shock to fully appreciate him. No longer the slim muscular baller I met, he's *all man* now. He's dressed in a thick black sweater outlining his mammoth physique. Wood toggle buttons run down the front, and the round collar lays flat, highlighting the corded muscles at his neck. Beneath clings a black T-shirt that shows a hint of his pecs. The rest of him, he poured into tight black jeans that accentuate his trim waist and muscular thighs, which he followed with black boots. He gelled his thick dark hair, which only draws me in further into the planes of his face, the sharp lines of his jaw. He looks like a mix of conservative and bad boy.

He's breathtaking, devastating, a man to drink in, slowly.

The truth of this is further reiterated once we hit the busy sidewalk, and the eyes of most female passersby cover him in appreciation. It shouldn't bother me, but it does. It's one of the reasons it was hard for us to be together in college. Well, one of the reasons it was hard for me. But back then, we were never public like we are now and…did that lady just run into a door?

"Jesus," I mutter.

"What's wrong?"

He's clueless or playing it that way when a group of girls passes us breaking their necks to get a seconds' long look at him.

I keep my head forward and let out a nervous laugh. "Nothing."

A woman hovering over a German Shepherd picks up his morning dump with the hand not holding the plastic bag as we walk past.

"Damn," she says before realizing her error. "Oh, shit."

"Literally," I grumble at her over my shoulder.

"What?" Lance looks over to me, drawing his brows.

"Are you serious right now?" The next onlooker, a woman somewhere in her mid-forties, stops mid-step on the crowded sidewalk to gawk, her cell at her ear. "Don't tell me you didn't see that."

"They probably know me from my fights."

I snort unattractively. "Yeah, because all women are so into *boxing*."

"They could be."

The woman's thirsty eyes roam from Lance to me, doing a long sweep, and I know her line of thought, I can read it clearly with her expression. 'What's *he* doing with *you*?'

The answer today is, I'm not sure. I hate this feeling. I hate that she has me questioning it myself. I hate that a complete stranger has this power over me. I hate that I let her have it. Sending up a prayer, I glance over at Lance, who seems completely unaffected by her and unaware of her reaction to me.

And I'm thankful.

Thankful he never knew just how hard it was to be loved by him. Thankful he doesn't see me in the same pathetic light. Thankful I didn't let my past insecurities break me entirely or the looks I got on campus at Grand, much like the one I just received, take their toll.

I want to believe that's the truth, but my scars begin to burn in afterthought, a reminder of the casualty. The evidence walks next to me, telling me my previous convictions are unjustified, and I don't have grounds enough to feel any type of pride.

The truth is searing. I didn't win that fight, and I damn sure didn't come out of it unscathed, or unbroken. I just came out of it, and I'm not sure what that makes me anymore.

"You have thousands of followers, and I'm willing to bet a good bit of them are women. Stop making excuses. You don't have to downplay your looks."

"That's not me. You know I don't give a damn about that," he says, nudging me. "You jealous, Priss?"

I am. Briefly, I wonder how many beds he's graced since our split. I had to force myself away from that line of thinking soon after our breakup, or I would've lost my mind. We make our way toward the subway, and the women's stares follow like dominoes. He's drawing the attention of a freaking movie star, and honestly, he looks the part.

"Seriously? You can't see this?"

He smirks down at his boots as we wait for our train. "All I see is you. And your flaring nostrils."

"Oh, shut up."

"Penn Station, this is us," I say as Lance scours our surroundings on the subway. I hide my grin at his discomfort. Though his expression is stoic, I know this man, and I pride myself on recognizing he's not so comfortable yet in this environment. It's as if at any second he's expecting to feel the rumble of Godzilla terrorizing the streets while picking off skyscrapers.

"I see you laughing at me."

Well, damn, maybe he can still read me as well. I can't help my giggle.

"Sorry, it's just funny to see you looking around ill at ease, country boy. I know you're used to more cows on the pasture than people."

"I saw a man in a diaper in Times Square on my run."

"Ah, I would have thought the Naked Cowboy would have brought you some comfort."

"Still have a mouth on you," he grumbles, poking his head out of the car, blocking my exit and looking both ways before allowing me off the subway. I laugh as he jerks me close to him by the elbow.

"It's okay, Lance. We're safe."

"That's subjective," he mutters as we step out, and he

follows my lead up the steps and onto the street until he sees our destination. Once we cross 8th Avenue, he stares up at the building, dumbstruck. "Madison Square Garden?"

"You said you already saw the city. Now it's time for you to meet the bones, come on." I take his hand, and he doesn't hesitate. I can't help but welcome the swarm of butterflies as he strokes the skin on the back of my hand with his thumb. Our eyes connect, and so do we, it's effortless. Lips parting, pulse thrumming, I pull my phone from my jacket using my free hand to send off a text. A few moments later, an entrance door pops open, and we're ushered inside by one of Nana's oldest friends.

"Hey, sweetheart," Charlie says before pulling me into a hug. "How've you been?"

"Great, Charlie. Thanks so much for this. We were hoping to take a look around if that's okay?"

"It's fine. I was happy when I got your call. How is Amelia?"

"Nana's doing well. I wasn't sure if you'd be here during the holiday."

"Leaving New York at Christmas? Blasphemy, but I have no big plans. They're about to start setting up for the show tonight, so I can only give you a few."

"That's all we need."

Charlie turns to Lance. "She doesn't call in many favors, but her Nana has been doing my taxes for thirty years and saved me a fortune, so you better be worth it."

"Hope so. Lance Prescott." Lance extends his hand, and they exchange a shake. Charlie leans in, Lance towering above him.

"Treat her right."

"I intend to," Lance says easily as Charlie walks us past a hall of concessions and into the arena.

Once inside, Charlie grins at Lance's reaction and turns to

me. "Doors will lock behind you at the entrance when you're done."

I pull Charlie to me and feel the frailty of his frame. When I met him, he had far more life left in his posture. "Thank you, Charlie. We won't be long."

"Anytime, sweetheart."

Once alone, we take the steps to the center of the Garden.

"A lot of the greats fought here," Lance says, mystified.

"I don't know if you're aware, but New York is quite the boxing mecca."

One side of his mouth lifts as he scans the space, eyes glossed in wonder. "I'm aware."

"On October twenty-sixth, nineteen fifty-one, Rocky Marciano beat Joe Louis here, knocked him—"

"Through the ropes. It was one of the biggest upsets in boxing history, Joe Louis was dethroned by the underdog." He lowers his gaze to mine. "How did you know that?"

"I got into boxing back in college, my boyfriend was kind of a badass. He was into Marciano."

"Yeah? What happened to him?"

"Marciano?" I shrug. "He became one of the greatest fighters that ever lived."

Lance rolls his eyes.

"Oh, you meant the boyfriend. He became a bigger badass. He's kind of the king of underdogs. He's going to win the heavyweight title one day."

"You think so, huh?" He follows me with his eyes as I begin to walk in a slow circle around him.

I shrug. "I know so. He's come so far already. And his dreams were so small when I met him. He wanted the NFL. Now? He's already advanced to professional fighting after two short years in the amateur circuit. He's about to start fighting for the title."

Lance shakes his head ironically.

"You think I'm crazy?"

"I think you're talking crazy."

"You thought so then too. But what if I'm right?" I'm still circling him as he takes in the whole of the legendary arena. "What
if…you're the next Marciano or even better, *Lance Prescott*. What
if you're the next great upset?"

"I love your faith in me, but—"

"But what? You think they weren't just as intimidated? Do
you think any of those fighters went into the ring without a trace
of fear or self-doubt? I promise you they didn't."

"I'm sure they didn't, but—"

"So why not you? Have a little faith, and picture it. Like you
did last time. Picture yourself here or *anywhere*, fighting for that
title. Visualize it. And don't stop fighting until it becomes a reality. You did it to get this far, you can do it again."

His hesitation is heartbreaking. "If you say so, Priss."

"You're going to win that title, Lance. Close your eyes."

Our voices are anything but intimate. They're more like
echoes upsetting the vibe in this sacred place, but that does nothing to stop the goosebumps from erupting on my skin. I'm standing in front of a world-class sportsman. I just need to make him
believe it. What I knew in my gut then about his fighting mate-
rialized into truth. I don't believe this conviction any less. Lips
upturned; his eyes close. I lift up on my toes, balancing myself
on his shoulders with my palms and whisper both our hopes for
his future. "Are you seeing it? Do you hear them? It's going to
be incredible."

"I don't care about all the noise."

"No man destined for greatness ever does. But by the time
you get to that point, you'll deserve it."

He opens his eyes, and in them, all I see is hope and longing.

In the next second, he snatches me to him, so I'm flush with his chest.

"Look at that speed," I manage through a laugh as he grips the sides of my face and leans down just an inch from my lips. I wet them in anticipation, but he backs away slightly, amusement dancing in his eyes. I do my best to hide my disappointment. "All this faith in me. I hope I don't let you down."

"You never have. Don't start now."

"I'll do my best. This is incredible, Priss. Thank you."

"Ready to see more of New York City?"

He slowly nods, his eyes searching mine before his lips lift into a serene smile. "Let's do it."

thirty-eight

LANCE

After touring a good bit of Manhattan, we walk Central Park for hours just talking in the freezing cold. None of the conversation is forced but it's mostly in circles when she asks about life in Texas. I've been tight-lipped about home for a reason, I'm here to escape. After dodging most of her questions, she fills me in on the last two years of her life. I haven't asked about her relationships because I don't want to know. A more mature man could handle it.

For the moment, that motherfucker ain't me.

The more I watch her, the more possessive I feel. It's growth that needs to happen, but the hardest of my pains when it comes to her.

I don't want to know just yet who's kissed her, touched her, fucked her. I'm liable to lose my head. But I know there's a part of me that needs to be okay handling whatever the truth is. Even after all our time apart, it's clear to me she's very much the same girl I fell for, just a little less naïve and more worldly. I can still read her, anticipate some of her words, her thoughts. So, when her breath sputters after seeing a man in wait at the foot of her building, I notice.

The guy catches sight of Harper and lights up when their eyes connect in a way that grates me, and I know without a doubt, this is the *new*.

Harper's ears redden, and it has nothing to do with the cold.

"New?" I ask, trying to hide the raw jealousy I feel.

I already know the answer, but she nods, looking on at him before darting her gaze back to me. "Just let me talk to him for a second, and then I'll introduce you."

"Can't wait."

"I'll be right back."

The guy lifts his phone as she approaches. "Hey, you, I've been trying to text you today."

"Sorry, I've been out and about."

Just as I was thinking it minutes ago, I know without a doubt I'm being tested, which is just my damned luck. Though he might be new, it's obvious there is a little history between them. I can read it in their posture and easy conversation as I size him up. He's tall, built, and dressed to dance in skin-tight black slacks and a matching button-up shirt. His thin pants leave nothing to the fucking imagination.

And the cherry on top? Well, that's the horse dick resting on one of his silk-covered thighs.

Instantly, I want to dismember him.

Horse dick looks past Harper's shoulder at me, and her eyes follow. She's nervous, and it's painfully clear. She's never juggled two men at once, and her attempt is shit. Even in my state, I swear to God I love her more for it. I'd be more amused if the guy wasn't staring at me like I'd just stolen his puppy.

After a few seconds of polite conversation, I make my way over to where they stand.

"So, who is this?"

"This is Lance. We went to college together at Grand. Lance, this is Casey, he's a choreographer for the show I'm in. He was just doing a promotional shoot at the park across the street for one of his upcoming shows. Isn't that a coincidence?"

"Sure is." It's a nice enough reply, but I play on the only words I truly heard. "Yep, old college pals," I say, grabbing his offered hand with a firm shake as he sizes me up. I'm only too happy when I see him swallow.

That's right, motherfucker.

"Just old pals. I played ball for her dad." I nudge Harper with my shoulder. "Though he got a little pissed when she Snapchatted my dick to him."

"It was your ass!" Harper says, close to hysterical as her eyes volley between us.

"That's right, my bare ass. My bad, *pal*." Casey is not at all amused, and I give myself a mental pat on the back. It's a hell of a lot breezier conversation than I thought myself capable of. But my point has been made, and I can safely leave it there.

"So, what are your plans tonight?" Casey asks Harper, dismissing me as though he's the bigger man. And maybe he is.

I hate everything about this situation but fight the inclination to show it.

Harper stands fish-mouthed for a few seconds. "Well, we're...I was going to take Lance to—"

"I'm training tonight, so she's free," I toss in, which has them both turning my way. Casey looks satisfied while Harper looks over to me, stunned. "You didn't tell me that."

"I've got a fight in less than a week. Can't pass up a chance to train. Tony's with me."

"He is? Here in New York?"

"I told you I fought last night. Can't do that without my corner."

"Uh huh. But you said this was a charity fight coming up."

"A fight all the same." I shrug. "Gotta have my trainer."

"A fight?" Casey asks.

"He's a boxer," Harper adds with pride, despite my shitty

demeanor. She's too proud of me to act any other way. "He's got his first pro fight in a few months."

Casey nods, eyes lingering on her face with the way she regards me. His disappointment is unmistakable, and I let myself have a little victory. I can see him mentally start to lay his weapon down before he persists, and I have to give him credit. He leans in toward Harper as I stuff my clenched fists in my jeans.

Casey tugs on her scarf. "Want to grab dinner?"

"I, uh," Harper looks back to me.

"You go," I speak up, unwilling to witness another second. I'm not giving up, but I'm tapping out before I let the thought of them gnaw at me. "I should head out now," I say, pulling Harper in for a brief hug, ignoring the eagerness in her expression.

I look over to Casey. "Good meeting you, man."

"Nice you finally showed," he mutters dryly.

"What's that?"

"Just as nice meeting you." He's no bullshit, and it's clear he has a set of nuts on him as well. He tilts his head as if he's trying to figure out my game while I keep my face as passive as possible. The hard part about becoming the man you want to be is owning the actions that entails. I've never been so fucking jealous in my life, but I know that if we are to ever have a future together, if we have any hope of having one anytime soon, I have to kill the territorial beast.

"See you later?" I ask Harper.

Harper slowly nods as I fight for every single step away from her.

"You left her, at her apartment, with a guy with a Moby Dick?" Tony asks, holding the bag.

"Yep," I grunt, running a combo on the tattered sack.

"Why?"

"To prove to myself I can handle it."

Again, I slam my fist into the bag, the momentum pushing Tony back.

"Props, man. I would have pissed a circle around her."

"Trust me, I fucking wanted to."

"I'm proud of you."

"Don't be, you don't know what I'm thinking."

"It's okay to think, as long as you never act. It would do you good to remember that. And you're making the bag bleed. I haven't seen you this amped up in a hot damn minute."

"I don't know what I'm doing here."

"Sure you do, you're giving her a choice."

"He's here. He's in her world. I'm not."

"I'm not much for girl talk, but if I remember correctly, at one time, you were her world."

"Right," I do another combo, and Tony's again pushed back by the force of it. "That's why she left."

"Easy, man. This is just a warm-up. And maybe that's why you're here. Not for another chance with her, but to finally front her out about leaving you so abruptly."

I shake my head. "You think I'm such a damned egomaniac I can't handle getting dumped?"

"By *her*, dumped by her. She's the difference."

It's the truth. Post breakup, I had to spend a lot of time training with Tony. He watched me fight through it all and has been around every minute since. He's one of the only true friends in my life, one I respect.

I tag the bag again with a hard right, and he shakes his head.

"Jesus, don't throw like that at the charity fight, you'll kill the guy."

"Why are we doing this anyway?"

"It looks good on the résumé," he answers. "And before you think about canceling it to spend more time in New York, think again, it may be a charity fight, but we're getting a decent paycheck, and we both need it."

"I know. I won't."

"I mean it, man."

"I fucking won't!" I roar as Tony steps back, and I lay into the bag.

"Chill, you're going to spend yourself on warmup, and we have a match in five."

We're training in one of the nastiest dumps I've ever been in, and that's saying a lot for having grown up in a town with one stoplight.

"Where did you find this shithole?"

"I trained here for a while before I went pro. Don't knock it, some of the greats stemmed from here. And anyway, platinum training doesn't keep anyone hungry. You stay in the gutter, you stay hungry."

"Wise words from the guru of boxing."

Tony grins, reminding me of Joe Pesci—who he could pass as a cousin for—just with added height. "Damned right, and it will do you good to remember it."

"Who am I fighting?"

Tony glances around the room and jerks his chin. "That guy. Three o'clock. He beat Otto once."

"No shit?" Otto Lawrence won heavyweight this year and is a fan favorite. His strength and speed are intimidating. He's one of the few who do that to me, but when it comes to boxing, I've never hesitated to step into the ring.

I size up my competition on the other side of the room, and

he gives a polite nod. His demeanor may be friendly, but his eyes say he's going to own my ass. My answering nod says, 'we'll see.'

"He's got the speed you lack. After he schools you, he's going to give you some pointers."

"Don't be so sure that's happening."

"I like your confidence, but he's next level. You aren't quite there yet."

I glance over to where he sits while getting his fists taped up, as an image of Harper and horse dick pops up, blurring my vision crimson. "Let's do this."

"Fuck, I look like Quasimodo," I say, eyeing myself in the mirror in the bathroom while making my way to Tony.

He throws his head back with a laugh. "That's what you get for squaring off with a professional."

"It wasn't that bad," I wince as he presses on my nose, my words coming out muddled. "I need a painkiller."

"Yeah, it was," Tony says, pulling out a bottle of ibuprofen and tossing two in my hand, "you came to New York pretty, but you got jacked."

My phone buzzes on the bench beside me as Tony tapes up the cut above my eye. "No stitches needed, the nose will go down overnight, and the tooth will reset itself, just don't touch it. Your eye, though," he whistles through his teeth, "well tomorrow, you'll have a face only a mother could love."

"You didn't tell me he's an ex-champ."

"You didn't ask."

"Am I ready for this?" I ask honestly.

"Don't doubt yourself now, asshole. He came at you with everything he knew because you didn't know of him. That's insulting. Know your opponent. I told you to start watching other fighters."

"I played football for fifteen years, I know football."

"And you've been in *this ring* for years, no more excuses. I know you have a shit ton on your shoulders, but we need to get in the head game. I'm serious, man. We, not just me, have to anticipate strengths and weaknesses. We'll attend more fights this year."

"Yeah, because we have the bread," I roll my good eye.

"We'll deal with it. You need some sleep. That's fatigue talking."

My phone rattles again, and I pick it up to see it's Mom checking in. I text her back and see a missed text from Harper.

Harper: Why did you run off like that and leave me there? That was a dick move.

"Shit, and it's just that damned easy for her to make you smile," Tony says, bagging his supplies. He lingers, and I can tell he wants to say something but thinks better of it. "Ice and heat. And sleep."

"Got it."

"See you the day after."

"Wait, you're giving me some time off?"

"Get your miles and weights in, but yeah, you're ready. Have a good Christmas. I'll meet you at the airport."

"What about you?"

Tony grins. "I'm covered."

"Like that, huh?"

"Yeah, like that. You forget this is home for me and I've got a house call to make. Besides, one of us needs to get laid."

I give him the finger and glance down at my phone.

Lance: How would you know? It's been a while since you've seen my dick move.

Harper: Har, har, still Shakespeare, I see. And that's not what I asked. Why did you bolt?

Lance: I told you I had a match. And I got my ass kicked. I don't look pretty.

Harper: That's karma. What time are you coming in the morning?

Lance: In the morning.

Harper: You are such a pain in the ass.

Lance: Admit you missed me.

Harper: Rolling eyes emoji.

thirty-nine

HARPER

"H OLY SHIT!"

"I texted you it wasn't pretty."

"You look like a pug dog."

"Thanks, and you look beautiful." Heart soaring from his compliment, I tug him into my kitchen to inspect his eye. Much like yesterday, he looks gorgeous, aside from the side of his face that looks mangled. It's a little grotesque. There's a cut above his eye, and his nose is a bit swollen. I order him up on the counter, and he hoists himself up easily, his biceps flexing under another form-fitting sweater. I pull one of my ice packs from the fridge and press it against his bruised skin. "Does it hurt?" I lift the pack and press on the area, testing to see if there's fluid behind it.

"Yes, because you're fucking with it."

I jerk my hand away. "Sorry. What does the other guy look like?"

"Hot, he's about six-one, two-thirty, mocha skin. It was a nice date. How was yours?"

"We didn't make it to dinner." Casey knew after laying eyes on Lance that he was the one I'd been waiting for. He'd said as much after I hesitated to accept his dinner offer before he bowed out.

"Shame. Are you upset about it?"

"No, he knows I'm not in the right place for commitment."

I pause because I can feel his body tense with my statement.

"And anyway, you took care of the rest with your lewd shit. Thanks for that. I had to spend five minutes explaining why I Snapchatted your ass to my father."

"Sorry," he smirks. "It slipped."

"Sure, it did. I can't believe you told him we did the horizontal hustle."

He tosses his head back and laughs. "You dork. Who says that?"

"Nana and I don't like saying..."

He quirks a thick brow. "Saying...?"

"You know," I say softly.

He leans in. "Nope, no idea."

"Sex."

Lance shakes his head slowly. "That's not what you were going to say."

We're close to eye level, his breath hot on my lips, his eyes tracking my every movement. "I remember it flowing quite nicely through those lips, many times."

"Fucking," I own it. "But I don't like to be that vulgar when I'm not in the heat of the moment or pissed off."

"I'm hurt, Priss, I thought we made love."

"Oh, shut up."

"'Sides, I thought I was a gentleman about the whole situation."

"You *almost* passed for one. And what's up with that? Who are you, and what did you do with Caveman Prescott?" I can't figure him out. His eyes and lips, even his language all scream intimacy, and yet he hasn't gone out of his way to touch me or claim me in any way, even for the moment, even if his visit is brief. Maybe his intention isn't at all to win me back. Maybe his point of visiting is just that. I swallow, tracing the light bruise on his jaw.

"Be proud of me, Priss," he says through thick lips. His eyes are drawing me closer as I inch my fingers around his face. Nipples drawn tight, I'm far too eager to give in one more inch and draw on his lips. The buzz between us is there, it's heavy in my limbs, my aching center, becoming harder to ignore. I never asked if he had anyone waiting for him back home. And the question is getting harder to pose.

"Proud of you for?"

"I'm a growing man," he says gruffly. "Speaking of which, I'm starving."

"O-okay," I stutter out reluctantly, pulling my hands away. "I'll, uh, get my purse. We're going to my nana's first if that's okay? I just need to show my face and spend a little time with her since my Christmas plans changed last minute."

"Sorry," he says, sincerely apologetic.

"I'm not," I say, sliding my purse on my shoulder. "Let's get you fed."

Lance and I take the steps up to the brownstone as I pull my keys from my jacket pocket before unlocking the door. "Nana, where are you?"

"Hey, Dove, I'm in the kitchen."

"I'm not alone," I call out in warning.

"The more the merrier."

"I bet she's making matzo ball soup," I say excitedly. "It's tradition. Today is the first day of Hanukkah."

Lance hesitantly steps into the house, glancing around.

"Don't worry, she's a little old school, but surprisingly

open-minded, and she'll love you. Take your boots off." Lance unlaces his boots and sets them on the doormat next to mine.

Nana calls out to us from the kitchen. "Come on in, I'm making matzo soup."

"Told you," I say as Lance takes his time perusing the two-story townhome I've spent most summers living in since I was five. He stops short of the entryway, fixed on a picture of me in a pale pink leotard and matching tutu. "That was my first recital. I was two."

He grins and grabs the frame to study it up close. "Cute."

"Yeah, well, it was a disaster. I sneezed and peed all over my leotard but kept dancing. That's showbiz." Setting the picture down, he takes a step forward and scans the wall of the staircase, which is basically a photo collage of my dance history. Dozens of pictures tell my story by photograph, showing my growth. He runs a finger over the latest addition. It was a showcase I did in Spain.

"This is cool."

"It's a little embarrassing. You would think I'm her only grandchild."

"She's proud is all."

"Yeah, that she is. She danced a little when she was young."

"That's where you get it from?"

"Most definitely."

He chuckles at a few adolescent photos, and I move to block his view. "Enough with this, we don't want to keep her waiting."

"Did you get lost?" Nana calls as I take the hallway that leads to the kitchen with Lance trailing behind.

"Nope," I say as she comes into view, her back to the two of us as she stirs the same metal pot she's used for years. In her home is where I feel the safest. The smells, the fact that very little décor has changed over the years. It's my place of peace, where I block out the outside world and exist in hers. I wrap my arms around her where she stands, inhaling her scented lotion. "Smells so good. Hanukkah Sameach, Nana."

"You too, Dove." She sets the spoon down and pulls me to her. "I've missed you."

"I'm sorry. I've been busy with the new show."

"Ah well, that's a good excuse. Speaking of, your mother called this morning. They won't be coming for New Year's either. Says she has to work."

I glance over at Lance, who follows our conversation carefully. "Maybe next year."

"Maybe." We both sound skeptical because when it comes to my parents, we aren't sure they'll ever be in the same room again, let alone celebrating the holidays. Lance hasn't said a word about Dad so far, and I've been thankful. When I release her from my grip, she turns and drinks him in. "And who do we have here?"

"Lance," he offers, extending his hand across the space before all five foot one of my nana pulls him in for a hug. She's in her late seventies but doesn't look a day over fifty. She takes immaculate care of herself. Today, she's dressed to the nines in cashmere and slacks, her hair artfully braided to frame her face. "Ah, Lance, well aren't you a surprise." She makes no show of ignorance to who he is. She's very aware of him and our story. I've confided in her more than I have René, which is why there is a spark of concern in her eyes when she asks the million-dollar question. "What brings you to New York?"

I spare him the lie and do so on his behalf. "He had a fight here."

"I can see." She pulls away from him, scrutinizing him for his life choice. "Are you in pain?"

"No, ma'am."

She huffs. "Grown men beating each other in a boxing ring. You don't think that's a bit ridiculous?"

Lance grins, taking her ball-busting for what it is. "It can feel that way at times."

"As long as you're aware. Seems like no one has managed to knock any sense into you yet."

"Nana!" I exclaim, eyes widening.

"I can see where Harper gets her candidness," he drawls amused.

"We Ancel women don't mince words," Nana offers without apology.

"I like that about her."

"She seems to like something about you too." I can feel the blush creep up my neck as she grills him. "So, you're staying in town just for the holiday?"

"Yes, ma'am."

"How nice. Well, let's get you fed. Dove, get the good china from the cabinet."

I do as I'm told. "Saw Charlie yesterday," I say before giving Lance a conspiratorial wink. Nana sighs. I've been trying to get them together for a few years. Grandpa died six years ago and left us all with broken hearts. I don't like Nana alone, but she assures me she prefers it this way.

"Where did you see him?"

"He let us tour the Garden. You know he's staying in town for the holidays. I think he might be alone."

Nana looks over to Lance. "And then you realize how much your pushy granddaughter is like you and wonder if you should have raised her different. Bring me your bowl, Lance."

Lance chuckles, bringing his bowl to Nana as she ladles in some soup. "Only as much as you need. Never a bite more."

"Yes, ma'am."

Once we're all sitting at the table, Nana doesn't hesitate. "In this house, we pray."

"We do much of the same at the ranch back home."

"Good."

After two bowls of soup and countless stories about me, Lance and I are hard-pressed to get a word in edgewise. This doesn't seem to bother Lance, but when Nana gets to a fun anecdote about my first period, which I suffered while in New York on my fourteenth summer, I draw the line.

"Nana!" I protest for the umpteenth time.

"Nothing to be ashamed of."

"Still not great dining conversation."

"Do you have any children, Lance?"

"Nana, what in the world?"

"What?" she shrugs. "Just asking."

"He's not married."

"That apparently hasn't mattered in decades. Ask him if his parents were married," she challenges me.

"Actually," Lance chimes in, "they were. But I can't say there aren't any bastards in the family." Lance and Nana share a grin. "And no, ma'am. I'm waiting on kids."

"For how long?"

"Till it feels right. I'm not ready to give them the attention they'll need."

"That's a good reason. Most kids say age. You know what I tell them? Don't wait until you're in your late thirties. You might have more money then, but nothing matches the energy of your twenties. Not all of us got it wrong." She clamps a hand on Lance's muscular shoulder. "But if you take good care of this heavenly body you have, you'll be fine at any age."

I want to disappear inside the wall.

"Nana!"

"What?"

"Please eat your soup."

Lance is full-on belly laughing.

"You are a bit of a primitive man, are you not?" Nana asks Lance.

"I am."

She turns to me. "You're in for a treat, Dove. Your grand-father was the same. There's a big difference between a passive man and a primitive man, passive men are horrible in the sack."

I'm choking now as she turns to me and rolls her eyes while pounding on my back. "I swear, you kids think you got here by immaculate conception."

Lance sips his kosher beer, all too enthralled as I try and catch my breath. I sip water, glaring at Nana as Lance gives me a slow wink.

"I'll keep all of this in mind, Mrs. Ancel."

"You do that. Nothing beats a satisfied woman. It would do you good to remember that. There's something to be said for happy wife, happy life."

"Nana, Lance is just in town for Christmas."

"Better make the most of it then," Nana says, eyeing Lance, whose chuckle slows as a seconds' long silent conversation en-sues between them. "I've got some babka if you're interested."

"We really have to go—" I pipe up.

"I would love some," he says, pinning me in my seat.

Lance helps me clear the dishes, and Nana and I stand at the sink when he excuses himself to the restroom.

"He's back for you."

"You don't know that," I whisper sharply, "and you didn't

have to lay into him like that. Really, Nana, periods and baby talk?"

"You know your grandfather and I met at a party. A mutual friend's party."

"I know."

"What you don't know is that he was engaged to another woman."

"What?"

"I was a friend to the woman he was engaged to. I was by her side through all of the planning. I was at the engagement party, and there when she picked out her dress. I was forced to watch all of it."

"That's horrible."

"I never spoke up, and neither did he because surely you shouldn't be in love and break off your engagement for a person you just met. It seemed like nonsense even though it felt like anything but. If I didn't say something, I was going to watch the man I loved marry another woman."

"What happened?"

"I spoke up. I told her I was in love with him and lost her friendship. We'd been friends for over ten years."

"I'm so sorry. What happened after?"

"She broke ties with me, trashed my reputation, so I withdrew. I no longer went to parties. I was miserable, and I allowed all of it. I went to him the week before he got married and told him I wanted him to choose me. He sent me away with a broken heart. But the night before he was to marry her, he came to see me. He was angry, confused. He couldn't understand what was happening. We fought, and we hardly knew each other. It was so strange, and still, I knew. I just knew that I wouldn't have affection for any other man or be as attracted to another like I was to him. I wasn't innocent. I was twenty-five. I'd had my share of fair-weather romances before I met him. But I knew with him, I knew, without a doubt, if he married her, I would never marry another. I just knew."

"So, he called it off?"

"Yes. And we were married a week later. That doesn't happen anymore. It's considered ridiculous now in this day and age to commit to someone you hardly know. And though we were together most of our lives, your grandfather died partly a stranger to me. There are some things about him I'm sure I never asked. Things I'm curious about even after forty-eight years together."

"So, you really think if he would have married her…"

"I would be an old maid. You and your mother wouldn't exist. If I'm old-fashioned, it's in that way. I don't ever want to move on from your grandfather. And you're very much like me in that sense."

She plucks the bowl from my hand. "I'll tell you this. He's far less shaky than your grandfather was the night he called off his wedding, and even though he wasn't as convinced as me, we got our years." I bite my lip as she takes the last bowl from my soapy hands. "This is where you speak up."

"Nana, you know what happened. I'm terrifi—"

"Speak up, Dove, or you'll be forced to watch."

forty

LANCE

"**P**ROPER NEW YORK HOT DOG FROM A VENDOR, CHECK." She swallows the bite she's talking around before crumpling her wrapper with mine and tossing them into a nearby trash bin.

"Jesus, it's cold," she says, blowing into her hands. I tug her to me by one of them, swiping the mustard off her finger with my lips. She watches, rapt, as I place a gentle kiss on the pad of it before I let go. It's been like this all day, lingering looks, stolen glances, sentimental words, endless eye fucking. Neither of us has given in, only been on the verge of. She wanted me to kiss her at the Garden yesterday, and I wanted to, but I'm not sure what the right move is. I'm still testing the waters. We've fallen back into us quickly, easily. She wants me to dream big, and the only time I've ever really done that was when I've been with her. She's always pushed me to want more for myself, aim higher. Maybe she does it with a gentle hand, but she pushes me, and I don't want to need that. Need her. I can't want to rely on her again if she won't be there.

She's in love with her city. Her dreams came true here.

And though there's a ton of truth to her words about New York being a boxing mecca, my future is the ranch. For the first time since I showed up here, I'm wondering if it was a mistake to come.

Because it's the same fucking predicament we were in two years ago.

"What are you thinking?" she asks as we cross the street from Rockefeller Center, making our way toward NBC Studios. She wanted to do a few touristy things today, so I got a full tour of the city. I'd passed on ice skating beneath the iconic tree, and she was fine with it. With her show coming up and my fight, we can't risk any injuries. We're both, in a sense, athletes. Instead, we drank hot chocolate and watched from the glass above, admiring the families around us as she tried to grill me about things back home. But I don't want to dwell there, not yet. Not at all, really.

"Lance, how is Jack?"

"He's good."

"Uh huh. And Trevor?"

"A little shit."

"And your mother?"

"Hanging in. I need to pick her up a present while we're out."

"Okay, we'll hit a few shops on the way back."

"Sounds good."

She turns to me as hordes of shaky skaters circle the rink behind her. "Now, tell me how things really are."

"Priss," I start, and she takes the hot chocolate from my hands before I can take another sip. "I'm not done with that."

"You are if you don't start talking."

"Things are good. We're making it work."

"That's generic and not good enough. Tell me about home."

"Well, there are cows and chickens. And we feed them. And when the cows get fat enough, we take them to auction."

"Smartass," she mumbles.

"Give me that hot chocolate."

"Not a chance."

"I don't want to talk about it."

"That's obvious." There's an edge to her voice. "But how can we really catch up if you aren't being truthful?"

"Still no bullshit, eh?"

"Have I changed much?"

"Not at all," I say with a smirk. "And neither have I, so if you don't hand that fucking delicious hot chocolate over, I'm going to throw you over my shoulder and redden that perfect ass of yours."

"Like that?" She beams, shimmying her perfect derrière toward me before taking a sip of my chocolate. "Mmm," she moans, eyes widening. "Why, it is fucking delicious."

"That's it," I say, charging toward her as she thrusts it at me.

"Here, you shit. I just wanted to know about the family."

"Should come see us sometime," I say. "Invitation's open. See for yourself."

"I just may do that."

"Tony's living there now."

"Really?"

"Yep. And the other guest room bed is really uncomfortable, so you would need to share a room with me."

She rolls her eyes. "I'd rather sleep with the cows."

I lean in and wipe the chocolate from the corner of her mouth with my thumb before sliding it over her bottom lip. "You sure about that?"

Her lips part and I know she's close to biting my thumb when I pull it away. She licks the chocolate from her lip. "I'm sure they're more conversational than you. More honest."

"I don't want to talk about it, okay? This is my break from all the bullshit."

"Is that what this is?" She asks with an edge of hurt to her voice.

"What did you want it to be?"

She shakes her head and hands me back my cup. "You win, I'm done with the questions." Not long after we leave the rink, I get lost in my head, and she's in front of me again as I stare at the entrance of Radio City. She taps my temple. "What's going on in there?"

"Nothing?"

"Doesn't look like nothing," she regards me carefully.

"It's been two minutes, Priss, and already more questions."

"Do you want to talk about it?"

"I just told you I didn't."

She shakes her head. "That's not what I'm talking about." She glances away, and I know exactly what subject she's broaching. She can feel my resentment, no matter how much I've tried to hide it.

Do I want to talk about it? Yes. But I don't think I can yet without unleashing some of the lingering anger I feel. But the longer I'm with her, the more resentful I'm becoming. Because of the way we fit, the way we've always fit. I hadn't imagined a single moment of it. I'd romanticized nothing. We were—and still are—as good as my memory of us, and even now, I can't understand why she walked away completely. "Nah, really, I'm good."

"You're a terrible liar." She squeezes my hand, and I didn't realize I'd taken hers again. Or that she'd taken mine. Either way, there's been little time today where we haven't been touching. But it's as if we're both too afraid to push beyond that.

"So, there's a tour here," she says as we walk inside the building. "It's about the Rockefellers, and it's crazy. When you see just how much of their agenda was hiding in plain sight, it's just…baffling. It's less touristy than the studio tour but still touristy. You in?"

"Sure."

Some time later, after walking most of the building while the tour guide explains the meaning behind every painted mural, I realize I've spent more time memorizing Harper than I have paying attention to the socialist agenda of the rich and powerful. It's surreal being here, knowing she was always just a plane ride away. She did everything she set out to do. I'm proud of her. In a way, I envy her. I feel like I have so far to go, and she's accomplished so much. Toward the end of the tour, we're led outside to see the Rockefellers' purposefully constructed middle finger amongst the New York City landscape. I stand transfixed on the statue just outside the building across the street from St. Patrick's Cathedral. A bronze Atlas stands a story tall, holding a globe-shaped sphere on his shoulders.

"Atlas was installed in 1937 and created by the sculptor Lee Lawrie. The piece has since been appropriated as a symbol of the Objectivist movement, the philosophy being the ideal man be a producer who lives by his own effort and does not give or receive the undeserved, who honors achievement and rejects envy. Objectivism holds that there is no greater moral goal than achieving happiness. But one cannot achieve happiness by wish or whim. Can anyone tell me who a major player was in bringing this movement forward?"

"Ayn Rand. *Atlas Shrugged*," someone pipes up from the mixed crowd.

"Correct. This is bold capitalist agenda…"

The tour guide's voice falls away as I look on at the statue.

"It's such a thin line, isn't it?" Harper whispers, standing next to me.

"What?"

"Between being a realist, believing only what you can see, and believing in what you can't, entrusting faith." She turns to look up at me, but my gaze remains on the statue. "It's you," she says softly beside me, grabbing my hand, "it's the way I've always seen you, Lance, with the whole world on your shoulders, but never aware of just how much you shine. It's like you're paralyzed by the weight when just a few steps away," she nods toward the church, "you can accept a little faith and just let some of it go."

It's then I take my hand from hers. "Maybe some of us only believe what we can see." My tone is harsh, cold, but I can't bring myself to apologize for it.

"I'm sorry. I overstepped. Maybe that's not you anymore."

"Yeah," I finally rip my eyes away and glance down at her. "You've said plenty. But I'm curious, Harper, where was your faith?"

"What?" She swallows as the tour guide prompts us all to follow him, but we remain where we are. "You talk a lot of gospel, but where was your faith?"

She searches my eyes, and I know she sees the hurt I've been holding for two years, just as clearly as I see the guilt in hers.

I let out a long breath. "Forget it."

"Lance, we can talk about it."

"No point, right? It's been over for years."

It's a low blow, and completely the opposite of how I feel, but at the moment, I feel weak, with only shaky ground to stand on. She's exposed me mere hours into our day together, she's always seen me, seen through me, stripped me bare, and I forgot how uncomfortable that can be. And all I feel now is…anger.

forty-one

HARPER

I**T'S BEEN AN HOUR SINCE HE CALLED ME OUT ON THE SIDEWALK** next to the statue. Since then, he's been a living statue himself. After the tour, I suggested we go shopping, and he agreed because he still needed a gift for his mother.

"So, after the show, it's back to auditioning. Nothing is ever guaranteed, but with *Retro* on my résumé, it could be a busy summer. At least I hope so." I have no idea if he's listening, but I've been rambling for five minutes, my nerves firing off. The start of our day was nothing short of spectacular, the last hour has been a fantastical freaking mess. He's angry, and it's apparent. When we were together, we rarely seriously fought, if ever. This dynamic between us hurts more because not only are we not together, but I have a feeling he regrets coming to New York.

"You have a lot going on, that's for sure," he speaks up finally, thumbing through some scarves.

"I've needed to be happy about being busy, right? Most dancers don't get this far. I'm proud of myself."

"Lots of *me* and *I* going on," he mumbles before picking up a jewelry box.

"What's that?" I heard him, and he knows it.

"Nothing."

"I've missed you, you know? More than you can imagine."

"Can't imagine it at all," he says, picking through a book he's not reading.

"Can I help you two?" One of the store sales associates asks, and I shake my head and smile. When she takes her leave, I look over to Lance who stands fuming on the other side of a table filled with loose items. We're in a mismatch shop full of mostly cheap junk, and I can't imagine him finding anything for his mother here.

"Lance, I have missed you. Horribly."

"Could have fooled me."

I can only take so much. Irritated, I lift a designer coffee mug from the table.

"You like this for your mom?"

"No."

"How about this?"

"Nope." He's not even looking at what's in my hands.

"You sure? It's a hide purse. Cute for a rancher's wife, don't you think?" This gets his attention, and stormy eyes lift to mine.

"Would you buy that for you?"

I look it over and shake my head. "Not really my style."

"Bet it's not."

I can feel my ears reddening. Fuming, I eye a box on the shelf, snatch it and shove it into his chest. "How about this giant freaking purple dildo and matching anal plug!? Think Mom will like that?"

He looks up completely unaffected, "Nope."

"I don't think we're in the right place." Tossing the box down, I stalk out of the cluttered shop and into the department store next to it. He's hot on my heels.

"Got that fucking right."

I turn back to see he's spoiling for a fight and release a stressed breath. Fighting with him is the last thing I want to do.

"Look, let's just…" I search around and pull a sweater from the closest rack. "How about this? Simple, elegant."

"You think Mom's simple, huh? I'll give her your regards."

"That's it." I hook the sweater back on to the rack and close the space between us, forcing his eyes to mine. "God, you're still a brute, aren't you? You haven't changed a bit. Still pigheaded as hell."

"Pigheaded?" He opens his mouth in mock shock and covers his chest with his hand. "How *dare* you."

I'm in between fight or flight, but I've been dodging this long enough. My heart can't take more confrontation. I've missed him too much. His eyes flare with satisfaction at my irritation. "Misery loves company, right, Lance?"

"Never said I was miserable."

"You don't have to. Did you come to New York just to torture me?"

"Maybe."

"Rub it in over what I'm missing out on?"

A voice sounds from next to us. "Is there something I can help you find today?"

We both turn to the woman with lasers in our eyes, and she swallows. I clear my throat. "We're fine. Thank you."

Lance winks at the woman, his eyes scanning her form. "Maybe you can help *me*?"

"You son of a bitch," I hiss, before walking away from the table. His voice rings out next to me as I rip through a rack of scarves.

"Good to know you care, Priss, gotta admit, it's surprising."

I reel on him. "Don't you dare! Leaving you was the hardest thing I've ever done in my life. I had to make a clean break. I had just lost everyone that mattered to me. I was losing my mind."

"I got pissed for *one day,* and you went off the grid."

"And you *let me go* because you knew no matter how much we wanted it to work, it couldn't. You have no idea what I went through!"

"What *you* went through? Do you know I spent six months ranting to an Uber driver named *Dave* because everyone on my team hated me when the truth came out?" He stomps after me as I pull sweater after sweater off the rack. "Troy jumped ship after he got drafted. I had no one but Tony and those fights."

I turn to him with twenty sweaters in my arms. "Jenner? When did y'all get so tight?"

"When shit got tough, and my fucking girlfriend bailed!" He glares down at me, his breaths coming out fast.

"Guys, we're going to need you to take this outside." A woman, whom I assume is the store manager, approaches us cautiously.

I look around the store and see all eyes are on us, especially the women sizing him up. "He's available, ladies," I snap, laying the sweaters on a nearby table, "I'm willing to bet he comes *really* cheap." He's on my heels as I push through the glass of the department store.

"Oh, was I supposed to wait for you? Must have missed that memo. That's it, you must want a saint. That's why you didn't stay."

"I was twenty years old and alienated from a place I didn't want to be anyway."

"Good to know."

"That's not the way I meant it. And you know damn well until you, I was only there to appease my dad, who I barely speak to now."

"I'm sorry about that, I am, but that's on him. And what in the hell are you talking about 'alienated'?"

"Forget it." I pull on my gloves as heavy snow starts to come down. "I think we've concluded our tour for today."

He glances around the sidewalk. "Well, no need to show me more, I hate this fucking place!"

"And why is that? Not enough free-range chickens?!"

His eyes flare. "You digging on the ranch now, Priss? I saw a damned rat the size of a cat on my run this morning!"

"Probably has better manners than you, shithead."

"Pulling out the big guns now, huh? There's that backbone. I was wondering where it went."

"Go home, Lance, you hate it here. And you obviously hate me."

"Just the opposite. It's impossible, and believe me, I'm trying!"

"Well, I hope you succeed! Thanks for stopping by, Mary Poppins. Best Christmas *ever*! Make sure to bulldoze the nativity scene on your way out!"

"Fuck this." He throws his hands up and eyes me warily before turning and walking away.

"Merry Christmas to you, too!"

forty-two

HARPER

"R**ENÉ?**"

"In here, Mami."

Blotting my face with my scarf, I hang it on the hall tree before making my way to his room. I find him shuffling through his closet. "What are you doing?"

"Looking for the perfect pajamas for this White Christmas! I want to have one of those nights where I'm comfortable in my pajamas and eat good soup. You know, cozy. I love those nights."

"Where is Ricky?"

"Working. But he's off tomorrow. You not going to Nana's?"

"No, I saw her today with Lance."

"Where is he?"

"At his hotel, I guess."

"Oh, well, you can join me if you want. I'll drink two, maybe three bottles of wine. We can watch the snow fall and plan my massive funeral. Pretend it's like Princess Diana's."

"You're the weirdest man ever."

"I know. Now, where did I put those damn pajamas?" He moves a pile of sweaters and glances back at me. "Oh no, have you been crying?

"Yes. Lance and I just had the biggest fight. It started in the department store and then turned into a street brawl. He's still pissed I broke up with him."

He doesn't look the least bit surprised. "Uh huh."

"And he's acting like a total possessive dick. Like he has any right after two years."

"Uh huh."

"Every time I say something about the show, about dancing, he starts getting snippy."

"Like he resents your life here, your career?"

"Exactly. And I've only been supportive and happy for him."

He turns to me with a sweater in his hands.

"Mami. Have you had sex with him?"

"No. He's barely touched me. I mean, we've held hands, but nothing beyond that."

"Uh huh."

"Why do you keep saying that?" He pulls out a small suitcase from the floor of his closet, unzips it, and puts one of his sweaters inside.

"What are you doing?"

"Packing."

"Why?"

"I told you my plans."

"You said you were going to get drunk and watch the snow fall."

"Oh, I am. But at Ricky's."

"Don't go. I'll get drunk and watch it with you."

"Sorry. No can do. Hand me my seashell bag on my dresser over there, would you?"

I hand him the bag, and he tosses it in the suitcase. "I don't understand why you're leaving."

He shakes his head. "You will very soon."

He adds his pajamas and another sweater to the suitcase along with a pair of jeans before he zips it shut.

"You told me that you'll be here no matter what!"

"Yes, and I mean it."

"But you're leaving?!"

"I'm making room for the other man in your life."

"What are you talking about?"

"Oh, baby. You are so blind sometimes. Sigh."

"You don't *say* sigh, you *text* sigh, or you actually sigh, and don't you dare walk out that door!"

"You don't need me tonight. When's the last time you got waxed?"

"What?"

"Humor me, Mami."

"Jesus, I don't know, four days ago, why?"

He kisses my temple. "Perfect."

"René, you can't leave me alone on Christmas."

"I'm not." I follow him out into the kitchen, where he plucks two cups of his Keurig coffee and shoves them into his backpack.

"Fine, go, but I'm keeping this wine." I pick up two bottles off the kitchen counter and hold them tightly to me. "You're leaving this."

He smiles. "All yours. To celebrate."

"Enough with the bullshit. What in the hell are you talking about?"

Arms full, I follow him to the front door, and he opens it before turning to me with a telling smile on his lips. "You're about to have the best sex of your life. I envy you." He kisses my cheek. "Merry Christmas."

I'm still gaping at the door, hugging the wine bottles to me when my phone pings in my purse from where it sits on the hall tree. Depositing the bottles in the seat, I pick it up to see René's just sent me a real-time pic of Lance, walking toward our building.

Shit!

Scrambling to the bathroom, I clear my face of my ugly cry makeup and swish mouthwash for a good fifteen seconds. I barely have time to rinse when a knock sounds on the door. Heart pounding along with my feet, I race toward it and fling it open, breath stolen when I see the look in Lance's eyes. Tears spill over my cheeks as he takes a step forward.

"Priss, I'm sorr—"

I launch myself at him, and he grips my face, holding me just an inch away from him, his eyes searching mine, a curse erupting from his lips right before he crushes me with his kiss. He presses in, my cries stifled by the pressure of his lips before he sweeps his tongue along the seam, and I open for him. Our kiss is endless, as he steps inside with me wrapped around him. I'm already drunk on the thrust of his tongue, so deep, so perfect as he groans into my mouth. A collective sigh escapes us both as he kisses me so intensely, I fight for more. My hands urgent, he pulls his away and pins me to the door, eyes hooded, his breaths coming out harsh. "Are we alone?"

Thank you, René.

"Yes."

"Thank fuck," he says roughly before he again claims my mouth, hungry. He's already grinding against me, and I'm matching every thrust of his hips as our tongues clash violently. I'm covered in desire, drowning in need. He pulls away, kissing every inch of my face as I rip at his hair, his sweater. He's just as eager, getting my blazer off before he begins to work on my shirt.

"I've missed you so much," I murmur between kisses.

"Fuck, baby, I thought I'd never see you again."

"Lance, please, please hurry."

"How many shirts do you have on?"

"Rip them off!" I practically scream as one of them catches, hooking my mouth like a fish. We burst out laughing until our mouths again collide.

When we pull away, he sets me on my feet, unhooking my bra and letting it fall away before covering my naked breasts with warm hands. Goosebumps erupt over my skin as he speaks to me in a dreamlike state. "I could never hate you, Priss, never." He scoops me into his arms and gazes down at me in a way I could only dream about. It's his eyes that convey so much. He gently deposits me on the couch, hovering above me, his fore-arms next to my head.

"I'm sorry. The last thing I want to do is fight with you."

"You love fighting with me."

His smile lights me up. "That's true."

I struggle to get his T-shirt off before he reaches behind him, gripping it with his fist, quickly discarding it.

"Harper," he murmurs as he hovers above, his face the pic-ture of restraint as I explore his chest, my palm roaming over the nuances, the indents of muscle on his torso. "Jesus, Lance, you're so…"

He quirks a brow. "So?"

"Hot," I grin up at him. "So…fucking hot."

"I missed you so much," he takes one nipple in his mouth and sucks, his eyes trained on his task while I observe the way his thick lips surround my taut skin. It's so fucking sexy. Gripping his hair, he trails his mouth down my navel, toying with the waist-band of my pants as he brings lust-filled eyes to mine. "How long do we have until we're not alone?"

"All night."

He nods and bites his lip.

I bite mine for a different reason. "Lance?"

He licks a trail over my skin, before stinging and soothing with his perfect mouth. "Mm?"

He pauses his movement sensing my question and guilty eyes meet mine before he drops his head to my stomach.

"I mean, of course you have," I attempt to say in a light tone, but instead, it comes out reflecting the hurt I feel. That I have no right to feel.

"René's got condoms somewhere." I move from underneath him to stand, and he lets me go. The sight of him shirtless on my couch does the most erotic shit to me. "I'll be right back."

René has a new box of condoms in his bedside table. I make a mental note to not only replace his wine but gift him everything on my dresser. Best friend ever.

Back in the living room, Lance sits on the couch, staring out the window, lost in his thoughts.

I approach him cautiously but decide not to let his change in mood deter me. I need him, and I'm not wasting another second fighting with him or worrying about what he did when we were apart.

I straddle him and grip his chin in my hand. "Don't get wrapped in your head," I murmur. "Please, not right now. Please, I need you to touch me."

He searches my eyes in question.

I shake my head.

"Priss—"

I unzip his jeans, releasing his cock, pumping his thickness in my hand. The hiss through his teeth and the lift of his eyes to mine is my undoing.

"Touch me, Lance. You're the only one…"

My words seem to break his heart, but he does, he lifts a hand and easily covers my breast with it. "So beautiful, Priss."

I pull away and stand, pushing down my panties and ripping open a condom as he slides his jeans down to his thighs. He grabs the latex from me and rolls it on, and I straddle him again, our mouths crashing together the instant I'm back in his arms. I lift, and he lines us up, our eyes connected. Wincing at the invasion, I sink onto him slowly, feeling every bit of the stretch.

"Jesus, Harper," he grits out, stilling me. "Easy, baby."

"More, more. Please more."

Slowly he thrusts up, stealing my breath and the last of my control. Ignoring the sting, I grind on his thick length, flicker turning flame as I begin to swivel my hips and meet his steady thrusts.

"Fuck, fuck," he grunts, gripping the back of my head, mouth parted, warm breath hitting my lips. With him, I feel it, the magnetic pull, the need, the want, the raw desire, the lust, the love. I ride him, slowly, our hearts syncing up as if no time at all has passed. In his eyes, I see answers to my every question, it's possession, love, and mirrored lust. "Harper," he murmurs before leaning in to kiss me, his strokes quickening as we both ignite. He's deep, hitting me perfectly, and I feel myself on the brink before he stills me, positioning me on my back while starting a slow drive into me.

"It's you," he says, pressing in deep, the couch dragging along the hardwood with his every thrust. "It's you," he repeats to the open wound I've spent years trying to heal. Tears threaten as I pull him down to meet my kiss, and he returns it with hunger, with fervor, with hope. It's then we combust, his thrusts quickening to a manic pace—hard, deep, so much friction. Our breaths and words mingle as I tip over and come, my fast breaths pumping into his mouth. The orgasm is a crushing wave that takes over the whole of me as Lance plunges once, twice, and gasps out my name until we both lay speechless.

forty-three

LANCE

"**L**ANCE…" SHE MOANS MY NAME, BREATHLESS. GRIPPING the back of her neck, I lean in, kissing her shoulders, buried to the root and grinding, doing my best to keep the sounds pouring from her. She's been starving for me. It's the best feeling of my life. I've never been this happy, and odds are this will be the highlight in my reel that sticks out the most. Harper is mine. At least for the time I have left. She saved her body, her heart for me. No one else has had her. It hurts, and it heals, and I can't imagine how she's feeling at my confession.

I should have held out.

I should have come for her sooner.

Regret eats away at me as I lick the shell of her ear before sucking her lobe into my mouth. Her moan muffled by the fabric as I press into her from where I bent her on the couch. We haven't made it long without using a condom since we gave in. We're running out of time, but I refuse to focus on that. Instead, I thrust into her, gripping her curvy hips and relishing in the sight of my cock disappearing inside her. She grips the back of the couch, her head tilted, her silky blonde hair cresting off the smooth skin of her back.

All I want to do is confess my love, pack her up, and bring her back to Texas with me. For now, I'll steal time, and try to possess her the only way I know I can, in the place she kept for only me. Determined to bat away my own sin against her, I brand her with long, thorough strokes. I've never been able to truly voice how I feel the way I want to. The words I come up with would never be enough, but she deserves to hear some. Instead of confessing what's on the edge of my tongue, I swallow it back and go dirty.

"You look so good stretched on my cock."

Reaching around, I spread her and press a finger into her slick clit. Her back bows and her legs shake as I go impossibly deep. She detonates, tightening around me, her body convulsing in pleasure as her pants and grip drive me over the edge. I come, hard, pulling her upright and capturing her mouth as I pulse inside her. I kiss the hell out of her before pulling out and sweeping her into my arms. She buries her head in my chest, her skin heated, rose-colored from my touch.

"Let's shower." I nuzzle her neck.

"Mmm," she murmurs back.

"Got anything to eat?" I carry her toward the bathroom.

"Sorry, I've been a shitty hostess."

"I would say you've been *very* receptive."

"Har, har."

"I mean," I shrug with her in my arms, "your *lover* has returned."

"Has he?"

There's a question in her eyes we both know the answer to.

"Today and tomorrow. Nothing else matters right now."

She smiles, and it lights up my heart. "We'll order Chinese, like old times."

I set her down to start the water before I take inventory of her bathroom. "How much does this shoebox run you?"

"Too much for not enough."

I nod. "I thought as much."

"As much as you hate it, I love it."

"I don't hate it."

She lifts a skeptical brow. "Really?"

"Not at all. I was just being an asshole. This city is interesting…alive."

"I agree."

We step inside the shower and barely fit. I chuckle. "Okay, this is going to be a test of wills."

She giggles, and the sound is music. "I can make it easy on you, shower quick and step out, or—" she takes a soapy hand and runs it down my cock. I'm already perking up, "—we can let the hot water run out. That's about four minutes from now."

"That's not long."

"Nope."

"Guess we better get to work."

"We both have *very* strong work ethics."

"Oh," I grit through my teeth as she pumps me vigorously in her hand, "I couldn't agree more."

"Finally, we agree on something."

Not long after our shower, we're devouring Shrimp Lo Mein in the best feature of her apartment, the window seat in her living room. Arms wrapped around her, she skillfully feeds me the soaked noodles with chopsticks and then stuffs her own mouth with the same mammoth bite.

"You're still a pig," I chuckle as she forgoes my mouth, stuffing hers instead.

"Yep."

"No shame."

"None. I work my ass off every day. When I stop dancing, I'll deprive myself."

I hesitate because the conversation keeps leading to future talk. "Me first," she says, setting down the container. "I picture a grand church, lined with large pillars with high arches hovering above. White roses showing little greenery everywhere. Everything white. All of my family and friends gathered. The perfect music."

"Are we really doing this?"

"Yes."

She lifts the box along with the chopsticks to my mouth, and I take the noodles eagerly. "It's so beautiful, right?" She nods toward the snowdrift falling outside the window next to us, both blanketing and shielding us from the world outside. When I pictured coming here, a night like this is more than I could have ever hoped for.

"Absolutely."

She hands me the container and stands. She has on a long sweater and thick socks, no panties. That was my stipulation for her getting dressed. She didn't put up much of a fight.

"I'm going to go grab some wine while you think about what you want."

"It's Christmas, and we're talking about our funerals."

"Play along, Prescott."

"Fine."

She saunters to the kitchen, and I stay put. The last few hours have been bliss, but I'm tired. I will much needed sleep away because I'm afraid to close my eyes.

I hear a little conversation as she opens a drawer and uncorks a bottle.

"Yes, I'm fine. Shut up. Okay, you were right. Whatever. Is

Ricky home? So, you're not alone? Good. I love you too. See you tomorrow night? Merry Christmas. Rainbows."

"René calling?" I ask, staring down the window at a surprisingly calm New York.

"Yes, he's just checking on us, making sure we haven't killed each other. I didn't even ask, do you like wine?"

Regret weighs heavy on me. As much as we do know about the other, we don't know simple things, everyday things that a couple would know if they were able to be together publicly. The irony is we don't have to hide anymore, and we haven't had long to take advantage of it.

"It's not my drink of choice, but I'll drink some."

"What do you drink?"

"Beer or whiskey."

"Huh."

"Yep. So, can I ask why you end your calls with him with rainbows? I was always curious when we were together but never asked."

"Yeah, it's nothing he wouldn't share. He got caught kissing a boy at dance camp, and it outed him early. We were eleven. He was mortified. His parents were called in." She shakes her head behind the counter, pulling two glasses from the cabinet. "Can you imagine? He was destroyed. One of the camp counselors—who was a pastor—called him an abomination, but there was another who stood up to him and told him he had no place preaching or speaking of love when he didn't understand the meaning of it."

"That's cool."

She walks toward me with two glasses in one hand and the uncorked bottle. "It was pretty spectacular the way he came in and consoled him. That counselor didn't leave his side or mine all night because I wasn't about to abandon René as distraught as he was. He talked him off the ledge. To this day, I think he saved his life, just by being there for him. I mean, I was there, but I wasn't an adult, so I think it meant a lot more to René coming from someone with more authority. He told him that as stormy and horrible as this time would be, there's always going to be that time after, that promise of a flipside, a rainbow moment that will make the trials worth it." She hands me a glass and pours. "So, no matter what we go through together, we just remind each other of that horrible day and that there's a flip side. Rainbows."

"That's awesome."

"We've been inseparable since."

"He's good to you."

"One of the absolute best people on this planet."

"I'm glad you have him."

"I thank God every day." She smirks. "You know he'll be home tomorrow night, and I would love it if you let him meet you. Like *really* meet you."

"I'm cool with that."

"Yeah?"

"Yeah. Why, did you think I'd be a dick about it?"

"I don't know. We've never talked about it."

"I'm not that asshole." I take the glass she offers me with one hand while running an appreciative hand over her ass with the other before pulling her back into my lap. "Love who you want, fuck who you want, as long as it's not Harper Elliot."

"Is that so?"

"Yes."

"Cheers." We clink glasses, and I take a sip.

She elbows me. "Your turn."

"Harper, come on. I can think of a thousand other things I'd rather discuss."

"Tell me."

"You're a pushy little chick."

She grinds her ass into me, and I groan. "Don't start nothing, won't be nothing."

"Mmm. Let's get drunk and have drunk sex. I've never had it."

"Fine with me, baby," I lean in and kiss her neck.

"Is it better?"

"No, it's sloppier, but your inhibitions go straight out the window. It can be fun."

"Well, then, drink up."

"You're crazy."

"You love it."

"I do."

"Funeral, Prescott."

"Jesus, fine. Bury me."

"Wow. Impressive."

"Next to my parents."

"Now we're getting somewhere."

"On the ranch."

"Makes sense."

"And my wife."

She nods solemnly.

"Is this depressing enough yet?"

"When René plays this game, it's a lot more fun. Elton John is there, and drag queens are pallbearers."

"Now that's a funeral I'd go to." I sip more wine, and my blood starts to heat. "Damn, is this strong?"

"A little. You feeling it already, lightweight?"

"I'm just…warm all over."

"Nice," she says with a giggle. "Are you a mean drunk?"

"Not tonight," I say, pushing blonde strands away from her shoulders.

She hops out of my lap and takes the other side of the seat to face me. "I want to look at you."

"Yeah?"

"Yeah, it's been a long time. You look good."

"So do you."

She sips her wine and looks at me wistfully. "Can you believe how far we've come since that day at the gym? I mean, we talked about me dancing here in New York and you going pro as a fighter, but now we're actually living it."

"If it weren't for you, I don't have any idea what I'd be doing."

"That's not true. You already had that inkling. You were boxing again. It would have come to you even if I hadn't hit you over the head with Tony."

"He's great, Harper, as far as trainers go. He's got me with an agent. I signed the contract on the plane here."

"That's awesome."

"I'm going to make some real money on this fight. Not enough to make me rich but enough to keep the ranch going for months."

"When do you get a title shot?"

"Depends on how I do. There's a lot to it."

"You'll get there, I know it."

I shake my head. "You have that much faith, huh?"

"Yeah, I do. You're going to be incredible."

"You dance for a living. That's incredible."

She nods with a smile. "To us." We clink glasses.

"We're mighty full of ourselves tonight," I say with a grin.

"When you work your asses off like we do, aren't we allowed to have a little pride?"

"Sure."

"We can be humble tomorrow and thankful tonight, but we can admit our status: badasses."

"Speaking of," I hop off the seat, still clad in my boxers and drain my glass before setting it down. Pulling my jeans from the floor, I pull out the box and make my way back to her.

"What's this?"

I place the box in her hand. "I saw it in the window on one of my runs."

"I didn't get you anything."

"You didn't have time between taking my head off and handing me my nuts."

"Sorry."

"Me too."

Her chin wobbles as she opens the box, and I weigh her reaction.

"It's…" She lifts the platinum and embarrassingly small ruby necklace from the box.

"A rose. I know the star of the show gets them after a performance, right? So, since I can't be at yours, I thought maybe if you wore this after, you would know I wanted to be the one to hand it to you."

"I'm never the star."

"But you are. You just got your first solo."

She lifts her hair as I take the necklace out and fasten it around her neck.

Her eyes shimmer with tears as I take my seat across from her, and she cups the necklace in appreciation. "Thank you."

"Don't cry."

"It's the wine. It's strong."

"Liar."

"Okay, it's because it's the perfect gift." A tear glides down her cheek as her eyes bore into mine. "I still love you, Lance."

Her confession steals my breath, striking deep. She leans over and kisses me.

"Jesus, Harper," I murmur before deepening the kiss, tasting her regret. Her words mixed with the salt dissolving on my tongue light me up with the hope I've been desperate for.

She pulls away and palms my jaw. "I feel bad, I got you nothing."

"That can be rectified."

She raises a suspicious brow. "Is this an *ass* thing?"

"No," I lift the word with my chuckle. "But is that on the table?"

She slaps at my chest. "Absolutely not!"

"Okay, okay, doesn't hurt to ask."

She smirks. "I might consider it."

"Really?"

"Sure, if I can do it to *you* first."

"Shit," I shiver. "We're good."

"Hey, that's where your G spot is, René says—"

"That's enough, Harper."

"Good."

"Fine."

We share a laugh.

"Now, what is it you want, my grumpy boxer?"

I pour some more wine in both our glasses. "I want you to dance for me."

"What?"

"It's been too long since I've seen you dance. I mean I've watched clips but—"

She palms my jaw. "Say no more. You want me to do it now?"

"Can't think of a better time."

This excites her. She tosses back her glass and hands it to me.

"Okay, what are you thinking? Fast and furious or," she waggles her brows, "slow and sexy?"

"How about your number in the show?"

"Yeah?"

"Hell yes."

"Okay," she jumps up from the window seat, her face animated. "You know I told you it's called *Retro*, right?" She makes quick work of connecting her phone to the large set of speakers in the room before pushing her coffee table out of the way. It's the only large room in the apartment, which I can now see had to be the selling point.

"Okay, so we all got 80s movie theme songs to dance to."

"Yeah? What's yours?"

"It's the "Love Theme from St. Elmo's Fire." Have you heard of it?"

"Nope."

"I hadn't either, but I loved it. Oh shit, I need some panties on."

"Not necessary."

"That'll be just way too graphic, even for us, Prescott."

"Fine. Five-minute pass."

"You're such a twisted pervert."

"I haven't seen or licked that pussy in two years. We've missed each other."

"*Primitive indeed*, geesh."

She disappears for a few seconds and comes back wearing shorts along with silky red ballerina shoes wrapped around her ankles.

"We said nothing about the addition of clothing."

"Shut up, Prescott," she says, stretching an arm across her chest, "do you want your present or not?"

"I do. A lot less mouthy and much more naked."

"That's after."

"Oh yeah?"

"The wine's kicking in, and René told me how to give a proper blowjob."

"On with it," I gesture impatiently with my hand. She throws her head back and laughs, and that's the moment I know I will never love another woman in my life the way I love her.

"So, this is a running song throughout the movie."

"Hence the title, "Love Theme Song." I think I've got it."

Narrowing her eyes, she stands in the center of her living room, the sweater swallowing her as she does a few more stretches. "I'm nervous."

"Don't be, I promise to give you roses after."

"Even if I suck?"

"Especially if you suck, but you won't."

She shakes her limbs out at her sides, taps on her phone, and takes position a beat before violins sound throughout the living room.

And then she begins to move…ripping my newly-content heart right out of my fucking chest.

The only light in the space is from a streetlight through the window next to me, which casts shadows of the snowdrift behind her. Her dance intoxicating, she leaps and spins, her body fluid. She's a master, her dancing weaving a story as she glides along the hardwood, not missing a single step. And she shines, God how she shines, her long angelic hair trailing behind her as if it's all part of it, highlighting her strength, her grace.

She's the most beautiful thing I've ever seen. A ball of regret lodges in my throat as I think of the way I've punished her in the last few days for her gift.

She's light, and you can't hide light, you can't hold it and keep it. It's unattainable. And maybe that's what Harper is for me—a light I can't keep. As the burn in my chest grows unbearable, I fight myself not to let the defeat show. A fighter I may be, but I am the threatening dark to her light, and this light I can't, I refuse to snuff out. As the song gathers momentum, she follows it in a surreal leap across the length of the room before spinning into a series of circles, her frame taut, her legs in a continuous rotation.

A saxophone chimes in, cuing the end of her story as she wraps herself back into position, and I sit there stunned until her head pops up and she peeks over at me, her skin shimmering with sweat, her cheeks heated.

"Merry Christmas?"

"Come here, beautiful," I whisper hoarsely, holding out my hand. She lifts, worry on her features, and takes my hand as I pull her to me and wrap her in my arms. I cradle her, so she can't see the expression on my face. I'm fighting like hell not to lose my shit. "I need you to forgive me."

"For? What's wrong, Lance?"

"I foolishly forgot just how magical you are. Harper," I manage, "baby, that was incredible."

"Really?" She tries to look back at me, and I keep her pinned where she is. Maybe it's the wine, but I can't help the threatening emotion, so I pull the damp hair away from her face along with her sweater and press a kiss to her shoulder.

"Can I ask for one more gift?"

"Anything."

"It's more of a promise. Please don't ever stop dancing. Not for me, not for anyone, not ever."

"I won't. Lance, what's wrong?"

"Nothing at all," I say, pulling her back to me and letting my lips roam.

"I'm all sweaty."

"I like you this way."

"Such a charmer, but still no Shakespeare." The rawness of

my voice has her on alert, but I just hold her to me, keeping my forearm locked around her chest.

"You're going to blow them away with that dance. I'm so damned proud of you."

"Look at you, getting all sentimental on wine."

It's the longest fight of my life. The minute it takes me to rein my emotions in. I've already lost her again, and the worst part is I completely understand why. I can't be in her future if it's here in New York. It's not impossible, but with her unwillingness to commit to anything but dance, it's improbable. I battle with myself to ask. I'll never feel this way about any other woman, I know it.

I know the unconditional love of family, the sincerity of a good friendship in its own love-like version, but Harper showed me—taught me—what love with strings feels like. Her strings pinpoint so many parts of the anatomy of my heart—desire, borderline obsession, need, want, but most of all, the capacity to be content, and that's something I've never had until her. I still love her the way she taught me how, and I don't want to ever know any different. It's her.

This fight is selfish. All my thoughts are selfish. The best thing I can do for her is let her dance, let her shine her light, and not taint her with the darkness I fight daily, the darkness that keeps threatening to swallow me whole.

Maybe my line of thinking is dramatic, but it's totally true.

"It's almost midnight, almost Christmas," she says softly before leaning back and drawing me into her kiss. I kiss her back, knowing the clock is ticking as I fight for just another minute with her. No matter how good we fit, no matter how hard we love each other, or how much I want it, she can't truly belong to me.

And it's that blow that leaves me defeated.

forty-four

HARPER

BOTH OF US ARE ON THE VERGE OF SLEEP, LANCE GRIPS ME tightly to him as we lay on my bed using my Mac as a TV. We put on my favorite Christmas movie after making love for hours. Hours I could never, ever forget. He'd showered me in his love, his need. I'll never fail to remember the way he hovered above me—his movement so deliciously slow as my entire body shook with the feel of him. My center throbs now as I think of the way he leaned in, drawing my kiss as he rolled his hips, his deep thrusts stealing my breath, in his eyes a gentle storm. It's utter completion being with him this way. I feel free, happier than I can ever remember. Nothing has ever felt so real to me, so right. My heart's been faithful for good reason. He's the one and my only, and he's leaving soon. I'm terrified. Terrified to speak up because I know what battles I'll face in the road ahead if I choose life with him.

Lance's fingers run along my scalp, and I cower away from his touch. Repositioning myself on his chest, I try and concentrate on the movie and the feel of his caress.

"Happy, you little bitch?"

I shiver in his hold, trying to bat away the images that keep surfacing.

"Do we have your attention now, Harper?"

Minutes into my fight, Lance's voice pulls me back to where he lies beneath me.

"She's too skinny," he says in sleepy observation.

"What?"

He juts his chin toward the screen. "She's way too skinny."

I lift to sit and peer down at him, unable to help the bite in my tone. "Is that all you see?"

He frowns. "What? What do you mean?"

I glance over at the screen. "Is that all you see when you look at her?"

"She's unhealthy. She looks sick."

"She's my hero. Vera-Ellen is a freaking legend, and is she remembered for this movie or her incredible dancing? No, instead, she's known as the anorexic dancer."

"No offense, babe, but it looks pretty true."

"You know what I see?" I say in a huff. "I see raw, unbelievable talent. A rarity. Someone worthy of a hell of a lot of praise, not your scrutiny."

Lance moves to sit, reaching for me. "Where is this coming from?"

"I'm just saying, look at her dancing, her *talent*."

"Whoa," he says, reaching for me. I stand, shying away from his touch before roughly pulling on his T-shirt.

"People don't get it. They have no idea what it takes to do something so damned complicated and make it look easy. You know what else I see," I look over to the screen, "I see that she probably spent months perfecting the transition into that fouetté turn, for *you*, for *me*, and you see a girl who needs a cheeseburger."

"Okay, what the hell, Harper?"

I shrug, trying to play off my crazy. "She's my hero. And comments like that ruined her."

"Point made. Sorry."

"Fine. I'm hungry."

I make my way into the bathroom and shut the door. Seconds later, a knock sounds on the back of it.

"I'm pretty sure you aren't going to find anything to eat in there."

I splash water on my face, humiliated. "I'll be out in a minute."

"Harper, open the door."

I open it to see Lance standing in his underwear, confusion etched all over his face and in his eyes. "Want to tell me what that was about?"

"I told you."

"Bullshit."

"I'm just hangry."

"Fine," he says, lifting me over his shoulder. "Let's get you some food then, brat."

"I'm not a brat," I say as he hauls me into the kitchen. "I just think it's wrong to look for the flaws," I mumble into his shoulder. "You look at anyone long enough, you'll find them."

He sets me on the counter and pulls the leftover Chinese from the fridge before offering me a bite, and I refuse it. "You know she lost a baby to SIDS a few years after *White Christmas* and stepped out of the public eye. Now she's just that anorexic dancer who went crazy."

He sets the box down and smooths his hands down my arms. "Baby, what's wrong? What is this really about?"

"Nothing."

He tips my chin. "Tell me."

It's on the tip of my tongue. It's the perfect time, but I can't bring myself to fess up. Terrified of his reaction, it's all I can do to keep my chin from wobbling. By telling him, I would only humiliate myself more, and not only that, it would change everything. "It just breaks my heart, that's all."

"If you say so." Unsatisfied with my reasoning, he forks another bite of noodles and offers it to me, and I refuse it again.

"So, not hungry, then."

"Guess not."

"Not even for a little dessert?" He picks up our unopened fortune cookies off the counter and holds it up. "I'll open yours, and you open mine?"

"Deal."

He pops one open, grinning as he reads the slip of paper. "This suits you."

"What does it say?"

"The early bird gets the worm, but the second mouse gets the cheese."

"That is so me."

"Totally."

He hands me his. I crack it open and shake my head, grinning.

"What does it say?"

"Meh."

"Not a good one?"

"No," I giggle, "it says Meh." He takes the paper from me. "Of fucking course."

"Let's do half and half."

He draws his brows. "You want half of meh?"

"Hell yes, I do."

We each take half of our cookies and pop them in our mouths, sharing a smile before he lifts me off the counter, looking down at me. "You're awesome."

"That's you. And I'm sorry. I didn't mean to lash out like that."

"Don't be." He kisses me. "Let's go back to bed."

I lift a brow. "Are we going to sleep this time?"

"Maybe," he grins, and I wrap myself around him, soaking in the warmth of his skin.

"You know, I could get used to this."

His reply is silence, and it has me on edge, but once we're in the bedroom, he kisses me back into our lull. After Vera's next number, he turns to me on his pillow. "Believe it or not, I get exactly what you're saying. She was incredible." I nod, wrapping my leg around him and pulling him close. Savoring the feel of him, I drift to sleep just as the movie credits roll.

forty-five

LANCE

HARPER SIGHS IN MY ARMS, CONTENT AS I STUDY HER profile in the morning light. I slept harder than I have in months. And it's the first time we've ever had a night in bed together in the entirety of our relationship. I'm way too comfortable. I need to break away. Get my head back on my future. One that will have to exist without her. It was foolish to come here, but I won't regret it. She's okay, she's better than okay, she's thriving. I saw the evidence of it in my time here. As much as I want to whisk her away and resume my life with her in it, I can't. She's barely scratched the surface of her dancing potential. She deserves to live her life the way she's envisioned it, and any entanglement between us now will only get in the way. I'll be an obligation she can't cater to. I've been acting like a lunatic in the few days we've spent together, jealous of the one thing she loves most in the world, dancing. It's immature and wrong of me. We managed to recapture what we lost, and it's more devastating than I can imagine thinking that very soon, I'll have to walk away from her and the idea of us all over again.

We were meant to be in each other's lives for the time we've had, that much I'm sure, but our paths are so completely different. Hers clearly paved while mine is muddled with what-ifs.

Inhaling her vanilla scent, I give myself another few minutes just to hold her. To kiss her cheeks, her temple, her nose. Pain sears through me as I pull myself away.

It's time to go.

forty-six

HARPER

I HEAR THE SHUFFLE OF CLOTHES AND WAKE TO SEE LANCE DRESSING.

"Hey, you," I smile, drinking him in, loving the look of him in my bedroom. "Merry Christmas."

"Merry Christmas," he replies, his voice void of the same life it had mere hours ago.

"It's early," I reach out to him, "Come back to bed."

"I can't."

"Where are you going?"

"I have all my stuff back at the hotel, and I need to get back to my dad."

This grabs my attention. "Is he…is it serious?"

"He's temperamental these days, it's always serious."

"Sounds familiar." I can't help my smile.

When he doesn't reply, I know something's definitely up. I feel shut out from a few hours ago. It's barely daybreak. Swallowing, I look around the bedroom because the idea of him leaving me has me scrambling to my knees. He pulls a sweater over his head and peers down at me.

"Can I use your restroom to wash up?"

"You were just inside me in that restroom hours ago, what's with the formalities?"

He half shrugs. "Just trying to be polite."

"By all means, Mr. Courteous."

He shuts the door, and I hear the water run. Dragging myself from my bed, I wince at the soreness between my legs as I pull on my sweater. He's leaving. On Christmas Day? Not just leaving, he's bailing. Why? He's been in a somber mood since he saw me dance and I can't understand it. Putting a K-cup in my Keurig, I feel my heart start to race as dread fills me.

I walk over to the bathroom and knock on the door.

"So, where exactly in the city was your fight?"

Silence.

"Was it around here? I sure wish you would have given me the heads-up. I would have loved to have seen it."

"Sorry, next time."

Tears surface as I fully rouse and realize what's happening. "I think we both know there won't be a next time."

The water shuts off, and he opens the door wiping his hands on the towel hanging on the back of it. "Probably right."

"Yeah, because this was, what? 'I'm in town and let me see if I can turn Harper's world upside down?'…to get back at me?"

"You know that's not it."

"Your dad doesn't need you home. Not today. You asked me to spend Christmas with you, and you're going to up and leave a day early? Why?"

He avoids my stare, pulling his wallet from the top of my dresser and tucks it in his jeans. "I just need to get back."

"Bullshit."

"I have a fight coming up."

"I understand, but it's not today."

"I need to focus."

"Lance, what did I do?"

"Nothing," he says, searching the room for his boots.

"You show up after two years, sleep with me, and now you want to leave without so much as a discussion about it?"

"I have to go home and train. You have a show. What's there to discuss?"

"How about the fact that your last fight was in Lubbock, not New York."

He still won't look at me. "I wanted to see you, Harper, is that such a crime?"

"You're hiding. You refuse to talk about home. There's more to it than that. And these two days have meant something. What we have—"

His head snaps up, and his eyes pin me. "If you wanted to make me a priority, you had the chance two years ago."

I swallow. "That was different."

"How?"

"It was…hard back then. Different circumstances."

He squares off. "And it's easy now?"

I give him the truth. "No, it's not."

"Why?"

"Several reasons, the first being I can't just leave. I'm in a show."

"Exactly," he shakes his head. "So, there's no point in getting upset about it. I'm not."

"Well, that's apparent. So that's it? Was last night a goodbye fuck?"

"It was a great couple of days," he says as if we're talking about his favorite brand of cereal. "Thank you."

"Are you really saying this—"

"I can't swing if I've got nothing to swing for." His voice is arctic. "Stupidly, I always hoped our break up was temporary."

"I felt the same way, I still love you. Lance, please understand I can't drop everything and go ringside right now. I just… I've been working for this my whole life."

"I'm aware. I'm not arguing with you."

"So that's it? Did you get what you want?"

"Far from it. But you don't want me to ask for what I want. And you can't give it to me. So why are you acting jaded?" He laces up his boots. "I need to be able to see you, touch you." He looks up to me from where he sits on the edge of the bed. "I need a commitment. You refused to commit to me then, you had your reasons, I guess. So, commit to me now, *right now*."

Awareness pricks up my spine.

He shakes his head ironically at my silence. "You preach a hell of a lot about faith but seem to have none in us, in me."

"That's not true. And that sounded a hell of a lot like an ultimatum, not a question."

"It is an ultimatum. And you've made it true. You told me dancing will always come first, and I didn't listen. But after last night, I can't be mad at you for it. I can't." He lets out a self-deprecating laugh. "I'll take your silence as another no."

"Damnit, Lance, it's not that simple—"

His silvery gaze cuts me off mid-sentence. "Just fucking once, I would love to hear you say it was a mistake to leave, to leave *me*." The guttural edge to his voice has my heart bottoming out.

"Look how far we've both come."

He closes his eyes, and I know I've sealed my fate. His voice gets so low, I barely recognize it. "When I'm on that plane on the way home, and I admit to myself I *do know* why you won't commit to me, I think it might just rip the rest of me apart."

"That's not it. Not at all. Lance, you're enough, you're more than enough, don't go," I reach for his face, and he grips my hands between his. "Just one more day. We've still got time. If you could just stay *one more* day!" I'm hysterical and humiliating myself. "Stay. Please stay."

He cups my neck before his full lips cover me in his kiss.

It's far too brief before he pulls away. I feel it then, the distance he's creating. Eyes intent on mine, he's still cradling my head when he speaks. "I think what mattered to me most about coming here is that I never got a chance to say I love you. And I do, I love you, Harper."

His words strike deep, lifting my heart to an immeasurable height before it plummets to the concrete.

"Please don't go," I grip his forearms as he releases me.

I hate my stupidity, my cowardice the most. I shouldn't have to squeeze the life I've made to fit inside his. It's unfair to me. But that's not what he's asking. And it's not the reason for my hesitation. It's never been the reason. Dancing was just the best excuse to leave him, to leave Grand.

SPEAK UP.

SPEAK UP.

Fear cripples me as I watch him make his way to the door.

"Lance," I croak my hopes crashing with his every step, "I swear to God, I love you."

He looks back at me with resignation in his eyes. "I know," he says softly. "You were good at it."

And with that, he closes the door.

The rest of his life starts now, and my silence just bought my front row seat.

forty-seven

HARPER

Six weeks later…

RACING THROUGH THE AIRPORT TO MY GATE WITH MY PASSPORT in hand, I stop short when I see my flight's delayed. We have our last show in Canada, and from there, I'm stuck auditioning again. Forever searching for the next gig. It's terrifying when your career jumps from a small place of certainty to the unknown. Shouldering my bag, I make my way toward the bar. I'm in a martini kind of mood and have been for the last six weeks. I can't, for the life of me, continue my life as if those days at Christmas didn't happen. Winter got colder, more dismal, more miserable, more colorless when Lance left my apartment. I'm done denying that I didn't make the biggest mistake of my life letting him walk out of it, losing him a second time. If it was for the best, then I could let go, but I can't hold a candle of an excuse, save one.

It's not just dancing. It's *never* been just about dancing.

I ran away from the truth then, and I'm still running from it now, but it's caught up with me in the most painful and colossal way. There's no more denying it. Lance Prescott is the love of my life, and I didn't need him to remind me, I was all too aware, but now, now I've twisted our separation reasons into a distorted version of the truth. I lived it for two years—lying— lying to myself, lying to him.

Pulling up my phone, I scroll through his feed, searching for anything new. He'd obliterated his opponent in his last fight. Tony's been quiet with him on social, only showcasing a few of his workouts. I'm sure he's prepping for his premiere heavyweight fight taking place in only two weeks. A fight I would trade everything to see. A fight I deserve to attend. Search empty, I unwrap my scarf as the bartender approaches.

"What are you having?"

"Grey Goose martini, one olive."

"Sure."

I thumb my necklace, a new habit as I stare at my phone, willing it to come to life with a message, a single word, but I know it's a foolish hope.

I can't blame him. He thinks I've been too quick to dismiss a future for us, *again.* I sip my fresh martini dreading the showcase in the days ahead. Even dancing has lost some of its joy.

"Harper? Harper Elliot?"

I turn to see the man calling my name from the opposite side of the bar.

"Troy?"

"I thought that was you, hey there," he says, picking up his beer and heading my way. Troy was my first real college crush, one I kept from a distance until an insanely handsome cornerback came crashing in and stole every bit of his thunder. Our friendship formed when I was with Lance, and he'd revealed to me Troy was covering for us. I hadn't realized how vital said friendship would be until the day he saved me. But along with all things I left in Texas, our budding friendship was cut short when the truth came out, dividing me from my life there. Troy takes the stool next to me and leans in with a light hug in greeting.

"How are you?"

"Good," I say, nostalgic tears threatening. I haven't been

back to College Station since I left. Not even when my sister begged me when things got worse. But Troy's presence now reminds me of the ever-present sun I miss with his bleached hair and year-round tan. He represents home so well that I have to turn away from him briefly to gather myself.

"Harper, not to be an asshole, but you're on the verge of tears, and all I said was hello."

"It's nothing," I sniff, cursing my inability to get my emotions in check. "Just memories. You look good," I say, trying to change the subject. "I was so happy for you when you got drafted, and I wanted to reach out, but I didn't know if it would be weird."

He frowns. "Why would it be weird?"

"Because I'm your ex-roommate's ex-girlfriend."

"We were, *are* friends, hence why I'm sitting with you and not on the other side of the bar."

"You know what I mean."

He sips his beer. "Aren't you the girl who taught my son to dance?"

"Yes."

"And, were you or were you not, the girl that talked me into trying cannoli?"

"That was me."

"Yeah, well, thanks a lot. Does my ass look fat in these jeans?"

We share a laugh, and I'm thankful for his attempt to lighten my mood.

"So," I take a sip of my drink, "where are you off to?"

"On my way to Canada. I've got an endorsement deal."

"I'm on the same flight."

"No shit? Cool. We can sit together." Troy is an absolute God, even with my heart tied up in one man, I can't help but notice the chisel of his features, the light ocean in his eyes. He's both beauty and charisma through and through and the opposite of me in so many ways. It's what attracted me to him way back when I still had a heart to offer.

"Aren't you flying first class?"

"Nope. My wife is an asshole."

This makes me full-on belly laugh.

"And why is that?"

"She said for every kid I knock her up with, I owe her a million for her trouble and a million in savings. She's a cheap millionaire."

"How many are you up to?"

"She's a few months along with our fourth. I'm hoping for another boy."

"Damn, you wasted *no* time."

"Exactly. Needless to say, she's pissed."

"But, you're happy."

"Hell yeah. But going broke fast," he nods at the bartender for a fresh beer.

"Ah, you'll be playing for a long time." It's the truth. When the Giants picked him up, I still remember the scene I made in the bar in New York. Unlike Lance, Troy was a shoo-in during draft time. Despite their losing season, Troy never dropped the ball and carried it a record number of yards earning him enough points to set a Grand record for the whole of his career there. Those points weren't enough to get him a bowl game, but it was enough to get him an invitation to camp and eventually snatch a lucrative contract that had the whole of TGU alumni in hysterics. I'll never forget the feeling of pride I felt for him that day. Or the six martinis I had after picturing the devastation on his roommate's face, who suffered the opposite fate. With the Giants, Troy landed himself in the playoffs this year, only losing by one point to get to the championship. He's already a star in his second year and making waves.

"So, what are you doing in Canada?"

"Dancing. I'm with a show called *Retro*. It was a short run, but The New York Times did a piece on it, and they invited us to Calgary for an encore performance."

"That's awesome. Have you been to Texas lately?"

I shake my head. "Not in a couple of years, no."

"You should go. Nothing like a visit home to shake the dust off."

"Yeah, someday."

"The sooner, the *better*." He drags out the word until I'm facing him.

"Have you talked to him?"

"Yeah. Things are rough at home with his dad. If you want honesty, he's a fucking wreck. But it's fuel for a guy like him. He'll come out of it fighting."

"Are you going to see him in Vegas?"

"Yeah. I'll be ringside. You should join me."

"I wish I could."

"Where will you be?"

I shrug. "I don't know. I don't have any commitments past this show."

"I know someone who could use you." He winces. "That came out wrong."

"I could use him too," I say, taking a gulp of my martini as a tear escapes down my cheek.

"It's not my business." He sips his beer, picking up my napkin and dotting my face before I have a chance to wipe it away. "But you know what? I do want to know. It was so damned obvious you two were happy together."

"We were. So happy. Did he tell you he was here?"

"Yeah. That's why I brought him up; otherwise, I would give you the ex-respect."

I sip my martini and nod.

"We've been talking a lot lately." He chuckles. "He probably couldn't get in touch with Dave."

I smile, even with fresh tears burning in my eyes.

"I don't get it, Harper. I really don't. Though he's not much for words, I gathered you weren't interested in long term with him?"

"That's not true at all."

I just made him believe it because it was easier. Though none of it was easy, agony is a better word.

"So, are you going to tell me why?"

"I just have my reasons."

He reads my posture, and his back goes ramrod straight. Accusatory eyes roll over me. "No fucking way, Harper. You never told him?"

"No, I left, there wasn't any point."

"You promised me you would. You need to come clean."

"I can't. He's got enough on his plate now, and then, it was a hell of a lot worse. I just couldn't," I bat away a few tears, my defenses crumbling. I feel like an idiot sitting at a bar crying, but all the ache has made me useless, and the fear that I'm too late, that he really did close the door, is crippling. Troy looks around the bar as a muffled sob escapes me. He pulls me to him as I cry openly, unable to hold it in, cursing my emotions and their freaking impeccable timing. Troy holds me close, never wavering in the strength of it, his voice steady. I know then he's probably an outstanding husband and father.

"It's okay, Harper, I'm so sorry. I didn't mean to upset you."

"I'm s-s-so embarrassed." I look around to see the bartender's eyes dart away.

"Jesus, don't be."

I pull away sniffing as two more drinks are delivered.

"From a fan at that cocktail table."

Troy nods. "Thank him for us, but please do me a favor and grant us some privacy. Keep them at bay?"

The bartender glances at me, and I drop my gaze. "Sure, man."

"Thanks." Troy takes our drinks from the bar and gestures to a nearby booth for more privacy. Once seated, he turns to me.

"Why didn't you tell him?"

"It's humiliating for one."

"I get it, but he never suspected?"

"No, and I was thankful. With his temper. He would have lost it."

"Aside from that day, what else did they do?"

"What didn't they do? Notes on my car, in class, and then that day, that day you stepped in, that was the worst of it. I never really got a chance to thank you."

"Don't thank me, ever. I'm still disgusted."

"I j-just, c-can w-we stop t-talking about this?"

"Harper, it's clear this is eating you alive. You need to talk to someone."

"I'm sure you have better things to worry about."

"No, actually, I don't. I was there. And I saw how they hurt you. I'm still pissed we didn't report it."

"It was just better if I left." I stab at the loose olive with my cocktail straw.

"I get why you didn't tell him, then. But why does it stop you now?"

"Let's just change the subject, okay?"

"Harper—"

"Because I don't want to be the champ's ugly ass girlfriend. That's why!"

"What?" Troy pales, his eyes going wide.

"Jesus," I sputter out, "if we're going to discuss this, then let's be real for a second. I'm not pretty enough for him. That was the perception then, and it will be now. I don't know if I can handle a target on my back again."

"What the hell, Harper?"

"Come on, Troy. You're being kind. With his looks and talent, he *will* get big, he will. Except this time, the *media* will be involved because he will become a champion. Boohoo, right? At least I'll have Lance. But what do you think they're going to say about me? It'll be the same shit all over again. I thought I was strong enough then, but I wasn't. And that was just college. I cracked. I left him. I believed them. And some days I still do."

"Harper, you're not ugly. Damn, is that what you really think?"

"No. But I don't think I'm pretty enough for Lance, and I know how pathetic that sounds. I have a good body image, and I work with what God gave me but standing next to him…it changes everything. And it does. It did. No one gave a shit about me at that school until I started dating him. At the home game before the one you helped me, these girls were openly talking about me a row down, saying how ugly I was and wondering what in the hell he could see in me? My sister was sitting next to me, begging me not to believe them, sobbing. But do you know why she was crying? Because it's the truth. The truth is that as long as Lance is in the spotlight, I'll be the ugly girlfriend who doesn't deserve him."

"Harper, you can't believe that."

"No offense, but you've never had a bad face day in your life. Being with him will make me a target, and I don't know if I can handle it. Last time, they assaulted me, this time…I'm terrified to find out. So, when he asked me to commit to him, I hesitated. Fear won. That's the truth." I toss back my martini intent on numbing that realization off my tongue.

He shakes his head. "I don't think that way about you."

"You care about me, and anyone who does never really has the guts, nor the will to hurt me like that. But here's the thing. I don't need you to tell me I'm pretty. I'm fine with the way I look, it's everyone else who will have a problem with it. I need a solution."

"Harper, this is bullshit."

"Troy," I stay adamant. "If it wasn't true, it wouldn't be an issue."

"Harper, you know that man thinks you don't love him enough to be with him. To even try?"

"I know. I've never told anyone but my nana what happened. Not even my best friend. Because I swore, *I swore*, I wouldn't throw this pity party, but here I am, in full-blown PTSD two years later."

"It's because you're scared."

"Terrified. You can tell me it's all going to be all right, and you can pep talk me all you want, but the truth is you know just how shitty people can be. And by being with him, I'm inviting that into my life. There is no solution."

"Shit, I don't know what to say."

"Nothing to say. I'm so sorry you were coming to have a beer and relax, and I'm shitting all over your downtime."

"I don't give a damn about that."

"You're a good guy, Jenner."

"That's a rare compliment for me, thanks. But I'm not dropping it. Harper, you have to tell him."

"So, what…he can tell me I'm pretty? That's not a solution either, Troy."

"You can't let them win."

"I handled it for months before I cracked. But it was more than that. My dad was terrified. That's why he reacted so badly to the news. He got it all wrong, but I was bullied before in middle school, and that was a cakewalk compared to what they did to me. My dad was partially to blame. They didn't just come after me. They came after my sister on social media first and then continued to harass her after the fact. And when it all came to a head, I had an escape route, and I took it. To spare Lance, me, my parents…everyone. It was just easier for me to leave than to let it go any further, you know?"

"Yeah."

"I wanted to be here in New York, Troy. I did. It was an easy out, a way to follow my dream with one exception."

"Lance."

I nod. "See," I sniff, "problem is, I can't stop loving him."

"You aren't going to outgrow him, Harper."

"I'm realizing that."

"You have to tell him."

"He thinks I'm above what people think about me, and for so long, I was, but that scared the shit out of me."

"It scared me too, even now, I'm terrified for my children and the world they're growing up in."

"I don't blame you."

"Can I give you a little of my own truth?"

"Sure."

"None of us really are tough enough, no matter how resilient we think we are. Someone in the newsroom had it out for me the other day, called me a fucking monkey, and I almost cried."

I throw my head back and laugh.

He narrows his eyes. "You asshole."

"Sorry, but I needed that laugh."

I sip my martini and finally put a voice to the rest of my fears.

"Even if I decide to hell with it and step into the spotlight with him, this is Lance. He's not going to get it at first because the man truly loves me, loves this face, and everything attached. But when he realizes what's happening, he's going to want to fight and not just in the ring. Because they *will* come after me again and again for a face God gave me, and some *will* go far enough to say it in front of him. I don't want him to feel these things. I don't want him to be embarrassed." I'm sobbing again. "If I would have fallen for a nobody, it wouldn't matter. But people are so damn cruel. You know that."

He pulls me to him and holds me there as I shake with the fear of the last two years. It's exhausting, and all I want to do is let it go.

"I don't think I've ever in my life met a man who so clearly loves and respects a woman equally as much as he does you. He's worthy of you."

"God, don't I know."

"He doesn't."

"I know. I just…"

"I understand you completely. It's a horrible situation, I hate the scrutiny, myself. Not just about the way I play, but my wife, my family. It's no picnic, but we've learned to ignore it. It will be the same for you."

He pulls up his phone and begins tapping on it, which sends me on high alert.

"Troy, please don't tell him."

He eyes me as he continues with his phone. "I'm not going

to lie to him anymore, Harper. If you're not going to put him out of his misery, I will."

"I will, I just need to figure out how. I don't even know if he'll talk to me."

"I wasn't texting him anyway."

"So, who are you texting, then?"

He turns to me, holding his cell phone in plain view. I study it closely and crack up laughing. "Is that *you*?"

"Yes. Google Drive. My mom was kind enough to scan and organize the family photos and saved this gem."

"Okay, so you had *one* bad picture day."

"And this is seventh grade."

"Geesh. Is, oh hell, Troy, are those your teeth?"

"Yep. Single mom. She couldn't afford braces. I was stuck with those fucking teeth until my freshman year of high school."

"Yikes."

"So. I may know a thing or two about feeling ugly."

"Yeah, well, you got them fixed. I'm not about to Jennifer Grey myself and get a nose job. Screw all that. But I did consider it briefly."

"Then don't. He would hate it if you changed a single thing about your face. You know that. But all of us at one point of our lives are on an insecurity streak, and there's always going to be some asshole quick to point out your flaws, even with a back-handed compliment. Then there are the people who see nothing but how they feel about you." He glances at the photo and grins. "Mom loved this fugly-ass kid. When she sees this picture, she sees the son she loves. And you saw—"

"Your teeth," I admit, feeling guilty, "your flaws."

"We're all guilty, Harper. Most are programmed somehow to be assholes and notice the flaws first. Even a saint would gasp at these fucking teeth. You just have to ignore the assholes who speak up and say, 'What the fuck is wrong with that boy's teeth?'"

We both burst into laughter. He tips his beer and shakes his head. "See, we're laughing, but if that boy wasn't me?"

"I know."

"He never saw your flaws, Harper."

"I know. I screwed up so bad.

"No, see, I think you're brave."

"How? I let my insecurities get the best of me, and I ran away like a coward."

"Maybe you did, *then*, I think you're brave now because you know you're not going to Canada."

ROUND
3

forty-eight

LANCE

I TAKE A PUNCH, APPRECIATING THE BURN IN MY JAW WHILE trying to lighten up. Jab, jab, hook. Chris's head snaps back with each blow.

I let my frustration overpower me, and then I'm flying, my fists the propeller, my legs, the anchor.

"Watch it," Tony growls as I dig into my sparring partner, my hooks landing too heavy for a friendly bout.

"Easy, bro," Trevor chimes in from the side of the ring.

I'm too in the moment to ease up, ready to unleash.

Body, body, body, uppercut.

"Ease up," Tony barks.

I charge forward cornering Chris, before unleashing another combination.

"Done. Time," Tony calls. "Enough!"

I pull away, extending my arms out at Tony in frustration.

"Jesus, man." Chris spits out a mouthful of blood after pulling out his mouthguard. "What the fuck are you doing?"

I blow out a breath, trying to steady my pulse. I'm still in the mood to brawl and have no outlet.

"Get him out of there," Tony barks at Rip, one of my dad's longtime retired ranch hands who now works in my corner. "He's not fucking listening today."

"I'm all ears," I grunt, spitting out my mouthguard. "I need a *match*."

"You need to work on your fucking feet. I'm done today, and so are you. What the hell were you thinking laying into him like that?"

"I'm thinking you need to get me someone in here that can fucking handle it!"

Chris tosses me a look. "Offense taken, asshole. Tony, I'm out." Chris gathers his gear and stalks out of the barn as Tony turns back to me with accusing eyes.

"It's called sparring for a reason." He pulls himself up eye level with me on the side of the ring.

I tap my gloves together, still alternating on my feet. "He's a welterweight! Get me a match!"

Tony crosses his arms perched on the side of the ring. "You know anyone else willing to come out to this cow pasture specifically for you?"

"It's your job to figure that out!" I throw up my gloves.

"This is fucking ridiculous," Tony says, sizing me up. "A hard hit isn't all you need. You still need speed. You think you're outclassing that guy? You don't have shit on the guy you're about to try to pound into submission. They might not land as hard as you, but it won't matter if you can't match their speed. And they will hit hard and land more."

I shrug. "It's working so far."

"That's it," Tony spits. "Rip, glove me up."

"What?" I laugh, incredulous. "You aren't serious."

Rip hooks Tony up with some gloves as my little brother snickers on the side of the ring. "Now you've done it," Trevor laughs. "You're about to get your ass kicked by an old man."

"Forty-two isn't old, you little shit," Tony says to Trevor pointedly. "I'm just smart enough to know when to stop running my damned mouth, unlike you and your brother. There's a lot to be gained from humility."

Trevor, being Trevor, spouts off. "He's practically undefeated."

"Yeah, except he's not."

Chris's tires crunch in the distance before he tears out, and I know I fucked up. Chris was doing us a favor. An apology is in order, I'm just too pissed off to fess up. I hate myself, but I need to get this out. Fill this gaping hole somehow. Tony's not the only one who's disgusted. I came back from New York City with a bitterness I can't shake. I still can't bring myself to admit it was a mistake to go, but I hate the fact that I have this knowledge now. I wasn't good enough, and though my actions are proving it now, I'm getting better at blaming her.

Tony stands on the opposing side of the ring. "Two rounds, asshole. If you can land more than fifteen solid punches, I'll shut the hell up for the rest of today."

"Done," I say as Trevor snatches the mouthguard at my feet and hoses it off with my water bottle.

"Don't take it easy on me now," Tony scoffs with a sinister grin before putting in his mouthpiece. He looks over to Rip, "Your count."

"On it," Rip says, just as entertained as Trevor, who has sprouted up to a man's height in the last year. He's almost got me beat at only sixteen, still wet behind the ears, but cocky as ever.

I bounce on the floor of the ring, the ring Trevor, Tony, and I constructed in my father's tractor barn where I train daily. The barn still houses our farm equipment, but within the large space is now my own arena, which makes it far more convenient to train at the ranch.

"Hey, bro," I instruct Trevor, "do me a favor and make the speakers bleed." He nods, walking over to the workbench where the stereo sits. The speakers start thrumming as I put my mouthguard in and wink at Tony before giving him a 'come hither' with my glove.

forty-nine

HARPER

WHITE ZOMBIE BLARES FROM THE BARN ADJACENT TO THE house as I pull up in my rental car. In a mere few hundred steps, I'm going to commit to the man I love. Either that or beg forgiveness. I'm terrified. Plain and simple. Not about the commitment itself, but for what it means for the future. Doubt creeps in as I eye the barn.

What if I'm too late? What if he's already moved on, at least in the physical sense and is seeing someone else? If so, it would be my fault, and I'm just going to have to deal with it. My hesitation might have cost me more than I can handle this round. Panicked, I leave my suitcase in the car and shut the door to the rental peering at the ranch house. It's still as spacious as I remember, heavy wood and stone, smoke pluming from the chimney. It's cozy, a picture-perfect home nestled amongst acres and acres of pasture. I shiver, the mid-February chill seeping through my hoodie.

One step in front of the other, Harper.

I can't swing if I have nothing to swing for.

I can't go through losing him again, that much I know. These last six weeks have been utter hell on earth. What we have, I won't ever be able to replace with anyone else in this lifetime or any other. He's worth it. And this time I'll have to fight for him, to be with him, longer and harder than I ever have. But first, I need to step in the ring, and of all the steps I've taken in my life, this is the hardest.

One breath, one step at a time.

Years ago, I swore no man would ever take precedence over my dancing career. This step makes me a liar.

But I'm no longer just a dancer in love with a football player.

I'm a woman in love with a man I can't and refuse to live without.

Everything has changed. I've spent the last two years dancing, I can spend the next few months of my life securing my place with Lance. Committing.

It's the phantom itch in the back of my skull that keeps me standing in the middle of his yard.

"Happy, you little bitch?"

Lance is fearless. Though not outspoken, he takes every task on in his life without reservation, regardless of how he feels. I can't let this fear win if I want to be the one to venture through life with him.

Searching for courage, I recall the surprising wisdom of René's words as I took the drive down from the airport. I finally told him the details of what happened back at Grand, and he was angrier than he'd ever been with me. After a thorough bitching out, he cried, and then helped me construct a game plan.

"We all need an end game, Mami. No one want to be alone forever."

"You want to get married?"

"Of course. Someday. Everyone needs a partner to finish this life with. When I get old and grey, I want the right person with me. The one who knows I'm too short to get the cup from the cabinet and gets it for me without me asking. Things like that. Someone who looks out for you without you being aware. You might be a dancer now, but the shelf life is short. You won't die one. You need someone who makes it sting less when dancing is over, makes you smile, makes things easier, inspires you."

"Lance is that for me. He's everything for me."

"The difference between me and you is that my end game has no face yet. Maybe it's Ricky, maybes not, but yours does."

"I love him. I want this. I don't want to be without him anymore. I can't."

"Then you show him the truth. Show him he is now a part of your dream. If he don't want to see it, you come home."

I run my finger between my braids, along the back of my head just as the front door opens, and Jeannie appears. "Harper? Baby, it is you!" She shuts the front door and wraps her sweater around her to ward off the chill. "Honey, it's freezing out here. What are you doing standing in the yard?"

"Jeannie, hi, I, uh, well," I fumble for words as she walks down the few steps toward me.

"Get over here, girl, let me take a look at you." She pulls me into her arms and hugs me tightly. I hug her right back. Her embrace is warm, comforting.

"How've you been?" She pulls back to study me.

"I've been good. Really good. How about you?"

"Holding up well. And you look beautiful."

"Thank you. So do you."

She glances toward the barn. "Nervous, huh?"

"Yes," I swallow.

Her son has her hair color, her nose, and lips. She's beautiful and wise. It's scary just how easily she reads me. "It's pretty terrifying deciding on someone, isn't it?"

If she only knew, but I don't explain my fears because I'm in the midst of facing them, so I just nod.

She pulls me to her side as she walks toward the barn.

"He's been waiting on you for some time." I hear the

warning in her voice, along with the plea not to torture her son unnecessarily. She eyes me cautiously as I take a step in the ring. "I'm not here to hurt him."

"I thought as much. Are you staying?"

"If he'll have me."

She lifts a brow. "Not going to lie, he came home a lot harder to get along with."

Guilt mars me, and she shakes her head. "You're here now, that's all that matters. I'm just about to start supper. Why don't you go say hi?"

"Okay." I swallow again, hesitation clear in my posture.

"I knew it the first time I saw him look at you. It doesn't solve everything, but it helps. Go on, go get him, baby." Jeannie heads toward the house and glances back at me with a comforting smile. "I'm so glad you're here."

"Me too."

"Give him hell," she says just before she closes the door.

Shaking all fear away, I take a deep breath. It's time to fight, for me, for him, for us, for what we both want.

Mind made up, I make my way toward the barn, guard down, and gloves up.

fifty

LANCE

"**S**HIT, TWELVE. YOU'VE ONLY LANDED TWELVE," TREVOR snaps off at the mouth just as Tony lands a right that has me dizzy. I see the pleasure in his eyes when he stuns me. Pissed, I come at him with a right hook that jars him.

"Now it's a fight," he mumbles around his mouthpiece, his eyes alight with satisfaction. Channeling the beast, I swing again, and he dodges it far too easily.

"Sixteen landed, thirty seconds left," Rip shouts from my corner.

Pissed, I do my best to corner Tony and run a combo on him just before time is called.

"Holy shit, you just got schooled," Trevor says with awe in his voice.

Tony pulls off his gloves and glares at me. "If you think I'm happy about this, think again. Your speed is shit. You've regressed."

I spit out my guard. "I don't give a shit what you're happy about."

Tony shakes his head. "You need to get right, kid. Head and heart. You need to shake it off and concentrate."

"And what is it you think I'm doing?"

"Brawling, not boxing. It's a sport, not a street fight. Lately, you've forgotten your form, and now you're just bloodthirsty."

"You know what, man," I shake my head my temper flaring, "you think—"

"I'll take a crack at him. *One* glove."

The sound of her voice has me reeling where I stand. I turn to see Harper at the foot of the ring in an oversized Giants hoodie and matching beanie. She looks beautiful and completely foreign standing here in my space. With as many times as I pictured her there, it does no justice to the real thing, which only angers me.

I stare down at her, incredulous as to how she got so close without me noticing her. All eyes on her, she stands with clear confrontation on her features, her hands on her hips. "Since when are you such an egomaniac that you get in your own way?"

Trying to mask the kick to my heart, I give her a listless stare. "What the hell do you know about it?"

"I know what I just witnessed, *isn't* you."

"That right?" I walk over to the side of the ring, crossing my gloves on the rope as I peer down at her. "Sweetheart, you haven't been around for two years, and what's it been now, six weeks? So again, what in the hell do *you* know?"

"I know enough." She's acting full-on pissed with no right to be. At the moment, I just want to pull her to me and smash the smartass off her lips before savoring it off her tongue. She's a much-needed fresh breath of air for my collapsed lungs, but I refuse to inhale because I know the cost.

I'm a man standing in the wake of lost love, bitterness in my heart, and singed beyond anything I can control. I was supposed to have left her there, in that apartment, in that city, but she's been with me the whole time, and her sudden appearance is only worsening the fact—I can't get over this damned woman.

But I'm determined to. And I refuse to let her fuck with what's left in my chest.

"Harper, what are you doing here?"

"I was invited by someone, right now, I don't think you would recognize him."

"Consider yourself un-invited. Surprised you found your way here. When you leave, go back the same way you came."

"Shut up, asshole," Trevor spouts before making his way to Harper. "Hey, you. Good to see you."

She gives him a grin with his greeting of "Hey, you," and he pulls her into a hug, lifting her off her feet. This lights me up as I feed on the animosity in the barn and the irritation at her sudden appearance. He doesn't know her. Not like I do. He's only met her once. But she's done nothing but wreak havoc on my life since the minute I fell for her. She can't be here, invading my space, burning more of herself into my memory. She has no right to weasel her way in with any sort of opinion or air of authority. I can feel my pulse thundering at my neck as Trevor hugs her a lot longer than appropriate. "Looking good, girl."

"Thanks. And look at you, all grown up."

"Yeah?" His grin is full of pride. "You'd be surprised how much I've gro—"

"Happy for the both of you," I snap, "and your reunion and all, but we're in the middle of something here."

Tony chooses that moment to make me hate him. "Actually, she's just in time. I'm done embarrassing your sorry ass today. Might as well let her take a crack at you."

She looks past my brother's shoulder, lifting her brown eyes to mine in challenge. "What can it hurt?"

"This is ridiculous." I hold out my gloves. "Rip, take these off. Harper, thanks for stopping by."

"I'm staying for dinner, your mother invited me," she taunts.

"There's a McDonald's thirty minutes down the highway."

"What the hell, Lance?" Trevor says, glowering at me.

"I'm not fighting her," I'm unable to keep the bitter edge

from my voice. "And she's got a *real* problem with making decisions. Not sure Mom's pot roast is enough. She might need variety."

Harper holds out her fist. "Just one glove, please, Trevor."

"Coming right up, my lady."

"You aren't serious," I scoff. "What the fuck are you going to do with that? It will feel like a mosquito bite."

"I've got speed," she says, winking at Tony. "Which is what you're lacking, right? What are you afraid of?"

That if I look at her any longer, my heart will stop beating and fall out of my chest. "You can't just come here—"

"Oh, *I can't*, huh? But you did," she says, entering the ring with her one glove, the scent of her invading my nostrils. Rip chuckles, eyeing Harper, fully amused. He likes her, I can tell. Tony pulls her in for a hug, and they exchange whispers before she smiles and turns to me. "But *you* can come to New York, right? You can just barge into *my* life," she says, jumping back and forth on her Nikes in an impressive show before ripping off her sweatshirt.

Catcalls come from all sides as she dances around me in nothing but leggings and a sports bra, her perfect tits pressed together in a way I refuse to indulge in.

"Saw Troy at LaGuardia," she gestures towards her discarded hoodie, "the shirt's for you. He said you need to worship more than the Cow*girls*."

"Hey, hey," Trevor said. "Them's fighting words in this house."

"Yeah?" Harper says with a smile before looking over to me. "Looks like I'm in the right place."

"Wrong, thanks for bringing it by, but there was no need to hand-deliver it. Mail would have done just fine. And don't you have somewhere you need to be?"

"Gloves up, asshat, I'm not fighting one of your cows."

"I'm not throwing a punch at a woman. You're being ridiculous."

"I love her," I hear Trevor say to Tony.

I do too. And at this point, I'm close to hating her because of the way she keeps making me fall for her, every single time I lay eyes on her before she rips my soul away from me. Tony grins over at him with just as much a fucked-up reply. "I'm getting hard just watching this."

"I can fucking hear you both." They both grin and shrug as Harper steps up to me in the center of the ring.

"Come on, champ, dukes up."

"You can pack it up, Harper. I'm done fighting with you."

"Punk," she says, stepping forward and landing a jab on my chin. I roll my eyes.

"This isn't cute," I growl.

"I agree. Your behavior right now is deplorable. Not to mention what you did back in New York."

"What *I* did?"

"You come to New York after two—" she lands another blow and another, and I don't flinch. It's like being hit with a pillow, "—years and expect me to just jump into your arms like a willing pound puppy."

Gloves down, I stand there taking her in, her solid body toned to perfection, her skin porcelain, twin braids hanging loosely from her beanie, dancing over her shoulders with her movement. All I want is to grab her and fuck her up, with my lips, my tongue, my cock, the way she's fucking with me. I'm in the mood to punish her, and it's apparent she feels the same.

She lands a solid right to the mouth, and the force of it without my guard takes me by surprise. Copper melts on my tongue as she attempts to unleash my beast. She's happily playing with fire, like I'm a joke, like we're a joke.

"Ahhhh," she says, crossing her gloves like she's in a karate fight. This time my lips turn up briefly as the guys chuckle in the corner. My smile only angers me further.

"You underestimate me," she says, landing another to my chest and stomach. I stand there completely limp as she dances around me, taking potshots.

"As I was saying, you come to New York after two years, ask me to spend Christmas with you, start a fight in a department store that turns into a street brawl, make these grand declarations and tell me you want me to just drop everything and come," jab, jab, jab, "back here, for what was it?"

"Harper, this is personal," I grunt, taking another right to the temple.

"Oh, well, you went BIG in New York," she turns back and winks at the guys, "quite often." She lifts a glove mimicking a puppet, "Commit to me now. I know I haven't seen you in over seven hundred days, but if you don't say exactly the right thing in my time frame, I'm leaving, and I'm taking my big dick with me."

She winces, tossing a look over her shoulder, "Sorry, Trevor."

"Don't be," he quips, "just so you know, that runs in the family."

"What the hell?" I protest as my entire corner snickers. "That's so not how it went down."

"Sorry," Harper pipes, "foggy memory. It must still be a blur because of how fast you came and went."

I step into her next jab. "You should talk."

"I deserved that, two years ago, when it was relevant to our relationship, now I'm just pissed." Another punch, this one lands squarely, and I have to give her a little credit, it had some pressure behind it.

"You're delusional."

"And you're still a caveman. You might as well have thrown me over your shoulder and slapped me on the ass," jab, jab, "oh wait, you did do that the *first time* we got together."

"Is this some fucking joke to you?"

"Should it be?" She asks, lifting a brow. "You come to my city, turn my life upside down, demand once again that I commit without once letting me catch my breath."

"That's not how it—"

She lands another right on my lips, and it stings.

"You deserved that."

Eyes blazing, I feel my anger brimming again. "You made your point yet?"

"Nope, gloves up, champ. You said you can't fight without something to swing for, well, here I am."

"Well, your time is up," I say, throwing my own invisible punch, I see it land, but instead of giving in to her quivering lips, her eyes light fire.

"Wow, that was fast. And you expect me to believe a word you say?" she throws a right, and I lift my glove to avoid another blow to the face.

"Ah, there you are," she says, too pleased with herself.

"You've got a lot of nerve."

"Touché, Lance. Get your freaking gloves up."

"I'm not fighting you."

"You love fighting me."

"I did."

"You do."

"Dancing, that's where you need to be. Not here."

"I am dancing," she says, doing a perfect impression of a boxer's footing around the ring.

"And she's better than you," Tony laughs.

This time I bite. "Why don't you guys fuck off and give us some privacy?"

They all reply in unison.

"No fucking way."

"I'm not missing this."

"Sorry, man, no can do."

"Dinner!" Mom calls from the house.

"Oh, good, I'm hungry," Harper chimes in, throwing another jab.

"You can sit next to me," Trevor spouts.

I'm too pissed at everyone in my life at the moment to see anything but red. "You sure you're staying? I mean, I wouldn't want to blink while we're saying grace and miss seeing that beautiful ass of yours walking out the door."

"Lance," Trevor protests as Harper holds up a glove tossing a look over her shoulder.

"I've got this, little brother." She turns to me. "And just how long do you plan on punishing me for *that*?"

"Not long after you see yourself out."

"Well, good thing we all agree, don't we, boys, that your grudges are getting old?"

All three of them speak up.

"This isn't fucking funny," I grit out.

"You've got issues." She taps me again with her glove.

"*I've* got issues?" I press a glove to my chest. "You're the *coward*. Sure you aren't going to tuck your tail between your legs again? I think we both know I'm the fighter here."

She shrugs. "Not much of one at the moment."

"You're making a fool of yourself," I seethe with venom. "You need to go back from which you came and forget about this place, me. You're out of your depth and league, sweetheart."

She stops her movement as Trevor curses in disgust. "Fucking asshole."

Harper walks up to me, tilting her head up, her eyes earnest, all amusement gone. "Maybe I am, then again, I know just how to handle you, Lance Prescott. Don't forget that."

"Think so, huh?"

"I know so."

In a blink, my trunks and underwear are at my ankles. Bare-assed and cock dangling, I stare down at her, mouth parted, as the guys howl with laughter. But she's not laughing, not at all. She's pissed.

"You want a worthy opponent, Prescott, you've fucking got one! See you at dinner, asshole. And you can watch my beautiful ass walk out of the barn all you want, but I'll be the one saying grace tonight."

And with that, she stomps out of the barn.

Buck ass naked, aside from my trainers and the trunks around my ankles, I watch helplessly as the guys follow her out.

"If you don't marry her," Trevor calls back over his shoulder, "I sure as shit will."

HARPER

DINNER ISN'T GOING MUCH BETTER THAN COCKTAIL HOUR. Lance sits at his father's side at the head of the table. Next to him, Jack shakes uncontrollably, fixating on his forkful of roast to get enough of it in his mouth. It's the most uncomfortable silence I've ever endured, even with Jeannie chatting me up. After a few painful attempts, Jack leaps from his seat.

"Excuse me."

"Sit down, Jack," Jeannie orders softly. "I'm willing to bet Harper would very much like to spend time with you."

"I'm, I'm m-making her uncomfortable."

"Not at all," I say.

Jack eyes me through the violent jerk of his head. "Since when did…you become a bullshitter?"

"I'm sorry if I'm making *you* uncomfortable. I'm fine, I swear." I prepared myself for this by watching a couple of hours of clinical videos as I waited for my flight here. Though no matter how hard I prepped, a part of me dies inside with every tremor that costs him an ounce of pride. He was frail when I met him, but now he's sickly-looking, pale and appears older. The more distinguished version of him is mirrored in his son, who sits brooding at the table and hardly spares me a glance. I'm fighting every emotion imaginable. The hurt from his response to me being here, the hardest to battle. I didn't expect open arms, but I didn't expect a hostile reception either. It's at the table where I realize the truth of what's going on.

Troy told me things were hard at home, and I knew as much with Lance's refusal to talk about it in New York, but I wasn't really hearing it. And the only thing I've really heard in the last six weeks is the irregular sound of my heart.

But I'm beginning to realize my reception wasn't entirely about us.

Lance wasn't lashing out at me as much as he is the life he's been living. His bitterness doesn't just stem from the hurt I caused, it's his situation. And instead of coming in with understanding, what did I do? I humiliated him. All I want to do is run. Grab my bag and walk out the door so I don't have to face the tragedy of this family, but I don't, and I won't because the man I love can't.

And with his playing indifferent, I can feel him slipping away with every second that ticks by. It becomes painfully clear to me that in order to prove I'm ready to commit, I need to do the one thing I've failed to do with Lance when things got hard—stay.

Jack slowly takes his seat, as Trevor turns to me with sympathetic conversation. "So, how's the dancing going?"

"G-good. The show I was in did great. We got asked to perform in Calgary."

"Really. How did that go?"

I dump more green beans on my full plate. "I don't know. They should be on right about now. I'll have to call and ask them."

I can feel Lance's eyes shift to me the minute the words pass my lips.

"You missed it to come here?" Trevor asks before glancing at Lance and then back to me.

I nod at my plate, too afraid to meet the grey eyes that haunt my every waking minute.

"It was no big sacrifice," I say. "But I saw pictures of the venue, and it looked amazing."

"Who danced for you?" Jeannie asks.

"No one, they just cut my number."

The loud clank of a fork sounds to my right before Jack explodes out of his seat. Jeannie immediately stands and looks at me. "This is not your fault." She follows him out of the dining room. "Jack," she whispers, "she's fine."

"She doesn't need to see. It upsets her," is all I hear before a bedroom door slams.

"I'm sorry," I say to everyone at the table. "I didn't mean to upset him."

Trevor chimes in. "No, I'm sorry. My brother's an asshole, and Dad's just having a day. It's okay, I promise."

I nod, tears threatening.

"Are you just going to sit there?" Tony says to Lance, though I don't look up, I can feel his gaze still on me. Forcing myself to take a bite, I look up to meet the livid eyes of my ex-boyfriend. He's so damned beautiful, dressed in nothing but black sweats and a hoodie, his eyes blazing, and jaw set in a hard line.

"Dance first. You promised me. We agreed."

I swallow. "No, you decided for me," I say, popping some of my dinner roll into my mouth, "like every other boneheaded man, you think you know what's best for me. Besides, it was a bonus show. It doesn't count."

"You shouldn't be here."

"That's not what you asked of me."

"I told you I was done asking."

I sip my water. "Maybe I have my own questions this round."

"I'm not doing this." He moves to stand, and Trevor shocks us both, his voice acidic as he scolds his older brother.

"You can't help him. You can't fight this, Lance. It's a horrible disease, but don't take it out on her, on any of us. You're fucking up, bro, and you won't stop it even when we're telling you how you're doing it. Do yourself a favor and take a breath."

"Do yourself a favor and save yours," Lance retorts dryly before stalking out of the dining room and slamming the back door.

Despite my need to go to him, I finish my dinner. Tony eats two plates while making conversation until Trevor excuses himself, his posture deflated.

"They grew up too early," Tony says, wiping his mouth when Trevor is out of earshot. He's an attractive guy, older. I've been fond of him since I recruited him for Lance years ago. He's an ex-athlete with heart and a good sense of family. It's how I knew he would be the perfect fit for Lance.

Tony throws his napkin on his plate and sighs. "I know what they feel right now. I went through similar shit."

I swallow. "Should I be here?"

"Do you want to be here?"

"More than anything."

"Then you should be here."

"Jack's gotten so much worse."

"Actually, he's been holding steady for a few months. Problem is they couldn't afford his medicine this month. It's eight hundred dollars with private insurance. That's a majority of what this is about."

I nod. I figured that was the case.

"I love him. But I don't know what to do."

"He knows it. But if you're itching for resolution, it's not going to come easy."

"I know."

"Just be there for him. This breakdown of his has been a long time coming."

"I can't believe it's gotten this bad."

"It's been hard, Harper."

I turn to Tony. "Why do you stay?"

"Because they took me in. My own family has never been so kind. And because I believe in Lance. I know what he's capable of. I'm just not sure he knows it anymore."

"He was a completely different man in New York."

"He was on a hope kick. Sometimes when that's stripped away, you hit bottom hardest."

I bat my tears away.

"Don't blame yourself. This is his life, and he has to work his way through it. You can't fix this."

"Okay."

"I'm glad you're here. This will be good for him."

"Thanks." I stand to go in search of Lance and double back to where he sits. "Tony, can you do me a favor?"

He looks up to me, puzzled. "Sure."

I find Lance in the back of the barn working on the tractor. Approaching him cautiously, I set down a glass of tea next to where he's dismantling a blade.

"Thought you could use something to drink."

"Thanks."

"I'm sorry." He glances up at me from his workstation, his jeans, and Grand T-shirt covered in grease spots. "About taking your pants down."

He grins, surprising me. "Nothing they haven't seen before."

"Still, I came in guns blazing. I should have texted you, but you would have told me not to come."

He sighs. "You're right, I would have."

"Lance, I'm sorry I didn't say anything in New York. My hesitation had nothing to do with the way I feel about you."

"Harper, I hear you. Okay. I hear you. But it changes nothing."

"But it does. I want to give you what you want." I shake my head, knowing I screwed up with the way I just worded it.

He tosses his wrench down, and it clanks loudly in the box. "What I want?"

"That came out wrong. What we both want. Lance, you're the only relationship I've ever been in. I'm not always going to do or say the right thing."

He sighs. "We ended it twice. It's not going to work between us, Harper."

"You asked me to come. I want to be here."

"I also begged you to give me any sign we might work out, and you kept that mouth of yours shut. But seeing you, being with you, it was… Those were the best two days I've had in years. But I'm in deep shit, Harper. And you aren't the answer, no matter how much I want you to be. My fists are my way out. And you're right, I had no business going to New York and disrupting your life like that. Make no mistake, I loved every minute I spent with you. But you aren't the answer. You're not. And I won't ask you to be. Your career is back there. There's no one to dance for here, but me. It's wrong, even I can see it. I won't ask you to sacrifice your first love for your second."

Tears gather in my eyes. "Are you sure?"

"I have to be, for my sanity alone."

"Is it that hard to love me?"

"I can't keep you."

Fighting the sting in my chest, I search for some common ground. "Let's table us for now. Let me be your friend."

"I've got enough of those."

"Don't shut me out. You're in a bad place, Lance, it happens. Let me be here for you, for your family. I can handle it."

"Think you can, huh?"

"I can handle anything for you, with you."

He sighs, wiping his hands on a towel before pressing his fists against his workbench. "I told you I was done. Why aren't you getting that?"

"You don't mean it, you can't, and I'm not leaving until you figure that out."

"Suit yourself. The guest bedroom is down the hall from mine. Night."

"Lance—"

"I've got shit to do." He splays his hands in front of him, and I nod, defeated. I've had enough rounds for one day.

"Okay."

Eyes watering, I make my way out of the barn into the cold and realize the temperature here is a hell of a lot more frigid than it was in New York.

Maybe it's too late.

fifty-two

HARPER

A LOUD SCREECH COMES FROM MY BEDROOM WINDOW, JARRING me from a dead sleep. I fall from the bed onto the freezing hardwood floor.

"Jesus Christ!"

I pat down my body to make sure I'm not bleeding or broken as deep chuckles come from the other side of the window. I open it to see Lance holding a rooster, laughing hysterically along with Trevor. I open the window letting in the freezing air, ready to pummel them both.

"You assholes!"

Lance's laughter dies in his throat as Trevor's eyes bulge. In the next second, the rooster is set free, and Lance is covering Trevor's eyes with his hands.

"Harper," Lance barks, "your titty popped out."

Trevor fights Lance's hold as I look down and see one of my boobs came free from my sports bra during my fall.

"I could use a morning feeding," Trevor laughs hysterically, pulling desperately at his brother's hands as I adjust myself.

"Get your chores done and get to school."

"Talk about backfire," Trevor says when Lance lets him go. He grins at me with his brother's breathtaking smile, and it tugs on my heart. "Morning, my lady."

I roll my eyes, unable to help my grin. "Morning, handsome."

"Sorry about that," he offers, stepping up to the window and nodding toward Lance, "wasn't my idea."

I glare at the man standing next to him in a grey, long john shirt and black marshmallow vest. A beanie covers his thick dark hair enhancing the chiseled, strong lines of his jaw. "I'm sure it wasn't."

"So," Trevor says, looking between us, "see you after a while?"

"I'll be here," I say defiantly, meeting the eyes of my ex. His nostrils flare, and he shakes his head.

"Wouldn't count on it, brother."

"Oh, I'll be here," I assure Trevor.

"Damn, I don't want to leave," Trevor says, grinning between us before biting his lip. "Maybe later tonight, you can tuck me in and tell me a bedtime sto—"

"Chores, school," Lance barks out, pushing him out of view.

"Fine, man, I'm going, Jesus."

Trevor takes off, and Lance and I stand there awkwardly on opposite sides of the window. It's barely daybreak and I'm not sure I've witnessed a sunrise in years.

"Thanks for that, friend. A cup of coffee would have been far nicer."

"Sorry, couldn't resist." His grin is devilish and infuriating. He's declared himself on the wrong side of the welcoming committee.

"So, what's on the agenda for today?"

He shrugs. "No idea. You don't work here."

"Do now. I'll be out in twenty to help."

He shakes his head as if I'm being ridiculous.

"I'm here to help, Lance."

"No one's asking for it."

He's determined to push me away. I'm not having it. This

little saga of ours has lasted long enough. I forgot how much strength I take from him. How being on the opposite of both his resistance and affection empowers me. And whether he wants to admit it or not, the draw is still there.

I can do this. I'm not giving up, not at all.

Game on, *Lover*.

Seeing the coast is clear behind him, I pull off my sports bra and stand there half naked as his eyes roam appreciatively down my body. I turn, glancing over my shoulder, lip caught in my teeth as I slowly peel off my sleep leggings to give him a clear view of my naked ass. Lance stands on the other side of the window, a storm brewing in his eyes as I turn, giving him a full-frontal view. I drop my grin just before I abruptly drop the shades, shutting him out.

A barely audible growl escapes him, but I hear it and feel the zing in my chest while prancing through the bedroom, wearing only a smile.

This round is mine.

"Morning," Jack greets me from where he sits at the table.

"Morning, Jack."

"You got a minute?"

"Of course," I say, taking the seat at the table next to him.

"I'm sorry for my outburst last night. It was a bad day. I'm hard to get along with lately." He looks toward Jeannie, who sets a cup of coffee in front of me along with an antique-looking sugar and cream set. "Thank you."

"Morning, sweetheart. I think what he's trying to say is—"

"I can speak for myself," he says to his wife.

"Sorry, baby," she says, a glimmer of hurt in her eyes before it disappears.

"Come here," he says to her, and she looks over at him, confused.

"Just a second," he tells me, jerking in his seat. "Come here, Jeannie." He holds out a shaky hand, and she takes it. He pulls her to him, and I can hear his whisper. "I love you."

The sentiment seems to take her by surprise. "I know you do."

"I'm sorry."

"Jack—"

He nudges her. "Tell me you forgive me."

"Nothing to forgive."

He hugs her tight to him, and she pulls away with tears shimmering in her eyes. "So sentimental this morning. I'll get your breakfast." I see then that Lance is Jack's apple. And Jack's just as much of a gentle soul with the same hair-trigger temper.

"I haven't been myself in quite some time. My boys are suffering, and they don't deserve it."

"No one is suffering," Jeannie chimes in, cracking an egg on the side of a cast-iron pan.

"Enough, baby. Let me talk to Harper."

"Fine."

Jack turns to me. "I know what you did."

"I'm sorry. I just can't watch you suffer."

"We can't accept it."

"It's only for a couple of months until Lance pays me back."

"We don't do well accepting charity around here."

"I'm aware. But it's a loan. I swear. Once he gets paid for his first fight, he's going to reimburse me."

"This is a deal you made with Lance?"

Jack weighs my expression as I do my best to keep a straight face.

"It's a deal we made a long time ago."

"You're bullshitting, Harper, but I appreciate it. You should know we've endured a lot out here over the years. This is just a hard time."

"I admire you for it. Both of you. It's amazing what you've built. I'm sorry for overstepping. But please take it." I don't look away because something tells me he would appreciate it more if I confronted his condition the way he's been forced to.

"All right. Thank you. It'll be nice not to be a human blender for a while."

Jeannie laughs as Jack chucks my chin with shaky fingers, another Lance trait I adore. "It's all right to smile, it was a joke."

Jeannie winks at me as she sets our plates down. "I hope you like rib-sticking food, that's all we serve around here."

"I'm a fan of it, thank you," I say, feeling relieved. "But please don't feel like you have to cook for me."

"Happy to, darlin'."

"You are welcome here," Jack adds, "no matter what my boy says. He's going through something right now, hard to get through."

"I know. Thank you, sir."

"Jack," he says, picking up a piece of bacon.

"Thank you, Jack."

After breakfast, I make the trek out to where Lance is on his tractor. He's rolling out hay on the frozen ground for the cattle. I flag him down to join him, and he ignores me, driving past as I fume, freezing where I stand.

"If you want to help him, grab a rake and spread it out some," Jeannie calls to me from the side of the fence where she scatters corn around for the chickens.

"Thanks." I make my way toward the barn and come back armed. I spend the better part of an hour thinning out the hay as Lance expertly lays it out in a trek for the herd. The sprawling estate looks gorgeous in the early morning light, the frost hitting the trees. When Lance is done, he hops off the tractor and stands next to it, watching me for a few seconds before walking toward the barn.

fifty-three

LANCE

"A NOTHER ONE," TONY BARKS AS I FLIP THE TRACTOR TIRE over. Four days. She's been here for four days, and from what I can tell, has no plans of going anywhere. She's done the one thing I swore I wouldn't let her do, weaseled her way into my world, and into my family's heart. Trevor is head over heels, at her beck and call, while my mother fawns over her nightly at the table, and Dad remains stoic, painting the best picture he can of his health. It's all for show, as far as I'm concerned. Everyone seemed to have remembered their manners the day after she arrived here, but as soon as she leaves, she'll take the light she brought with her. I'm refusing her help at every turn. Only looking at her when she addresses me in polite conversation. She's letting me do my thing, showing up to every workout without fail as silent support while biting her tongue. I know her tactics. She thinks I'll come around and eventually we'll work it out.

She's wrong.

I have a life-changing fight a little over a week away, and I need to win, regardless of the payday. I have a family to support. I'm not a fly by the seat of my pants kind of guy. Every move I make matters. New York was my first whim in years. Despite her attempt at showing my reflection in a statue, it was no big epiphany. I'm very much aware of the weight on my shoulders, and I'm doing everything in my power to keep my head up, to keep that weight from crushing me.

I'm done pretending sticking a bow on it will pretty up this life of mine. I need to think about my future in the realistic sense. And so, she can stay as long as she wants, but it won't change the facts.

I have to admit, it's been nice to have the help, to be able to concentrate more on my training than the daily duties at the ranch. But I know what's coming, and I dread the fact that I'll have to turn her down. Where she's concerned, I'm resigned. Love solves nothing. It's just another catalyst for shit that can go south. I need to protect us both from more heartache, especially since she's too blind to see it. I've been chewing on the truth since I left New York, and since she arrived here, I just can't bring myself to swallow the fact that when she drives away from this ranch, it will be the last time I ever see her. With her talent, her future is unlimited.

"Good," Tony says as I get the tire over again. "Get in a few more, and I'll see you ringside in about thirty."

I nod just as Harper walks up, in jeans and a hoodie, perching herself on the fence.

"Hey, guys, how's it going today?"

Tony smiles at her. "Hey, going good. I'm going to head in. See you ringside in thirty?"

"Wouldn't miss it."

Lifting the tire, I push it over effortlessly, my irritation at her arrival, giving me a burst of energy.

"I was hoping we could talk sometime today."

"Busy at the moment," I say, lifting the monster tire in an attempt to tip it.

Commotion stirs up behind her, and she glances back at the herd.

"Why are they locked up today?"

"We've got a few heifers in heat."

"Ah," she says, turning back to me and lifting a brow. "Bow chica wow wow."

I shake my head, fighting my grin. "Harper, I'm busy."

"I can see that, but last time I checked, you didn't need to have your arms to waggle your tongue."

"What?" I challenge, turning the tire over again.

"I just wanted to see if maybe you would take me out of here. You know, go somewhere. Get dinner or a beer."

"Bored already?"

"No," she says adamantly. "Not at all. I'm still sore from yesterday."

She's been doing more than her fair share, and guilt riddles me that I let her.

"You don't have to help."

"Well, I consider it paying for room and board."

I put my gloved hands on my hips. "And just how long do you plan on staying?"

"Until you can look me in the eye and mean what you say."

Grunting, I lift the tire. "Don't you have an apartment to pay for?"

"Don't worry your head about me. I'm just fine, right where I am."

Right at that moment, one of our herd decides to taste her cheek, and she jumps off the fence, screaming bloody murder. "Jesus, buy a girl dinner first, bleh," she says as I wipe my hand down my jaw, trying to hide my laugh. She glares at the cow and shoos her away, resuming her seat on the wood post, swinging her mile-long legs.

"Come on, Lance. One beer? It will do you good to get out, have a little fun."

"I don't need to have fun. I need to concentrate, and you're fucking that part up nicely."

"I'm just trying to help."

"You know how to help," I snap. "You just can't believe it's the truth."

"Leaving you again is not an option for me, sorry. Name something else."

Commotion erupts behind her, and I freeze in awareness.

"Harper, get down." I'm halfway to her when I see the bull stiffen and rear back.

"No! I'm not going anywhere, you ass! I know it's going—"

"Harper, get off the fence!" I yell just a second before the bull charges.

"Lance!" she cries hoarsely just as I snatch her off the fence and hear the crash of the horns. She laughs hysterically in my embrace as she eyes the bull.

"Hey, man," she calls out to the bull, "what did I ever do to you?"

Giggling in my arms, she turns back to me, cheeks pink from the cold, eyes filled with laughter and lips turned up in a serene smile. Her fingers brush along the growing stubble on my jaw. "My hero. You saved me from a raging bull."

"It's not funny!"

She jerks in my hold, eyes widening at my venom.

"If he would have nailed you, your career would be over!"

I drop her to her feet as she gapes at me.

"Why is everything a joke to you?"

"Hey. Hey!" She holds up a defensive hand. "That was close, I agree, and I'm thankful to you for saving my ass, believe me, but what in the hell is your problem?!"

"You, you're my problem. You take *nothing* seriously. You make light of everything, and it's ridiculous. You act like a child."

"I'm just trying to snap you out of this funk, Lance."

"It's not a funk, Harper, this is my *reality*," I hold my hands up. "This is inescapable, and I have to deal with it every day. So, while this may be a vacation for you, this is my future, and I'm here, day in day out, trying to hold onto it. I'm losing my father," my voice cracks and it only angers me further, "to an illness I can't afford to help him fight. My little brother has nothing, nothing, a guy his age should have. He's still running on smiles and hand-me-downs, and even when he gets a job, he won't have shit because we're sticking every dime we have into a sinking ship. So no, Harper, I don't want to go break free and have a few beers because it won't help shit."

I leave her there in the middle of the field and head toward the barn.

fifty-four

HARPER

S ENDING OFF A FACETIME REQUEST FOR THE THIRD TIME, RENÉ finally picks up.

"Hey, Mami! How is Texas?"

Just as I open my mouth to speak, my face crumbles.

"Oh shit, Ricky told me it was home of the steers and queens, maybe I'm the one who should of gone to Texas."

Laughter bursts from me as I try and suck up some of my disappointment. "Not exactly the saying, but if only that were true, it'd be a much happier place. Can you come?"

"No can do. What's wrong, sweetheart?"

"I need a rainbow day, bad."

"He's still punishing you?"

"Yeah," I look across the pasture at Lance, who's slinging rope with Tony. Today was substantially warm for mid-winter, and I've been roaming the grounds by myself since Lance has spent most of the day avoiding me. "I don't know how to get through to him."

"Come home. He came for you once, maybe he will do it again."

"He's talking to me less and less. I've tried everything. He keeps telling me I'm acting like a child and that I think this is some sort of vacation."

"Oh shit. This is bad."

"He won't let me get close enough to tell him the truth. He's, I don't know, he's a steel wall."

"It can't be all that bad. Show me this cow ranch." I lift the phone and scan the ranch from one side to the other.

"Lower," I move the phone lower. "Ah, no wonder you're depressed. Oh wait, I see, lower, to the right. There, much better view."

It's then I see what he's fixated on. Lance has his shirt off and is rinsing some mud from his chest. I turn the phone back over to see several notifications that René has taken a photo.

"René!"

"What?"

"I can see you taking screenshots!"

"I'm not."

"You so are."

"Fine, I'll erase them."

"No, you won't."

"We can fight about this later. In the meantime, why are you not snooping in his room?"

"What? Why would I do that?"

"Because you don't know him, not really."

"Yes, I do. We were together for months."

"Uh huh, oh months, huh? Do you know I found out Ricky likes Pink Panther movies? Like really likes them? Thinks they are funny."

"Okay. So?"

"This is news. We've been together for years, Mami. You don't know that man. Snoop. Find his bones."

"Skeletons. And no way."

"Trust me and do it. I gotta go, I have a shift in an hour. Rainbows."

"Rainbows," I say deflating.

"Mami," René looks on at me with a small smile. "Remember this is not the case of dickedgood."

"What?"

"Dickedgood. It means this isn't about sex. You aren't some crazy ex with a sex crush. He came for you. That means something. You are there to claim your man, your partner, be the 'take no shit' bitch I raised you to be and win him back. Make me proud."

I'm snooping. And so far, the only thing I've discovered is Lance uses dandruff shampoo.

Detective freaking Holmes, right here, folks.

I have no idea what I'm looking for. But I take René's advice and look for his skeletons. Prying him for any information at the moment seems impossible. Current location—closet, and it's huge. Inside, I tug on the light switch and see a stack of old notebooks along with his yearbooks. I pull one down and start flipping through. I find him easily, his face unmistakable as I trace it with my finger. He's not smiling, in fact, he looks a bit pissed.

"Can't say much has changed," I snort ironically. "Do you have any bones, Prescott?" I mutter in René's accent.

I flip through his senior yearbook and see no signatures. He said he has plenty of friends but does he? He was known as the mute in college, gorgeous and broody. We never ventured out much in public, aside from his training, and he wasn't quick to converse.

I assumed it was all due to his temper. Didn't he have any friends here? I shut the book and rifle through a stack of sweaters and find a bottle of whiskey and decide what the hell. Why would a grown-ass man have a stash of bourbon in his closet? Does he have a drinking problem? I decide to create one for myself because I down half of the pint in a few gulps.

With the fresh buzz, I go through each shelf one by one, searching for clues as I nip at the bottle.

Halfway through his jacket pockets, I find a dirt-encrusted utility bill envelope. It's when I see the signature on the bottom that I tense up.

Lance,

I made a mistake. Please stop punishing me. Please meet me again tonight. I can't stop thinking about you.

Channah

"Sounds familiar," I spout sarcastically, flipping the top off the bottle and taking another swig of the contents.

I flip through the yearbook until I find her name. Channah Dickson. Gorgeous. She was all the things, cheerleader, swim team, debate, and of course, prom queen. I hate her. Instantly I'm on edge. The more I think about it, the more I realize René is right. Lance never really spoke much about home, and he had a whole life here before he met me. What else don't I know? Is she why he turned me down flat when I arrived? Then again, this letter could be ancient. I study the North Face jacket and don't recognize it from our Grand days. I sink when I realize it's relatively new.

I rip through more hangers, feeling stabbed.

I swore to myself I would never get wrapped up in any man like some needy nymph, and here I am in a freaking closet pilfering through his clothes and yearbooks, the jealousy in my chest burning as much as my cheeks, due to the whiskey. But I have to be mature about this.

I toss back more of the bottle.

"Yeah, no, freak that," I hiccup, before finishing the last of his bourbon. The liquid no longer scorching my throat. And then I'm sorting through his clothes because who in the hell puts their jeans in the middle of their hoodies and shirts? It's just not right. I've developed a drunken case of OCD. And why in the world does one man have such a big closet?

"Bet Channah does, in her big fat vagina," I hiccup again and FaceTime René.

"Mami, I'm on a shift."

"He's had sex with a Channah!"

"What's a Channa?"

I flip open the yearbook and point to her picture. "This, *this* is a Channah."

"Ah, so we hate her."

"Yes!" I smart. "We hate her. See, this is why I didn't want a damn man in the first place. Man-free, problem-free, but noooo, here I am, all hormonal and jealous as hell in a closet! A CLOSET!"

"Calm down, Mami. If he was into her, he wouldn't have come to New York."

"But you were right, he has this past, and I don't know a damn thing about it."

"You have not been honest with him either."

"I have about other people."

"He probably don't want to hurt you. You need to think—"

Lance's bedroom door opens, and I cut René off mid-sentence hanging up on him.

I shut the light off, hoping that he can't hear me stuffing the note back in his jacket and hanging it up before carefully taking a sweatshirt off his rack. I'm waiting like a drunken closet ninja clothes sorter, my hackles rising, as I pray that he bypasses me to get to the shower.

The door opens a second later, and Lance gapes at me where I stand ready. I thrust the sweatshirt toward him. "I'm borrowing this!" He jerks back as I step forward, and a burp slips out of me right in his face. "Okay?"

"What the hell are you doing in here?" He takes a step forward and pulls the bottle from the floor. "Drinking?" He looks past my shoulder, "And rearranging my clothes? In the dark?"

"I just told you what I was doing. And not in the dark, I just turned the light off, duh."

After a long pause, he drops his head, his shoulders shaking.

"Is that…laughter? Lord help me. The boy may be healed! Thank you, Jesus!"

His chuckle slows. "You're the worst liar in the history of ever."

"I told you that when we met."

"Answer the question."

"I have a gay best friend."

"I'm aware."

"And he puts dumb ideas in my head."

"So, what were you doing?"

"Why do you have hooch in your closet? Are you a closet drinker?" I snort.

He rolls his eyes. "That's Rock and Rye. It's whiskey and lemon. I keep it for when I get congested and didn't want Trevor to find it. And that bottle you drank was a hundred years old."

"Seriously?" I ask through another hiccup. "Will I get sick?"

"Doubt it. Will that be all today? Or do you want to go through my bathroom shit too?"

I hiccup again. "That was the plan. I didn't get much time in there."

He steps aside. "By all means."

"You know," I say, strolling through his room, "I didn't want a boyfriend when we met." I open one of his drawers and pull out his razor and carefully inspect it. He hasn't used it in days, his beard growing in at a rapid rate, and I love it. He grew one when we were together back in college. A faint memory of the feel of it against my thighs has me rubbing them together. He crosses his arms at the door of the bathroom, as I continue my rant. "I didn't want to be involved."

"I remember."

"You didn't want a girlfriend either," I pick up his cologne off the side of the sink and inhale his scent. Big mistake.

"Nope. I didn't. What's your point?"

"But we happened anyway," I pull out another drawer and find a platinum chain covered in years of debris. "Really?"

"That's old as shit."

"You really should clean your closet out. Lots of *old shit* in there too."

"I'll take that into consideration."

"As well you should." The last of the bottle kicks in, and I turn to him, pulling an old Chapstick from his drawer. "Now, this is just disgusting." I drop it in the trash next to his toilet.

"I use that!"

"Yeah, well, you'll thank me later."

"Seriously, are you that bored? Or is this just a new hobby?"

"Well, the cabana boy around here isn't being very hospitable." I hiccup. "Worst vacation *ever*, by the way. Definitely no room service."

"I can book you a flight in ten minutes."

"Nope, I'm good here, I just won't be giving a high hospitality rating."

"Harper, I want to take a shower."

"Don't let me stop you. Finally, some entertainment." I pull up my phone and hit my Spotify playlist, circling my finger. A second later, "Boss" by Little Simz fills the bathroom. "Make this good."

"Bro," Trevor walks in and looks between us with a goofy grin. "What's going on in here?"

"Nothing, trust me. I've had better dates with my gay roommate."

Trevor chuckles as Lance speaks up. "Harper is leaving."

"Oh no, I'm not," I say, hopping up on the sink counter.

Trevor studies me, taking a step into the bathroom, his smile widening. "You drunk?"

"Lil' bit. Rock and Rye apparently. I have questions."

Trevor leans against Lance's bathroom door. "Fire away."

I look to Lance instead. "You said you had enough friends." I lift my hands. "Where are they?"

"What friends?" Trevor looks between us.

"His friends from high school."

Lance clears his throat. "Harper, I need to shower. I have shit to do."

"Me too. So?" I raise a brow, looking between them.

Trevor speaks up. "No one really stays here unless they have to."

He's covering for him. I can tell. It's a sibling thing, and I know it well because I have my own. "Is that so?" I say like I'm concluding a point, which I'm not. It's then I realize I got drunk in my ex-boyfriend's closet, snooped through his things, stole his clothes, and am currently interrogating his little brother for absolutely no reason. Whatever skeletons Lance has, he's not about to give them up, save his nasty Chapstick. René is insane, and I'm officially on the same train.

"Is that all?" Lance prompts, and I bob my head.

"For now."

Trevor laughs as Lance shakes his head. "I see why you love her, brother. I really do."

"At least one of you has some sense," I hop off the sink as the first wave of nausea hits. "Now, if you'll excuse me, I need to freaking throw up."

"Shit, grab her," Lance says, just as I start sinking toward the floor.

I wake up in bed in the pitch dark, unsure of the time, and hear the noise of dinner. It's seven. Jeannie runs a tight ship. Mealtimes do not vary. Head pounding, I make my way to the bathroom to pee and check my appearance. I look like I feel. My complexion ghastly white. I don't have drunk amnesia, I re-member vomiting—very, very well—while Lance held my hair.

Chalk resting in the back of my throat, I crank on the sink to get a quick drink and freeze when I see the color of my tongue. I lean in and inspect it to make sure my mind isn't play-ing tricks on me.

"Oh my GOD! OH MY GOD!" I scream as I begin to in-spect my teeth. I hear the thunder in the distance of two in-coming Prescott boys as I furiously rinse my mouth. "Oh my GOD!" I gag out while I squirt half a tube of toothpaste on my finger.

Lance is the first to reach me and bursts into the bathroom on bated breath.

"What, Harper? What is it?" He darts his gaze around the room as I furiously scrub my teeth.

"Oh, God, Lance," I'm gagging again, my heart thundering as I inspect my mouth. "Something's wrong, Lance. Something's so wrong!"

"What? Harper, you're scaring the hell out of me." I furiously wash my mouth as he presses me, putting his head level with mine at the sink as I cup water into my mouth. I'm struggling to get more in as Lance stills me and pulls me upright.

"Damnit, spill it."

"I think," I gag again, "I think I ate a bug." I stick out my tongue just as Trevor pokes his head in. "Is she all right?"

"Out," Lance says, closing the door on him, his back to me. Seconds pass, and slowly he lowers his head, pressing it into the door and rolling it back and forth before he turns to face me. And then he's laughing. And though it's the most beautiful thing I've ever seen, I'm too busy freaking out to fully appreciate it.

"It's not funny! What if it was a spider?! A cockroach?!"

"You didn't eat a bug."

"Then I'm dying. My tongue is fucking black, it's BLACK! And how would you know if I ate a bug or not? Haven't you seen those videos?"

He's hysterical. "What videos?"

"The ones where on average, a human eats such and such amount of bugs a year!"

I squeeze the toothpaste into my hand and massage my gums with it as Lance wraps an arm around me, pulling me away from the sink, his chuckle slowing at my back. "Okay, calm down because I'm pretty sure you're having an anxiety attack."

"My whole tongue is black! It's black. I ate a bug! A very

big bug! You don't think it will happen to you and bam! Jesus, if I find a leg in my teeth, I'll never recover."

"Harper," he says through another chuckle. "Your tongue is black because I gave you Pepto tablets before you passed out, which, when mixed with acid, can sometimes turn your tongue black."

I still my fingers, my hand covered in toothpaste and glance over at him. "What?"

"I gave you two Pepto tablets."

"I don't remember that."

"Probably because it was before you took a Rye nap."

"Right...," I study my hands and the mess I've made at the sink. "Okay, well, that's not common knowledge. I can't be held responsible for that reaction."

"Can I go back to my dinner? Or are you planning on heading to the roof with a bottle of jack and a roman candle?"

I swallow as my cheeks heat. "I apologize for my behavior today."

He sets me down and shakes his head. "I'll have Trevor bring you some of the chili."

My stomach turns. "No, thanks."

He looks me over. "You need something in your stomach. I'll figure it out."

"You don't have to."

"Don't worry about it."

He eyes my hoodie. And that's when I look down to see it's a Grand sweatshirt. "That feels like a million years ago now."

"Do you ever miss it?"

He darts his gaze to the tile between us. "All the fucking time." Before I can open my mouth to reply, he opens the door and knocks on the frame. "Get back in bed, I'll see you in a bit."

I take a shower and brush my teeth for ten minutes, hoping, praying that the look in his eyes and the conversation was the beginning of an olive branch. I've been here nearly a week, and I haven't made much progress with him at all. It's when I make it back to my room, I see two hot pockets and a Diet Mountain Dew waiting on my dresser that my hopes fall away. He dropped the food and left like I'm some sort of prisoner. And I have to admit, loving him is starting to feel like a sentence.

fifty-five

LANCE

I WALK PAST HARPER'S BEDROOM AND SEE IT'S EMPTY. IT'S THE suitcase in the corner of the room that has my heartrate evening out. The kicker is, I'd be surprised if it wasn't packed. Half of my problem with her is that it's always seemed easy for her to leave. The longer she stays, the harder it is to admit to myself she might be serious, but if that's the case, what's changed? I reach the kitchen to see my dad sitting in his chair, sipping coffee through a straw, and staring out the window.

"Morning, Dad."

"I think we've got one missing," he says, eyeing the pasture.

"There's no way you can know that."

"Test me. I heard the coyotes last night. It's my body betraying me, not my eagle eyes."

"Motherfucker." I know he's right. He's been doing this longer than I've been alive.

"You'll find 'em. You always do."

"I don't need this today. We have a delivery at three."

"Better make good time then."

"Yes, sir."

Dad never minces words when it comes to the ranch, so when he smiles, I follow his line of sight to see Harper…dancing in the middle of the pasture.

"What the hell?" I say, stepping toward the window to see

Harper doing a fucking ballet in the middle of the herd. She's prancing around like she's in a field of lilies. I scrub my hand down my face. "She's insane."

"She's a hoot. That's for sure. She's been at it for the better part of an hour. I'm willing to bet she's covered from the knees down in cow shit." He chuckles, and I can tell he's smitten with her. Another one down. I roll my eyes and sip my freshly poured coffee.

Dad keeps his eyes trained on Harper. "She's good for you."

"She's young."

"Your mother was younger."

"It doesn't work anymore the way it used to. She doesn't fit in this life."

"She seems to be doing a good job." He looks up to me. "Go talk to her, I swear she just carried a conversation on with one of them."

"I've got shit to do."

"Talk to her."

"Like you have all the answers."

Dad lets out a harsh breath. "Son, I know I messed up—"

"Is that what you want to call it?" He looks over to me with guilty features. "Forget it." I scrub my hand down my face. "I have work to do."

"Does that hurt?" Harper's voice sounds out as I tag the cow.

"A lot less than making it a steak."

"Jesus, Lance."

"Just another reason you wouldn't make it out here. Too much empathy for dinner."

"I'm making it just fine, thank you. I got my coveralls today. Amazon Prime. Gotta love it. They deliver everywhere."

Straddling the fence, I glance down to see her in faded pink coveralls, her hair in braids. She looks fucking adorable and gives me a wink when my gaze lingers on her a bit too long.

"Don't you have something to do?"

"I'm doing it."

"What's that exactly?"

"Observing the angry bull in its environment."

"There are no bulls in here."

"Says you."

I roll my eyes. "Make yourself useful and hand me that tag."

She lifts on her toes and manages to get it in my hands.

"You want to tell me what you were doing this morning?"

"Cow shit ballet. It's something I'm testing out for the future. What did you think?"

"You know there was a cleaner pasture, not a hundred yards over."

"Yeah, but I like the cows. They're chill creatures. What are you going to name this one?"

"I don't name hamburger meat."

"Okay, okay," she shakes her hands at me. "Well I'll name her. Channah-nan-na-nan."

I pause, peering over at her. "Any specific reason why?"

"Seems like as good of a name as any. You like it?"

"Not particularly."

"Seems to be good *meat*."

I lift a brow. "You have something you want to ask me?"

"Nope," she pops her glossed lips and leans in. "But your ass looks amazing perched on that fence."

I hang my head. "Harper."

"What?" She drawls out. "I've been invited on an expedition, a date, you'll have to save all that negativity for later."

"A date? With who?"

"With me," Trevor says, sauntering up and handing Harper a loaded rifle. "We're going to catch that 'yote."

"The hell you are."

"You know I know what I'm doing," Trevor says, indignant.

I kick back on the fence. "This girl couldn't shoot to save her life."

"I resemble that remark, fully." She turns to Trevor. "Really, I do, I was raised in a tutu." I can't help my smirk. "But I'm also a Texas woman, educated in football, nursed with beer and other manly shit, so, have some faith, Lance. I'll kill your cow eater."

"No."

She wrinkles her nose. "This isn't up for debate." She checks the chamber of the gun. "I know the basics."

"And I'm saying, no, fuck no, and no way." I glare at my brother, making my way down the fence. "Your crush is cute, but you don't hand a lady a gun when she doesn't know how to use it."

"Back off, dick, I know enough for the both of us."

"No, and no," I say to each of them individually in an attempt to make my point.

Harper lifts her rifle. "You're outnumbered. That concludes this debate."

Cursing, I charge toward her. "Give me that."

"No." She turns away from me as I glare at Trevor, who's smiling like Alice's Cheshire cat. "I may be in love with her. I think this is the only woman who has ever said no to you."

"Interesting," Harper says, her cheeks heating.

"Trust me, none of them had him tied up the way you do," Trevor says, jutting his chin toward me.

"Good to know. Channah-nan-na-nan," she cocks her rifle, eyeing the cow with disdain, "enjoy your Lance since your days are numbered." And with that, she leaves the barn with Trevor hot on her heels.

"They aren't working, damnit, they aren't working. It's like tunnel vision. I can't see shit," She whisper-yells next to me. I take the goggles from her and flip them over before switching them to night vision. "Oh. Jesus. How did I miss that? Blonde moment, for sure."

"Shhhh, lady love, not so loud," Trevor chuckles, and it grates me. I know he's doing it just to screw with me, though some part of me does think he's smitten.

"So, what are the signs?" Harper asks.

"Well, that would be a 'yote coming into view," I say under my breath. I'm supposed to be doing a hundred other things aside from entertaining this bullshit.

"Smartass," she spouts, lifting her night vision goggles to scan the herd. "I just meant, is there anything in particular to look for?"

"A coyote," Trevor and I say together.

"I've always wanted to do this," she ignores our sarcasm. "And shoot pool. I've never done that."

"We've got a hall up the road," Trevor says. "Lance use to stomp around up there. He's good."

"How good?"

"Really good," Trevor supplies.

She nudges me. "Will you teach me?"

"Don't have the time," I say, imagining her bent over the table for a shot, her long legs in a short skirt. I hate every minute of this. This conjured image just another I'll need to wipe, along with the one of her in those coveralls. She's pressed against my hip, laying on her stomach with Trevor on the other side of her. She's on watch while we each have a scope on the herd.

"You bring the hooch?" Trevor asks.

"Yeah, you have hooch?" Harper mimics. You would think *they* are related.

"No, because this isn't a party."

"Could be," Trevor quips. "God, you used to be so much more fun, brother."

"I can't drink that shit so close to a fight, and oh, you're sixteen."

"That didn't stop you from giving me that moonshine not too long ago," he smarts.

"It was two shots, enough to shut you up, which you two apparently can't do now. If we have any chance of catching them, it won't be due to this circus."

"I think we're doing a fantastic job," Harper says, her binoculars up.

"You are," Trevor says.

Harper scoots in closer to me for warmth, and I allow it. It's freezing tonight, but clear, clear enough that we have a real shot of catching the culprit responsible for the dead heifer I found today.

"I see it," Harper whisper-shouts. "There's two, three of them."

"Bullshit," Trevor says, looking through his scope.

"About fifty yards away from the barn."

Trevor chimes in. "Yep, she's right."

"Damn," she pipes up, "they look like *dogs*. I was expecting something a little more epic."

Trevor chuckles, and I sigh. Three is the worst possible number. He reads my thoughts.

"Three," he says, "if we take two of them out, it may solve the problem, but you never know."

"Damn." I train the scope on one of them and look over to Harper, who I know has a waiting smile on her lips.

"Did you want to ask me something, Lance?"

fifty-six

HARPER

"**W**E GOT 'EM, DAD," TREVOR ANNOUNCES PROUDLY as the three of us enter the living room. "And our girl here got the third." Trevor and I share a grin.

"Good job," Jack nods toward me as I take off my jacket.

"To be fair, Lance took my aim. All I did was pull the trigger."

Lance removes the gun from my hand and Trevor's and locks them up in the cabinet next to the fireplace before securing the key in his pocket. He and Jack share a look I can't decipher from where he sits in the recliner as Rip picks up a guitar on the couch next to him.

"Where's Mom?" Trevor asks.

"She picked up another shift," Jack replies before taking a sip from his tumbler.

It wasn't until I got to the ranch that I found out Jeannie went back to work years ago to help out with the bills. She bartends at the only hotel in town. Not one person in this house ever stops, even retired, Rip comes out to help with the workload. He lives on the edge of town with his wife but is over almost every day. On the Prescott ranch, everyone is considered family. Rip's talent takes me by surprise as I watch him run his fingers effortlessly along the strings.

"Wow. You're good."

"That's nothing," Trevor says, hanging his coat next to the roaring fire where I heat my hands behind me. "You should have seen him and Dad when they used to play. We have videos."

"Yeah?" I look down at Jack.

"We used to open for Lynyrd Skynyrd," Rip says.

Lance sighs as if he's heard the same story a thousand times. He told me when we were dating that when his dad was younger, he played in a band, so chances are, that's the case.

"Why did you stop?" I ask, knowing it doesn't have anything to do with Jack's Parkinson's diagnosis. It was too long ago.

"Jeannie got pregnant," Jack says as Lance looks over to me. "And we played when we could, we just never got anywhere. I wanted to settle down anyway, and no one was beating down our door to sign us."

"Good times," Rip says, clinking glasses with Jack before they both take a sip.

"Lance, pour yourself some," Jack gestures to the bottle of whiskey on the table.

"Can't. Training."

"One drink, son," he insists.

Lance shakes his head. "Got shit to do."

"Bullshit." Jack stands with his drink in hand and moves toward Lance before he loses his footing, falling to the carpet as though he's been tripped, his tumbler spilling over.

Lance curses and is at his side in an instant, helping him up.

I feel the embarrassment, the tension, as Trevor looks on frozen, while Rip keeps picking his guitar. And then I'm on Jack's other side as we secure him back in the recliner. Unable to handle another second of the tension, I pipe up. "Jack, that was the absolute worst Cupid Shuffle I've ever seen." Lance's head snaps to mine as I dig in. "You have a dance professional living under your roof, the least you could do is ask for help."

Lance's eyes bulge as Jack looks up to me speculatively before he starts to laugh. Rip joins in as I pick up the empty glass and hand it to Trevor, who's smiling at me. "Get him another one." Trevor doesn't hesitate, he pours two fingers of the bottle in the glass and hands it to his dad. I look over at Lance and see him repeatedly swallowing before he turns and makes his way down the hall.

"Will you play for me when I get done changing?" Rip nods, and I turn quickly, making my way down the hall to catch Lance.

"Lance." I'm at his back at his bedroom door. He pauses with his hand on the knob. Without a second thought, I wrap my arms around his waist and lean in, inhaling his scent. He smells like evergreen, and I become instantly addicted. He doesn't pull away from my touch, he just lingers there with me.

I'm sorry. I love you. Please, give me another chance to prove I mean it. But I don't say it out loud, words seem pretty useless these days. Actions speak a lot louder. And he needs actions, he needs solidarity because he's always waiting for the other shoe to drop. It's clear to me he's gotten to the point where he believes in trade. That in order to be successful in one area of life, you have to let go of another. He believes that all things can't go well at once. And that's the most heartbreaking part of it. I too thought that at one time, but I'm here to prove it's simply not true. Warm hands cover mine as he finally speaks.

"Thank you for your help."

I squeeze him tighter, willing him to open up, to give me something, anything.

But he releases me.

"I'm going to go help Trevor with dinner," I whisper at his back.

I've been in the kitchen for hours, making Jeannie's apple pie. I pulled it from an old recipe box after I did the dinner dishes and just got to work. Lance ate in his room—to avoid me—I'm sure. I got close today. I can't remember a time in our whole relationship where he resisted me so damned much, even when we'd had an argument.

It's not about you.

It's not about you.

It's not about you.

But it feels personal. I fucking love him. I deprived myself of two years without him, the whole time unsure if he felt the same ache. Him coming to New York was affirmation. And now the space is killing me. I don't want to sleep down the hall from Lance. I want my place at his side. A couple of years ago, he made love to me all night long in that bedroom he's holed up in. Now it seems like a lifetime ago. I'm close to cracking after just a week.

I need him. I want him so badly I'm aching, limbs heavy, my center a constant throb. He brought that part of me back to life.

The need is debilitating. It's all resistance to us. I've made him smile, laugh, and that's been no easy feat. Even with those leaps, it feels like he's sinking further into himself. I pull the second pie out of the oven just as Jeannie walks in the kitchen after her shift.

"Hey, you," I say, pouring her a cup of coffee. "I borrowed apples, cinnamon sugar, butter, flour, an egg, and some electricity. I'll pay you back."

She grins at me, her posture showing her fatigue as she takes the coffee and kisses my temple.

"Thanks, darlin'. And I'll settle for a slice."

"Coming up."

"How was today?"

"I did a ballet for the cows, killed a coyote, and baked two pies."

Jeannie throws her head back with a laugh. "Bet you never thought that would ever be your day's summary."

"It's different," I grin. "That's for sure."

"Do you like it?"

"For the most part, yes."

She smirks into her coffee. "But not at night."

I bite my lips. Do I really want to be talking sex with Lance's mom?

Hell to the no. "You could say that, yes. It's a bit lonely."

"Hang in there. He loves apple pie."

I grin. "I know."

"It's another of the few things he can't resist."

I quirk a brow. "Are you telling me to go seduce your son with apple pie?"

"Whatever gets me a grandchild."

I set a piece in front of her. "I need him speaking to me first."

"He's good at hiding."

"Tell me 'bout it." I sigh, wiping the counter before rinsing out the dishrag.

"He comes alive with you around. It might be hard for you to understand because you haven't watched him from the beginning. He spent the first two years of his life covering our mouths to shut us up. He didn't like the noise. Matter of fact, his first words were Mama and shut up."

"Funny, shut up were his first words to me too."

We both laugh as I pull a seat at the table.

"But when that child cracked a smile, he lit up the room. When he laughed, he laughed hysterically. I was so in love with my little boy." She sips her coffee and sets it down. "He didn't play with other children well and isolated a lot until Trevor came along. He claimed his brother the minute we brought him home. He's always been quiet. Always, until he started getting in trouble at school. And it wasn't words he was using that got him in hot water."

"Fighting?"

"Yeah."

"He likes his own noise, communicates in his own way. He seemed to blossom some in college, but when he came back, it's like he went into himself again. Over the last few years, I've watched his smile fade and heard many more shut ups. But with you, it's as if he's picking up a conversation that he's been having his whole life."

I fight the threatening tears. It's true. The man I met was confident, moody, self-assured, and highly opinionated, but only around me. To others, he was an introvert.

"Sometimes, I wonder if we did right by him. Should we have done more? Got him counseling or pried more into his life or something."

"He's an amazing man," I say honestly.

"He is. But I'm not at all happy about the fact that he's lashing out all the time and isolating more. But he's still talking, and I've seen him crack a smile a mile wide since you've been here. His heart isn't closed to you, Harper. You keep managing to find a code very few have access to. Don't give up on him."

"I won't." I stand, the rattle in my chest hard to bear. "I'll get Trevor and Jack a piece."

"Let me do that. Take one to Lance." She stands and cuts

a mammoth piece of pie and plates it along with a fork before handing it to me.

I reluctantly take it. "You're setting me up for failure."

"It's pie. What's he going to do, throw it at you?"

We give each other a look, and both burst into laughter, knowing it's a real possibility at this point with his hot and cold.

"If he does, come get me, I'll kick his ass."

"Deal."

"You two will work it out," she says, stretching. "I need to go pry my drunken husband from his recliner." She looks down at the pie. "This should do it."

"Night, Jeannie."

"Night, darlin'."

I make my way down the hall toward Lance's room and hear Trevor groan. "Jesus, not that fucking song again." His door closes, and that's when I hear it. The music coming from Lance's room. Just outside his door, I hear the opening lyrics to "Rest in Pieces" by Saliva. It's while standing there that I realize the words are meant for me. He's talking to me.

It's how we've always communicated. It's the way he showed me who he was, told me about his struggles, his demons. It's the same way I showed him what I was about, showed him the ways I wanted him.

Lance always said he would get better at communication when I dubbed him Shakespeare in jest, but this is his way. I listen to the lyrics, my heart breaking when he tells me I'm beautiful, but I've messed with his head long enough, and he needs me to leave. It's unbearable.

After a quick knock on the door, I open it to see him tossing a football up. He's bare-chested in long johns, his hair damp, and it knocks the breath from me. His olive skin looks incredible stretched over the muscles of his chest, his barbed wire tattoos stretching along his biceps with each spiral he throws up. But it's the sight of that pigskin ball that does me in. It hammers home just how far we've come and how much our relationship has cost him. Silver eyes cut me to the bone as he follows me from his door to his nightstand. I set his pie down and lean over to hover above him where he lays in the bed. His beard's grown darker, thicker, outlining his full lips, and I run my hands along his jaw to trace it. Stormy eyes regard me with a mix of hostility and love. It's insane how much I can clearly see when he lets me. And this look tells me that this time I cut him deep, and he's not willing to forgive so easily. He no longer trusts me with his heart. It's not a question of love. It's his trust I've lost.

"I'm sorry." I lean down, the necklace he gave me grazing his chest as I hover above him. He doesn't move, doesn't flinch, he lays there, looking up at me. In his eyes, I see a rare vulnerability. It breaks my heart I've hurt him so badly. "I'm sorry," I whisper, just before I lean in closer and press my lips to his. I can feel his restraint as I pull away and stare down at him with all the love in my heart.

"I love you," I sniff as a stray tear falls down my cheek, splashing onto his chest. He closes his eyes on impact. I wait just long enough for his rejection before I move away. Heart splintering, I gather myself from him and make my way out. I can feel his eyes on me when I shut the door.

In my room, I stare out the window at the pasture, knowing the confession I came to make may be the only way to get through to him. My phone buzzes in my hand as I lift it, sure it's René, but it's the last person I expect to hear from.

"Daddy?"

"Harper," he rasps out, his voice a million miles away. "We need you to come home."

fifty-seven

HARPER

THE NEXT DAY, I PULL UP TO THE RANCH JUST AS THE SUN SETS. It's been one of the worst days of my life, and I have no fight left in me. I wipe my eyes of debris and sit in the car going over the last few hours.

"We can't make it work," my mother says, barely able to keep the anger out of her voice. "I've filed for divorce."

I look over at my dad, who stares out of the kitchen window. He's been absent since his stint in prison, where he served eighteen months. Mom had come to New York the first few of them to avoid the media in Texas and any immediate threats. She was forced to sell the house to pay his fines and lawyer's fees. Now they have a tiny one-bedroom apartment an hour away from College Station. Mom spent the whole time in New York going over years of finances with Nana, trying to find a way for them to come out of it. But the truth is my father sunk us and took away our lives with his selfish decisions. And we were all still paying for his mistakes.

"Dad?" Kandace prompts from where she sits.

"It's for the best," he says as if he's on autopilot. As he has been since he got arrested for racketeering. My father has always been a betting man, but a gambling addiction is the last thing I expected. And the fact that he was gambling with his team, and our lives was the most shocking. After ten years as a reputable coach whose morals were based

on family and trust, nothing was more jarring than the media coverage of seeing him taken off campus in cuffs.

"Why, Daddy, just tell me why?" Kandace asks, in tears at their kitchenette. "You had everything. You had all of those people counting on you."

"It's a sickness," my mother explains, her voice lifeless.

"And we're just supposed to accept it? You can't," Kandace says, reading her the riot act. "You can't forgive him. Twenty-six years of marriage, and you can't forgive him."

Dad scrubs a hand down his face wiping away stray tears. "I don't deserve it." He looks down at me. "Not from anyone in this family. The things I said, the things I did, they're unforgivable. I didn't mean it," he assures me. "I'm so sorry."

"I know you were just trying to protect me."

"My reasons for my behavior were all selfish. I don't expect you all to forgive me, now or maybe ever, but just please know I love you. I can't give you excuses that really don't make a difference. I have none. I ruined this. Your mother deserves to be happy, and I'm not the man who can do that for her anymore." They share a look, and my heart cracks. I can still see the love between them, but there's far too much water holding them both back.

"Fine, you're getting a divorce, that it?" Kandace stands and turns to me. "I have my own family to get back to."

"Kandace," I say as she shoulders her purse and makes her way toward the door. "Kandace, stop," I order as she hustles toward an SUV I don't recognize. "When did you get this?"

"A year ago." Guilt covers me. When everything happened, I all but deserted her. She'd come to New York for a few days to visit when Mom came, but our dynamic was off because of my absence. We never addressed it because we were too busy focusing on Mom. Not only did I run from what happened, I went completely MIA on her.

"I'm sorry."

"What are you even doing here?"

"I came to be with Lance."

"Lance?" She gapes at me. "Are you serious?"

"He came to New York weeks ago, asking for a commitment. I've been staying with his family."

"Well, good on ya. Guess you don't have to worry about your own family falling apart anymore."

"Kandace, I miss you."

She eyes me. "You cut me out. You left us all here to deal with the mess."

"I know."

"You think I didn't need you?"

"I'm sorry, I threw myself into dancing. I didn't…I wasn't myself."

"Selfish."

"Yes," I say, moving toward her. "It was."

"That seems to run in the family." I reach for her and she jerks away. "Don't," she says, wiping her face and avoiding my touch.

"I was planning on coming to you after I sorted things with Lance. But you should know I left because I didn't want it touching you anymore. The less you had to do with me, the less you would've had to deal with it."

"Are you serious? I was terrified for you. I spent so many nights worrying about you, did you for once think of me? I'm your big sister. I wanted to be there for you, to protect you and you just shut me out."

"I'm sorry."

"Yeah, well, aren't we all today."

"I love you," I say softly. "I miss you so much. I needed you too. I just…handled it wrong. Lance is mad at me as well. I just didn't know how to keep you all away from it and stay in your lives. I was trying to protect you all."

Her posture breaks, and she finally lets me wrap my arms around her. "I'm so sorry."

"I'm so mad at you. You broke your nephew's heart too, you know." She pulls from my embrace. "But don't ever do that again."

"I'm sorry. It was just so hard to come back here."

"Baby, I know. I know. I just wish you would have talked to me."

"Please forgive me," I say, crying in her embrace.

"I will, eventually. But, I'm proud of you," she sniffs, pulling away from me, her eyes swollen. "Just so you know. I saw you dance on TikTok. Zane showed it to me."

The thought of my nephew finding me on the app to watch my dance videos breaks my heart.

"Can I see him now?"

She eyes me. "I'm about to pick him up from school. You want to come with me?"

"I'd love nothing more."

We collectively look back at the apartment building. "You think we should tell them we're leaving?" I ask.

She shakes her head. "Let them hash it out."

"Okay." She unlocks her SUV, and I climb in. "I can't believe it."

"I can. Neither one of them are the same anymore. I hope I can forgive Dad one day."

"I just…don't you feel sorry for him?"

"He made his bed. Maybe one day I'll see it another way." She adjusts the rearview and wipes her eyes. "So, you came back for Lance?"

"It's complicated."

"Tell me everything."

A knock on my window has me jumping in my seat, and I see Trevor and roll it down.

"I was hoping he didn't scare you away. He's been a mammoth dick for months. Thought you had left there for a second until Mom found your suitcase in the laundry room."

"No, I went to see my family. My dad called last night, and I dropped everything. I didn't think about leaving a note."

He eyes my tear-stained cheeks. "Want to talk about it?"

Sweet Trevor, he's just a sixteen-year-old kid, and he's spending most of his time trying to keep his own family together.

"The short of it is that my parents are getting a divorce."

"I'm sorry."

"Yeah, me too. But it's been two years, and it's time to close that chapter. I'm okay, really. Just getting past the sting."

"I read about your dad, what a mess."

"Yeah. It was."

I roll up the window and lock my rental up. Stepping out, I glance around the ranch as the sun begins to set.

"It really is beautiful here."

Trevor nods. "It is."

"You like being a rancher?"

"Honestly, I don't know life without it, but I love it. I do. And so does my brother. Definitely in our blood."

"I can see the appeal. It's peaceful."

Trevor looks over at me, evident concern on his face. "Mom made meatloaf. It's really good. I saved you a plate in the microwave. Lance has been hitting it pretty hard today. He's blown up a few times. I think he thought you left too."

I realize then how stupid it was not to send a text. He's probably been expecting this. I'd rolled my suitcase into the laundry room before I left when I discovered I had nothing clean to wear to face my parents. I'm in the Grand hoodie I stole from him and my last pair of leggings.

"Is he still in the gym?"

"No."

"Good. I want to work some of this out."

"Okay, well, I won't tell him you're here. Give you some time."

"Trust me, he's not coming after me." Trevor doesn't

hesitate, he pulls me into his arms. I hug him back and break down a little.

"Sorry," I sniff.

"Don't be. I would be devastated if my parents split. It's got to feel weird."

"It does." I pull back and manage a smile. "You're going to be an awesome husband one day."

"Damn right, I am. I assure you not half as pigheaded as my brother."

"Well, that should do you good."

He looks worried when he asks. "So, you aren't leaving?"

"I'm tired of running from the things I'm afraid of. Doesn't make it any less hard to deal."

"You're perfect for him, you know."

"And he for me."

He hugs me again and makes his way toward the house as I square off with the barn. I'll get back to fighting in the morning, for now, I have my own shit to work out.

fifty-eight

LANCE

"H EY, DICKHEAD?"

"In my office."

"It's Dad's office."

"Whatever. I'm in here."

Trevor turns the corner with an apple in his hand and takes a bite.

"That's my apple."

He presents me with the bitten fruit, and I wave him away.

"All yours. What do you want?"

"Nothing."

"Then get out. I have work to do."

"Let me save you some time, we're broke," he says matter of fact, "you're welcome."

"Yeah, well, bills still have to be paid. You might want to sit down and learn how to cut a check."

He takes another bite of my apple. "I'm good with manual labor, for now, especially if paying bills makes me look as constipated as it does you."

"Get out," I grumble.

"Okay, but I came in here for a reason."

"You came in here to fuck with me."

"Whatever."

Music sounds from the barn, and I look up from Dad's books. "Rip out there?"

"Nope, and since when does Rip listen to Evanescence?"

I turn to look out at the barn, trying to ignore the pickup in my chest. I've been a fucking wreck all day, and it's only made me realize what she's capable of doing to me.

"Mom found her suitcase in the laundry room. She didn't leave, she just went to see her family. It was an emergency."

"What happened?"

"Not my place to tell."

All I want to do is release the breath I've been holding. A part of me relieved, a larger part of me angry. When Trevor noticed her bed unmade this morning and her car missing, I hated that I wasn't surprised.

I expected to miss her again the minute she set foot on this ranch, which is why I wasn't quick to welcome her. But the truth is, I'm not testing her.

"She doesn't belong here."

"Bullshit."

"Trevor, she doesn't. She's a successful dancer in New York. This place will only drag her down. It's too complicated. She needs to go back."

"You make it sound like you have nothing to offer. She could be happy here."

"She'll be happier doing what she was born to do."

"I think you're wrong."

"Am I? Come on." I get up from the desk and walk past him, and he follows me to the barn where we enter through the side door, so as not to alert her that we're watching. Harper leaps across the ring just as we get the door shut and then begins turning in circles covering the length of the elevated floor, executing each spin with precision. The song is fucking depressing, the lyrics hard to listen to. And I know they're for me. I feel every single word. I want so much to believe her, to let her back in, but she's made it hard to trust her. The longer she stays, the harder it's becoming to love her at arm's length. She's torturing us both, and I'm struggling to do right by her.

"Jesus," Trevor says, amazed by mere seconds of her dancing. And then I'm pulled in, rapt as she throws herself into it, every single one of her limbs poised perfectly, her physique controlled. But it's her face that has me on high alert.

She's crying.

Guilt consumes me as Trevor looks on awestruck by her raw talent.

"She's so good."

"Yeah," I say, hearing the pride in my voice. "She's incredible."

I look over to Trevor. "So, tell me honestly, little brother, would you be the guy to take that ballerina and put her back in the box?"

Trevor doesn't miss a beat. "She wants to be here, with you."

"And I don't want her to hate me for it."

"I might not be as hardheaded as you, but if you can watch this without an ounce of feeling, maybe I'm looking up to the wrong guy." He glances over at Harper and shakes his head. "This is fucking sad. I'll be inside."

"See? Definition of complicated. Maybe don't be so anxious to grow up."

He rolls his eyes, but leaves me there, just as Harper stops moving and starts sobbing into her hands.

In seconds, I'm pulling her into my arms.

fifty-nine

HARPER

LANCE SURROUNDS ME IN HIS EMBRACE AS I CRUMBLE IN THE middle of his ring. "He screwed everything up. For us, for you, and I can't stay mad at him. I want to be so mad at him, Lance. And I am, I'm furious, but I love him more than his mistakes, and now he's just gone. He's not my dad anymore; he's a shell. A fucking shell. And I can't stand watching it. Everyone he loves has abandoned him. And for good reason, but his own family? They're getting a divorce. I don't know why I'm surprised, but…God," I pull away from him, and he lets me go. I look up to him, emotions running rampant. "I know you hate him. You couldn't care less about Ryan Elliot."

Cloudy eyes peer through me. "I hate what he did, but I knew him before, and I saw how he changed. I genuinely liked him as a coach. I'm sorry you're hurting."

"Are you?" I glare over at him and see the honesty he's giving me. "I can see you are. I didn't mean that."

"Tell me what to do," he says, and it's apparent, my pain is his.

"Let me back in." It falls so easily from my lips. I close the space and lift on my toes, kissing him. "Touch me, Lance," I beg. He goes solid, tensing beneath my fingers. "Kiss me back," I press my lips to his and get nothing. "I need you."

He shakes his head and grabs my hands, pushing me away gently.

"So, you regret New York?"

"Partly."

"Leave."

"What?"

"Leave. I'm not buying what you're selling. I don't believe you. Mere weeks ago, you wanted this, wanted me. Whatever has gotten into you, isn't the truth. You're believing the lies you're telling yourself."

"I believe what I can see," he yells angrily. "That's the truth."

"Then fucking look at me!" I scream at him. His eyes roam me, my breaths coming fast before he darts them away. "*Believe me*, Lance. I know I hurt you, and you're punishing me for it. And you're hiding behind my dancing as an excuse to get rid of me, but that's all it's ever been, an excuse. I'm here because I want to be. I want you. I want *us* back. You can trust me, Lance. Let me back in."

His answering silence is deafening.

All fight leaves me as I walk over to him and again lift on my toes covering several inches, so we're eye level. I'm on pointe now as I glower at him. "It's a thin line, Lance. And so, I'll believe for both of us."

Defeated, but only for the moment, I leave the ring, this round goes to him.

Dinner and a hot shower do wonders for me. Though I'm still reeling from the news about my parents, deep down, I always knew the day Dad got arrested was the day it was over for them. I expected it, but it didn't make it any less hard to hear. Now maybe they can move on, both of them. And perhaps it's for the best. Running a comb through my hair, I crack the bathroom door to let the steam out and hear Trevor down the hall on his headphones, talking shit on his video game.

"Yeah, me and the wife are going to do the usual tonight. It's Friday, so that's tacos and fetish porn."

I burst out laughing when he pipes up again. "You ever tried mayo? It's an edible lubricant."

"Shut the hell up, punk," Tony grumbles from his bedroom, and I can tell there's amusement in his voice.

"I'll get to you soon, honey," Trevor quips. "Grab the new jar of mayo, it's in the cabinet."

Giggling, I smooth the goat's milk lotion Jeannie gave me—made by a local farm—over my arms. It smells of Lavender, like Nana, and somewhere between the lewd jokes Trevor's making, the atmosphere of family, and the comforting smell permeating the bathroom, I feel the same level of ease as I do in Nana's brownstone. It's the ease in which Lance now dismisses me that has tears threatening, but I bat them away. I came to fight for my place in his life, and he's not making it easy. But I refuse to let his determination overtake my own.

I know he loves me. Just as much as he did seven weeks ago, two years before that and the years during, but lately, he's making it incredibly hard to believe. The longer I stay, the angrier he seems to get. But I have to hang in there, especially when times are hard. My parents may no longer be a shining example of longevity, but his are. And they've overcome improbable odds. I'll never stop dancing, and I will resume my breakneck pace once I've earned my place with Lance. There's a future for us. We loved each other across space and time before, we can do it again. I just have to get him back in that mindset. Mustering up my strength, I open the door and catch Lance on the other side.

"Can I have a word?"

"Sure."

He nods over his shoulder. "My room."

Cloudy eyes roam my body. I've got on a long tee and tiny sleep shorts. My hair is wet, and I've just applied lip balm. Heat stirs below as I watch him clench his fists. He wants to touch. I'm his to touch, but I won't give him home field advantage or the leverage to kick me out of his room. He's not here to mend fences, it's evident in his demeanor.

"Not finished yet, come in." Reluctantly, Lance steps in and closes the door behind him.

I draw a dollop of lotion from the jar and hike my leg up on the side of the sink before rubbing it in.

"So, what's up?"

"You paid for Dad's meds and told him we had a deal."

Shit.

Double shit.

"He needed them, and I had the money. It's simple math. Don't ask me to apologize for it."

"You had no right."

"I'm a part of this family."

"No, you aren't."

"Fine, I *want* to be a part of this family. And I didn't do it for you, or because I think I have some say in anything, or because I think you'll love me more for it. And I can't believe you would want to deny him that comfort for foolish pride. You're being an idiot."

"And when we don't have the money next month?"

"Jesus," I say, turning to face him. "That's next month."

"You'll be gone then, and he'll be just as helpless. You can't put a Band-Aid on this, Harper."

"Stop it. Don't make me feel bad for doing something that helped. I'm glad I could, even if it's only temporary."

"Stay out of this."

"It's a recurring charge."

"What?"

"You can pay me back."

"Cancel it. I mean it. I don't know what's going to happen from now until my next fight."

"Whatever happens, I want him to have those meds. I don't give a damn if you pay me back, I'm just saying it for the sake of saying it, kind of like the way you're ignoring the fact that you love me."

He snatches me to him by my wrist. "You aren't wanted here. Go. Home."

"You love me." I palm his face, and he rips it from my touch, his breaths coming fast. Undeterred, I step away.

"Look at me."

Jaw locked, his hostile gaze drifts up to mine.

"You love me. You're full of piss and vinegar because you're sick of life. I get it. Take it out on me." I slide my hand between the valley of my breasts, and his eyes follow as I rim my shorts. I feel the shift, the tension growing unbearable as he watches.

Slowly, I begin the descent of my hand before sliding my fingers between my legs. "You love me, and you damned sure want me. You're jealous of my fingers," I say, increasing the pace. "I want you here too." I bite my lip, my eyes hooding before he jerks my hand out of my shorts.

"You still think this is a game?"

"No, Lance. I'm pretty fucking serious. Though I desperately miss your sense of humor. But I'll give you a pardon because it seems you've lost every bit of sense in that thick ass head of yours. So how about we ease some of that tension. Take me.

I'm right here. Take it. I want nothing more than for you to take it out on me." I grab my towel. "I can bite into this. No one will be the wiser."

In seconds I'm bent over the sink, scalp stinging due to his fist full of my hair.

"Atta boy."

He commands my eyes in the mirror. "You don't want this. You don't know what you're asking. You don't want to know this level of depravity."

"I'm not the inexperienced little dancer you met. You changed that. You keep changing it." Reaching behind me, I grip his thick cock and feel he's hard. "You made me a fighter too."

"You want to be fucked and used?"

"Used? You're incapable of using me, but if that's what you want to call it—and if used feels as good as it did in New York—I wouldn't mind it."

"Damn you, Harper," he hisses, and I sense him weakening as I stroke his length. I can feel the anger rolling off him.

Loving Lance has always meant embracing his demons. Two years ago, we were able to keep them at bay. That no longer seems to be the case. "You want to play devil?" I taunt, "I'll be your greatest advocate. If this is what keeps you fighting, so be it. Whatever it takes. I love you. *All* of you. Even the asshole who seems to have taken up permanent residence. I'm not leaving. Fight me, fuck me, it's your decision. But I'm not leaving." I stroke him again and feel his fingers at the top of my shorts. His grip on my hair tightens as his cock jerks at my touch. Breasts heavy, I stand in wait as he jerks his sweats down, and murderous eyes meet mine. He's at my entrance when a knock sounds on the door.

"I have to piss," Trevor says from the other side.

Lance jerks away from me, his voice coated in arousal when he replies. "Use mine."

I straighten, heart hammering as he steps away, shutting me out.

"Go home." It's a new tone, one I've never heard from him, and I can't help the crack I feel in my foundation.

Singed, I open the door, steadying my voice. "I am home." His eyes are still on me when I shut the door. Seconds later, I hear the crack of drywall.

sixty

HARPER

I NEED TO TELL HIM. BUT I DON'T WANT THE TRUTH ABOUT what happened to be the reason we get back together. I want to tell him when we've mended our relationship to the point I feel I can open up. I don't want his pity or his guilt to be the reason he forgives me. It's a battle I fight daily. But he needs to hear it. He needs to know why I left. And it kills me that it may be the only way he lets me back in. And if so, will his perception of me change?

It's a risk I'm going to have to take. There's too much space, far too much space.

Heavy bass rings out through the pasture as I make my way from the house toward the barn. I can feel the weight in the air as screeching guitar riffs draw me in. I know what's just behind the door, but the sight of it is just as paralyzing when I open it, and Lance comes into view. Tool's "Sober" rings out as Lance's powerful fist connects with the bag. It draws me back to our beginning. He's no longer caged, the barbed wire at his biceps flexing with every powerful throw of his arms. He's liberated himself. The side of him he used to hide from me has taken front and center.

He's always prided himself on keeping his demons, his anger on a leash, but it seems like in the last few months, they've swallowed him whole. For the past day, I've watched him closely and weighed his words carefully. The thing about knowing someone so intimately and having them pull away is this, you have the power of perception few others will ever have. And with this knowledge, with every move he makes, I know this isn't the same version of the man I fell in love with two years or even two months ago, but his mirror. He's now living the perception of his reflection.

He's giving up the fight and letting it consume him, and we're all in the path of his implosion.

It's not going to go away overnight. This is depression. He's barely living. Mechanical. Easy to anger and quick to blow up. There's no solution. He might be living in his reality, but he's also drowning in it and has been for way too long. When I arrived in Texas, I thought the hard part of the battle would be convincing him I'm sincere, and it has been, but the real battle will be to show him his mirror.

I can't confess anything when he's in this state.

A full minute into the song and he's not winded in the least, his combos coming out at a machine gun pace. Body, body, uppercut. He's hungrier than he was when we met, more jaded, less willing to believe in the dream, in any dream.

Strong torso twisting with each step as he charges forward, his speed increases with the weight of his throws. Covered in a sheen of sweat, his body glistens like he's covered in kerosene as he catches fire. His bruises and scars just as visible to me as the first time I saw him, but they've multiplied.

The words of the song bleed in my ears and trickle down to fester in my chest as the bag jerks on the chain like a piñata. I'm certain he's never hit this hard in his career, in his life.

This is thunder, a warning.

"Jesus Christ," Tony mutters, appearing next to me at the door just as the song peaks and Lance cracks through the leather of the bag. It's then I see it, the awe and fear on Tony's face. Neither of us has ever met this side of Lance. Just as I'm about to speak up, Lance knocks the bag off the hook, and it lands with a thud clouding up the dust on the floor of the barn.

sixty-one

HARPER

THE CRUNCH OF GRAVEL ANNOUNCES A NEW ARRIVAL AS A FORD pickup pulls up next to the barn. A guy who looks around Lance's age and build jumps out. I'm in a folding lawn chair next to the ring and am the first to greet him.

"Hello."

"Hey there," he says with a smile, heading towards Tony. Lance barely glances up before resuming his strikes on the bag.

"Hey, man," Tony greets as the guy nods toward Lance.

"That him?"

"Yeah."

"This should be fun." The guy smiles, and it's then I realize just how good-looking he is. He pulls off a ball cap, revealing light blond hair and tugs off his hoodie, uncovering his ripped form. He's so hot, a nervous laugh erupts from me. All eyes shoot in my direction, including those of my ex-boyfriend.

"Sorry," I lift my phone. "René…" I trail off. Lance isn't buying it, and a grinning Tony isn't either. Rip makes the introductions. "Lance, this is Nick Regis—your sparring partner today."

Lance nods, slapping the side of the bag with his fist and making it jump. "'Sup. Thanks for coming out."

Rip starts taping Nick's hands as my eyes dart between the two. "No problem. Heard you're coming up quick."

"Working on it," Lance grunts out, tapping the bag twice more.

"Might want to save some of that for me."

I can't help my wicked mouth. "Oh, he's got stamina."

Lance bites his lips to hide a smile. I consider it a small miracle. We haven't spoken in a day, and though still aloof, we've worked alongside each other in a sort of silent truce, neither of us willing to give in. I'm still working out a way to bridge the gap since he's become untouchable.

"I didn't mean that as a compliment," I say dryly, turning to Nick. "He's full of hot air."

Lance rolls his eyes. "Ready when you are."

Trevor pulls up a few minutes later in his Dad's beat-up truck, hauling ass to Lance's corner. "Damn, I would have been pissed to miss this." He glances over at me and blows me a kiss. "Lady love."

I give him a wink. "Hiya, handsome."

Lance grumbles and places his mouthguard in. The barn goes eerily silent as Lance's background music dies down. "I'm on it," Trevor says as he and Lance exchange a look.

"No music," Tony says.

Lance shakes his head in protest.

"Tough shit," Tony retorts, "you don't get your crutch, and we're going all rounds today."

Lance looks surprised. "I've been at it half the day."

"That's the point. It's time to mix it up."

Nick steps inside the ring and looks around. "Nice setup, man."

"Thanks," Lance grunts, seeming unimpressed with the whole situation.

"That yours too?" He nods over to where I sit. I wait with bated breath as Lance's eyes roam over to me. My heart is beating in my throat. I know what answer I want him to give, what I desperately want to hear, but know he won't give it to me. In his heart right now, he doesn't believe it to be true. But it doesn't affect the sting of his answer.

"No."

"She's mine, actually," Trevor says easily.

Nick chuckles. "Sure, kid."

"You can suck this kid's nuts," Trevor quips.

"Easy, killer," Tony chuckles.

"Give me a few to warm up," Nick says, walking to his corner.

"Sure," Lance says, his eyes finding mine.

"Tony," I say, keeping my eyes locked with Lance. "Would you have a beer with me after dinner?"

"Sure."

"Nick, how about you? Would you like to join us? I looked up this bar down the road a few miles. I want to shoot some pool."

Nick eyes Tony and nods. "Sure."

"You're going to the Rust Hole?" Trevor says with a sour look on his face.

"Sorry, buddy," I say. "I've been working my ass off. I need to blow off steam."

Lance taps his gloves together, soaking in every word. I know I'm walking a dangerous line, but I can't help but fixate on his answer to Nick. I'm at my limit. I love him, and I know he loves me. But if he won't even admit to a stranger who I belong to, how in the hell will we ever get out of this mess together?

I'll stand my ground, but I can only stand so much punishment.

Air thick with tension, Tony orders at Rip to take Nick's corner while Trevor stays back with Lance. The guys face off in the center of the ring as Tony gives them a rundown. And with the ring of the imaginary bell, hell unleashes.

I'm on my feet as Lance throws a combination, dazing Nick on the ropes. Nick shakes back to in enough time to dodge what I'm sure would have been a knockout blow. Lance is wholly concentrated on the fight, channeling his fury into his fists as Nick rises to the challenge, landing one blow after another. Tony had told us at the kitchen table last night that Nick was going pro in a few months. Lance finally has a worthy sparring partner and in the last six rounds of boxing, he's proven himself, but I can see the fatigue growing in his steps, in his throws. Lance's stamina is obliterating his defense, every punch he throws wearing him down. It's a fair fight, but I can physically feel the air change when Jack steps into the barn ringside. Lance throws one combo after another, swiping Nick's headgear askew.

"Round," Tony yells as both men exhale, retreating to their corners. Nick's eye is swelling as Lance swishes and spits a mouthful of blood.

Trevor's whispers carry slightly as he encourages his brother. I'm on the edge of my senses, admittedly and ridiculously turned on at the display of testosterone. Both men are in insanely good physical condition, and I'm having a horrible time keeping my head in the fight, instead of in my overactive sexual imagination. I think of the first time Lance made me come, the intensity in his eyes, the way his lips felt, the feel of him on top of me. And later, when he pressed into me for the first time, the burn, the ache I felt for him after. The ache I feel now just watching him.

Does she belong to you?

No.

But I do. Head and heart, body and soul. I need him. He needs me, and I can't do anything but pray he comes to the same conclusion.

He's hurting me in a way he never has before with his denial. It's bitterness going down and numbing my heart. I would do anything to erase it. To drown the pain with the love I feel. I'm not giving up. But it appears, he isn't either.

Tony calls the next round as Lance's family and I watch him exhaust himself, throwing himself into the fight as if his life depends on it. Nick taps out at the end of the round, and Tony proudly declares Lance is ready.

He will reign the ring. That, I'm sure of.

And the only place I want to be when that happens, is by his side.

But on this day, he leaves the ring silent and alone.

sixty-two

LANCE

"Damn," Trevor says as Harper enters the living room from her bedroom.

"You look beautiful," Mom chimes in as I keep my head down. I'm set up at the kitchen table with Dad's books. I've got hours of this shit to work on before I can get some sleep. I don't bother looking up as Harper thanks them both, walking past me toward the kitchen while the scent of vanilla drifts to my nose. I won't even entertain this bullshit, this attempt to make me jealous.

"I'm going to grab some coffee to go if that's okay?" Harper asks from the kitchen.

"Sure, sweetie, I have a new travel mug in the cabinet. It says, 'Beautiful and Badass.'"

Harper laughs. "Don't mind if I do."

Out of my periphery, I see her struggle to reach the mug. Pushing away from the table, I walk into the kitchen and feel her freeze when she senses me behind her. I extend my arm above her, and she turns to face me and softly says, "Of course."

Unwilling to try and decipher whatever that means, I snatch the cup from the shelf, feeling her eyes on my profile.

"Please, look at me." I lower my gaze to hers and see her eyes brimming with tears. They're outlined in dark shadow, her lashes curled up, making her look painfully innocent. She looks beautiful in a light pink sweater and jeans. Her long hair flows over her shoulders. "I miss you. Please come with us."

"I've got shit to do." I hand her the mug and catch the slight wobble of her chin. I capture it between my fingers, trying my best to ignore the shimmer of her lips, the sting of her tears. "If this is too much to handle, I understand if you pass the bar and head on out."

"Please stop punishing me. I just want to go and have a good time."

"Then go."

"I'm not doing it to make you jealous."

"We aren't together."

"I belong to you."

"Stop," I snap. "I need to get back to work."

"Please come with us."

"No."

She slowly lifts before pressing a kiss to my jaw. "I love you."

"Have a good time, Harper."

"She's twenty-two," Mom pipes up when the front door closes. I look up from the books to see both of my parents' eyes on me.

"Drop it."

"You need to get your head out of your ass, son," Dad says. And that will be the only thing he says. He's not much with words, and we're alike that way.

"Lance," Mom says, drawing my attention to her. "She's still a baby. She's still sorting herself out."

"Drop it."

"Don't you talk to me like that, you little shit. You're still my kid, and you'll give me the respect I deserve."

"Sorry." I drop my eyes back to the books.

"She's been working her ass off for the last ten days trying to prove herself to you, to this family, and you just can't stop giving her hell."

"Mom, please just stay out of it."

"You need to give her some grace, room to grow."

"Mom!" I say, boiling over. "It's not your business."

Standing from the couch, fists at her sides, her eyes narrow in the scariest of ways. My mother does something she hasn't done in years. She...*moms* me.

"Lance Alexander Prescott, get your damned ass in that truck right now and go have a beer!" Laughter bursts from me as she walks over to the table and snatches the books up. "I've got this."

"Mom, stop, okay? I know you all love her, but it's just not going to work out."

"*You love her*, you fool. And you're throwing her love away, to what? Prove you don't need anyone? Bullshit. Get up! Get up! Now!"

"Fine," I huff, standing and making my way down the hall where she trails after me. I know my mother, she's long-winded when she's pissed, and it's apparent I'm in deep shit.

"I've had enough of this crap. You won't listen to anyone. You need to snap the hell out of it. You think parading around on a pedestal makes you the more mature adult? You think throwing judgment at me and your father for our past mistakes makes you a better decision-maker?"

I pull a hoodie on and gape at her. "I'm not judging you."

"Bullshit. The way you're talking to me," she points to the living room, "to the man who's given you everything," her voice wavers, and my heart cracks right down the middle. "We're your parents. Us. And Harper's heart isn't the only one you're breaking."

"Hey, Dad," Trevor calls from the front door. "Got you some of the ice cream you like."

My mother's eyes water as she steps up to me. "I've never been so proud in my life as I have of you boys in the last year, but no matter what happens, Lance, no matter what happens to this damned ranch, we have each other. And I won't lose you to this. So, keep it up, I'll sell this damned thing out from under you."

"What?" I can't believe what I'm hearing. Anger simmers low as she faces me head-on. "You heard right. Your father and I have been discussing it. We're thinking about selling."

"Why?"

"Because it's not worth losing our son!" She cries out hoarsely.

"What's going on?" Trevor enters the room and looks between the both of us.

"Tell him," I demand as my mother's tears fall. "Tell him what you just told me."

"Trevor, give your brother and I some privacy."

"No, tell him you're thinking about selling his birthright because his brother is fucking it all up!"

"That's not what I said."

"Is that true?" Trevor looks between us for answers, and I give a gruff nod. I can feel his heart breaking from feet away.

"Don't you dare, Mom," Trevor pleads with her. "We've been working day and night. Haven't we, Lance?" He looks to me helplessly, and I feel the failure down to the center of me.

"I won't let you lose yourself the way your father did," Mom whispers, her eyes on mine. "I won't let it drag you down anymore. You deserve the life you choose."

"I choose this life, over and over again," I swallow.

"Then don't let it eat you alive." She walks over to Trevor and grips his face. "Neither of you."

"I won't, Mom, I swear," Trevor assures her, his eyes spilling over. It's the look on his face that is eating me alive.

"Don't, Mom," I swallow again and again, "don't do it. Please, don't do it."

"Then prove to me you can handle it," she says between the both of us. "Without losing yourselves." She peers over at me with my eyes. "You always told me you didn't want to be *one thing*, right?"

I nod, feeling the rug being ripped out from under me, just another thing I can't control.

"Then don't be one thing." She leaves Trevor shaking in her wake, and I walk over to where he stands.

"Don't worry, I won't let it happen."

He wipes his face. "What are you doing? When's it going to be enough?"

"Dad—"

"You're my dad," he interrupts. "I lost him years ago. You had to take over, and I'm sorry for that," his voice cracks, and he shakes his head. "I can't lose you too."

"I'm not going anywhere."

"What the hell are you saying…you're halfway gone already."

He kicks at the edge of my dresser and scrubs his face. "I just went to get ice cream. What the fuck happened?"

Harper. Harper happened.

sixty-three

HARPER

Tossing back a shot with Tony, he grins over at me as I turn the glass over and set it next to the others. "I needed this."

"Me too."

I pinch the edge of the stick and take aim, the way Tony taught me. "Three ball, corner pocket."

"You're stripes this round."

"Crap."

I reposition, take a shot, and miss as Tony steps up for his turn.

Nick sits silently in the corner of the ripped pleather booth, next to where we shoot, his face swollen from rounds of Lance's brutal blows. My insides match his outsides, feeling just as battered. But I refuse to dwell on it tonight as I look around the decade's past-prime bar feeling the upbeat vibe before glancing over to Nick.

He's got an easy smile, but he's not much for words, much like his recent opponent. Though he has caught the eye of one of the women in the booth adjacent to us. They've been going back and forth with lingering looks for the last few songs. "Hey, you," I say to Nick, who draws his eyes from hers to look at me. I push two of the shots his way. "Take one over to her."

"Not a bad idea." He winks in thanks, and I giggle. Vodka does that to me.

Nick saunters away on the prowl while Tony nudges me that it's my turn.

"How are you doing?"

I scan the table and line up my stick. "Hanging in there."

"He's making it tough."

"I can handle it."

I look up to see he's calling my bluff with his expression.

"I can. I'm just having an off day."

"If you say so."

I miss another shot. "Is he really ready?"

"Yeah, absolutely. I've never seen anyone hit as hard as he does. He wants you to think being here isn't helping, but since you showed up, he's thrown himself back into it. I think knowing where you are is help enough."

"That's so barbaric."

"True." He clasps his hands around the top of his stick, planning his next shot. "But think about it this way, how would you feel trapped in a corner of the world where nothing existed but your job, your two very hard jobs, knowing the girl you want is living this great life without you, and possibly with someone else? I call that fucking torture."

I scrub my face, forgetting my makeup. "I just want to be with him."

"He just wants it to be real." He takes a shot and sinks it before his eyes lift to mine.

"I'm all in. He's not just my first, he's my *only*. And it's terrifying because I'm not sure what I'll do if he won't let me love him anymore."

"You've only been here a little over a week. He's still thawing."

"You saw him in the barn the other day. He's doing anything but."

Tony sighs and lifts his beer from the tall cocktail table we've congregated around. "I need to tell you something."

This has me pausing, and I lift my eyes to his. He gestures toward the seat, and I take it. I look up puzzled by his expression when he speaks. "I'm trusting you with this, which may end Lance and me if he ever finds out."

"Okay, you're scaring me."

Tony blows out a breath. "He's scaring me."

I grip his forearm. "Tell me."

He looks me over carefully and shakes his head. "Fuck it. Three months ago, Lance found Jack alone with one of his hunting rifles."

It takes me the length of a second to realize what he's saying, and suddenly, there is no air in the pool hall. My whole body cringes as I try to grasp the idea of what that was like for Lance.

"I don't know if he was really going to do it, but I know there were shells scattered around him."

"Jesus, Tony."

"Jeannie and Trevor don't know, and the only reason I do is because I happened upon them at the right time. Lance has slowly come unglued since."

Reeling, I try to reason with it. "Not Jack. He wouldn't, he couldn't do that to Jeannie, to his boys."

"He wasn't in his right mind. Even so, I really don't think he could have gone through with it, but then again, I don't have a disease taking over my body and ruining my brain."

"Oh my God, Tony. What if he had—"

"Damn, he's here," Tony whispers before his pleading eyes meet mine.

I try and give him as much reassurance as I can. "You have my word, Tony, I swear it."

I turn in time to feign a smile for Lance. "You came."

He's not planning on staying, that much is clear when Tony lifts a fresh beer in his direction. "One won't kill you."

Lance jerks his head before he eyes me, his voice clipped. "We need to talk."

I look back to Tony, and he grabs my stick and lays it on the table. "Go on, I'll tab us out."

"Okay."

Tony makes his way toward the bar as I look back over to Lance. I physically feel his flinch when his name is called from across the bar.

"Prescott, that you?" I hear a guy call out from a booth across the way. He stands, and that's when I see the brunette at his side, her eyes trained on Lance like she can't tear them away.

Channah.

On instinct, I know she still wants him. It's written all over her face. I wonder if the same desperation laces mine. Fighting the sting of jealousy, my stomach drops as the man draws near, a sinister grin on his face.

"Thought that was you," he says, sidling up to Lance. I can feel the air thicken around us as Channah pulls at his arm.

"Mark, you promised."

"And who do we have here?" he says, ignoring her and looking me over.

"Mark," Channah begs, "Please don't."

"Don't what?" His eyes cut back to her as she pulls at his bicep. He's attractive, but dressed business casual, and looks out of place in the bar. "Just making friendly conversation." He shrugs. "Haven't seen this guy around lately, have we?"

Her eyes dart away, a sure sign of guilt. I feel like I just walked into a wall as I realize my assumption was right.

"Gotta pay our respects to our hometown hero, our football star, don't we? Oh, that's right," he clamps a hand on Lance's shoulder, "you didn't get drafted. Damned shame, probably why you're back home crying in your beer."

"We're leaving," Lance says, grabbing my arm possessively. I glance back over my shoulder to look at Channah, whose eyes are trailing Lance. Following him out of the bar, I study him. His face is impassive.

"You want to tell me what that was about?"

"It's history."

"Yeah, well, history has a way of repeating itself, doesn't it?"

"Not this time." He turns to face me once we've cornered the bar, his eyes granite. "Harper, leave. I'm not asking anymore. I'm telling."

He might as well have slapped me. "What?"

"We're done. I don't want you here. You've already cost me too much. I'm done with this. Us. *Leave.*"

I feel like I'm having an out of body experience. He can't be saying these words to me. And meaning them.

"You really want that?" If I thought he was impenetrable before, it's nothing compared to the arctic indifference he's showing now. It's as if I'm some groupie gnat he can't seem to bat away.

"My mother's going to sell the ranch if I don't get my shit together, and I don't have time to play patty cake with you anymore." Heat climbs up my neck as I try to grapple with the weight of his words.

"I'm going back inside."

He grips my wrist to stop me. "I mean it, Harper." I cut my eyes to his.

"Enough. You're scared. You're afraid things won't pan out

this time. You're terrified of what's around the corner, and I can understand this more than you will ever know. You're afraid I'll hurt you again. Well I'm fucking scared too, but Lance, this is just life trying to put us at odds again. These are our circumstances now. Not forever. We can deal with this together. If you would just let me in."

"You aren't what I need."

"That's a lie. Jesus, and if she's threatening to sell the ranch, it's because you've turned into a raging dick void of personality. You don't get to pin this on me. This is your fear talking. I'm not going anywhere. I'm not here to hurt you."

"I don't want you anymore!" His voice booms, humiliating me, and I flinch on impact. I barely recognize my own voice when I counter.

"That's a lie. I'm not going anywhere. You're acting a fool."

"I don't want you here."

"Lie."

"I'm going to hate you if you stay much longer."

"Lie. Lance, there's something I need to tell you if you would just—"

"Prescott, I'm not fucking done with you," Mark rounds the corner of the bar as Channah continues to plead with him.

Lance turns to me without hesitation.

"Go, get in the truck."

I don't move.

"Got to say," Mark drawls, his eyes on me. "I would love to settle the score, but it looks like slim pickings. My, my, how your standards have changed."

In an instant, Mark is pinned to the brick of the building, his smile growing wider at the reaction he's drawing from Lance. It doesn't take much to recognize this is an ongoing war waged long ago. Point only proven when Mark spews more venom. "Still the same inbred fucking piece of shit you always were."

I stare at Lance, shocked by his silence.

His eyes scream murder, but his lips remained sealed. And that's when my stomach drops. "Your whole family is shit," Mark spouts as Lance releases him and turns to me.

"Get in the truck, Harper."

"He's been drinking all day," Channah attempts to excuse, pulling at his arm. Mark grins over to me, and I can feel the coil in Lance's posture as he keeps his own gaze zeroed on me. "This guy wore my hand-me-downs for years. My mother gave him my old clothes. I guess it's only natural that he tries to second hand my fucking girl." Lance grimaces, but not at the insult, at *my* reaction.

"Had to fuck her, huh?" Mark says, taking a menacing step forward.

All the blood leaves my face. Channah looks over to me, and I can feel her confusion, see the question in her eyes. It's the same damned question every woman's piqued gaze asks. *What's he doing with you?*

"Had to fuck her to show me. You sure showed me, didn't you? But what exactly did you prove? Didn't get drafted, your ranch is in shambles, you're bankrupt. You aren't going any-where, Prescott, and so you just couldn't keep your filthy hands to yourself."

"Mark!" Channah begs, tugging at the sleeve of his shirt while trying to drag him back.

Lance remains mute, his eyes trained on me. Blinding anger shines through, but it's mixed with fear. It's then I see everything he's been hiding.

I saw all the signs, I recognized them because I've lived them for years.

I close my eyes as the shock wave runs through me.

Not Lance. Anyone but Lance.

Introvert. Mute. No social media. Tight inner circle.

He's been dealing with this his whole life, and he didn't want me to know.

A part of me dies inside as it dawns on me why. Mark isn't Lance's nemesis, but his bully.

Reeling, I grab his bicep and squeeze. "Let's go."

Eyes forward, Lance stalks toward his truck, and I follow. So does Mark, who easily discards Channah with the jerk of his arm.

"You're a shitshow, always have been. Won't ever amount to nothing."

Silence. Unbearable silence is Lance's answer and it rips me apart.

This is not the confident man I met, this is his shadow, a shadow he's been fighting for years. In a sickening second, it occurs to me he might actually believe the hateful words being spewed at him.

"And your girl is fucking ugly."

Lance turns on a dime and spits on the ground just as Mark takes a swing, and Lance leans into it, begging for the contact, for the greenlight. He counters with his right landing squarely on Mark's jaw, taking him down with one blow.

Channah screams just as Lance charges to get to him, where he lays sprawled on the ground. In the next second, Tony has Lance in his hold, pulling him back. "I'm going to fucking end you," Lance explodes, fighting Tony's grasp to get to him.

"Your goddamn fists are deadly weapons!" Tony roars as he hooks Lance around the chest and manages to get him in a lock barely a foot away.

And then he's in his face, Lance's deadly stare fixed on Mark where he sits on the ground dazed as Tony commands his attention. "You fight him, and it's all over! Everything we've worked for, over. Wake the fuck up!"

Channah looks over to me, face ashen as she kneels in front of Mark. "I'm so sorry. I'm so sorry." She hoists Mark up, and he sways to his feet before Channah wraps an arm around him. He spits out a mouthful of blood, his satisfaction with the spectacle he created unmistakable. "You're still a fucking loser Prescott, always will be."

Tony doesn't budge in his hold on Lance, his back ramrod straight, his voice laced with venom as he addresses Mark. "You better get the fuck out of here, man. I assure you, you don't want what you're asking for."

"Stay the fuck away from her," Mark warns, which would be comical since he can barely stand from the weight of Lance's blow, but it's anything but. "You were just a means to an end," Mark spits again, lifting Channah's hand to showcase the obnoxious rock floating on top of it.

"I'm coming for him next, if you don't get him out of here," Tony barks out to Channah, who wastes no time walking him back toward the bar while he continues to mouth off.

Tony steps up to Lance, who's seething. "If you're going to throw everything away for that piece of shit, then you're wasting both our fucking time. Last warning, Lance, wake the fuck up! Or I'm out."

"Take her home," Lance grits out, his breaths coming fast.

Tony sweeps his hand out, clear accusation in his eyes. "After you."

Crippled by the last few seconds, I stand by helplessly as Lance clenches his fists, his eyes roaming with lividity from Mark's retreating back to Tony.

"You go after him, your life is over," Tony says in desperate warning.

Lance's gaze finally drifts to mine, and in his eyes, I see the bite of humiliation. I know that look. I've felt what he's feeling a hundred times over. Heart clawing its way out of my chest, I move toward Lance just as he lashes out.

"You fucking happy? Did you see what you wanted to see? Did you get what you wanted?"

"Lance—"

"It's a damned shame you had to see what you bought into, isn't it?"

I shake my head. "I don't believe that. Not any of it."

"Yeah, well, you should. Who's the fool now?"

"D-don't say anything else. Please."

He levels me with his cold, dead stare. "You aren't wanted here. Leave!"

And that's when the levee breaks, and rage overtakes me.

"I hate you," the words are guttural, stemming from a hurt I've never experienced. It burns like acid, my skin recoiling as bile climbs my throat.

"Good, take care, Harper."

All at once, I'm broken, sick with grief. This final blow he delivered with precision, and I feel the betrayal to my core.

He moves towards his truck when I charge and begin to pound on his back. "You didn't have to come back to New York! Why? Why did you do this to me?"

He takes my blows, his steps sure as if he's not stomping on the remnants of what I believed about us.

He's not this man, he can't be this man.

Lance shrugs me off effortlessly, pulling his keys from his pocket. "Get her home."

"You bastard," I cry as Tony wraps around me, tugging me away. Sobbing uncontrollably, I let the anger win, and the flood-gates open. "Lance!" I scream at his retreating back. Something in my voice has him pausing to turn and look at me. "You're becoming what you hate!"

Physically, I see him flinch at the truth. "And you win," I choke out. "I made a mistake. I should have never left Texas! I should have never left you! I didn't want to! I didn't want to leave! I had to!"

"What are you talking about?"

"This is what you wanted, right? Well, I'm admitting it." An eerie calm overtakes me, and I go limp in Tony's hold before he lets me go. My boots crunch on the gravel beneath my feet before I stop to face him head-on, lifting enraged eyes to his. "I had to leave. They ran me out. They terrorized my sister, my family, me, that's how my dad found out about us, he was worried about your motives. I was fourteen all over again. But the breaking point was when they assaulted me at the Amhurst game."

Lance visibly sways, as if struck, while Tony swears behind me. "Jesus Christ."

"If I hadn't left, you would have fought them all. I came here to commit to you. I love you, Lance. You. Fucking. *Idiot.* But being with you made me a *target.* I fought them then as hard as I could, and I was willing to fight them now to be with you… but now…God," I sob out, "I hate you."

His voice is barely a whisper. "They—"

"They—as in your teammates and their girlfriends—they came after me, blaming me for their losing season, or maybe it was just for sport. If Troy—"

"Troy knew?"

"Don't. I begged him not to tell you. And if he wouldn't have stopped it that day, it would have been a whole lot worse. You were worth it, *then*," I shake my head in disbelief. "I don't know you anymore."

"Harper," he whispers hoarsely, searching my eyes. "They *hurt* you?"

"Jesus, Lance, despite what you think, you're one of very few who think I'm beautiful. Your teammates didn't share the same opinion. Did you not hear that man just call me ugly? Maybe you recognized a part of yourself when you looked at me the first time, or maybe you just loved me too much to see it. But that made you worth it."

He stands stunned as I wipe my face free of years of humiliation.

Unable to deny it anymore, I admit my truth. "I didn't want you to be ashamed or be in the position to defend me. You would have blown your shot. And when you came to New York, I got scared. I got so scared that when you again get caught in the spotlight, I will be too. Being with you would, without a doubt, hurt me."

He stares at me, jaw slack, absorbing the truth.

Body trembling, I fight to get the words out. Words that are too late, words that are the crux of us. His words from years ago. "You see, my love, it's a cruel world without you in it."

His face falls as I lift, so my truth hits his lips. "My leaving had little to do with dancing, despite what I promised myself. I wanted your love so much more than the look on your face right now. But what you just did to me…" I lift my chin in defiance, showing him his mirror, "makes *you* the bully." All the fight leaves me as I utter my defeat, "no longer worthy of this *ugly girl's* love."

For the first time in my life, my legs fail me as Tony sweeps me into his arms and drives me back to the ranch.

sixty-four

LANCE

"Lance, man, it's late."

"What the hell happened to Harper?"

"She finally told you?"

"I was halfway to the highway when I realized I had no idea who I was going to murder."

"You're talking crazy."

I uncap my bottle. "I'm feeling a little crazy, *brother*."

"I'm not telling you shit until you can handle it. But I'm glad she told you."

"Why didn't you?" I grit out. "You're supposed to be my friend."

I drain some of the whiskey sitting in my truck parked behind her rental. I refuse to let her go, though she hasn't walked out of the house since Tony brought her in. I'm lucky she had too much to drink or else she'd be long gone.

"I'm sorry, man, she begged me."

"Motherfucker!" I slam my fist into the dash.

"Lance, you have to calm down. I know it's the last thing you want to hear, but going off the rails isn't the solution."

"Tell me what happened."

"You going to chill?"

"I'm not going anywhere tonight. I make no promises for tomorrow."

Troy sighs over the line. "I get it. I really do. Let me change the baby and get her a bottle. Hold up. I have to set my phone down."

Troy's voice sounds up again a second later. "Hey, baby girl. You hungry?"

I hear the answering coo of his daughter. She's desperately trying to discuss it with him. I can hear the kiss he gives her before the rip of a diaper.

"Look at Daddy's baby. Look at you. You're a hot mess," he coos back. "Stinky too, but I'll forgive you because you're so damned pretty." She's wide open now, her wordless conversation coming out in breaths and grunts. I can picture her, fists raised and flying, helpless and utterly dependent on him. My emotions shift as I listen to their exchange, and I do my best to steady myself for what I'm about to hear. A few minutes later, he's back on the line.

"Hey, man, you still there?"

"Pretty manipulative using your kid like that."

"I have no idea what you're talking about."

"Tell me what happened, Jenner."

He lets out a long breath. "It was in the parking lot, after the game. She told me she was on her way to wait for you."

I sip the bottle, my vision blurring in a mix of pain and rage. "They threw a full soda can at her head at the end of the fourth and split it. She was on her way to get help when they pinned her to her Toyota in the parking lot. That's when I walked out."

It's everything I can do to keep from ripping the cab of my truck apart.

"It was Yates and his crew. He was threatening her. Telling her, it was her fault and that she had fucked up a whole football season because she couldn't keep her legs closed. I lost it."

"Jesus Christ," I rub my temple.

"I went to the ER with her as she was stitched up and…"

"Don't hold out on me, man."

"There was a lot of blood. She was hysterical. She refused to report it. She knew you would blow a gasket." I think back to that night. I remember her making an excuse for not picking me up after a game. It was nearly a month before we broke up. She'd been hiding it that long?

"I'm so sorry, man. It was fucking horrible to witness. I damn near killed Yates, but it wasn't just him. They came at her from all sides."

"Why? Why didn't you tell me? I could have protected her."

"No, you couldn't, and she was protecting you. Tell me she's there. That you're working things out?"

"I don't think that's happening, man." I'm seconds from exploding but have no outlet. I've damaged everything. My relationship with my parents is strained, Trevor thinks I'm off my rocker. Even Tony is fed up. And Harper, the love of my fucking life, is disgusted by me. I've ruined myself. I've ruined damn near everything good about my life.

"I've done some pretty fucked up things to Clarissa. She forgave me. Don't give up."

"I don't know if she's capable of loving me the same."

"You'd be surprised. But trust me when I say, I got him, and I got him good. I didn't want you to blow your chance at the draft, either."

"Yeah. A lot of good it did."

"Big oversight on their part. You know how I feel about that. But you're where you belong now. I believe that, and you do too. She was right about you, and you were about her. Lance, she's one of the good ones."

My eyes burn as I try to put myself in her shoes. "All this time, she never told me."

"Would you want to admit it?"

No. And I didn't. For years I've kept my own shit to myself. And the fact that tonight she saw what I dealt with growing up was humiliating.

"Do you think…" I swallow because it shouldn't matter, but the words feel like acid coming off my tongue, "she's ugly?"

"My opinion never mattered to you before. And that's what she didn't want to open your eyes to. Honestly, she's not *conventionally* beautiful, but no, I don't think she's ugly at all."

"She believes she is," I say, heart obliterated. "I think she's fucking perfect."

"That's all that matters. You think I give a shit if you think my wife is pretty?"

"Troy, how…*how* could they hurt her?"

It's then I see the livid eyes and hear the voice of Ryan Elliot years ago in my driveway.

"She's not like other girls. She won't recover if you rip her heart out. She's been through a lot, and you're subjecting her to a lot more."

He thought I knew. He thought I knew they were hurting her.

"People are fucked up, man. It's not because of the way she looks, it's because of the way she looks next to *you*."

I choke on my emotion, and he hears it.

"Hey, you know I've got some time off. I can come down."

"Fuck, Troy, what am I going to do?"

"Love her. That's all she wants."

"That's not a problem." I'm breaking apart, piece by piece, as I stare at her window.

"Look," he says on an exhale, "you were there for me when I needed you, and I'm trying to do the same. I'm just asking you to think, okay? Think. Absolutely nothing good can happen from you going after them now. Get some sleep, man. You'll get her back tomorrow."

"Damn," I run a hand down my face. "Jesus, I'm so fucked."

"You're not, it just looks bleak. She's your reason to fight, always."

It's then I crack wide open. Because it's the truth. It's the absolute truth.

"I gotta go."

sixty-five

HARPER

"*YOUR GIRL IS FUCKING UGLY.*"

He didn't even hear it. Well, he did, that's what drew his violent reaction, but he didn't acknowledge it. The words didn't resonate because he doesn't believe it. He's never believed it. He's blind to the scrutiny. If I'm honest with myself, it's one of the things I love so much about him. It's the only thing that leads me to believe some part of the man I fell for still dwells inside him, but it's not enough. Not anymore.

Painfully sober, I creep down the hallway, my bag in hand, and push the note to Trevor under his door. It's going to be impossible to forget this family I've fallen so comfortably in love with. It's only been ten days, but I feel every bit a part of it. I can't face his parents. I assured Jeannie I wouldn't hurt him, and there's a chance I won't with my leaving. He's become a stone too hard to penetrate.

I don't want you anymore!

Who's the fool?

Yeah, I'm out.

To hell with love. It's been no picnic. I need my flats and a clear dance floor. I need a martini that doesn't taste like dish soap. I need to be able to order Chinese at three a.m. I've been delusional, this isn't home. Home is New York. My future is there, and I'll resume it there.

One agonizing step at a time.

I creep out of the front door, hearing the creek and wince, hoping I can get out undetected. Outside, I make my way to the rental car. I'm at the driver's door when I realize there's less than an inch between my bumper and Lance's truck. I'm trapped. His headlights click on just before his door opens, taking me by surprise. I drop my suitcase, pissed by the ambush.

"Let me out. Right now."

"Just let me talk to you." His voice is jagged glass. It's guilt or sympathy or both, and I want no part of it.

"Just getting home? I guess I shouldn't be surprised. Don't worry, message received."

"Priss—"

"Don't. You. Fucking. Dare. You haven't called me that since the day I set foot on this ranch."

"I'm sorry."

"I *don't* care. Move your truck."

"Please hear me out."

I slam my handle into my suitcase and click the fob to unlock the car. "This relationship has turned toxic. I'm no expert, but I think it's safe to assume we can't come back from this. And you seemed to have moved on anyway."

"It was a year after our split. I haven't touched her or another woman since New York. Haven't wanted to since you. I don't give a damn about her."

"Well, she's clearly still in love with you," I say, tossing my case in the back seat and slamming the door. He steps forward, caging me to my driver's door, and I refuse to look up. I can't because I know it will take all my strength away.

"And I'm in love with you. You're the only woman I have ever loved."

He inches forward, and I jerk my chin.

"Doesn't matter anymore. Just move your truck."

"No."

"Fine, I'll wake Trevor and get him to do it."

"Don't go." It's the plea in his voice that brings my eyes to his.

"Lance, I can never forget what you said to me."

"I won't expect you to, but you gave me no reason to believe…you made me think we had no future. Will you just tell me…why, why didn't you tell me?"

"You know I couldn't. Move your truck. I know we're shit at communication these days, but it's clear now, what we were—we aren't anymore."

"If that were true, you would still be in New York."

"Well, we've gotten good at making things bad, haven't we?"

Lance lifts his hands and cradles the back of my head, his fingers searching until he finds the scar.

I jerk away from his touch. "I see you spoke to Troy."

"Harper," my name cracks across his lips, "I'm so fucking sorry. If I would have known…"

I turn away from him and open the driver's door, and he shuts it in the next second.

"Don't leave." He hangs his head on my shoulder, his heart beating wildly at my back, his scent engulfing me as angry tears emerge.

"We can't work now. I'm not what you need." He pulls at my arm, so I'm facing him and desperately tries to wipe my tears with his fingers. I jerk away from him. "Don't touch me."

"Don't say that. Fuck. Please don't ever say that to me again. I fucked up. Jesus, I fucked up."

"I can't watch you destroy yourself anymore."

"It ends now. I swear. I'll make it up to you. I'm still in here somewhere. I'm still the man you fell in love with." He places his hands on his chest. "I'll do anything, I'll be anyone, Harper, don't leave."

"I can't help you. You won't let me. I need to save myself before you ruin me for good."

"I won't."

"You just did. God, you bastard," I sniff, wiping my nose with my sleeve, *"you already did."*

Hot tears run down my cheeks as I try to steady myself. "You know, no matter how ugly it got, I was never afraid of you. Never, until tonight. And now I know what you're capable of doing to me." I cup my chest. "I can't take it, okay? I just can't. I'm not a worthy opponent, not at all. We agree on that."

"Not true." He rakes a hand through his hair, and I see freshly dried blood on his knuckles and know it has nothing to do with his fight with Mark. "This is the worst I can do. Harper, I swear it."

"Move your truck." He tilts my chin, and I rip it away from his grip. "Let me go."

"Never. Never again. *Fucking ever.*"

"You've been humiliating me since I set foot here, dead set on pushing me away. Mission accomplished."

I turn and open the door, and he closes it again.

"Don't…" he chokes out. His chest at my back as he closes in, pressing me to the door, his arms capturing my lower half. I exhale as he wraps himself around me. Silence lingers, and then I hear the hitch of his breath. "Jesus…don't go…I fucking… I n-need you."

He's beautifully broken, the floodgates opening as he cries out his apology. "I don't deserve you," he weeps against me.

"Lance—"

"I c-can't do this without you, Harper. I'm just so fucked up. I've been a slave to money my whole goddamned life. It's ruining me. The lack of it is ruining my family. Dad, I f-found him..." his chest bounces against my back, and it's all I can do to keep standing. "I found him with a g-gun. He...if he gives up." The lift of his voice followed by the agonizing sob that leaves him is too much to bear, and I grip his hands feeling every second of it with him. "I don't...I can't keep fighting if I can't see the end. This is the worst I can do."

He crushes me to him. "It wasn't true. P-please don't believe the lie. I w-want to marry you. I want to grow old laughing with you, Harper. I've never loved anyone so much in my life. No one can love me like you do. No woman could or will ever be you. That's why I went to New York. God...I-I-I just never wanted you to see me like this." He buries himself in the back of my neck, his tears soaking me, my heart. "Your opinion is the only one that has ever fucking mattered to me. P-please. Don't, d-don't leave." He beats on the top of my rental. "I don't have the words! I still don't have the fucking words! Tell me what they are. P-please, tell me what they are."

Defeated for the second time tonight, I turn in his arms and pull him to me before we slide down the side of my car. He's still wrapped around me, and I lay drenched in his confessions, my mind reeling. "You just said them, Lance. You just said them."

I pull him tighter to me, and he clings to me for life where I am his anchor, his face buried in my neck, his own body shaking with release.

"I'm so fucking tired," he croaks, breaking me further along with him as I try to steady myself. He's hitting rock bottom, and I'm relieved it's happening. It was always going to happen. It was just a matter of when.

"I'm spiraling," he whispers hoarsely, "And I can't seem to come out of it. I'm so sorry. Please don't stop loving me back."

"I'm so mad at you," I sob, thrusting my fingers in his hair and tugging at it until bloodshot eyes meet mine. We're both hemorrhaging, the pain of the past eating us alive, our need for the other undeniable. And I won't. I refuse to deny that a large part of my happiness is in his hands. And I gave it all to him. All of it, because he is worthy, even if he isn't acting like it.

Nothing else matters but putting our pieces back together. Not my hurt tonight or those of the past.

He lashed out in anger, and I felt it. But I fell for a man with a horrible temper, and I knew someday I'd have to face his demons with him.

It stung worse than anything I've ever felt. But the hardest part of a fight is staying when it's over, no matter the outcome. The sweep up of the aftermath, and then finding the will to fight again. He is my will, and I am his. This is where I show up if I want to prove it. I run my fingers through the dark locks on his forehead.

"I'm so fucking tired, baby. I'm so…*tired.*"

"It's okay, Lance. Breathe. Just breathe."

"I can't fight anymore."

"Then tonight you put the gloves down," I say, covering him in my touch. "Tonight, all you have to be is Lance." I run my fingers through his hair. "Not Tony's fighter, and not Jack's son. Lance. That's who I came for. That's all you'll ever have to be for me."

The guttural sounds coming from him tear me apart. "Breathe, baby." I run my hands along his back, up his neck, tracing his beard and stroking his hair before I speak.

"When I was fifteen, this is just months after that crap went down, I was still struggling to get through every day as if nothing had happened. I had this dance instructor, Ms. Fennan, who was a saint compared to most others. She didn't drill us as hard, but it didn't matter, I was pushing harder than I ever had," his breath hitches as I continue to stroke his hair in a long sweep, "I was struggling because I was trying to do too much to make up for what happened. When she realized how hard I was pushing myself, she put a stop to it. She took the time to slow me down."

I lean down and press a kiss to his temple, and he grips me tighter. "She told me, 'Harper, you aren't going to get everywhere at once. You need to stop living for the what ifs and start living in the what is, one breath, one step at a time.' And that stuck with me. It changed me. It *slowed* me. And in a way it saved me. If it hadn't, you wouldn't have met the version of me that you did." I continue to soothe him with my hands, my fingers, as he molds us together. "I would have been a distorted version of me, and no doubt a lot less healthy. She saved me that day, I think. And I've lost sight of that again recently. But that's all over," I stroke his arms tracing his hands. "But it's a good plan, Lance. So that's how we're going to do this. We, both of us, *together*, are going to stop living for the what ifs and start living for the what is, one breath and one step at a time. That's how we're going to do this."

Slowly he raises his head, lifting his eyes to mine, the look in them something resembling hope. "So, marry me, Lance, grow old and laugh with me and don't ever, *ever*, hurt me like that again."

Relief covers him as another of his tears fall and another, and my heart breaks at the sight of each one.

"I fucking love you," he croaks, "so much."

"It's a good thing you made that clear back in New York."

"Harper," he cups my face, his thumbs brushing my cheeks. I feel so much love in his grip as he searches my eyes,

"Don't believe them. Please don't believe them. They're fucking blind."

I shake my head. "I don't believe them, not anymore. That's why I'm here. Because I believe *you*."

He leans in and takes my lips in a kiss that says it all.

Mine.

I am his. I'll always be his. Since the day I met him, he boxed his way into my heart, my champion, my fighter, my nemesis, my undoing, my everything.

"I love you," he murmurs again, and again, pressing gentle kisses to my mouth as he opens himself fully and lets me back in. Heart stuttering, I cling to him, knowing that from this moment forward, all my steps will always lead back to him. This isn't commitment. This is forever.

His kiss goes from sweet to feverish before he dips to suck the skin at my throat. I'm on fire when he lifts me into his arms. It's freezing, and his cold nose nudges mine as he dips to kiss me again. I return his fevered kiss, heart alight, future both mapped and unpaved. I'll do anything to keep his love and have him this way.

He walks me toward his truck, his lips descending over and over with his kisses. "Where are we going?

He sets me on my feet and hands me his keys. "Away. Get in the truck, I'll be right back."

"Okay." Instead of leaving me, he presses me against his truck door and kisses me again, the sweep of his tongue lifting me until I'm floating above ground. When he pulls away, he whispers, "I'm such a fucking idiot."

"You'll get no argument there. Then again, don't talk about my man that way."

"Yours," he pledges earnestly. "I swear to you."

He makes quick work of going inside the house and comes back with an armful of blankets and two water bottles.

"Where are we going?"

"Just drive out to pasture."

"K," I kill the headlights and circle the house, and he grips my hand and brings it to his mouth, kissing it feverishly while repeating, "I'm so sorry."

The instant I park, I'm in his arms, his mouth crushing mine in a kiss that sweeps me back into a time where things were a lot less complicated. Every thrust of his tongue a beckoning to remember, and I do. I answer because when hard times happen in the future, it will be moments like this that keep us together. The truth is, there's rarely a right time for everything at once, and very few moments in life where you get a cue to take important leaps. This is what I've learned loving Lance Prescott.

He kisses me for endless minutes, our hearts syncing as the hurt slowly dissipates, he strokes my scar with his thumb, cradling my head while he possesses my mouth. And then he's touching me, my limbs growing heavy as he strokes me with calloused hands, the lust in his voice causing goosebumps to erupt over my skin. He lays me on the seat, lifting my sweater and caressing the swell of my breasts with his palm.

"Naked," he murmurs, the heat coming from the vent the only sound in the cab. I unfasten my jeans, and he helps me pull them off along with my panties. "I wanted to take my time, but it's going to have to wait. I need to taste this pussy," he slips a finger inside me and I damn near combust. And as if I weigh nothing, he lifts me to meet his mouth and dives. I gasp at the contact, my hips bucking as he licks me furiously, his head moving back and forth along with his tongue in a maddening pace. Thighs shaking, I'm close to coming when he lifts his head, his eyes boring into mine, the cab light illuminating his features, "I've imagined coming down the hall to you a thousand times or more," he dips down and licks me from center to top before roughly sucking my clit. I explode on his tongue as he milks me.

"Lance!"

"Fuck, yes, baby, I've missed that so much," he murmurs as I cover him in my kiss, unbuckling his jeans on my knees as he slides a warm palm down and massages my ass, pushing my hair out of the way so he can watch me take him in. The act so intimate, I feel it down to my toes.

"Damn," he grunts, his hands covering me in a caress. I lick and suck, pumping with my hand as his fingers slip inside me. He presses them in and out, the sound of my arousal spurring him on as I fully fit him into my mouth. I bob on his rock-hard cock, loving the power the position wields me as his fingers quicken, and his breaths come faster.

"Fuck, Harper."

"Exactly," I whisper, flicking my tongue out over his crown. "Fuck me, right now."

"Jesus." He grips me by the arms and pulls me into his lap. I lift as he lines himself at my entrance before I ease down on his cock just as he thrusts up. I lose my breath as he fills me to the brink, and we both call out to the other. It's fucking perfect, better than perfect, it's surreal.

His jaw goes slack, and I feel the whoosh of his breath.

"Move, oh, my God, Lance, just move." It's sensory overload as he thrusts up slowly and I detonate, I'm already coming by the time he drives up again.

He watches me convulse, one hand guiding my hip as I ride it out and the other tangled in my hair. We gaze at the other without breaking as he builds his rhythm.

"Harper," he groans, "I don't have a condom on."

"Those days are over. Come inside me."

"Baby," he stills my movement, cupping my face and taking over, his thrusts achingly slow, I feel every inch of him. "I've never felt so close to anyone, have you?"

I shake my head. "Never."

He brushes a finger over my lips as he pulses inside of me. "I love you, Harper, over everyfuckingthing."

sixty-six

LANCE

I T'S BEEN ONE OF THE WORST NIGHTS OF MY LIFE, BUT THE aftermath has been pure bliss. After the first time I took her, we loaded up in the back of my truck bed, where I both fucked and made love to her until it got so cold, we had to retreat back into the cab. From there and for the first time in an eternity, I looked up at the stars and was happy I felt so damn small.

Now, even with the sun fully up, we've refused to burst our bubble though Harper insisted we dress. From the time on my dash, I know Trevor left for school an hour ago, and since then, I know Tony's been up and looking for me. He'll have to search twenty acres to find me. It won't be that hard, but I assume the fact that we've both disappeared will be enough to stave him off.

"I love you," I murmur, running my fingers through her hair and along her scar as she looks up at me from where her head lies on my lap. I can't stop touching it, knowing she needed me and I wasn't there. Over the course of the night, she told me the horrors she went through and I can't imagine what I would do. It was hard to hear, but at the same time, I finally got to release the resentment I've felt over the years. "I'm so sorry."

"I know, Lance. I know."

The sun beams into the truck, and I wince.

"Hungover?"

"Little bit. Not too bad."

I stroke her temple with my thumb.

"Lance?"

"Yeah, baby?"

"Why didn't you fight for yourself?"

"What?"

"You didn't do anything until Mark insulted me. Why didn't you defend yourself?"

"You know I'm shit with words, at least I was back when it started. So, I figured it out early. If I don't acknowledge it, they start the fight."

"So you can lash out?"

"I know that's wrong, but that's how I fight back. Well, that reason, and you can't teach an idiot what to think about you."

"How long…" she swallows, reaching up to cup my jaw.

"Since I was eight. When it happens, I lock up. And then get physical when I reach my breaking point."

"I'm so sorry."

"Don't be. It made me."

"I freaking hate that."

"It's fine. I don't lose sleep over it."

"Is he the one you put in the hospital?"

"Yeah. You would think he would learn."

"Was it over her?"

"No. He messed with Trevor. She was a crush for me when I was young, but I was *her* drama when we got older. Not the other way around. I don't feel for her like that. At all."

"I saw that last night. And he's a miserable human."

"I felt his jaw crack. Maybe he'll finally learn to shut his fucking mouth." I shrug. "Probably not."

"He's an idiot." She gently traces my lips. "I think you're incredible."

"And I think you're fucking gorgeous."

A thin tear runs down her temple. "We almost lost this."

"Yeah, but we didn't. I won't lose you again for any reason. I'll give it all up. All of it. I don't want back in that headspace again."

"So would I, but we don't have to." She cups my neck and lifts to kiss me, and I meet her halfway. "And we can't avoid life forever. We should go back to the house, I bet they're wondering where the hell we are."

"You aren't stopping dancing," I say, drawing her attention back to us.

"Nope, I'm not, but that's just geography. And that's not the truth of what's kept us apart."

"Nothing will again. You hear me? We're going to make this work."

"I want nothing more. So, should we go?"

"Yeah."

"So enthusiastic," she drawls.

I shrug. "It's just that we're all on such emotional high alert, I don't think any of us are keeping it together anymore."

"Lance, it will get better. And I know just because we're going to be okay, doesn't mean everything will, but it will get better."

"I know. It has to, but Dad won't."

"Parkinson's isn't a death sentence. And they're creating new medicines all the time."

"I know."

"Just don't give up."

"I can't," I grin. "You won't let me."

"Damn right, I won't," she says, lifting to straddle me and yawning. "Aren't you tired?"

"Yeah. Want to move into my bedroom and nap with me?"

"Sure."

"I think I'll give myself the day off."

She traces the bruise underneath my eyes. "Does this hurt?"

"No."

She presses on it, inspecting it closer.

"Does now, oww," I say, playfully slapping her hand. She giggles and it's music. It's relief. It's a thousand other feelings only she's made me capable of. Maybe she is the fucking answer. Maybe I got it right all along. "You know buzzed or not, I remember every second, and every word I said."

"I know."

"I'll have to ask you proper," I brush her sides with my fingers. "I just have to wait for the right time."

"No kids until after I hang up my flats, okay?"

"Yeah, no rush. I want to kind of earn my way out of poverty first."

"You know that doesn't matter to me."

"I know."

"Do you feel like everything's changed?" She asks, brushing the hair at the back of my neck.

I nod. "You?"

"I'm not afraid anymore. But Lance, we are going to have to talk about it at some point."

"We will. I swear, I just don't want to think that way. I just don't want to believe… You," my heart aches at the thought of them hurting her. "I just don't understand it." I brush my lips against hers.

"We don't have to understand them. That's part of breaking the cycle."

"You're right." I glance down at her necklace while she studies me.

"What are you thinking?"

"You know how last night you said your instructor's words changed your life?"

"Yeah."

"You did the same thing for me."

"I did?"

"I couldn't handle another day without seeing you. And it became clear when I heard your voice so clearly before I jumped on that plane."

"What did I say?"

"What if this moment, right here, is the one that changes your life?"

"You make me seem like a hero," she says, smoothing my bottom lip with her thumb.

I gaze back down at her and tell her the truth.

"Maybe because as much as I want to believe it's the other way around, in this story, you are. Let's go home, baby."

"Lead the way."

Minutes later, I silently usher her into the house and into my bedroom. Within seconds, I'm uncovering her, spreading her, worshiping her, replacing tears of last night's devastation with elation. She cries softly out to me as I hover above her, lifting her hand to my chest so she can feel what she does to me, pressing deep into her while I give her the last piece of my soul. It's when her brown eyes lift to mine with complete trust that I realize that despite my best efforts, I will be *one* thing for the rest of my life, *hers*.

Lance Prescott wins first heavyweight bout taking down Romeo Andreas in the 3rd.

Up-and-comer Lance Prescott, aka The Blanket, a title earned in his formative football years as a cornerback at Texas Grand, won his first bout with veteran Romeo Andreas last night. The fight, which took place in Las Vegas, marked the start of Prescott's career on the heavyweight circuit. Prescott released a series of devastating blows in the first round, winding the veteran within seconds of the bell. In a press conference held shortly after the fight, Prescott said he was reprimanded for his exertion in the first round by his long-time trainer, Tony Willis. Willis won the title in 2004 and is a two-time Glove Champion. Despite their difference of opinion, the two were clearly pleased with the outcome and Willis claims that he's certain Prescott will make a name for himself in boxing. All eyes are on Prescott for that verdict.

epilogue

LANEY

"**A**LMOST GOT IT," THEO SAYS, TYPING OUT A MESSAGE AS I usher him into the arena.

"Look, man, I love you, and you're an okay husband and all, but if you don't stop working so much, I'm going to have to find a replacement for date night."

Theo glances over at me and grins, he looks sexy as hell with his full beard grown in and trimmed close to his face, at my insistence.

"Don't smile at me like that. I mean it. I need attention."

"All yours."

"Lies. All lies," I wave my hand in annoyance. "It's a miracle we made it to the plane on time. You love playing the tortured artist too much."

"I had to make sure his new anthem was legit."

"It's incredible. He'll love it."

Theo lifts my hand to his lips and softly kisses each of my knuckles, his brown eyes boring into mine. The plans I see rolling in his head have my lips parting.

"Cut that out, Houseman, I'm horny from weeks of neglect."

The couple passing us in the aisle bursts into laughter. Theo stiffens and jerks me closer to him, scolding me in a harsh whisper. "I said I'll make it up to you tonight."

"Yeah, well, saying and doing are two different things. I just may hold out, give you a taste of your own medicine."

He stops me mid-aisle and cups my face, placing a slow, full-lipped kiss to my mouth surprising me when he deepens it until I'm breathless.

When he pulls away, he smirks at the effect it has on me.

"You smug bastard."

"Not being replaced today."

My legs are Jell-O, and this time it has nothing to do with weed. Though I did give him a pot brownie on our anniversary, just for old times' sake. We locked ourselves out of the house that night and ended up grabbing the tent he got me on our first Christmas. It was an amazing night. I stare up at him, utterly stupefied for the love I feel for him.

This makes him grin wider, and he takes my lips a second time. When he pulls away, he pulls up his phone.

"Is this a test?" I grumble. "Because I'm about to fail."

He encases me in his arms and lifts the screen for me to see as a few people brush past us.

"What is this?"

"A preview."

"Of what?"

"Our vacation."

He moves the hair away from my shoulder and leans in, whispering to me as the goosebumps pebble my flesh. "Because you're the pillar of patience, I'm rewarding you."

"Smartass."

"Look, baby, it's where we're going when we leave here."

"I don't understand."

"What don't you understand? Allow me to demonstrate."

He pulls up the picture of the luxury bed in a swanky hotel

room and hits the editing tab before drawing an arrow to the middle of the bed and writing MRS. HOUSEMAN next to it.

"I see. And, where are you?"

"My arrow would be inappropriate."

"And where exactly is this?"

"Paris, and that's after Fiji."

"You're taking me to Fiji and France?"

"And Spain."

"What?!"

"And Greece."

"Oh my God!" I turn in his arms, and he grins down at me. "You've been plannin' this how long?"

"A month. Still want to replace me?"

"I was kidding. When do we leave?"

"Midnight."

Tears threaten as I try to collect myself. "You really aren't a bad husband."

"I know."

He tugs me behind him, leading us to our ringside seats. Once settled, I look to our left and see the rest of the row is mostly empty.

He laces our fingers, brushing my wedding ring before he lifts his eyes to mine. "I'm sorry I've been working so hard. I promise you I'll slow down soon."

"I'm so happy you're thriving. Please don't think I'm not. I just miss you sometimes." Theo is one of the most sought-after modern composers in the country. His knowledge of music and his incredible talent have taken him to great heights in the four years since we graduated. He's made a small fortune with his advertising jingles and his very first large purchase was upgrading my wedding ring. He says it's the accomplishment he's most proud of. I told him it was too much, but I can see the amount of pride in his eyes when he admires it on my hand.

And me? Well, I still haven't figured out what I want to do with the rest of my life career-wise, but I do my part, even though I'm now married to a wealthy man. He doesn't hold it against me that I change aprons and hats every few months, though he did very much like my stint as a sex toy rep. That was just for some side money for my newest business venture, which I don't have the heart to tell him I've changed my mind on just yet. Maybe I'll be a butcher, or a baker, or a candlestick maker, but he'll be my maestro, always, and that's truly all I give a shit about. I turn to my husband under the blaring house lights in the Vegas arena thinking about how far we've come since that drunken night next to the bushes and tears spring to my eyes.

"Jesus, Houseman, you make me pathetic."

"Yeah, well," he whispers warmly, "you make me happy."

"I meant that too," I sniff. "I love you…a ridiculous amount."

"I know."

"Forever."

He squeezes my hand. "And ever, Crazy."

My thoughts border indecent as I study him, tempted to do very unpublic things.

"*Before* midnight," he promises, keeping his stare ahead. He didn't even have to look at me to know what I was thinking, but I guess that's the gift of marrying your best friend.

TROY

I push the damp hair away from Clarissa's face as she rests at my neck while I pulse once more inside her. We've been fucking like rabbits for the last five years and haven't slowed down a bit. Tonight was no exception.

The minute she stepped out of the closet of our hotel room in the sparkling dress I'm running my hands over, I knew I wouldn't make it to the casino without having her.

It's still far too much fun to seduce her. And she'd resisted me well until I got her alone in the limo. Our marriage changed everything about what I thought marriage would be. But the truth is, I think we might be an exception to par. And really fucking lucky.

The chemistry is there, without us trying. It's always there, every single day, without fail. Maybe it will fade eventually, as I assumed it would, but so far it hasn't. I hold onto it because there's really nothing in the world I love more than making love or fucking my wife, except the result of it.

The minute she sank onto me, I lost my shit driving up into her until she was calling my name. I made it last as long as I could, but she got the best of me. My emotions won out, and I got lost, the way I always do. It's this time, after I'm spent, and I know she's sated that I love the most. The silent moments where we feel so fucking close nothing could ever separate us. I live for moments like these. Amongst the chaos of our life, I live for this time with her.

"Mon cherie, darling, you are zee apple of my eye, the fruit of my loins, the quarter to my back. You make little Pepe sing. You know, we will spend zee rest of our lives making all the love."

She giggles into my chest shaking her head. "Lord."

"Have I not satisfied you? Muah, muah, muah." I say as she laughs in my hold. "I love you, darling."

"You're so crazy."

"Crazy for youuuu, always," I drawl out in the Le Pew I've mastered over the years. She jerks as I tickle her sides and suddenly stills. "Oh my God, I think it ripped," she twists to run her fingers along the hem of her dress.

"What?"

"My dress. I think it's ripped. I can feel air."

"You're feeling the air because it's around your waist."

"Baby, I need you to check."

She lifts, pulling the dress down before she raises up in the seat of the limo bringing her sparkling ass directly in front of my nose. If I let out a laugh, I'm a dead man. Instead, I focus my fingers on her inner thigh and ride them up until she gasps.

"Yep, still no panties."

"I'm talking about my d-dress, Troy, s-stop it."

"No way."

"Please just look. I know I should have gone a size up."

I carefully inspect the dress. "No rip, and you're not even showing."

She turns on me, freakishly fast. "Pregnant. Again. I don't know why I love you."

I pull her to me, and she collapses in my lap as I push her auburn hair away from her shoulders.

"I'm sweaty and disgusting."

"You're fucking beautiful. So beautiful."

She sighs, looking up at me with clear blue eyes from under her lashes.

"And I promise not to get you pregnant again."

"Really?"

"No. Not at all."

"This makes five! FIVE CHILDREN! We're done." She shakes her head. "I'll deny you."

"You cannot," I drawl in impressive Le Pew.

"I'll divorce you. I will. I'll refuse you and divorce you. You aren't all that. Self-made, superstar athlete with an amazing penis."

"I'm sure you can do better."

"Piece of cake," she murmurs. "Please, baby, promise me, after this one, we're done."

"I promise."

"You're lying."

"I am."

She takes great pains in cleaning us up before opening her purse to apply more gloss. I watch her carefully line her lips before my phone pings. I lift the screen and chuckle.

"Dante sent us a progress report."

"Let's see it." Clarissa leans in, smiling as I hit play. The video is set to Jeopardy music, and Dante stands to the side of the screen, only half his face showing, his eye rolled up to the ceiling of our kitchen as Parker stands at the stove, a box of mac and cheese next to the pot, our daughter in her arms, our other two boys crying in jealousy at her feet. She looks perplexed as she tries to juggle them. Dante did several shots this way, his eyes always up as if he's at his wits' end while Parker moves in fast forward around his steady frame, doing her best to keep up. We laugh hysterically until the video ends with Parker passed out in the recliner. The footage then picks up as Dante takes over, pacifying all three of his younger siblings before wrapping Parker in a blanket. We shoot off a collective text of '**Good Job**,' and he replies with an eye roll emoji followed by dollar signs.

"That boy."

"He needs a raise," I say, chuckling.

"He's such a good kid," Clarissa murmurs. "We hit the lotto with that one."

"With all of them," I murmur, kissing her neck.

We pull up to the entrance of the hotel just as she shuts her compact. When the car rolls to a stop, I pull her to me and crush my mouth to hers, ruining her efforts and hearing her protest a split second before she melts into my kiss. The door opens as I steadily devour her, not giving a fuck who catches sight of us, and she lets me. I'm obsessed with my wife.

"Troy," she murmurs, looking up at me with a lusty gaze when I pull away, "haven't you had enough?"

"You know the answer to that. Come on." I make sure everything is covered as I gently escort her from the limo. The driver gives us a grin as I pull her into the breezeway of the hotel. We're only a few steps past the door when a man approaches with his wife trailing behind him.

"Hey, Troy? Can I get your autograph?"

Clarissa smiles, making small talk with the wife as I usher the guy to the side of the busy walkway and take the pen from him.

"Killer season, man. Next year is our year. I can feel it."

"Thanks, hope so." I scribble my name as I've done thousands of times and still can't believe this is my life. It's been a crazy ride from that blue rental house to get to this point.

"Thanks, man," the man says as we take a quick pic before he's on his way.

"I've never gambled before," Clarissa says as I walk her through the barrage of noise in the casino.

"Let's fix that."

"No way."

"Come on, baby, loosen the purse strings a little."

"Maybe tomorrow."

"We're leaving in the morning. We have to get back, or we'll lose Parker."

She smiles. "Can't have that." She looks around skeptically. "I just don't think I'm a gambler."

"Then we won't do anything risky." I pull out my wallet

and slide a hundred at the dispensary window attendant in exchange for some chips.

"That's a hundred dollars."

My wife still does our grocery shopping, she still buys our kids clothes at TJ Maxx. She's frugal with our millions, and the irony is she brings home enough salary to support us all. I love that she's a cheap millionaire. I love that she's fretting over a hundred dollars.

"One bet," I tell her, handing her the chips.

"Just one?"

"Yes." I scan the room. "Over here. Roulette." I guide her to the table. "Red or black. Easy choice."

"What do you think?"

I tug a strand of her hair. "My bet will always be on red."

"God, you're awfully romantic tonight."

"Just wait until I get you alone again. That dress is a one and done. I'm going to make sure that fucker rips."

"Damn," she whispers, squeezing my hand as we side up to the roulette table.

"Okay," she chews her lip, "let's bet on Dante's birthday."

"Sounds good."

"Five on red?" She looks at me for guidance, and I nod before she places the chip on the table. In seconds, we lose a hundred dollars. I laugh as she curses under her breath. "I don't see how people do this. That used to be a fortune to me."

"Me too."

"Still is," she says as we step onto the escalator.

"I love that about you."

She stares down at me, perched on the mechanical steps, and we share a look that says it all. Neither of us thought this life would be ours. I take her hand and kiss it. "I know."

By the time we make it to our seats, the arena is mostly full. Theo and Laney are there to greet us.

"Hey, man. Can you believe this shit?" Theo and I do the man hug.

"He deserves it," I say honestly.

"No argument there," he says, looking around the packed arena.

Since we've graduated, Theo and I did little to keep in touch, but when Lance became a premier fighter, I decided to gift him with his own anthem and knew just the right maestro. Since then, he and Laney have come to a few of my games and even stayed at the house a couple times. Our new dynamic completely different than years before. He doesn't even blink when I hug his wife in greeting.

"Another one!?" Laney says to Clarissa with one hand on her belly and another wrapped around her in a hug. "You look beautiful."

"I feel ridiculous. This is a hoochie dress."

"You look hot," she insists.

"I agree," I add, looking her over with the lust I feel. "So fucking hot."

"Me too," Theo says, the next in line to hug Clarissa. We take our seats, and I scan the crowded room.

"Crazy, isn't it?" Theo says, reading my thoughts the seat over.

"Wouldn't change a fucking thing," I say honestly.

"Me neither."

"I have to pee," Laney belts breaking the sentiment, and we both chuckle.

"I'll go with you," Clarissa offers. "I'm sure I'll have to *again* by the time we get there."

Before they're out of sight, I grab my phone and shoot off

a text. A few seconds later, Clarissa reaches into her purse and looks back at me with glassy eyes.

Troy: No need to gamble when you've already won the lottery.

Clarissa: I love you so much.

HARPER

Standing just behind Lance and his crew, he shakes his arms out and rolls his shoulders before turning back to me. I'm sweating from head to foot in my tight-fitting dress and pray he can't see the nerves on my face, but of course, he does.

He gives me a slow wink. "First knockout of the night."

I bat away the compliment, too worried about how he's feeling. "You've got this."

"As long as I've got you."

And that's all it takes to straighten my spine, pride filling me where doubt just threatened. We're stronger than we've ever been. The last few years, especially this one, has been insane. I've danced in a few shows, in addition to being ringside at all of Lance's fights. His earnings as a heavyweight have relieved most of his burdens.

But it hasn't been easy.

We've missed each other to the point we've had a few fantastic fights that led to the most incredible make up sessions. But fighting across the miles isn't easy, either. But we have what it takes now to make it through. We now consider those tumultuous days at the ranch the ten days that made us.

And they truly did.

We hold absolutely nothing back from the other, even if it

causes problems, even if it hurts, even if it tests us, and on the other side is a closeness I've never felt with any other.

Lance splits his time between the circuit, the ranch, and New York while I split my time between the stage and wherever he lands. It's been hard, and wonderful, and paid off in spades. But nothing in the world, no stage, no spotlight could keep me away tonight.

And one day, very soon, he'll call New York home. Our end game is the ranch, but time is what we have, and we're making full use of it. We're living the next five years in the city and then moving Nana to Texas when we go. We have plans, loads of them, which include expansion of the ranch.

Tony sidles up next to Lance with last minute suggestions as Trevor takes in the packed arena. Lance is wearing a new and cranked up version of the robe I bought him years ago. It fits him perfectly, along with the trunks. Amped and rattling, Trevor stands next to him. I've never seen so much pride in his eyes. Lance is his hero and it fills me so full of joy to see them in this state. These two boys turned men have single-handedly kept their parents' legacy alive. Trevor will attend Grand this fall, thanks to his brother, who is picking up the bill.

Covered in nerves, I jump out of my skin when Lance's new anthem sounds out. Moving instinctively, I can't help but appreciate the vibe it brings. It's a mix of rock and rap, and it's so distinctly Lance. Stomach turning, I see Lance repeatedly nodding to Tony's words. And then we're off, collectively walking down the aisle together as his corner while the arena roars to life. It's the same buzz as it has been in his fights before, but this one I feel in my stomach. When it's time to leave me ringside, I move to take my seat when Lance unexpectedly turns and pulls me to him with a gloved hand. I freeze, knowing all cameras, all eyes, are on us.

"Look at me, baby," he says roughly. "It's just us."

"Gross understatement. Hundreds of millions of eyes, Lance. And they're waiting. What are you doing?!"

"Let 'em wait. There's no fight without you. I'm here because of you."

Adrenaline spiking, I glance around us.

"Well, you can thank me later."

"Look at me, beautiful," he commands, and I do. My eyes drift to his.

"I fucking love you."

Heart pounding, I nod. "I love you too, knock 'em out, baby."

"If I do, will you marry me?"

Eyes widening, I check his expression and realize he's serious, his eyes full of surety. "I've been waiting almost two years, and *this* is the moment you choose to propose?"

"Can you think of one better?" The man cares absolutely nothing about outsider's opinions at this point, and I admire him for it. I'm not quite there yet, but I love that he keeps pushing me and always will. This is the biggest of tests, and I refuse to let it cripple me. He's pushing me the way I have him, refusing to let me lurk in the shadows. And he's the source of the strength I need to dwell with him in the spotlight. I shake my head, smiling.

"So, Priss? Will you be my wife?"

"Marry you? Fine. One condition."

"Name it."

"I want KO by the sixth round."

"Fuck, you drive a hard bargain."

"Nah," I scrunch my nose, "you just need a little faith."

"I believe what I can see, and damn have you shown me." He chucks my chin with a gloved hand before he's whisked away toward the ring where his opponent waits.

It was a little under a sixty-second exchange, and the most exhilarating seconds of my life. High and dazed, I join the gang who're holding my seat.

"Hey, woman!" Clarissa says, pulling me into a hug as I stand stunned, half-assed greeting them all and returning their embraces. When Troy releases me, my eyes land on Trevor, who has grown into a monster, his build similar to his brother's when I met him. He sticks out his full bottom lip in a pout. It's then I know Lance's proposal was planned. I lift my shoulders in a helpless shrug and he gives me his brother's breathtaking smile. I match it before averting my gaze back to Lance.

"He looks incredible," Clarissa says at my side. And he does. He's put on more muscle in the last few months. He's a trim gladiator at this point. I'm still dumbfounded at times I'm his.

And so are others.

My reception was just as grueling as I expected it to be. The irony? Being the champ's girlfriend got me some national attention as a dancer. The nightmare of constant ridicule turned into a sort of blessing. But it hasn't been fun. None of it has. I've had to cut ties with social media. Lance forced me to turn mine over to his PR after seeing the backlash of our coupling. He's gotten downright vicious with a few reporters despite our game plan and had to apologize publicly for addressing some comments on Twitter. He may not give a shit about what others say about him, but I'm a different story. Together we've been his publicist's worst nightmare. At times, I thought I would never be able to show my face in public again. But here we are, still fighting, still standing, still us. The microphone lowers into the ring and my stomach turns as Clarissa grips my hand.

"Ladies and gentlemen, in the red corner, standing six-foot-two and weighing two-hundred and twenty-four pounds, with a record of eighteen and oh, Lance 'The Blanket' Prescott."

I'm already on my feet, screaming for him as he lifts his arms up and gives the crowd a short nod.

Otto is announced next, and that's when Lance goes business. In his eyes, a determination I've seen countless times before. The beast is there, locked up, waiting for the gate to open. His opponent is a warrior and has an undefeated record as well. This is going to be a fight, but Lance has an edge, most of his wins being knockout, Otto's technical.

Lance is very much the comeback kid in the ring. Heart in my throat, I'm too nervous for small talk as Clarissa leans into me.

"What's going on in your head right now, girl?"

"It's just…nothing."

"That's not nothing."

I turn and give her a smile. "This is going to be good."

"Yeah?"

"Yeah."

The first bell rings, and Lance comes out last, light on his feet, his movements drawing Otto in, who misses his first throw. Lance begins his dance, his head bobbing, his muscular legs shifting easily from one foot to the next. I've never seen him so fluid, so confident. It's been months since his last fight, but I can't believe how much he's grown in just that short amount of time. I'm in utter awe as I watch him handle himself in the ring with the two-time champ.

Lance lands a one-two combo dizzying Otto, and shortly after Otto lands his first punch. The camera pans in on Lance's face at that exact moment, and when Lance smiles around his mouthguard, the crowd goes apeshit.

"He's playing with him," Clarissa says in shock and awe. "This guy is toast."

"Easy, killer," I say, looking on in a daze as Lance dominates the first round. He's fighting a two-time heavyweight champion and making it look like a day in the park. I couldn't be more stunned. Otto seems…intimidated, his posture as weary as his expression. It's as if Lance has broken some barrier within himself and we're all bearing witness to it.

And then it happens. Otto finds his groove, and it becomes a fight. An uppercut wipes all amusement out of Lance's eyes, but he doesn't waver, seeming satisfied with the progression. He wants to earn it.

In round two, Lance's steps are slightly heavier, but he remains controlled, Tony's fighter.

"He's still fucking with him," Troy's voice booms across the space between us. He's just as in awe as everyone else in the row. Troy's been to several of his fights and can see the growth himself.

When they break for round three, Laney chooses that moment to holler her support in her deep twang. "Knock his fuckin' head off, Prescott!" We all turn toward her, laughing hysterically. Theo shakes his head, and she shrugs.

"What? I wanted to make sure he heard me."

"The world heard you," Theo says, eyeing his wife with love and amusement. And then the camera is on the five of us, panning in on Troy and Clarissa, and for a moment, I'm thankful Troy is here to take the focus off me. He's been a hell of a support to Lance and me over the years. A solid friend. We couldn't ask for better.

Tony hovers above Lance as Rip wipes his face and waters him up. And then the camera is panning in on me. Did they read his lips? Did they see our exchange? Was it Lance's intent that the world know we're getting married? A wedding will only intensify the scrutiny.

I stare at Lance in his corner who's all too ready to go gloves up and something comes over me. The solution.

Who the fuck cares?

About *them*.

They who hurt us without knowing a second of our story.

Without knowing the struggles we've faced, that we'll continue to face, together, fight for together.

And what we won is each other.

Fuck them.

Let their hate fester.

Let *them* watch.

Let them choke on that hate.

We won't ever respond to it again.

It's then I think of my dad, who's sitting alone in his apartment watching my future unfold. I imagine right about now he's regretting his mistakes where Lance is concerned. But Lance no longer harbors ill feelings toward him and reached out to get no response. He tried, and that's all I can ask.

By the fifth round, we're all on the edge of our seats, the momentum shifting again, and Otto is dominating. Lance avoids a jab, but Otto lands another uppercut I feel to my bones when Lance dizzies to the point he's leaning on the ropes and he goes down on his knees. Heart sinking, I stand and begin screaming my support. I know I'm impossible to hear, but I will him to anyway. From where he kneels, I can feel his struggle, and within seconds, I'm at the side of the ring.

The referee starts his count as Otto celebrates, his arrogance rousing the crowd.

Tony curses in the corner as Trevor screams for his brother, and I do the same.

"This is yours, Prescott! Don't let it in!"

As if he hears me, he's on his feet within the count of six.

After a brief exchange with the ref, his dance is back. With Lance still dazed, Otto lands a slew of punches until the bell rings.

When round six sounds, everyone in the arena is losing their minds. Lance and Otto are back and forth, delivering blow for blow until Otto gains the upper hand. I'm close to regretting my demand when Lance pushes Otto back with one glove to the forehead.

"HOLY FUCKING SHIT!" Troy exclaims just before Lance pounds his gloves together and unleashes the beast. No longer Tony's fighter, but the man I met in the gym six years ago. The true fighter he is. The true fighter life made him.

Lance is giving it everything he is, he has, landing one solid punch after the other dodging Otto's attempts. Otto looks very much like a punching bag jerking on the chain. And with each of his strikes, I see a flash of the past, of the first time I took a closer look at Lance in his element at our gym. Another right hook from Lance has Otto's mouthpiece loose, and there's only enough time for him to secure it back in before Lance delivers another. More memories flood me as my eyes water, and I picture him with his eyes closed while I circled him at Madison Square Garden.

"Through the ropes!" I scream, my eyes flooding as Lance picks Otto apart, punch by punch, not just fighting for the title, but winning against the odds that were stacked against him since the beginning.

"Through the ropes, baby!"

Lance lands another and another, dominating until he has Otto on the ropes.

I'm screaming at the top of my lungs. "It's you, Lance, you're the next big upset! This is yours! This is your legacy! Fight, baby!" I scream through the thousands of other voices shouting their support. With the uproar from every punch, I realize Otto is no longer the favorite.

"It's you, Lance! It's you!" The minute the words leave my lips, Lance delivers a right, and Otto goes down.

Everyone in our row mimics the ref's count. "One, two, three, four, five, six, seven," Otto does a slow climb back to his feet and nods to the ref. Undeterred, Lance takes two long strides to get to him and delivers one last blow that I know everyone watching felt. Otto goes down and in the next second, Lance's glove is raised.

All of the fights, the sacrifice, all of the hurt, the heartache, the need, the failures, the faith he lost, the faith he found, it all comes down to this moment. The moment he thought impossible until he saw it for himself and earned it.

Lance Prescott. The heavyweight champion of the world.

Seconds after Tony pummels him in celebration, Trevor meets me at the side of the ring, hoisting me up as Rip guides me through the ropes. I rush to Lance, who's already fighting the growing crowd to get to me. He's swollen and bloody, but I can read every emotion in his eyes.

"You did it!" I scream hysterically as he captures me and lifts me effortlessly into his arms. We hug for long seconds as I sputter out everything I'm thinking. "I'm so proud of you. We all are. He saw it, Lance. Your dad saw it. He saw it. Oh my God. You did it."

"I know, baby, I know. I love you, I love you," he murmurs again and again, ignoring the celebration around him.

"I always knew this was yours," I say, sobbing into his chest.

He pulls away and grips my head with his gloves as his belt is set on his shoulder. "And that's why I'm here. Because I believed you."

Seven months later...

LANCE

I stand in wait for my bride at the end of the aisle with Trevor, Troy, and Theo by my side. The church is only half full because we wanted the wedding intimate, but everyone who matters to us most is here. Three weeks after I won my belt, I moved to New York. From then on, it's been a whirlwind. Endorsement offers came in, and my staff is losing their shit to keep up. On the other side of things, I keep busy training to defend my title while Harper dances at various shows of her choosing. She's at the stage where her door is being knocked on now, not the other way around.

I've never been prouder of her than I was on her last opening night before she accepted the roses I brought to her feet. She's a star, no longer able to mask her talent, she's now sought after, thriving. Just like I knew she would be.

Mom leads Dad down the aisle, he shuffles his steps before they take their seats in the first pew. She's already choking up, and I have to force myself to look away from her, so I don't do the same. I'm not nervous, just ready. Ready to give this woman my last name, though our life together started years ago.

"You nervous, brother?" Trevor whispers from next to me, clad in his fitted tuxedo.

"Not one bit."

"Proud of you," he says, cupping my shoulder.

"Don't do that shit now."

He chuckles, knowing I'm on the verge of getting emotional.

He's caught up with me in size, surpassing my height by an

inch. He's all man now, and cocky as ever, but he's excelling at school. And I'm pretty sure he's smitten with one of his coeds. He goes home every weekend to help out at the ranch like I did, though he doesn't have to. I've managed to find capable hands, and as of now, the ranch is in good shape, though I anticipate ups and downs. But Trevor watches just as closely over our legacy. He's a lot like me, family first, and I can't think of a better man to be at my side. Troy and Theo stand next to him in matching tuxes, eyeing their wives across the aisle. Laney shifts in her boots, her eyes fixed on Theo as Clarissa shifts uncomfortably in her dress, looking every bit the eight months pregnant she is. Troy chuckles at her constant fidgeting and clears his throat when he catches her answering glare.

On my side, my parents, Rip, a few guys Troy and I played with at Grand, and all of our ranch hands sit idle, waiting on Harper's entrance.

Harper's side is full to the brim, with half of the dance population of New York. Her mother sits upfront along with Nana, who's next to René. She winks at me, and I wink back. René mistakes my wink for him and blows me a kiss. I roll my eyes and surprise him by puckering up. I can't hear him when he speaks, but I know whatever he's saying is not fit for church. Though I did promise him a dance after the wedding.

Not looking forward to it.

Soft music is playing in the background as I take in the décor. Harper went all out, put her soul into this day, planning every detail. It's then I really notice the sprays and sprays of white flowers that line the pews, and it dawns on me.

"I picture a grand church, lined with large pillars with high arches hovering above. White roses showing little greenery everywhere. Everything white. All of my family and friends gathered. The perfect music."

She wasn't planning her funeral that night. She saw the end, or rather our beginning. Even when we were unsure of every move we were making, her faith was unshakable.

Determined not to let my emotions get to me, I avert my eyes from the eager faces lining the pews when the music starts.

Fucking hell.

It's the theme song she danced to years ago, the song that I thought would lead to the end of us. Within a few notes, I can clearly see Harper gliding across the floor of her old apartment, the snowdrift behind her, her angelic hair trailing her frame.

Determined to keep my shit together, I slowly inhale to steady myself.

And then she appears, knocking the fucking breath out of me.

Flowers in hand, walking slowly toward me down the aisle, her dress hugs her every curve and trails in a bed of soft lace behind her. Her hair is down, flowing over her shoulders. Glowing, her brown eyes dart along the pews as she greets everyone with a serene smile. She beams at them in welcome before her eyes drift over and find mine.

"Damn it, Priss," I cough out as tears I can't hold glide down my face. She's perfect. In every fucking way. This love I feel for her has taken me to incredible heights, and right now, I feel the highest I've ever been. Her love has also pressed me, pushed me outside of being comfortable, built me up, tortured me, but not once has it ever left me. It's the most spectacular fucking emotion imaginable and I could not, would not, have ever felt it like this if it wasn't for her. Her tears spill freely down her cheeks as she pauses at the end of the aisle, the man who guided her pulling her into his arms and holding her there. His face soaked as he whispers to her before turning red-rimmed eyes to mine.

"I've got her. I swear to you."

"I know you do," her father says as he joins our hands together the way we rehearsed it last night. But in this moment, it means a whole hell of a lot more.

It's been a long road of redemption for Ryan Elliot, and he's still nowhere near together, but we've made peace for Harper. Though I don't expect much of a relationship with him, I'm good with the gift he's giving me as he puts her hand in mine. He steps away, wiping his face, and I turn to my bride, whose own face is streaking from her tears, eyes searching mine, all too tempted to take her lips.

"You're beautiful."

"I love you so much," she says as I do my best to clear her tears with my thumbs. I'm a fucking mess myself, and I'm not the only one. As the music dies, Harper and I hear sniffs coming from all directions and turn toward the pews with concern as laughter fills the church.

Grinning like fools, we collectively turn back to the priest to guide us. The second I slip the ring on her delicate finger—I feel a sense of peace wash over me. She squeezes my hand, reciting her vows earnestly with a tearful voice, her eyes alight with love as I do everything I can to keep from crushing her to me. I take in her every word. But in a way, I feel like we've already been living these vows.

We've been there at our best and worst, through my dad's sickness, in health, through poverty, and our new wealth, we've lived it. We've survived it. We fell in love in the thick of adversity and managed to make it to the other side stronger, better, and more in love than ever.

Feet away from the statue that mirrors the struggle, I marry the woman I love in a room filled to the brim with faith. Faith she kept, faith she still has, faith I now share. Faith that manifested itself because of this love we have and became something I can see.

"By the power vested in me by God and the State of New York, I now pronounce you man and wife. Lance, you may kiss your bride."

I cup her face, stroking the sides of it with my thumbs before I take her lips to seal our union. As I kiss my wife, I can still hear her voice, as clear as the day she said it.

"What if this moment, right here, is the moment that changes your life?"

THEO

"And now, ladies and gentlemen, a groomsman request. Would," the deejay cuts off laughing, but you can still hear it on the mic, "Crazy Laney, would you please join your husband on the dance floor?"

I search the room for my wife and see her head pop to the side of Lance's broad shoulder before her eyes narrow where I wait for her. And then she smiles when she hears the first few notes of "You've Got the Touch," and I swear I feel every step she takes in her smelly boots towards me. She looks so fucking beautiful in her dress, reminding me of the first night I claimed her.

Seconds later, our hands are clasped, and we start to move to our song.

"You walk a thin line, husband of mine."

"I'm aware. Have to keep you on your smelly toes."

"Enough with that. I put odor eaters in."

"Those boots stink. Your feet *stink*."

She rolls her eyes. "I met you in these boots. They're lucky. I'm not ditchin' 'em."

"Let's compromise. You won't ditch me if I buy you *new* boots."

"I don't need new boots. And that's not a compromise."

"Laney," I say, turning her so her dress swishes behind her.

"Fine. Okay, I've done everything. They stink."

"Bad. It's time to let go."

"Okay, later tonight. We'll give them a proper burial."

"Thank Christ."

Her chin wobbles and I hate the sight of it.

"Come on, babe. You can't be that attached."

"I am. And that was the most beautiful wedding."

"So was ours."

She smiles. "Ours was perfect."

"Weddings are good luck for us."

"True."

She glances over my shoulder. "I have an idea."

"That's never good."

"Shut up, Houseman. You think Courtney will mind if we do a realest life post?"

"Who gives a shit if she does? We started it."

She grins at me. "True, we did. And look, everyone is back at the table." She grips my hand and pulls me from the dance floor.

Minutes later, we're all groaning as Laney lifts her cell phone at various angles to take pics.

"Just one more," she presses in as Lance, Troy, Clarissa, Laney, Harper, and I crowd in for the selfie. It's when I study the six of us in her screen that nostalgia kicks in hardcore.

The friendships we have now are far more solid compared to the days where we were finding ourselves and fighting for these women who turned us into the better version of the men we've become. In the midst of low self-esteem among giants, I found a woman whose insides shine so fucking bright, all you can see is her. And somehow, I've managed to keep her amongst my madness, the chaos I've created with my music. The best part is she can hum along to every song because she's half of my melody.

Troy managed to woo Clarissa while fighting his own battles, facing his lowest points, gunning for the life he'd always imagined for himself, even when he wasn't sure he could have it.

And Lance, well, he's been the biggest surprise of the three of us. In the worst circumstances imaginable, he fought to become a champion amongst men, a hero to other fighters, to his family, and bride.

Back then, I didn't think I knew my roommates so well. Didn't think I had a thing in common with them. Turns out I couldn't have been more wrong. Though our stories are vastly different, we all longed for the same thing—to belong—all the while figuring out who we were, trying to prove ourselves and win the affection of the women who would help us figure it all out. We may not have had the friendships we do now, but I have zero doubts crossing paths the way we did was a coincidence. Our stories stemmed from the same place, intertwined, and wouldn't be what they are if it weren't for each other. And we'll be there for each other the way we have been the last couple of years and moving forward. Through every milestone, I'm sure of it.

"One more guys," Laney pipes up, and everyone groans and gives up as she continues her search for the perfect picture. Lance and Harper get lip-locked in the back while Troy drunkenly starts talking to Clarissa's stomach as she rolls her eyes. Laney grins, switching angles in an effort to get it all in. "Now we're getting somewhere."

"Would you be done already?" I strain, my face close to hers in the front.

"I'm just trying to get a good shot. I need a selfie stick."

"I forbid it. And you've taken seventy. Choose one."

"A few more. It's not often we get together like this. Oh, I forgot to tell you. I've accepted a new job."

"Awesome, can you take the pic and we can discuss it later. Wait, you *took it,* and you're just now telling me?"

"The position just popped up."

"What is it?"

"Mother."

CLICK.

#theunderdogsofoharadrive #awardwinningmaestro
#NFLdream #heavyweightchampionoftheworld
#mrshouseman #plusonecomingsoon #mrsjenner
#mrsprescott #grandgirlsstaygrand #grandmanlegacy
#friendsforlife #livingourrealestlives

#THEEND

about the author

USA Today bestselling author and Texas native, Kate Stewart, lives in North Carolina with her husband, Nick. Nestled within the Blue Ridge Mountains, Kate pens messy, sexy, angst-filled contemporary romance, as well as romantic comedy and erotic suspense.

Kate's title, *Drive*, was named one of the best romances of 2017 by The New York Daily News and Huffington Post. *Drive* was also a finalist in the Goodreads Choice awards for best contemporary romance of 2017. The Ravenhood Trilogy, consisting of *Flock, Exodus*, and *The Finish Line*, has become an international best-seller and reader favorite. Her holiday release, *The Plight Before Christmas*, ranked #6 on Amazon's Top 100. Kate's works have been featured in *USA TODAY, BuzzFeed, The New York Daily News, Huffington Post* and translated into a dozen languages.

Kate is a lover of all things '80s and '90s, especially John Hughes films and rap. She dabbles a little in photography, can knit a simple stitch scarf for necessity, and on occasion, does very well at whiskey.

Other titles available now by Kate

Romantic Suspense

The Ravenhood Series
Flock
Exodus
The Finish Line

Lust & Lies Series
Sexual Awakenings
Excess
Predator and Prey
The Lust & Lies Box set: Sexual Awakenings, Excess, Predator and Prey

Contemporary Romance

In Reading Order

Room 212
Never Me (Companion to Room 212 and The Reluctant Romantic Series)
The Reluctant Romantics Series
The Fall
The Mind
The Heart
The Reluctant Romantics Box Set: The Fall, The Heart, The Mind
Loving the White Liar

The Bittersweet Symphony
Drive
Reverse

The Real
Someone Else's Ocean
Heartbreak Warfare
Method

Romantic Dramedy

Balls in Play Series
Anything but Minor
Major Love
Sweeping the Series Novella
Balls in play Box Set: Anything but Minor, Major Love, Sweeping the Series, The Golden Sombrero

The Underdogs Series
The Guy on the Right
The Guy on the Left
The Guy in the Middle
The Underdogs Box Set: The Guy on The Right, The Guy on the Left, The Guy in the Middle

The Plight Before Christmas

Let's stay in touch!

Facebook
www.facebook.com/authorkatestewart

Newsletter
www.katestewartwrites.com/contact-me.html

Twitter
twitter.com/authorklstewart

Instagram
www.instagram.com/authorkatestewart/?hl=en

Book Group
www.facebook.com/groups/793483714004942

Spotify
open.spotify.com/user/authorkatestewart

Sign up for the newsletter now and get a free
eBook from Kate's Library!

Newsletter signup

www.katestewartwrites.com/contact-me.html

thank you

#thankyouforreading #thankyoutobexkettner
#thankyouautumngantz #thankyoudonnacooksley
#thankyougreyditto #thankyoutomyincrediblebetas
#thankyoutomyeagleeyeproofers
#thankyoutomyincredibleasskickers
#thankyouamyforanotheramazingcover
#thankyoutomyfamilyandfriends #thankstomyhusbandnick
#thankyoubloggersforallyoudo #somuchmoretocome

Dear reader and friend,

Thank you. The love you've shown for these characters propelled my one little comic relief book into a series that's become one of my favorite writing ventures to date. It's a gift you gave by voicing your love for this world, and the last two books would not have happened without you. Thank you so much for taking a chance and staying on this journey with me. #icouldnotdothiswithoutyou

XO
Kate